The Matchmaker

Catriona Innes

TRAPEZE

First published in Great Britain in 2019 by Trapeze
an imprint of The Orion Publishing Group Ltd
Carmelite House, 50 Victoria Embankment
London EC4Y 0DZ

An Hachette UK Company

1 3 5 7 9 10 8 6 4 2

A CIP catalogue record for this book is
available from the British Library.

ISBN (Mass Market Paperback) 978 1 4091 8837 7
ISBN (eBook) 978 1 4091 8838 4

Typeset by Born Group
Printed in Great Britain by Clays Ltd, Elcograf S.p.A.

MIX
Paper from
responsible sources
FSC® C104740

www.orionbooks.co.uk

The Matchmaker

Catriona Innes is currently features director at *Cosmopolitan* where she commissions, edits and writes the features section, including award-winning long-read investigative reports. She's been named Best Print Writer by BSME and recently won Best Feature Idea by BSME.

To Ian Hunter
For always playing 'guess the ingredient' with me

Chapter One

She tugs at her sleeve, causing orange lint to float off her jumper and circulate around her, like smoke from a cigarette. Her cheeks are rosy, sprinkled with freckles, and when she smiles one dimple appears. It's impossible not to fall in love with that smile.

Except, I've not seen that much of it since I arrived in this restaurant, twenty minutes ago. I've been watching, counting on my fingers each time it appears: once, when she got here; the second, when the waiter brought her wine; and the third, when she spotted me, in my itchy wig, tucked in the booth next to hers.

I'm straining my ears over the buzz of conversation around me, catching snippets of what's happening on her date, trying to figure out what's gone wrong. Why she's sitting there, not so much with a frown on her face but an impassive look, like she'd rather be anywhere else. From the mirror, strategically angled and placed near them a few hours ago, I can see the way he swirls his wine glass, his hand peppered with black hairs. I'm trying to assess the body language – he's leaned in and I can hear his laugh every now and then, nervous and throaty, but she never joins in.

An Aperol Spritz is clunked down in front of me, the ice cubes jangling together and in slides Bobby; he smells of garlic and butter, and even the sight of him makes my tummy grumble.

'Ah! It's the Matchmaker!' he booms and I fly my finger up to my lips, shhhing him. He side-eyes me, sheepishly. 'Sorry,' he whispers. 'I always forget you're meant to be a mystery.' Then he tugs at my wig: a black bob that's less Uma Thurman in *Pulp Fiction* and more Edward Scissorhands. 'Not your finest,' he says, shaking his head.

'You're telling me,' I say, ducking under a napkin to scratch underneath the wretched thing.

'So.' He rubs his hands together. 'Who are we spying on tonight?'

I point to the booth behind us.

'Ah, pretty,' he says of Elena, my client.

'Smart too, I just know they're perfect for each other.' I smile at him, proudly.

He laughs, easily, heartily. 'That's sweet, but it's not been going so well for you of late. I miss all the kissing.'

I elbow him in the stomach, playfully. 'You do not miss all the kissing,' I say. 'You're the one who phoned me up every night, "Caitlin, duck, please, I can't stand it, they're slobbering all over my best booth".'

'Better than, "Caitlin, duck, you've set him up with his brother".'

'It wasn't his actual brother,' I squeak. 'Just someone who looked, emmm, a lot like him.'

We settle into silence, listening in on them.

'Well, I had to tell her to put the cheese in the oven,' James is saying, guffawing slightly. 'It was the only place you couldn't smell it! You can't have that stinky cheese ruining the palate of a fine Bordeaux. What a ridiculous thing to bring!'

Bobby grimaces at me, shaking his head. 'He's a vintage wine importer,' I whisper. Bobby nods, then sings, 'That don't impress her much,' under his breath.

'She's a chef,' I add, defending my match. But looking at Elena it's clear that Bobby is right. Her eyes dart all over the restaurant each time James speaks, and now she looks down, staring intently at the menu.

'He's nervous,' I say. 'He's funny, I swear.'

He had been when I'd phoned him earlier in the week, one final assessment to see whether he was right for Elena. His job had sounded so interesting then, he had so many anecdotes that he filled me in on, poking fun at himself as he did so. There was the time he was paid to find what his client insisted was an incredibly rare, Portuguese wine . . . and James found it on the bottom shelf at a large branch of Sainsbury's. Or when he was on a trip to France and was encouraged to smash the grapes with his feet, and halfway through he remembered he had a verruca.

'Can't you step in?' asks Bobby.

I shake my head. 'Not unless she asks me to,' I say. I know the signal: Elena will excuse herself to go to the bathroom, and I'll follow her in there for a debrief. But I do really want to help. This isn't quite as bad as the brother story, or the woman who mainly wanted to use her dates to rope people into an aloe vera pyramid scheme, but it's not going well.

'Go over there and spill a glass of wine,' I say to Bobby.

He side-eyes me. 'How will that help?'

'I promise it will!' I say, grinning just slightly at him. But I'm not so sure.

He holds his hands up in defeat and slides out, pulling his notebook out of his striped apron with a flourish. 'If I get a bad TripAdvisor,' he says, 'it's on you.'

I watch as he goes over, adopting his 'Italian Grandfather' personality. It doesn't fool anyone. He thinks claiming he's first-generation Italian is what keeps his customers coming back, in truth they just love that Bobby even tries to pull it off: his hair is a shock of ginger curls and he calls everyone 'duck' in a strong Yorkshire accent.

'Ah, if it isn't my favourite customer!' he says, patting James on the back. James looks up, confused. He's never been here before. 'Can I get you anything from our special menu? Something for the lady, perhaps . . .?' He reaches over to the menu, expertly knocking James' glass.

Elena jumps up, causing the wine to splash all over the floor. James leaps up as well and begins to fumble in his pockets, as Bobby tries – and fails – to mop the mess up with flimsy paper napkins. 'I know I've got a handkerchief in here somewhere,' James is saying. Which is perfect, as it will show Elena how much of an English gent he is: she listed Hugh Grant as one of her celebrity crushes.

Then I hear her say: 'Hold on, what's that?' Her voice is sharp, and both Bobby and Elena are staring at the table. James has gone bright red.

'They're, they're . . .' I can't see what's in his hand in the mirror. I try to poke my head over the booth, to get a better view. Bobby has begun to laugh as James glares at him.

'I'm going to the bathroom,' she says, firmly. I follow her as three waiters flock to the table, jiffy cloths in hand.

'What the fuck was that?' she shrieks at me as soon as I walk through the door. She's standing by the sinks, both hands on her hips.

'Um. You'll have to tell me, I didn't actually see what happened.'

'He mopped up the wine with pants, Caitlin. Pants he'd pulled from his pocket.'

'What type of pants?' It's the only thing I can think of as I try to scramble for an explanation.

'What does it matter?' she says, exasperated. 'I'm going. I thought you were good at this.'

'I am good at this!' I say, even though – thinking about it – Bobby is right. I've not been on fire lately.

'That man out there' – she points to the door – 'is not a Harry.'

'He could be a Harry, if you gave him a chance.'

She begins listing James' traits on her fingers. 'Boring, obsessed with wine, has a slight monobrow—'

I interrupt her. 'Hey, that's not fair. You said you liked a hairy man.'

She continues with her list. 'Tells strangers to put their cheese in the oven, has a big-knicker fetish—'

'Wait, did you say big knickers?' My mind has stumbled upon something that could save this whole date.

'Yeah, huge. Like old lady ones, covered in roses. It'll be a fetish, trust me. I have the worst luck in men. I once was dating this guy, right, shagging loads of women and he kept their bras as souvenirs. I went to his house and he had a drawer full of them. Stolen, Caitlin. That's why I went to you, to weed out the shitheads.'

'No, it's not that!' My voice is raised, triumphant. 'He is a Harry!' Harry is my husband. The man every woman wants – or thinks she wants. It was our wedding day, so perfect the pictures went viral, that helped my business get off the ground.

Elena raises an eyebrow at me. 'How?'

'Those pants are his mum's. I remember now, she's very frail. He looks after her, visits her every day and does her washing.'

'Bullshit!'

'Not bullshit. Go back out there and ask him, say, "I'm sure there's a reasonable explanation for this" and he'll tell you the exact same thing.'

That's if he even is still out there. If I were him, I would have scampered by now.

'Well, that's nice,' she says, reluctantly. 'But that doesn't stop the fact that he's boring. Wine is all he's talked about.'

We're now back on even ground. I have well-worn lines to help with boring dates.

'You know, people are rarely one hundred per cent themselves on first dates,' I say. 'They get nervous, and they try to show off. I think that's what he's doing, as he is an amazing match for you.'

She wrinkles her nose. 'That guy?'

I put my hands up. 'Guide's honour. Look, I don't blame you for thinking he's dull. I've been listening and he's not really selling himself. But trust me, go back out there, get to know him and you'll see he's someone really special. He's not one of your old dickhead exes. I promise.'

She pulls out her mascara, begins piling it on. 'You'd better be right about those pants.'

A cubicle door clatters open, and a woman in towering red heels comes out. 'Hey,' she says to Elena. 'A big-knicker fetish ain't so bad, you ever tried to squeeze yourself into PVC? Uncomfortable as fuck.'

We all nod in unison. 'OK,' says Elena. 'Tell me one more thing about him and I'll go back out.'

'Has he told you about his fish tank yet?' This was what I matched them on, they're both fascinated by tropical fish. I was so excited when I found out, it was so rare to find two people, in my piles and piles of applications back at the office, who both had such a niche hobby.

6

She looks at me quizzically. 'He's got an aquarium? Does he . . .' She pauses. 'Does he like Tetras?'

'Yes, he absolutely does.' I have no idea whether he likes Tetras or not. I'm assuming it's a kind of fish . . . but then it could also be a nineties video game.

'And what's more, Elena, is that when I put you two together, I felt it . . . the Kick.'

'The one you felt with Harry?'

'The very one.' This is my USP. The 'Caitlin Kick.' It's like this rumble in my stomach, not quite a nervous flip, more like a little earthquake. As if the ground beneath me has shaken, just slightly. I first felt it with Harry. I remember looking at him and just knowing that he was going to be someone special in my life.

'But it's up to you to decide if you feel something for him too,' I'm saying to Elena, but her eyes are glazed over – it's like I've handed her a reason to go back out and try again. I think most people just want a guarantee that it will all be worth it: the small talk, the first arguments, the bravery of putting yourself into someone's hands, knowing they could hurt you at any given moment.

'An aquarium, eh? Who'd have thought it?' she says, almost rushing out.

'Whatever turns you on,' says the woman. I laugh and follow Elena out.

James is, by some miracle, still at the table. It's all been mopped up now, and I see Bobby, over in the kitchen. He waves the wine-sodden knickers at me. I give him my best 'don't be mean' glare.

'You came back!' James says as Elena sits back down. 'I didn't know whether to order us another bottle, so I've got a beer coming your way. I remember you said you liked it.'

I settle myself back into the booth, smiling. 'Now, the pants . . .' James is saying. I can almost hear the flush in his cheeks. 'There is a reasonable explanation . . .'

He tells her. That his mum is struggling, arthritis has taken over her body and she finds most things difficult. 'She doesn't bake any more, hasn't really since my dad died,' he's saying, while Elena makes caring tutting noises.

'I understand,' she says. 'Now, shall we start again? Tell me about some of your hobbies . . . apart from wine, that is.'

'OK.' He nods. 'Well, you might think this is boring, most women do, but hey! What do I have to lose? This date couldn't get much worse.'

She laughs. 'True. Go on, tell me.'

'I have my own fish tank, an aquarium.'

She gasps, overdramatically. 'No. Way. I have a fish tank, too!'

His eyes widen, and he leans forward, conspiratorially. 'What's your favourite fish?'

'Tetras! Yours?'

Please, James, say you like Tetras. I'm willing him on so much that I almost don't hear his answer.

'Oh, I love Tetras . . . but I'm also really fond of the clownfish.'

They begin to chat excitedly about the different person-alities of their fish and Bobby – sensing the shift in mood – gives me a thumbs up. I mock-wipe my brow, feeling the wig shift to the side. I begin to tuck into my spaghetti – it's gone cold but it doesn't matter. Bobby's tomato sauce (or 'red sauce' as he calls it secretly to me) is the best in town. The chatter and the laughter in the booth soothes me – it won't be long until I can go home. Elena requested that I only stay for the first hour. That's almost past now but I want to stay a little longer: he's leaning forward, listening intently to something she's saying and she's smiling now, her face lit up by the candlelight. I love basking in that excitement, that chemistry.

I chuck some cash down on the table and write Bobby a little note, thanking him for the evening. He's over in the corner enthusing about how the streets of Rome inspired his decor. I don't want to interrupt, so I slip out, giving Elena a discreet wave.

Outside, there are huddles of people spilling out of pubs, clutching beers and laughing. The first signs of Christmas are beginning to show: Bobby's laced fairy lights around his doorway, and I can see a few trees in windows above. A couple are snuggled up on a doorstep, the smoke from their breath in clouds around them. They clink their Corona bottles and peck each other on the lips. I glance quickly away, just as they spot me staring. The line of taxis is tempting . . . but I wrap my scarf tighter around my neck and begin to walk home. It's about half an hour from here but I like sneaking glances in pub windows, looking at who is inside, sensing the excitement of the season.

I glance down at my engagement ring. There are flecks of red in the milky opal that are lit up by the street lights. It's meant to be bad luck, to have an opal engagement ring, but I'd wanted one since I was a little girl. Harry must have known this somehow, maybe from my mum, and he played on the idea – the night he'd proposed I'd come into our living room to find him knelt on one knee surrounded by open umbrellas. Pink ones, spotty ones, see-through ones, all scattered across our living room floor. The cat that always showed up at our back door, a sleek black thing, was wandering around, and Harry had placed the ring on an upturned broken mirror, which he'd sprinkled with salt. He'd thought of everything, there had even been a ladder propped up on the inside of the door that I'd walked under without noticing. 'No day can be unlucky if I'm with you,' Harry had said. I'd been so happy I'd not been able to stop crying for two whole hours.

I think back to Elena and James, the way he was looking at her. I try to hold onto that, tight in my heart. I hope they'll end up, one day, feeling as lucky and happy as I did that evening.

Chapter Two

'Verity, what's going on?' I'm shouting for her to hear me; the music channels are on and Whitney's pumped up, dancing around on screen in a purple dress. I take a sip of my wine, fully expecting to wince at first and then slowly get used to the pungent flavour. But instead it goes down smoothly. I reach for the bottle. It's usually just plonked at my feet so I can help myself. But it's not there.

'Where's the wine?'

She pokes her head out the door, bringing with her a waft of melting cheese. 'In the fridge, you need a top-up?'

'No, just wondered what it was.'

'Pinot, from Marks and Sparks, I think.'

She retreats back into the kitchen and I look at the carpet. I don't think I've ever seen this much of it before. The magazine clippings she uses for her look books – usually spread out all over the floor – have been neatly stacked and shoved to one corner. I reach down through the sofa cushion's gaps, which are usually stuffed with chocolate wrappers. But nothing rustles.

Last night Verity had made it clear that I would not be spending another Saturday night working. I was to come over for tea. 'Do not come over unarmed,' she'd announced. I'd shown up with a bottle of good wine but the fridge was already stocked up.

She settles in beside me, clutching a Snoopy mug filled to the brim. 'Who you looking at?' She snatches my phone off me – I'm two years back on Polly Lee's Instagram.

'Do not like anything!' I yelp, trying to grab it back off her.

She laughs. 'Oh, I just might . . .'

'You wouldn't dare!'

I look over her shoulder – it's Polly Lee's daughter's fifth birthday party. She set up mini long wooden tables in the garden and covered them in vintage tea sets, and there were little French fancies at each place setting – the child's name iced on them.

'Can you believe these cakes are vegan?' Verity's reading the caption allowed. 'And sugar-free.'

'I had two . . . gotta treat yourself,' I say, filling in the rest from memory.

'I want to smash five Mr Kiplings in her face,' Verity says. 'Who is this smug bitch?'

'She's not that bad, she was the PR exec at my old firm.'

'Have you had a lobotomy? Everyone was hideous to you there!'

'OK,' I sigh. 'She was actually really mean. But look at her life, it's just perfect.'

'There's nothing perfect about living sugar-free – remember when I tried it?'

'Remember? I'm still scarred from it!'

It was back when Verity and I lived together – in this top-floor, tiny flat that we rented simply because it had a balcony. The floor of every room – even the hallway – was covered with an array of fabrics: sequins, velvet, denim, and we survived on ready-meals and two-for-a-fiver wine from our local shop. One January Verity decided to kick sugar, going cold turkey. She lasted three days – and, on the second, I had walked into the kitchen just as she had smashed a glass in anger at something someone had said on the radio.

'Is that lasagne I can smell?' It had to be an M&S ready-meal, that was all Verity lived off of. Verity can't cook, she's resolute that there are better things she could be doing with her time.

'Yep, just something I, y'know, rustled up.' She tries to keep her face straight, before pealing into giggles. 'Ah, you know me, Jeremiah cooked it, OK? I just put it in the oven.'

'Demanding your boyfriend cooks for us . . . clean house . . . clean wine glasses, what's the occasion?'

She looks away, her eyes boring into the TV screen. Now an old Backstreet Boys number is blasting out.

'No reason, just thought it'd be nice. Been a while since we hung out at mine together. Go on, show me who else you've been stalking so I can hate on them.'

I grab my phone back and pull up Morwena Star's profile. Morwena Star is ridiculous but I kind of love her. She describes herself as a 'crystal healer', and her account is full of selfies and shots of her perfectly manicured hands holding up crystals, spouting on about how 'opal fixes my crown, makes me ready for the day' while citrine helps her 'cultivate my sunshine'.

'Nobody looks like that doing yoga,' says Verity, pointing at one of her doing a back bend on a sunset beach. 'Wait, click on that one.'

I pull up one of Morwena sitting cross-legged, under a tree, her eyes shut. I read the caption: 'Be in the moment, in the now, take time out in nature, away from your phone.'

Verity snorts with laughter. 'And who's taking the photo?!'

'I know it's stupid but at least she's created a brand for herself. She's almost got a million followers.'

'But it's all fake, did you not say she's from around here?'

I nod. I'm not quite sure where she manages to find the beaches or luscious forests, as, after some investigating, I've discovered that she lives in Sheffield. A grey hilly city that's so far from the beach kids have taken to playing in the fountains in the square in the centre on hot days, running in and out screeching while their knackered parents sit on a park bench, sipping cider cans.

'Fake in a way that's making her a fortune. She'll get paid loads for these posts,' I remind her, thinking of my own feed and how hard I was trying to get the follower count up.

'Ugh, it's so depressing,' Verity replies. 'I just couldn't do it.' She takes a swig of her wine. 'Show me something that'll cheer me up again.'

So I flick to the folder containing all our old snaps. There's one of us fresh out of university: I'm wearing a pair of cut-off green tartan tights, a hacked-up denim miniskirt and a blue spotty hoody, and Verity's in denim hot pants, neon yellow earrings and a black vest. She was going through her Amy Winehouse phase, and had darkened her eyes out and painted her lips red.

'Still gutted I can't tame my hair into a beehive,' she says, patting her Afro.

We begin to scroll through together until we get to the more recent ones. There's a picture of Verity and I at a hairdresser opening. Verity had been invited by one of her clients, a WAG who'd just been given a hefty divorce settlement and was setting up her own business. I'm in a pinstripe black and white knee-length dress and heels that – you can tell from my face – pinched, while Verity is in a floor-length vintage seventies dress covered in orange flowers. Harry had said she looked like his nan's carpet, and Verity is throwing her head back laughing . . . In the background you can see one of the other customers giving her evils. Verity's laugh is so loud and unapologetic, you're either caught up in it or you're wondering where on earth that strange honking sound is coming from.

Then there's the three of us at my business launch party – Harry's eyes are two grey circles: he'd been working all day and then helping me all night for weeks in the run-up. He'd ended up falling asleep in the toilets at about 1 a.m. that evening. Next to that there's the pair of us, holding up the keys to our house, on the doorstep – my hair in pigtails and Harry covered in dust.

She looks at my glass. I've taken about four sips from it. 'Oh, you need topping up!' She gets up and bustles through to the adjoining kitchen. She's wearing jeans with bright pink tassels hanging from the butt – they shimmy as she walks, like a twenties dancer in feathers. When she comes back through she squeezes my knee, an old habit of hers, picked up from her grandma. I brush it off. Harry's face is still dominating my phone screen. She gently takes it out of my hand and places it on the floor.

'You'll never guess what happened on set today . . .' And she's off. Telling the story of Jenna Self, an old *Love Island* contestant she was styling this week. She's not supposed to tell me this stuff – if any of it got to the press she'd be in big trouble – but she just can't help herself. We've both been celebrity-obsessed since high school. When we lived together we'd spend days curled up on the sofa bingeing on reality TV. Verity would always sit there, analysing the outfits of all the contestants, saying, 'When I get my hands on her . . .'

'Every single outfit I pulled out Jenna would say, "Jenna no likey", sticking her bottom lip out! Then later on the make-up artist found out she'd nicked all of her nail polishes. She must have slid like twenty bottles into her handbag.'

'Oh my God,' I say, my mouth open. 'Is she still with . . .?'

'Chris? Yeah, he picked her up at the end. I swear that guy must be on steroids or something, he's literally built like a triangle.'

'It's so obvious he's cheating on her,' I reply.

'You mean the other week where he was caught in a toilet cubicle with two blondes, and his response was he was "helping them unblock it"?'

'Yeah, right, Chris the Plumber,' I say, looking under the sofa for the pile of *Heats*, *Closers* and *Now* magazines that live there. There's just a faint trace of dust. 'I mean, I hate her but nobody deserves to be with a cheat.'

Verity's sitting, picking at the tassels attached to her jeans – one has become frayed and she plays with its ends. 'Mmmm-hmmm,' she says before jumping up again. 'That'll be the lasagne ready!'

'Want help plating up?' I ask, but she insists she's fine and that I need to relax.

'How was last night's date?' I hear her shout through over the clattering of plates.

'Total disaster at first,' I shout back. 'But I saved it!'

She comes through, hands me a plate, steam rising from a generous slab of lasagne. 'And how was the wig?'

Verity gets the wigs from her styling jobs, lends them to me each time so that my client's dates don't spot me as their chaperone.

'Not great,' I admit. 'I don't know where you've been getting them from recently. The last few have been absolute horror shows.'

I see a smirk appear on her face as she chews her lasagne. 'No!' I cry. 'You didn't, did you?'

She begins to honk. 'I did, I'm sorry! Bobby thought it would be funny if we gave you shit wigs for a while, keep us amused.' She pulls her phone out, shows me a picture of me sitting in the booth, with a smug little grin on my face, as I concentrate on James and Elena's date. The black wig is curled all around my cheeks, and in the next snap I'm trying to discreetly scratch underneath it without anyone noticing.

'God, I thought I looked like Edward Scissorhands, but now I see it's much worse—'

She interrupts me, gripping my arm in hysterics. 'It's Hayley Cropper!'

'I can't believe it,' I say, in mock dismay. 'My best friend has been deliberately making me look terrible, for her own amusement.'

'Hey,' she says, sincerely. 'I told Bobby we couldn't do an Instagram. He wanted to call it . . . The Wigfluencer.'

'Hashtag look of the day, Hashtag Hayley Cropper is my style icon,' I say. She reaches down the side of the sofa, pulling up a green M&S bag. 'Snacks! We got the whole gang in here . . .'

She begins to unload the haul onto her coffee table. 'Percy, Percy's girlfriend, Percy's lover—'

'Not Panda!'

She nods solemnly. 'Penny has no idea.'

'Poor thing,' I say, tearing open the packet, shoving a gummy in my mouth. 'Still maybe she could cop off with Colin, revenge shag.'

'Oooh, I've got a good "who would you rather",' she shouts. It was our favourite game growing up. We could spend hours, sitting on the park green, sucking on 5p ice poles, our mouths all blue, asking each other who we fancied more – often choosing the worst-looking guys or teachers in our year to pick between. 'Colin or Percy?' Verity says, triumphantly.

'You're asking me to choose whether I'd rather shag a cake or a gummy sweet?'

'Yep,' she says. 'And you have to answer. Thems the rules.'

'I'm a lady,' I say, grinning at her. 'I'm not answering that.'

She playfully hits me with her cushion. 'Bullshit! Coming from the woman who confessed to a crush on Ursula the Sea Witch.'

'I did not!' I hit her back.

'Did so.'

'OK, once, after loads of gins. And, hey, Ursula is a very sexual woman.'

'Ursula is an octopus crossed with a drag queen.'

'I'm not the one who fancies Foxy from the Bingo adverts.'

'I stand by that,' she says. 'Foxy has a sexy charm to him, and great taste in suits.'

There's a pause and tomorrow looms up on me.

'Remember that night a few weeks back when you came to my office with a bottle of white?'

She nods. 'That was a fun night.' We'd ended up getting in another bottle, and then heading to the rock pub a few doors down from my office, where we did tequila shots with a biker called Gaz. It's all a bit hazy after that.

'We made a match that night before we went out, remember?'

'Wait, it's coming to me. They had the same drinks order!'

'Yes, but that's all they had,' I reply, remembering how Verity had yelled, 'dry martini with a twist,' and dinged the little copper bell I use for when I find the perfect match. I'd laughed, said, 'Fine, matched. Now let's get to the pub.'

'It was for Elijah,' I continue, 'you know, the hairdresser?' She nods. 'Fussy little bugger, he is.'

'Precisely. And we matched him with this filthy rocker guy, Tom. I've got to chaperone their date tomorrow – it's going to be a disaster.'

'So, just go to the restaurant, see how they get on, if they don't work, tell Elijah it was a clever experiment to make him see how wrong some guys are, or some shit like that.'

'I don't think you get how my business works,' I say, smiling at her. 'But I can't even do that, as I've arranged for them to go to the zoo tomorrow.'

'The zoo?' she says. 'There's not one for miles. What? Why?'

'I know,' I say, remembering the day I decided Elijah's date would be held somewhere new and different. He was sitting in my office reeling off how he always went on champagne bar dates, with men who pulled his chair out, who paid the whole bill. 'And how have you found the guys who do this for you? What's happened with them?' I asked. 'Oh,' he'd replied, his hand jutting to his mouth as he giggled. 'They've all turned out to be total bastards.'

'He's so particular, I just thought it might be good for him to go somewhere different. I obviously regret it now.'

'You'll be fine.' She squeezes my knee. 'You're the expert on this. Think of how many people you've made happy.'

'I know. I just really want to take the business to the next level, just not quite sure zoo dates are the answer.'

'Maybe not,' she replies. 'But you're still achieving what you set out to do. Don't be too hard on yourself.'

I breathe in, remembering one summer where all we did was sit squashed into our balcony, excitedly planning our futures. It was halfway through July, when one hazy evening I first saw Harry. Verity was wearing an emerald-green ball gown and trainers and the sun was just beginning to set, casting a golden light on the both of us. We were drinking cheap fizz and Verity spotted him first, pointing out a guy down on the street carrying a red tatty armchair all by himself while the girl in front of him, dressed in head-to-toe bubblegum pink, played on her phone. 'Nice ass,' she'd said, and I'd giggled. Later, I'd run down for more drinks when I'd heard this voice behind me. I'd turned round and seen him. His curly brown hair, flopped over blue eyes; his wiry frame and bobbing Adam's apple; his skin, lightly tanned; the stack of elastic bands around his wrist. I'd wanted to absorb all of him. He was laughing and I loved his laugh – like a dog barking. My stomach had dropped down, right down, and then something in it had come alive, like it was having a party. I tried to smile at him but didn't quite manage; instead I rushed back upstairs, desperate to tell Verity about him.

She'd just laughed and said, 'Hopefully you'll bump into him again.' We'd carried on drinking, looking out at the sky, which was turning from blue to pink, into the colour of pick-n-mix sweeties. Verity had made us write our dreams onto bits of paper, and then we'd folded them up into paper planes. She'd jotted hers down easily: fashion has been a part of her dreams since she first tried on her mum's velvet evening gown. I'd struggled. I had this feeling in my shoulders that hadn't quite reached my head that the path I was on – PR – wasn't the right one. But there had been something I'd wanted: stomach flip guy. Harry. I'd jotted it down, not even knowing his name then, and quickly folded it before she could see. The sky was cornflower blue by then, and we threw the planes, shrieking as we watched them plummet down into the street below.

Chapter Three

'Arrrk, arrrrk, arrrrrrkkkkkkkk.' Three monkeys are screaming at me, one sitting down in a pile of sawdust, holding onto his ears and grinning. I'm rushing towards Tom and Elijah but the monkeys are following fast. Clambering along the cage as I move. With them comes a crowd of people, all 'ooohing and aaaahhing' at them.

'Monkeys,' I say to a woman dressed head to toe in khaki, holding her camera right up to its face. 'They're not great for a hangover.' Verity had, inevitably, opened up more wine, for 'just one more glass' last night, which had led to us finishing off the bottle and me leaving hers, giggling as I fell into a taxi, at 1 a.m.

'Well, they certainly like ya,' she says, snapping away at them. 'They've been going crazy every time you move! It's why I'm sticking with ya . . . I think it's that gorgeous red hair of yours.'

I reach up, my hand springing off the wig: it's a short, red, curly number – Annie mixed with Ronald McDonald. I'd taken a selfie this morning, sent it across to Bobby and Verity. *This is the last time you bitches are doing this to me,* I'd typed, knowing full well they wouldn't take the least bit of notice.

I can see Tom and Elijah more clearly now, and how ripped Tom's jeans are, and how his Converse are caked in mud. Elijah is in a pair of baby-blue trousers, brown brogues and a thick green parka jacket. His hair, coiffed above him, adds about an inch to his height. Why did I let Verity match these two? Was it just because they have the same drinks order, or was there something else?

They've approached the camels now, the big brown beasts staring woefully at them, under long eyelashes. The camels are clearly not a star attraction here: despite a wooden nativity laid out in front of them, and some lamp-like fairy lights strung around the top of their enclosure in an attempt to make them more like a nativity. I duck behind a fence, staring through a gap in the wood. Tom is grinning but Elijah has his back to a brick wall and is frantically pumping hand sanitiser gel into his left palm.

'Come on,' Tom was saying, leaning forward to him, his arm outstretched. 'They won't bite.'

'They might SPIT!' shouts Elijah, rubbing his right hand ferociously. And there's something in the back of my mind that I can't quite grasp. I try to picture Elijah's file or our first meeting but it doesn't work. It's that hand movement, the rubbing like he wants, eventually, to scrape all the skin off. That's what is triggering this flurry of pebbles sloshing about in my gut.

Tom looks slightly annoyed now. His brow is a little furrowed, despite keeping a smile on his face. 'Come on, they're gorgeous . . .'

Tom's used to mosh pits, to people treading on his forearm in studded boots and then pulling him back up again. He's used to armpits in his face, dripping with sweat, and plastic beer cups filled with wee being thrown over him. So of course Elijah's serious, almost OCD phobia of germs won't make sense to him. Then it hits me: Elijah's almost OCD phobia of germs. This was the worst place possible for him to go. I have to get them out of there.

I glance around. How will I do this? I know Elijah, he may hate every minute of being there, but he's stubborn. Once he's agreed to do something he will stick it out. He'll just resent Tom for it. And that's not fair, this is all my fault.

It turns out the fence I ducked behind is a sort of makeshift storage area, which houses a huge pile of tangled plastic dinosaur limbs. On top of them, balancing precariously, is a dinosaur head. Maybe I could use it as a disguise. Tell them there's a dinosaur show happening? Herd them away?

I pounce upon the pile, tugging off my wig and abandoning it on the ground as I begin pulling out an arm and then a leg, hoping to lower the pile so I can reach the head, which is currently too far up for me to reach. It looks down at me with its dead, unforgiving eyes.

'What the hell do you think you're doing?'

I spin round, now clutching the claw. It was too sudden a movement, and all the limbs come tumbling down around me, like Jenga pieces. The head rolls and clatters and lands, right at my feet, its eyes boggling up at me. Also staring at me is a sturdy-looking woman. She's holding a bucket of fish. Her mouth is creased downwards. If smoke could come out of her ears, it would.

She just looks at me, until I find words escaping my mouth. 'George, George told me to tidy these up.' I look to my feet. Point to a red, bumpy tail. 'He said they're not needed any more.'

George is a manager's name, I'm thinking. She shakes her head.

'Are you the new girl? Joanne, is it?'

I smile, in what I hope is a sheepish manner. 'Well I don't know why the hell she'd tell you to do that,' says the woman, who I now notice has a name-tag. Kitty. 'Louis has been waiting in the penguin enclosure for ten minutes now. The show starts in five.'

She hands the yellow bucket to me. 'Take these to him and hurry up. And for God's sake, get your uniform on.'

Opposite the now-dismantled pile of dinosaur heads are three boxes containing caps and jackets – all with the zoo's emblem on them. Why didn't I notice them first? I can hear Tom saying, 'Fine, let's just go to another enclosure, if that's what you want,' as I struggle the forest-green coat on, shoving my own hair up into the cap. I stride out, towards Tom and Elijah, clutching the bucket. I've met Elijah lots of times, even before he hired me for my services. His hair salon is on the same road as my office. Thankfully, I've only spoken to Tom on the phone and I'm praying that he won't recognise me from the website. I pull the cap lower down on my face before speaking.

'Excuse me, sirs?' I say, and Elijah's eyes widen, and he stops rubbing at his hands. Tom grins, then sniffs, quickly pinching his nose. Elijah looks down at bucket, horrified. Some of the fish are still squirming. 'I'm afraid the zoo is closing. There's been a bit of an accident with the gorilla enclosure. You'd be best to leave right away.'

'Oh no!' Elijah says, touching his heart. 'We'd best go now.'

'Terribly sorry to interrupt your day,' I say. 'How about going to the coffee shop across the street? It does an excellent hot chocolate with homemade marshmallows.'

'That sounds delicious, and don't worry, it's not your fault,' Tom says, cupping Elijah's elbow and leading him towards the exit.

I follow, hurrying them along, when Elijah turns to me and says, winking: 'Shouldn't you be letting other people know what's going on?'

I glare at him. But he's right. This has to look believable to Tom. 'Ladies,' I say to a group of three. 'The zoo is actually closing, there's been a problem—'

'With the gorilla enclosure,' nods Elijah. The blonde of the group frowns at me. She's wearing a badge that says 'Fifty Is The New Forty.'

'But I just paid for these tickets, fucking joke this place.'

Her friends all tut in agreement. One of them, I notice, is drinking from a straw stuck into a miniature wine bottle.

'You will be given a full refund, but your safety is paramount.'

A man in his fifties turns round. 'Safety? Is there a problem, miss?'

'You're perfectly safe, it's just a precaution, but we will need you and your mother to evacuate,' I say, smiling at the elderly woman in a leopard print coat beside him.

'Excuse me,' she says. 'But I'm his wife.'

I'm about to apologise, when I feel a tap on my shoulder. A weedy teen, a scattering of acne around his chin, faces me. 'What's happening? I haven't heard about this gorilla thing,' he says, his voice coming out in a squeak. Clipped to his belt is a black radio, chattering away about how the penguins still don't have their food. I reach over, unclip it and put it on my jeans waistband.

'Yes, we have to evacuate people now . . . Take these,' I say, handing him the bucket of fish. 'Gorilla outbreak or not, the penguins need feeding. I'll radio and let people know what's going on.'

I hadn't meant to say outbreak. It just slipped out. 'The gorillas have escaped!' shouts someone behind me, which causes a ripple effect. Like dominoes being pushed over. One person begins to run towards the exit, followed by the next, until I'm being jostled back and forth as a swarm of people race past. Tom has started to do a gorilla impression, and Elijah joins in, the pair of them being pushed out the way as they lumber slowly along with the crowd.

I'm trying to calm people down. 'Honestly, gorillas are friendly beasts,' I say to one man who races past me, before turning to a woman who has gripped onto my arm and won't let go. 'Yes, I know what Attenborough says, he loves to exaggerate.'

Kitty is standing at the zoo gate holding a megaphone. The mob keeps running towards her, but she steps out in front of them – placing a hand in front of her, like a traffic warden. The crowd – as if they were speeding cars – comes to a stop. I begin pushing backwards, trying to get to the back, so she won't spot me.

'Everybody CALM DOWN,' she yells. The megaphone is crackly but her voice through it is clear. 'What is going on?'

'The gorillas have escaped!' shouts someone from the front.

'What? No they haven't,' she says, putting down her megaphone and scolding the person directly. 'Don't be ridiculous.'

'Yes, two members of staff told us.'

There's a murmur of agreement. 'Not our fault,' mutters one person. 'Just doing what we were told,' shouts another.

'Who?' she demands. I start to slowly remove my cap, my blonde curls tumbling down around me.

'Him,' someone in the crowd says, pointing to my unwitting accomplice. 'And the girl with the curly blonde hair.'

I duck down before anyone can spot me. I'm on my knees, wedged between a pair of red Doc Martens and some plain white pumps. Down here with me is a little girl, clutching a hat in the shape of a sparkly orange tropical fish. She gives me a little wave.

'Hello,' I whisper. 'I'm Caitlin.'

'Violet,' the girl whispers back. 'Are you a zookeeper?'

'I am,' I say. 'What's your favourite animal?'

'The sloth,' she says. 'Did you know they can swim really, really fast?'

'And they only poo once a week,' I reply, and she giggles.

'Have the gorillas really escaped?'

I shake my head, but hold my finger up to my lips. 'But let's keep it our secret.'

She mimes zipping her lips. Then beckons me in, speaking into my ear.

'I want to be a zookeeper when I'm older,' she says, earnestly.

'You would be a fantastic zookeeper. You already know so much about sloths.'

'And snails. Did you know they can sleep for three whole years?'

'I did not. I would love to sleep for three whole years.'

'I wouldn't,' she says, shaking her head. 'Sleeping is boring.'

'It is more exciting when you're older. Hey, Violet, do you know what you'll definitely need to be a zookeeper?'

'Sloth food,' she says resolutely.

'Well, yes, you will need that. But you'll also need a uniform.'

She opens her mouth with a gasp, as I plonk my cap on her head and wrap the coat around her.

Above me, in a thick Mancunian accent, I can hear a woman say: 'I don't care what she says. I'm not risking anything.'

A man's voice then says: 'But we just paid. Violet's been looking forward to it all week.'

Violet, who is clinging to a denim leg, begins to move with it.

'I have to go,' she says. 'But you can have my hat.' And she hands me my saviour, in the form of an orange fish head.

'Thank you, Violet,' I say, pulling it on, tucking all my hair into the back of it. She sticks her tongue out at me. 'You look silly,' she says, and then is pulled away.

I brush myself off and stand up: everything has calmed down a bit. I can't see Tom and Elijah anywhere. I hope this whole thing worked. I can't shake the thought of them running out together. The way they'd both found fun in the situation, linking arms and joking around with all the other tourists. It made me think that they're not so ill-suited after all.

I begin to walk towards the exit. Kitty's distracted, talking into a walkie-talkie: 'It was the new girl, Joanne. No, I don't know where she got that idea from either!' As she talks, my belt buzzes. The radio sitting on my jeans. I break into a jog, racing out of the zoo and round the corner, where I unclip the radio and place it on the wall. Hopefully someone will find it. I spot Elijah. Leaning against a lamp post and pointing at me. I tap my fish head and begin to laugh, and he joins in pulling me in for a hug, as we both gasp for breath.

'Well . . . that escalated quickly,' he says.

'I'm so sorry, I should not have suggested the zoo! And I just wanted to get you out of there . . . I guess I just didn't want my mistake stopping the two of you getting to know each other.'

'You're very sweet, Caitlin Carter.'

I shake my head. 'But the worst matchmaker ever. It didn't work . . .' I gesture to the space around him. 'You're alone.'

'He is terrible for me,' he says. 'Absolutely terrible. Have you seen his hair?'

My face drops. 'I know, but with a quick clean-up he'll look great. And, and I really think that you two could connect, if you just got to know him.'

'As for those muddy trainers . . .'

I must look devastated, as Elijah grins. 'OK, I can't do it to you! He is terrible for me, but that's why he's at the coffee shop, waiting for me.'

'You're giving terrible a chance!' I jump up, hug him again.

'Perfect wasn't working out for me, and hey,' he says. 'At least if it goes tits up I'll have a funny story to tell. And you, you have a brilliant hat. You should keep it, it suits you.' And with that, he turns on his heel and begins to jog in the direction of the coffee shop.

Chapter Four

The following day I wake up early. I stand at our bedroom window and watch a plane cut through the dark sky. Shadowed in a window opposite me, I see a woman staring out foggily, clutching a feeding baby to her chest. The cars on our street are covered with frost. Everything is silent. I haven't slept well, the adrenaline from the day before still twitching through my body as I lay in bed, eyes squeezed shut, willing sleep to come. But I don't feel bad, I feel renewed. Like a fog that's surrounded me has lifted, just a little. Tom had texted me as soon as I'd arrived home. *He's the best, I'm obsessed with him!* it had read, followed by three heart-eye emojis. Elena had also emailed saying she and James had lined up their next date.

Matches, that's what I need to do, make as many matches as possible, I'm thinking as I pull on layers: a black polo neck followed by a grey jumper and then an even bigger fluffy black jumper on top of that. I shove my feet into Uggs, 'Moomin shoes', Harry calls them: he hates the noise I make when I wear them, the constant drag and shuffle of my feet.

As I step onto the street, the birds have just started to sing. I begin to walk, head down, furry hood up, until I'm on West Street and everything feels that little bit more alive. Trams trundle past me, and Boots is just opening its doors – a woman in a white tabard, marked with orange foundation around the collar, smiles wearily at me as she rolls up the security shutters.

I climb the steps to my office two at a time: it's a small space, above Costa Coffee, that I started renting six months ago. It's a blush-pink, copper-themed haven. I'm here most days now at 7 a.m. I make myself a tea: Tetley's, sneaking in one sugar, even though there's no one here to witness it, and begin to print out the new applications that have come in overnight: all forty of them. I print out every single application I'm sent in, and file them away. I love it, makes the whole thing seem much more real somehow – reminds me I must take care of these people's feelings, that they're not just some 3D image on my computer screen.

I began the business with just friends, and friends of friends, who'd heard I had this knack for recognising who was right and who was wrong for each other, and slowly the word began to spread. I always remember that first email I received from a stranger. I'd been convincing myself for months that once I ran out of acquaintances that would be it, the business would be over, but there was Jana. She had tight curly hair, just like mine, but hers was chocolate brown, so glossy it was like it had melted. She had big, pond-green eyes and her smile spread right across the bottom of her face. I wonder if she knew how much she meant to me. I hope she's still happy with her match: the owner of a local party supplies store, who I met when buying balloons.

Ade will be here soon. It's almost 10 a.m. and she tends to come rolling in between now and midday, usually smelling of stale white wine and full of stories from the night before. I should probably be stricter with her: give her a proper start and finish time, and make sure she sticks to it. But, even as her boss, I'm fond of her haphazard ways: how she comes in like a whirlwind of energy and breaks me out of whatever daydream I'm stuck in.

To my surprise, she arrives bang on the hour: dressed in a leather pencil skirt, a white t-shirt that screams THIS IS WHAT A FEMINIST LOOKS LIKE and her hair, with its one blue streak, pulled back into a bun, a few strands escaping. She swaps out of her muddy Converse and into a pair of pointed courts.

'Hey, Ade, nice night? Coffee?' I say, wandering over to the Nespresso machine.

'Nope, no time,' she says, pulling her laptop out. 'I have come up with the best action plan.'

She's a social media manager who's worked with some of the biggest brands in the country: doing stuff for Google, Snapchat and Pepsi, before she packed her stuff up, choosing Sheffield for her next adventure because, as she told me when we first met 'I, like, really love *The Full Monty*.' When pressed further about her sudden move – almost a year ago – she simply shook her head. 'Too many lost souls,' she'd said. I'd known in the way she'd looked down, fiddled with her fingers, that there was a break-up involved somehow. But I didn't press. She can tell me when she's ready.

I hired her two months ago, setting her up a little desk opposite mine, which she's mostly just sat at, typing away, while occasionally showing me a meme or an online article that's made me choke with laughter.

She taps a long, freshly manicured purple nail onto the screen. I've never understood how she can type with those things. 'What's this?' My Instagram is up, the picture is of a mocktail, which I'd captioned, 'Who needs alcohol to have fun?' with all the sober hashtags lined up underneath it.

'Sobriety is cool at the moment! Everyone's doing it
. . .' I reply, glancing down at my desk. A photo of a girl
sits on top of my pile of applications: her button nose and
parsley-green eyes are calling to me. I want to pick up her
application and read it in peace, but Ade is still talking, so
I look at her and try to listen.

'But you're not sober,' she says, raising one eyebrow at
me, pointing to the pink mini-fridge. 'What's in there?'

'Wine,' I answer dutifully. There's also Diet Coke, a
half-eaten Caesar salad that's probably gone off by now
and, for reasons I can't explain, a tube of tomato puree.
But I understand what she's getting at. She then begins
discussing the power of 'authenticity' and 'building a
loyal following', reciting words and phrases I see scattered
across the internet but which I don't pay much attention to. I caress the pile of papers in front of me; button
nose's application reads that she wants to take up boxing
lessons. Jordy, I'm thinking, doesn't he teach kids boxing
each week? If I could just get his application, it's in this
bottom drawer . . .

'You're not listening to me!' she says, pointing one
menacing fingernail at me.

'I am!' I protest, quickly pulling my hand up and away
from the drawer, settling both palms on my desk like a
child emptying his pockets to show there's no forbidden
sweeties in there.

She smirks at me. 'OK then . . . what was I saying?'

I look at button nose, who just grins sweetly at me.
She's giving me no answers. 'Hashtags,' I say, confidently.

It's wrong. But at least it makes her laugh. 'No, silly,
I was saying you need to post more pictures of you and
Harry. They're always the photos that do the best. Honestly,

the stories you tell me about you guys, it makes me want to run off and marry a dentist.'

'It's not worth it, you don't get that much free dental treatment,' I say, suddenly wishing that Ade was a puppy and I could just throw a red ball at her and she'd run after it, distracted. 'Go, Ade, go play,' I'd say, and I wouldn't be sitting here feeling pins and needles erupt all over my body.

'I don't like to post pictures of him,' I say, pushing my chair back and going to click the kettle on. It lights up blue, and I stare at it, my back to Ade.

'But you used to,' she's saying. 'Look at this one, it's so cute.' I can't help myself, I turn round and go to her desk. On her screen is a picture of us at Halloween, coated in fake blood and holding plastic daggers. I'd made us tops by stapling cereal boxes together, and when I brought them through, shouting, 'Serial killers!' Harry had fallen off the sofa laughing.

'That was a fun night,' I nod. 'We love Halloween.'

I always buy sweets for trick or treaters, strictly instructing Harry not to touch them until at least 3 November – when he gleefully pounces on the many, many bags left over, as I always get too much. I pick a new theme every year for us to dress up as and make us go out on the actual day, even if it's a Monday.

I get my love of tradition from my mum, who always made a big fuss of everything growing up as it was just us two: Dad left when I was five. Verity would come round on Halloween and we'd bob for apples in the washing-up bowl, and on Bonfire Night we'd have jacket potatoes with chilli before heading to the local football ground to watch the sky explode with colour. I glance at the calendar hanging on the wall. The picture is of neon purple and pink fireworks, breaking out across a city skyline: November. I can't quite remember when the season began to change, when the trees turned orange.

'What did you dress up as this year? We could probably still post it?' Ade asks, breaking me out of my stupor as I try to remember the day.

'Oh, um . . .' I think back to the calendar picture the month before. 'Pumpkins. But I think it's too late now and I, uh, looked fat in all the photos.'

She laughs, this tinkling noise. Like a small bell ringing. 'You were dressed as a pumpkin, wasn't that the whole point?'

'Yeah but I thought it'd be cute . . . it just wasn't. Verity laughed so hard when she saw me.'

Ade shakes her head, begins to type something and I wander back to the blush-pink armchairs. They're situated in the window overlooking the bustling street below, where clusters of students weave their way along the pavement, wearing bright beanie hats and clutching coffees. I pick at my chipped nail varnish, catching the edge of the lacquered maroon, peeling it off in one satisfying strip.

'Funny,' Ade's saying, still typing away. 'I saw Verity a few days after Halloween. She said it had been a quiet one.'

It's like suddenly someone's pumped fog into my ear, and it's filling my brain up, working its way down through my limbs. I can't feel anything: I can't hear the chatter from outside, the beeping of the car horns that are the usual soundtrack to my day. The chair I'm sitting on, soft to touch, feels cold beneath me. I look over at Ade, it's like her fingers are typing in slow motion. All I can think is: Verity, Verity, why did she see Verity?

I take a breath. I want to control my tone, not let this feeling escape my insides. I swallow, which feels like choking back sticky green slime. 'Last week? Why did you see Verity?' I've failed. I sound acid-sharp.

Ade pauses, her hands hovering in mid-air. She picks up her phone, jabs at it, her eyes glued to the screen. 'No reason,' she mutters. 'She invited me for a drink, that's all.'

This is what Verity does. She befriends people, waifs and strays she's worried about. We'll arrange to catch up for drinks and Verity will bring along a vacant-eyed, plump-lipped model who'll spend her time staring at her glass of wine, but not touching it. 'She refused to eat on the shoot,' Verity will whisper to me. 'I was worried about her, I had to invite her.'

Ade is new to Sheffield. She doesn't have many friends here. Verity will just have been being thoughtful. I'm trying to reason with myself, think practically, but the fog has gone and now I'm a frazzle of nerves, questioning what Verity could have said, what the pair could have discussed.

'What did you talk about?' Ade is still looking at her phone, her thumb scrolling quickly, as if she's flicking through pictures.

'Nothing,' she says. She shakes her head, just slightly. 'We know some of the same people in London, that's all.'

'Who?'

'No one important.' Her voice breaks slightly at that. She pulls off the stack of bracelets around her wrist and places them on her desk with a clatter. She looks, suddenly, like a deflated balloon.

'Ade, you OK? Why are you being weird?'

Her head snaps up. And she's back, full of air again. 'I'm not being weird, you are.' She lowers her voice down to a whisper that I can only just hear. 'Verity said you'd be like this.'

'Like what, Ade?' Then I sigh. I don't like the feeling in the air – it feels like a radio out of signal – all crackly and irritated.

Ade is supposed to be lightness, a bubblegum pop song. I can't let her become another muddy, complicated thing in my life.

'Let's change the subject,' I say. 'Leave Instagram alone for now.'

'OK.' She nods. 'But we have to do it sometime, it's just as important as everything else.' She flicks to the next page of her notebook. 'Ah yes! I think you need to get a celebrity client, someone who can chat-about you in interviews. It could help get your business in the papers.'

We begin to chat about who's single and who's not, and I manage to distract Ade by leading her down a few tangents about who's cheating on whom. There's a pause. I decide to chance it. 'I've got loads of matches to make, Ade, why don't you go home early?' I suggest, keeping my voice light. I hold my breath. But she reaches for her notebook.

'You're kidding, right? We've still not decided on celebrities to approach, or what pictures of Harry to post.'

'If,' I say, 'if we decide to post pictures of Harry.' She rolls her eyes at me. Click-clacks in her heels over to the window.

'I think we should do a photo shoot,' she says. 'We could do it in the skate park, the one down the road? It'd be really cool. A True Romance kind of vibe. Be great to get some actual posters and ads out there.'

'No!' The word just flies out. I clamp my hand over my mouth. Ade doesn't seem to have noticed. She's asking me if Verity would do the styling for a favour, if she knows anyone who could do the make-up, and I'm just sitting, trying to scramble my thoughts together. The match bell sits on my desk, a little copper thing that feels delicate in my hands. The ting, ting, ting of it stops Ade's run of thought.

'I just had an idea,' I say, 'Morwena Star! She'd be perfect to approach to be a client. She lives here, in Sheffield I mean.' I'm blurting words out, trying to get Ade on another track. But she's locked in now.

'Yeah, yeah,' she says, waving her hand. 'You get started on that and I'll get on with everything else. I'll get the website redesigned, I know a guy. And just give me your passwords, I'll take over the Instagram.'

I try to practise saying the words in my head. 'No, Ade, I don't want you to do this.' But she'd press further, ask more questions about Harry. She doesn't need to know any more about him – just that he's camera-shy.

'You've gone quiet.' There's a small furrow in her brow. 'OK, fine, we don't have to do the photo shoot. I maybe got carried away with that one.'

'Thank you,' I reply, mustering brightness. 'You know me, just find all this marketing stuff a bit much. I just want to set people up, that's all.'

'Then let me do it, send me everything I need and I'll just do it. I'll even talk to Harry myself, explain how important it is.'

'Good luck with that,' I mutter. I've started picking at another crack in my polish. Ade comes over, slaps my hand away.

'Stop that,' she scolds. 'You need to get yourself a new manicure, the place is just down the road.'

'I know—'

'But you don't have time.' She tries to impersonate my accent. Crossed with her south London twang it comes out almost Australian. We giggle in unison.

'Look, I do need you to pay attention to all this stuff, just a little bit,' she says. 'You're losing followers by the day and I looked at your application rate. It's OK for now, but it's dropping too . . .'

'We had forty applications this morning!'

'After your wedding you had hundreds every week.'

We got married in The Winter Garden. A huge, curved, wood-framed greenhouse, right in the centre of town. It's always been a hidden haven, as all year round palm trees stand tall, and forest-green plants climb up the beams. I hadn't known, but Harry had arranged for butterflies to be released – just as we said our vows – and they had circled all around us, landing on our noses as we spoke. They nestled in my hair, these bright jewel-coloured accessories, and stayed there, fluttering as we sang our own version of hymns – Disney songs that caused everyone to laugh as we struggled to remember the lyrics. The whole day felt like being in a cartoon – and you couldn't tell, from the pictures, that we were in the centre of town, in a cold, grey city. It looked as though we were on a tropical island. That's not what I'd liked about the pictures though; it was how Harry looked at me. Like I was a shining jewel, something precious to be cherished.

Our photographer had sent the pictures off to a couple of wedding blogs – and one, *Wedding Belle*, did a post on us. That was then picked up by BuzzFeed, then the *Independent*, even the *Guardian* did a piece on how perfect the whole day was. My application rate shot up – everyone wanted to be matched by the woman who'd had the perfect wedding.

'We need some of that wedding magic,' Ade says. 'Otherwise these numbers are going to keep falling.'

'Look, is there nothing else we can do? How about a snap of Verity with Jeremiah? They were my first ever match, we could big that up?'

'Yeah, they'd do all right.' She's got some weird charts up, leaning in close to the computer. 'But just not as well as the ones of you and Harry.' She sighs. Pulls her chair closer to mine. 'Look, this is what works. Why do you think people sign up?'

I think of all my matches. Tom who dresses in this tough, torn-up rocker way, showing his tattoos and piercings, and how underneath it all he wants someone to lie with, curled up, stripped off and naked, whispering about his day. Or Elijah, all sassy comebacks and finger-snapping, and how he's secretly looking for someone who can give him a comeback that will make him howl with laughter. 'That's easy, they want love. I'm good at finding it for them.'

Her whole body is like one big eye-roll. 'Come on, you can't seriously think that? Everyone signs up because they want what you have – gorgeous husband, perfect wedding – that's what you're selling.'

I didn't think I was touting that. My life. My husband. I knew it reassured them, I'd drop his name in and let clients, like Elena, know how wonderful he is, but that's not why people sign up. Or so I thought. I saw a couple the other day, both of them wearing orange North Face fleeces, holding tall sticks – I didn't know what the sticks were for. Maybe some climbing thing? Quidditch? But that didn't matter. The most important thing was that they'd found each other, and they were off to do something they loved together. That's what I thought I was selling; finding that jigsaw piece, the one set aside just for you. But how do I explain that to Ade? This number-focused image creator? I want to shut my eyes. Fill in my tax return. Clean the bathroom. Anything to get me out of this conversation.

'The company isn't sinking, is it?' I squint, trying to make sense of those numbers and charts on the screen. 'Those are tiny losses, nothing.'

'If they carry on that way, they'll just get bigger, one client loss at a time.' I think of our launch night, the way Harry had squeezed my shoulder when everyone began arriving and whispered, 'It looks perfect.' The speech he'd made, his throat crackling and the paper in his hands juddering back and forth, telling me how proud he was of me. I really don't want all of that to be for nothing.

'Fine,' I say. 'I'll email across my log-in details. But please, Ade, keep the posts of Harry to a minimum.'

'OK.' She nods. 'At least until I've spoken to him. And you can choose the photos. I'll just do the captions, the right timings. Anything that keeps you away from posting about mocktails or any other boring shit.'

Better to post boring stuff than Harry, I think. But I keep quiet, start to scan some applications. She's staring at me, as if she's waiting for something. I look up just as she clicks her fingers. 'Caitlin!'

'What?'

'Send me some photos, will you? And Harry's contact details.'

My heart begins to race. She comes over, extracts the application from my hand. 'Harry's number, come on. I want to get started. I'm bored,' she whines.

She's not going away. I reach across, grab a pink Post-it, jot his number down – but at the last digit I write an eight, rather than a seven. 'There you go,' I say. 'But he probably won't get back to you for a few days. Surgery is super-busy right now.'

'He has time to reply to a message to do with his wife,' she says as I begin to tear at the Post-it note pad, ripping notes into tiny shreds. I muster a smile.

'Let's hope so,' I reply.

Chapter Five

The first time Harry cooked for me, he set up a picnic on the floor. It was when I was still living with Verity and he arrived, brandishing a tenner for her. 'First round is on me, Verity,' and she'd stood, her hands up in mock protest and said, 'All right, all right, I get the hint.'

He then sent me through to my bedroom for five minutes, and when I came back through he'd laid out a blanket and scattered it with cushions. Dotted all around it were metal lanterns, candlelight twinkling through them and casting golden impressions of stars across the walls. Grey streams of smoke snaked through the air, the smell of incense heady and strong. The blanket was a yellow-and-red tartan one that was only ever used for barbecues down the park, and even despite the incense, I could still smell the stale Strongbow and cigarette smoke lingering on it.

Harry propped the cushions behind me and began to pull Tupperware out of his backpack. He placed each tub gently on the blanket, pulling off the lids to reveal the contents: couscous dotted with raisins; a gloopy, orange tagine; feta nestled between fat butter beans. 'How are you enjoying your holiday in Morocco, ma'am?' he'd said, grinning at me. I'd played along. 'I saw the most incredible camel today, he had the knobbliest knees.' We'd riffed like that for a while, realising how little we actually knew about Morocco. 'We should go sometime,' Harry said,

43

and I liked that – it was only our third date, but it was a sign he liked me as much as I liked him. Then he told me to close my eyes. I thought he was going to kiss me, but instead he handed me a spoon. 'I bet you can't guess the mystery ingredient,' he said. Now, if I try really hard I can still feel the ridges of a raisin under my tongue. And the surprise kiss that finally came as I tried to figure out what herbs were in the dish.

We've played it ever since. Even if it's something simple like cheesy pasta we make a show of it, teasing each other and pretending there's something fancy in it, like rare truffle or an expensive blue cheese.

I've just stirred a tablespoon of barbecue sauce into the Bolognese. Elton John's blasting out on the radio and I'm singing along, stirring the sauce. When I usually make this dish I just shove everything in a pan and leave it to bubble on its own, watching *Friends* repeats on the telly. But I'm doing it properly tonight: chopping the tomatoes thinly and precisely, adding red wine and letting it simmer slowly. I'm massaging butter into oats, while keeping an eye on the Bolognese and the cooking apples, which are bubbling away in a pan. The crumble can go in the oven while the spaghetti is being eaten. It's Harry's favourite pudding, especially served with custard so thick it sticks to the spoon.

Dust flies off the tablecloth as I shake it out over the little round table shoved in the corner of our kitchen. The tablecloth is red-and-yellow tartan: a present from Harry within the first few weeks of us moving in together, so as to always remind me of that happy floor picnic. I'd unwrapped the present and put it on the table straight away, making sure we had raisin couscous for tea.

I pull out the thick white china bowls and copper cutlery that we were given as a wedding present – and that I keep in a separate cupboard from our everyday stuff – and then light a candle. It flickers violently at first, before settling down, filtering the smell of white lilac through the room. Harry always has his fork on the left, so I make sure to arrange everything in the right order, before pouring a glass of red for him. Earlier, I had asked the assistant which one was best. 'Special occasion?' he'd asked, and I'd replied, 'No, not really, but my husband has been working really hard recently, so I wanted to treat him.' I'd liked saying that, how the word 'husband' sounded on my tongue.

I sit down, pour myself a glass of white and stare out at the black night. Darkness seeps in from outside. A shiver runs through me. I'm thinking of what Ade said earlier, how it's my life I'm selling. I look at the clock, quarter past seven. He'd usually be home by now. 'People really want this?' I say into the cold, quiet air.

The Cat saunters in, looks at me disdainfully. He's a rescue we got a few years back, and despite trying out many names on him, 'The Cat' just stuck. My stomach gnaws, a grumble that fills up the room. The Cat jumps up onto my lap, nudges at my fork with his head.

'You're right, The Cat, may as well start.'

I turned the radio off earlier, Harry's not a fan of music while we eat, but now I long to jump up and put it back on again. But it's on the kitchen counter and The Cat has just started to purr. It vibrates through me. I don't want to disturb him.

'Let me see, tomatoes, obviously,' I say to the wall. I'll hear the door any minute, the whirr of his bicycle wheels coming to a stop. May as well start the game. 'And mince – but Quorn or real?'

The Cat mews, I've just started rubbing his ear with my other hand. 'Yep, you're right, The Cat, it's fakey mince . . .'

I keep playing, chattering up the air as the silence of it threatens to choke me. The Cat indulges me. Staying there, curled up on my lap and knocking the fork out of my hand whenever I stop stroking him. 'Basil,' I say, 'tomatoes, fresh. Butter, probably too much, you know me – can never resist another knob.'

I'm slowing it down, deliberately chewing fifty times before making another guess. All these ingredients are obvious, that's how we'd always begin, guessing not so much on the flavour but on our knowledge that onions are always in sauces, that we can see the pasta shape right there on our plates. I hold off saying 'barbecue sauce'. That was put in for Harry, to challenge him. I imagine him at work, grumbling because Kimberly, his receptionist, has put a last-minute late appointment in. She's always doing that. She's just not strict enough with the patients. 'He's making those teeth shiny,' I say to The Cat before resuming the game, listing every ingredient, and even saying 'salt' after a thoughtful chew.

Still the door remains closed, the air in the house as undisturbed as it was when I bundled in earlier, shouting 'coo-eeeee' and trying not to look at the empty space where his bike always sits. I shut my eyes, picturing what I will see when I open them: him, standing there, in black Lycra, his silly clip-on cycling shoes clicking across the wooden floor as he comes over to give me a kiss. I won't shout at him, or tell him off for not texting me. He'll just sit down, his pasta whirring in the microwave, and I'll tell him about my day. That's all I ever want to do really, have slightly dull chats with my husband about our days. I open my eyes. He's not there.

The food, thick, heavy and comforting, was supposed to weigh me down and help me sleep. One glass of wine usually helps, too, but I'm halfway through my second and I don't feel sleepy at all. The alcohol in my veins has left me wired, the butterflies in my tummy reminding me of last time Kimberly put a late appointment in. I'd roasted a chicken that night and ended up leaving it in too long, so it was dry and flaky by the time he got home. Oh how we'd screamed at each other that night. My mum raised me on her own, distilling in me the notion that you should never sit around waiting for a man. She won't even let me set her up with anyone, even now, decades after Dad left. 'I'm not some fucking Stepford Wife,' I'd shouted, to which he'd yelled back: 'Even if I was here you'd be on your bloody phone anyway.'

Which is why, as soon as I got in tonight, I plugged my phone in upstairs. I knew, otherwise, I'd end up sitting at dinner looking for photos to send to Ade – ones I approved of, before she starts pulling ones off Facebook herself. Or I'd want to comb Morwena's Facebook for clues. I'm determined to hook her in as a client and I know I can, but I haven't quite figured out how yet.

I look at Harry's bowl, the sauce congealing, the spaghetti limp. I push The Cat off, admitting defeat. I scramble around the cupboard, looking for the lid for Harry's red lunchbox, the one he always carries his sandwiches in. It's wedged right at the back, and has something sticky and unidentifiable on it, which I have to rinse off before tipping the contents of his bowl into it. Then I pad over to the table, unscrew the bottle of red and pour the whole bottle down the sink, watching it swirl in the plug hole, the liquid as dark as blood. I turn the oven off: inside the crumble sits, the top black and burnt to a crisp.

Chapter Six

It feels as though my blood has been replaced by concrete as I drag my legs – left, then right, then left again – through the frosty early-morning air to the gym. I haven't been here in months, and I feel disorientated at the sight of it, embarrassed to have to ask the bleached-blonde trainer at the reception desk where exactly the changing rooms are.

'I'll go all the time,' I'd said to Harry when I joined. 'The yoga classes are led by some of the best instructors in the country.' When he'd asked how I knew that and I admitted it was because of Morwena Star's feed, he couldn't believe it.

'You'd fork out eighty quid a month for a gym membership because this girl told you to?' he'd said, exasperated. I'd just shrugged, convinced I'd prove him wrong by becoming a green-juice-sipping, yoga-loving fitness queen.

I didn't know I had to book in advance, and today the yoga class is full – lilac light bouncing off the bodies lying on their backs, each person completely indistinguishable from the next.

When I joined I was sure that I'd have a flat tummy by summer. But work got so busy that I could never quite bring myself to uncurl from Harry's warmth in the morning. When our holiday that year rolled around, I'd been so cross with myself as I packed the same old tankinis and sarongs as the year before. Now I feel my stomach and it's so flat it's almost concave. I switch from finding food foul to suddenly feeling ravenous and swallowing barely without chewing, shovelling chunks of whatever I can find in my mouth. It was easy to roll out of bed this morning and now, I miss my padding.

My phone, rested against the treadmill's display, beeps with a message from Ade: *Why haven't you sent me those pictures yet?* I slow down, typing out: *Not had the chance to ask Harry yet. Post this instead.* Then I whizz across a photo of Verity and Jeremiah at last year's Tramlines festival, their faces caked in gold glitter. Followed by: *Morwena Star plan in action! ;-)* Then I turn my phone off.

I pump the resistance up until I'm walking at an angle so steep it feels as though I'm wading through treacle. I find, as I pound my feet against the rubber beneath me, that I am suddenly angry. Why should it be all about Harry? This is my business: I'm the one who wakes up at 6 a.m. most days, who approaches investors and emails local press with my most unusual and romantic matches. Just because Harry looks good in photographs, does that mean he gets to be the focus of the entire rebrand? 'What you're selling,' Mum once said to me, 'is the idea that people have to find their other half, which is just codswallop! I love being on my own.' I'd had to push the pile of applications I had resting at my foot underneath the sofa: they were all men Mum's age that I really wanted to set her up with.

I'll have a word with Ade, tell her that her new plan is sexist and that she should think of something else. The focus will be on other couples, my previous clients and that's it. I'll tell her that tomorrow. But first I need to calm down, blood is rushing through my ears, and I need to be zen for this to work.

The lilac bodies are now sitting upright, legs crossed. A low 'ooohmmmm' vibrates out of the studio. I scan the ponytails but they're pretty much all ice-blonde; it's tough to differentiate Morwena from the rest. Then I spot her, and jump off the treadmill, falling in line with the stream of women she's a part of. Up close, her skin looks more blotchy than it does in her photos, her jawline less defined and her bum, in Clingfilm-tight cranberry leggings, isn't quite as peachy. She looks, I realise as I follow her down to the changing rooms, like your average popular girl in school. The type you idolised as a teenager, someone you were desperate to emulate, but then later on in life you saw an old photo of and realised she wasn't all that – it was just status that made her glow.

I'm speeding up now. Dodging my way past the slower walkers, so I'm almost in line with Morwena.

I keep my head down, as if I'm reading my phone. The women swing through the doors and into the wooden-locker-lined changing rooms. Morwena is heading to a middle bench and I angle my body, just a tad, grazing my shoulder with hers.

'Oops, oh my God, I'm so sorry!' I say, releasing my hand, letting a tumble of stones fall to the floor. 'Argh, my crystals!'

I crouch down, begin scooping them up: a soft-pink one, a pearlescent white smooth round ball and one that's so shiny and black it reminds me of solid oil. They really are beautiful objects: they almost make me want to believe in the life-altering properties Morwena pretends they have.

'Your rose quartz.' She's bent down to join me, and hands me back the pink one.

'For I—'

'Love! I've got the same one.' She reaches into the grey pocket of her hoody and pulls out a near-identical stone. 'See! So you're single, too?'

She speaks in the same children's TV presenter voice she uses on her channel, relentlessly perky and squeaky, a smile glued almost manically to her face the whole time. 'Human cocaine,' I think, 'you're like human cocaine.'

'Married, actually, but I'm a matchmaker so it's important to keep the love vibes around me at all times . . .'

I'd written this conversation down in the middle of the night, the orange street lights serving as a lamp as I jotted them in my diary. They'd seemed natural then but now they sound stilted, like they're hanging in the air. 'I also have opal, you know, to keep me always inspired, and Apache tears, well, that's to help me in the gym today.'

'I love them! Opal is, like, there for fixing your crown and . . .' She pauses, then lets out this giggle that's almost as if she's blowing bubbles it's so light and airy. 'As if you brought a crystal to help you with your work out, that's so cute!'

I don't say anything, try and let the pause hang in the air, hoping that she'll fill the silence. Ask me more questions about what I do.

'Anyway, best go shower now – see you later . . .'

'Caitlin.'

She spins on her heel, almost whacking me in the face with her ponytail. I could trudge home, but they have rainfall showers here and a selection of Molton Brown shower gels. I grab my fluffy white towel and walk barefoot to the showers. Everyone else has flip-flops, some have even got their own robes.

When I return, my hair tied tight in a turban, Morwena's sitting on the bench that I dumped my rucksack on. She's in a brand-new gym outfit, full face of make-up, a squeaky-clean and fresh version of the person she was thirty minutes ago. Like she's about to go and do a class again.

'Hey,' she says, with a little wave.

'Hey.' I'm still in my towel. I hover, unsure what to do. Others around us are stripping off with ease – one woman is contorting her body round to rub thick white lotion on her naked buttocks. They're pert and lifted, almost as if her bum is smiling at me. The weight loss has left my own bum saggy and sad.

I begin to pull my clothes out very slowly: my black Converse, black jeans, black polo neck. I fold them neatly on the bench beside Morwena. Then I take out my bottles – blow-dry creme, foundation, mascara, deodorant – and place them on the ledge beside the mirror. Morwena watches me. I can almost see the words trapped in her mouth as she tries to figure out the best way to release them.

'Did . . .' She coughs. 'Did you say you worked as a matchmaker? Like . . . for couples?'

'Yeah, that's right, odd profession, I know – but for the last few years I've run my own business, Cupid's Caitlin.'

She glances at her hands. Stretches out her ring finger, fiddling with the skin there.

'Does it do well?'

'We've had a few babies, engagements. I'm like Cilla,' I say, observing her face to see if she gets the reference. Her face remains blank. 'Always buying hats.'

She twiddles with a gold unicorn charm around her wrist. 'How do you know who's right for each other? How someone's right . . .? When I pick for myself I just end up with duds . . .' She attempts a chuckle but it comes out strangled, her hands darting quickly up to her throat.

I take the seat beside her, pull the towel turban out of my hair.

'Instinct, I guess. I have this thing, a kick in my stomach that I've learned to tune in to over the years—'

'Like a psychic?'

No, I want to say. Not like a psychic. Psychics are bullshit, and they fool poor grieving people into parting with their money while they spout lies plucked from the darkest depths of their imagination. But I know what she wants to hear. So I nod.

'I guess, a bit. I first felt it with my husband, Harry. We saw each other in a shop and I just knew he was special. I thought it was a fluke, but then I felt it again – this time with a man for my best friend, Verity.'

'Wow, so you're married? And your best friend is still with that guy?'

I remember my lines. 'I am, she is . . .' I pull my phone up, my background picture is of The Cat, and I scroll back, way back, to find some nice pictures of me and Harry. I find one of us, decorating our house. I'd worn dungarees as that's how I'd always imagined the moment would be: pigtails, splodges of paint on our noses and denim dungarees. I'm holding a brush up and grinning. I'd ended up painting in my underwear, dirty beige pants and a sports bra. The dungarees had been too restrictive, and the day finished with a row as I got paint on our new floors.

'Here he is.'

She snatches the phone out of my hand. 'Wow, he's absolutely gorgeous . . . great teeth.'

'He's a dentist, so kinda has to have great teeth! Never thought I'd end up with a dentist, but there you go. My type used to be super-creative. Do you have a type?'

'Not really, but I'd want to be with someone kind, someone who believes, works hard, takes care of himself. . .'

'By that you mean six-pack?'

There's that giggle again. 'Maybe, but there's nothing wrong with that.'

Takes care of themselves is a common request with my clients. I hate it. It's a sly way of saying 'hot' without seeming too shallow. I tend to ignore it; other matchmakers do what's asked of them and make matches on appearances only. But I want my couples to last, all the way to old age.

'Of course not, but I work in love . . . not lust,' I explain. 'It's cheesy but I'd want to find the right soul for you, not the right body.'

'Oh,' she says, standing up. 'I was more asking hypothetically.' She smooths her ponytail down. 'I don't need help finding a guy. Anyway, best dash. I' – she raises her chin – 'have a photo shoot to get to.'

And just like that, she's up and gone. I thought I had her, but she's slipped away and now I sit here, my hands empty, my mission incomplete, feeling like a lost sock, a deflated balloon, the word 'failure' stamped across my forehead. 'You've got this,' I whisper to myself, but I don't. I don't at all.

Chapter Seven

I head home straight after the gym, ready to just climb back into bed and sleep off my failure. The covers are heavy on top of me. I've dragged our spare duvet into our room, and the two together feel like the weight of a person, holding me down and in. The back of my brain is telling me that I can try again, that it wasn't a failure, that she did seem interested. But every other inch of me is screaming at me for fucking it up, for it not going exactly how I'd planned it. I know it must be because I am tired and didn't sleep, but I can't stop the memories flying at me, thick and fast, of the other times I made plans only for them to go in the exact opposite direction . . .

The excitement of the Royal Wedding made it all the way to Sheffield. I'd helped Betty next door string up red, white and blue bunting all across the street and promised her I'd make a coronation chicken. I'd been buttering up Bill from three doors down with the allure of scones piled thick with cream and jam, telling him that Prince Harry and Meghan were a more modern Royal couple, that it wouldn't be against his beliefs to come along to the party, just for a bit. Mum, who lives on the outskirts of town, was driving down the night before. She was going to stay at our house for the whole weekend, and Bill – with his sandy-coloured hair and staunch left-wing politics – was the perfect match for her. She may always insist she's fine on her own, but I never stop trying.

Harry was being so grumpy about the whole thing. The first thing he said upon waking was how much it was costing the tax payer, grumbling about cuts and the Prime Minister, all sorts of moans that – as I told him – he could talk to Bill about. I just needed one picture of him, the plastic crown that I'd bought rested on top of his curls. I was going to caption it: *She may have her prince, but I think my Harry is even better, don't you?* The wedding, the whole of the UK being enthralled by romance, was perfect for business. But Mum, Harry, even Verity didn't get it – outwardly she seemed to be joining in, rocking up in a silver tiara and a torn white wedding dress, while getting stuck into the Kir Royales at 10 a.m., but I could see her rolling her eyes and muttering to Jeremiah about it as well. I'd walked past twice and heard them going on about the state of the NHS. I had wanted, just for one day, for everyone to forget their problems, for Harry and I not to fight and to ease my worries about Mum being lonely. But she cancelled, saying she couldn't be arsed with the drive and would prefer to sunbathe in her garden. By 2 p.m. Bill was fighting with Betty about how the monarchy should be abolished, Verity was so drunk she couldn't stand and Jeremiah was attempting to take her home, and I had retreated to our bedroom, where, when Harry came to find me, I blamed the whole disaster – even the fact that no one had touched my coronation chicken – on him . . .

My phone has rung three times now as I lie here trying to squeeze away the memory of being on this bed, the sound of laughter and conversation floating up from outside, and crying in that gulping, hysterical way while Harry just looked on, completely baffled. Like he didn't quite know where his wife had gone. I push one hand out from under the duvet. Verity's name lights up on the screen.

'Biiiiiiiiitttcchhh,' she's yelling. 'We're at the pub, you have to come.' I hear her ask someone for a light and explain that she's on the phone to me. 'She has to come, don't you think?'

'Can I come in my pyjamas?' I say, while struggling to figure out what clothes I can put on.

She laughs, her honk forcing a smile on my face. 'Why the hell not? Hey, bring me a pair! I'll join you.'

'OK, I'll be there in five.' I roll out of bed and run a brush through my hair: a ball of tangle is beginning to form, right at the crook of my neck, that I've been meaning to deal with, but just haven't somehow.

Verity screams when she sees me, a green parka shoved on top of my jammies. 'Oh my God, you absolute legend, you did it! Druncle Jack! She did it.' Jack, who is one of a group of locals who frequent this pub so much they've earned the nickname 'The Druncles'.

There's a bottle of white on Verity's table, so I just ask Julia for a glass. 'Nice to see you, Cait,' she says as I fiddle with a bar mat. 'It's been a while. Hope you're all right.'

'I'm fine,' I say, blushing now – suddenly realising what a stupid decision it had been to come in pyjamas. What impression it gives off. Back at the table, I hand Verity the tote bag. 'You have to change into these now,' I hiss. 'People are looking at me funny.'

'Course, can't wait, pour yourself a glass, Ade's just out having a fag.'

'Ade's here?' I say, but before Verity has the chance to reply I see her – unwrapping a stripy scarf from around her neck and waving at me. She wanders over, tugging her jeans up, and plonks her bag down. Ade's never without a brown leather holdall that's bursting with stuff, but never quite what she actually needs.

She pours herself a glass of wine as we both watch Verity wobble her way to the toilet. 'She showed up at the office looking for you,' Ade says with a shrug. 'Persuaded me to stop working and come for a drink.'

'She's impossible to say no to.' I fiddle with the stem of my wine glass as Ade roots around in her bag, pulling out her phone.

'I've made good progress though, check out the feed.' And there, in bright colours and plastered-on smiles, is my life with Harry. There's us, jet-lagged at sunrise in Mexico; curled up on the brown floral sofa at Mum's house; backs straight, champagne glasses in hand at various weddings . . . All photos taken from my Facebook feed. The top image, the very last one she posted, is Harry – plastic crown on head – his smile giving away no trace of how, just before it was taken, he'd yelled: 'Fine, if it means that much to you.'

'Ade, he's going to go mad.' I'm shaking my head, trying to get some power back into my voice. But Harry's just staring at me through the screen, a twinkle in his eye. It makes my heart hurt but it feels good, looking at our life together on that tiny screen.

'I'll speak to him, but honestly, I don't think he will even notice,' Ade says, as I stare more intently at the photos. She's done it – my life does look perfect. 'Did you not say he still uses, like, some ancient phone?'

The Nokia 3310. 'Who needs apps when you've got snake?' he'd say to me, waving the navy brick in my direction.

'You guys better not be discussing work,' Verity screeches, back from the bathroom and resplendent in her pink polka dot pyjamas, which she's accessorised by keeping on the pile of pearls she was wearing earlier. She downs her wine in two gulps then fills up all our glasses. I can hear a phone buzzing. I pull my phone out: no calls, but there is an Instagram notification: Morwena Star has sent a message.

'Oh my God,' I say, then read her message aloud: '"Hey, it was great to meet you at the gym earlier. Been looking at your photos, that couple look so happy . . ."' I pause, look over at Verity. 'That's you and Jeremiah she means!' Verity just rolls her eyes, takes another gulp. Someone's phone is still buzzing. '"I'd love it if you could do that for me. Email me . . ."' Then she's given her email!'

'That's amazing!' Ade looks so delighted and has pulled out her notebook. 'We have to get the website redesigned as soon as we can. I'll message Stu right now, meeting tomorrow . . .' She's jabbering away but when I look over at Verity, she's just staring into space, her head cocked to one side.

'You OK?' She snaps her eyes back onto mine. 'Fine,' she replies. 'Great news, but let's leave work alone for a bit. Ade, we're supposed to be sorting out your love life.'

Ade puts down her notebook, glares at Verity. 'I'm fine,' she says, her eyes wide as she nods her head in my direction.

'What's going on?' The pair look at each other, as if deciding who gets to speak first.

'I told you, Caitlin won't care.' Verity's reached over and placed her hand over Ade's, who looks close to tears.

'Seriously, what's going on?' I'm wondering how a mood can flick so quickly. It feels as though someone's thrown a dark cloud over our table. Druncle Jack has begun singing 'Wonderwall' out of tune, swaying on his seat.

'I didn't want you to know,' Ade says, a fat tear trailing down her cheek. 'But I'm heartbroken. Well, I wasn't, I felt I was finally moving on . . . and then, and then . . .'

'I went and put my foot in it,' Verity says, filling in the words that Ade suddenly can't manage. 'Turns out I know her ex, mentioned her casually one day when I was round at the office, and Ade burst into tears.'

'Oh Ade,' I say. 'You should have told me.'

'I didn't want you to know, nobody wants some heart-broken mess working at a matchmaking agency,' she says, as Verity looks over at me – unsure of what I will say.

'I've . . . I mean, I . . . We've all been heartbroken,' I reply, taking a gulp of wine. 'It doesn't affect the work.'

'Good advice, that,' Verity says, staring right at me.

'So,' I ask, ignoring her. 'Tell me about her.'

'Her parents don't approve,' Ade says, explaining that they'd been dating for about six months when Hannah told Ade they'd always have to see each other in private. That they could never get married or live together. 'It made sense, she was funny about going to certain parts of London and she always evaded the question when I asked where things were headed.' She looks around. Jack has now broken into 'Tiny Dancer'.

'Did you want to? Marry her, I mean?'

Ade nods. 'I'm a romantic at heart, really. And I decided I couldn't carry on seeing Hannah if it wasn't going anywhere. So I broke it off, packed up my things and moved here. I thought I'd moved on. But I haven't. I still love her.'

'Love is hard,' Verity says. 'But maybe it's better this way, this passionate bright spark of an affair, an explosion!' She releases her fists, creating fireworks with her hands. 'Marriage often means things fizzling out, realising that someone has slowly fallen out of love with you . . .'

I look down at my hands, twist my wedding ring round

my finger. Verity spots me, shakes her head at me. I refuse to meet her eye.

'Maybe,' Ade says, emptying the bottle of wine into our glasses. 'One more?'

'We need something to pull us out of our funk,' Verity says. 'Look at us, we're in pyjamas. We're supposed to be having fun and we're supposed to be finding you someone new to sleep with!'

I look around. 'And you brought her here?' Druncle Gary has begun to harmonise with Jack, and he's surprisingly good. Julia is polishing glasses, trying to ignore the man in the corner, who is 90 per cent beer belly and fast asleep.

My phone bleeps. Jeremiah. *You with Verity?* it says. I whizz a reply back. *Yep, at The Hope. Come!!*

We've moved on to gin and tonics by the time Jeremiah arrives. Verity's in the bathroom and he bundles in, his bright white smile plastered across his face. He's wearing a burnt-orange jumper, which he pulls off to reveal a geometric print t-shirt, with shoulders that poke out in odd directions. I stand up to cuddle him, introduce him to Ade.

'Another one of your creations, is it?'

He pulls at the fabric. 'Yep, still not got the hang of it.' Jeremiah's been trying to make his own clothes the whole time he's been with Verity. He loves colour and odd patterns: garments that are near impossible to find in the tiny Topman in town.

'What are you doing here?' Verity looms over Jeremiah, who is skinny as a rake, his skin so white it's almost blue. They look so odd standing next to one another, but that's always been part of their charm.

'Cait invited me,' he whips back. 'Why are you in pyjamas?'

'We thought it'd be funny, joke's clearly lost on you.'

Ade pushes her chair back. 'Just going to go, ummm, smoke,' she says.

'Me too,' I say, pulling my parka on.

'You don't smoke.' Verity's tone is still sharp.

'Need the air.' I hurry to catch up with Ade, who is already heading towards the door.

We watch them through the window. Verity's got her arms crossed, while Jeremiah talks, waving his hands around. At one point he reaches for her gin and she bats him away. He picks up one of the almost empty bottles from earlier and drains the dregs. Verity looks on, her lip curled up.

'Eeeeeeeshhht,' says Ade. 'They don't look good.'

'It's fine, they're just fighting. All couples fight.' I say the words more as a reassurance to myself, rather than her.

Ade blows out a stream of smoke. 'Still, I think I might go home.'

I look through the window again. Verity's at the bar, clinking a shot glass with Jack, while Jeremiah sits at the table, sipping from her glass. 'Free yourself and go now,' I say. 'Verity never lets someone go home without a fight.'

Back inside, Jeremiah's at the bar with Verity and Jack, looking unhappily at a tequila that's been lined up in front of him. 'Verity, I've got work in the morning,' he's saying but she's not having it.

'So? You used to stay out with me till five then get up an hour later to get shit done, ah!' She spots me, turns her back on Jeremiah, who tentatively picks up the salt. 'Julia, pour a tequila for Cait and Ade, will you? Oh, and one for yourself, of course.'

I shake my head. 'Ade's gone home . . . and I've got a big day tomorrow. I have to find someone good for Morwena to date.'

'Fuck's sake, not you too! God, when did everyone get so boring?'

Jeremiah wrinkles his nose up guiltily at me. I make an overexaggerated sad face back, while Jack picks Verity up and swings her around, plonking her back on her feet, where she wobbles precariously. 'I'm not boring, sweetheart,' he says, leaning in that bit too close.

'No, but you are a drunk.' Julia places three tequilas down anyway. 'And it's time for you to go home.' Julia's five foot, with witch-black hair, has three nose piercings and tattoos snaking up and down each arm. She may be approaching sixty and always complaining about her hips, but the Druncles know not to mess with her. Jack throws his arms up. 'Fine, fine, same time tomorrow then, love,' he says and shuffles out. I spot Jeremiah mouthing, 'Thank you,' to Julia . . . at the same time Verity does.

'What you saying thank you to her for? Jack was just having a laugh.'

'He was hitting on you,' Jeremiah retorts as Julia and I exchange glances. 'He's been doing it all night.'

'At least someone is,' Verity mutters and then they're off, Jeremiah reverting to sarcasm as he 'apologises' for not showering her with attention 'all the fucking time'. While Verity – directly quoting Beyoncé – reminds him that he's 'not dating some basic bitch'. I begin to back slowly out of the door, waving goodbye to Julia, who just shakes her head and turns back to polishing the wine glasses. The three tequilas on the bar remain untouched.

Chapter Eight

'Wrong, wrong, wrong, wrong, WRONG.'

I'm sitting on the floor of my office, surrounded by pictures of men. Men with black hair, men with tanned, rugged faces, men standing next to zoo animals . . . The floor is covered in them, all grinning out at me from their paper prisons. The printer in the corner is humming, churning out more images and profiles for me to choose between. My laptop is open at my feet, Morwena's Instagram on the screen. When I shut my eyes I can still see her pastel coordinated grid swimming before me.

I've been here since 6 a.m., searching through profiles to find the right man for Morwena. I stifle a yawn. After I left the pub I changed into a new pair of pyjamas and then stayed up until 2 a.m., Harry's side of the bed empty beside me, scrolling through her profile trying to get a better sense of her, the blue light from the screen burning into the back of my eyes and my phone hot in my hand.

The Nespresso machine buzzes into action as I try to think of Morwena. Morwena likes the beach, Morwena likes yoga, Morwena likes turmeric tea, Morwena thinks meat is murder and sugar is the devil . . . I take my cup and sit back down, looking at Paul. Paul stares back at me. Paul plays rugby and volunteers for the Labour Party. But his profile picture shows him holding up a pitcher of lager the size of his head. Beside him is Tyrone, who has two little dimples and a small gap between his teeth. He's cute, he knows a lot about climate change. Maybe? But maybe isn't good enough. I need someone perfect for her. Tyrone won't do.

I begin picking up the pictures, staring at them intently, willing myself to feel the kick. But . . . nothing. My phone sits beside me, I pick it up. There's ten unread messages from Verity – but she'll just be hungover and paranoid about last night. I can chat to her later on, once the hangxiety has settled. Instead I dial Harry's number, listening as it rings out.

'Hey, it's Harry. I'm probably with a patient, leave me a message. Bye.'

His voice, as it always has, causes my stomach to flip-flop.

'Hi Harry, it's me. Look, I know this is silly, but I need your help with a match. A hippy-dippy type, oh my God, I wish you could meet her. You'd hate her so much! Anyway, I hoped you might be able to help. OK, um, bye.'

Harry has helped me with tough clients so many times in the past. He always asks his patients in the dentist's chair whether they're single or not. I love to picture it, their heads tipped back, mouth open, the little plastic cup of blue liquid beside them and Harry quizzing them jovially about their love life. They must find it so awkward! But it's paid off. Once I had this teacher, Gwynn, who was so shy she spoke in a whisper and trembled every time I asked her anything about herself. It made finding someone for her to date nearly impossible. I'd choose chatty men for her and then find that on the dates she didn't say a word. So then I moved on to shy men, but they'd just have these excruciatingly awful dates where neither of them spoke, just giggled softly into their starters. I didn't know what to do with her, and came home most nights ranting about her. Then Harry told me about one of his patients, a softly spoken but assured man, who ran his own charity helping fund guide dogs for those who couldn't afford them. He had such a calming presence, Harry was convinced Gwynn would relax in his company. And she did! They now live together, with their golden retriever Heather, a seeing-eye dog who lost her sense of smell.

Ade's coming in at lunch with her web designer friend, and I really want to find someone for Morwena by then. I should have a proper sit-down interview with her, find out what she's looking for. But I've spent all morning looking at her – and it's as if I can see a clock ticking behind her eyes – I don't want to be another fad that she gets obsessed by, like aerial yoga, and then abandons just as quickly. Plus, I'm at an advantage as she's already told me so much about herself through social media. There's no need for me to do my usual pre-interviews.

I can hear Ade stomping up the stairs, her footsteps so loud I can't hear if anyone else is with her. The next man I pull up has a strong jawline, floppy brown hair and he smiles out at the camera in a self-assured way. I click through to his next photo, in which he's holding a ginger kitten.

'What is it with men and pictures of them with baby animals?' I say to Ade, without looking up.

'It's because they want to seem sensitive but also tough.' It's not Ade's voice, but a soft Irish lilt. I swivel my chair round to see the most gorgeous man standing behind me. Then, before I've even noticed I've done it, I've swivelled back, my eyes glued to the screen. I know that if I look at whoever this is for too long I will lose the ability to speak.

'What's tough about a kitten?' I ask, in a slight squeak.

'Flick to the next picture, guaranteed it'll be a lorry or a . . .' The image flashes up. 'Ah see, there's your man, on a motorbike.'

I'm so aware of this man's presence, right behind me, his woody aftershave filling up the air. I take a deep breath in, but nope, nothing remotely interesting or witty comes to mind – and I still can't bring myself to turn round again.

Thankfully, Ade comes bustling in and spins my chair round. 'So rude, Caitlin,' she scolds. 'Honestly, she's hooked on finding matches for people. It makes her forget her manners.'

There's a silence. Ade elbows me in the arm. 'Right, Cait?'

I manage to cough out a 'right' and then, without meeting his eyes, or standing up from my chair, offer my hand for him to shake. 'I'm Caitlin,' I say.

'Stu,' he offers back.

Ade and Stu settle on the sofas, and I choose the pink pouffe, angling towards Ade. My eyes dart every now and then to Stu's arms, tanned and toned, where I can see that even the muscles in his forearms are well defined, his skin wrapped perfectly around them.

'I met Stu when I was working in London. He worked on the same floor as my team, designing the big company websites,' Ade's saying as I practise nodding in a normal fashion. 'We got on, he likes a drink as much as I do so I was so happy when he moved up here to Sheffield, a few months ago.'

He grins, the skin around his green eyes crinkling. 'I just missed Ade too much.'

The words float out of him and remind me of a strong whisky. How it catches in your throat.

Ade laughs and I find myself feeling eternally grateful that she's a lesbian. He's not here because he's in love with her. I could – I think – have a little flirt. I need cheering up. Except I can't flirt, I don't know how. And flirting would be a lot easier if I could at least look at him. Which I can't do without losing total control of my entire body.

'It's the climbing,' he explains. 'I love rock climbing and the scene is good in Sheffield.'

'Oh I had no idea there was even a wall here,' I say, peeling my eyes away from his arms.

'Funny what you miss out on when your idea of exercise is picking up a wine bottle, eh, Cait?' Ade jokes and I'm instantly annoyed. This toned, glowing man will think I'm a lazy couch potato. A lush.

But he just smiles at me. 'I imagine you don't have much time for hobbies. How quickly you've built this business is seriously impressive.'

Now the blush has reached my cheeks. I can feel them, hot and burning.

'And that's why we're here,' Ade says. 'To discuss taking it even further. I want to redesign all of Caitlin's online presence: so there's more focus on her, building her as the brand, focusing on her relationship with her husband, Harry. What everyone wants.'

She emphasises the word husband, and says 'Harry' even louder, as if she's trying to remind me he exists. She needn't worry. Stu may reduce me to a puddle of nerves, but I don't want to get to know him. There would be very little point.

'The problem is Harry, he's quite camera-shy. He doesn't really like being the focus of attention at all.' I need to say this to Stu, as every time I say it to Ade she doesn't seem to listen. She waves her hand, as she is doing now, and says: 'I don't understand why he doesn't want to do something so small to help out his wife.'

But Stu nods. 'I get it. I'm sure we can find a way to do the rebrand that matches Ade's vision but without pushing a shy man into the spotlight.'

This time I can look at him. I give him a small smile and mouth 'thank you'. Ade, however, doesn't seem to be listening to anyone.

'I'm thinking we get some nice photos of the pair of them, put some money into it and get some bus posters made up. Stu, honestly, they're so cute together, they should be the entire focus of the website.'

I try to harness how powerful I felt on the treadmill a few days before. The words I'd rehearsed about this being my business, and that Harry shouldn't take up all the focus. But I only manage a weak, 'Absolutely not.'

'Don't worry, I've looked into it – bus posters don't actually cost that much money.'

I press my hands onto my eyes. When I open them again Stu has begun to fiddle with his laptop. 'It's not the money, Ade, it's Harry.'

My heart has begun to flutter and the red spreading across my body has turned from embarrassment and lust to rage and fear. She can't make me do this. Why won't she listen?

'What if I spoke to him? Told him how important it is for the future of the business, for his wife's livelihood.'

'Now you're being dramatic. The business won't crumble if we don't do a photo shoot with some guy who's not even part of the company.' Stu's tone is firm, as if he's talking to a child or a puppy. Ade flashes him a look that's ice cold, daggers flying towards him.

'Hey! You're meant to be on my side.'

'I'm on no one's side, I just want to get the job done right. And this poor guy isn't going to give us the best material if he's hating the whole thing.'

It's funny to hear them go back and forth about Harry. I wonder what he'd think if he could hear them? I usually do anything to get away from conflict but I like hearing this lively debate about what he'd want, it soothes me in a strange way. I imagine him coming into the room and saying 'Eh, eh, eh what's all this fuss about me for?'

'Earth to Caitlin, Earth to Caitlin.'

I flash back into the room. Stu and Caitlin are staring at me expectantly.

'Sorry, what did you say?'

'I said I'd still want to meet Harry, check with him the bare amount of photos of him we do use are all right.' She rolls her eyes. 'It's a compromise.'

I shut my eyes. I'm suddenly very, very tired. My lack of sleep is catching up on me. Stu squeezes my elbow.

'Hey, are you all right?'

'Fine, sorry,' I reply. 'I've been up all night trying to find a match for an important client. Sorry, not very with it today. Um, what were we talking about?'

'Harry coming in to meet us all?' Ade says, looking at me.

'Oh right. Yeah, I can't see that being a problem, but he's, um, away at a conference at the moment. A big one. In California.'

'OK, so when he's back then?'

'He's not sure when it'll end,' I say. 'But go ahead, like you say we can deal with it later. But stick to social media for now, until I've figured the budgets out.'

Anything to get her away from the idea of bus posters. 'Finally you're listening to me!' she says, shooting Stu a triumphant look, and saunters through to the kitchen. 'Now, more coffee,' she shouts through to us.

'She's far too persuasive for her own good,' Stu says, winking at me. I notice he has feathers, inked in black and white, behind his left ear. I try to swallow my nerves down, deep into the pit of my stomach. He's just a man, an ordinary man, I say to myself, letting the words circle my head.

'So, what client is so special she's got you up half the night?' he asks, and I feel settled. I can talk about my work, that's easy.

'Oh, so she's this celebrity influencer, Morwena Star?'

He shakes his head. 'Unless she's the star of a nineties cult movie, I won't have a clue. But hey, why don't you show me who you're thinking of?' He pushes himself up, crouches down beside me. I can almost feel his hot breath on my shoulder.

'I've vetoed all of these guys', I say looking at the paper-strewn door. But there are more potentials on the computer over there.' I point to my desk, aware of the crumbs of salt and vinegar crisps that are scattered all over its wooden surface. I'm also aware of how tight my jeans are, and I'm suddenly worried I won't be able to get up off this pouffe in them. I manage though, quickly filling Stu in on Morwena's key details. He jumps up, goes over and peers at the strong jawline guy. 'He won't do,' he shouts over my shoulder. 'He's an atheist.'

'Who's an atheist?' Ade is clutching three cups in one hand, a packet of custard creams in the other.

'This guy who's not perfect for Morwena Star,' he says, a wicked grin settling on his face. 'We're looking for matches!'

She groans. 'We're supposed to be looking at your website design, Stu.'

'Yeah, yeah,' he waves his hand. 'There's plenty of time for that. This is fun!' He gets up, wheels two chairs round. 'Come on, ladies, let's find Morwena a match.'

An hour later and Stu is proving to be just as fussy as I am. 'Wrong!' he shouts, at a carpenter who has sent in a picture of him doing a bungee jump.

'Too adventurous?' I ask. 'Or is it that you think she won't like snakes?' In another photo he has a python wrapped around his arm.

'I don't feel he is ready to commit,' Stu says, laughing.

Ade has flung her feet up on my desk and is flicking idly through her phone. 'Can we please hurry this along?' she says. 'I'm bored and I need a drink.'

'We'll go to the pub once we've found Morwena's match.' He side-eyes me. 'You coming?'

'Maybe,' I say, my stomach flipping round once and then twice. Before I can say anything else, a guy flashes up on the screen. 'Wait, stop,' I yell, just as Stu's flicked on to a guy with a goatee. 'Go back one.'

'Him?' Stu asks – he's gone back too far, a red-headed schoolboy who I'd told to come back to me when he was eighteen, is on the screen.

'No,' I laugh. 'Can you imagine? Just before him, the guy in the white collar. Make the picture bigger.'

A professional photo fills the screen, the background a pale cornflower blue. The man's cheekbones are so defined they look drawn on, his face pensive, his gaze to one side. His hair is the colour of Dairy Milk, as are his eyes. The suit he's wearing fits him to a tee. It looks so expensive, I can almost imagine what he smells like.

'Rowen Garrett,' says Stu. 'Great name.'

'Scroll down,' I instruct.

'You're bossy when it comes to this. I like it,' he replies. But I barely register what he's said: I'm scanning the information Rowen has provided me with. Jeff Buckley is his favourite musician, Tolstoy his chosen author . . . and there – I see – listed under profession is the thing I'm looking for, the thing I can almost feel in my bones when I look at this man. His profession: clairvoyant and aura reader.

'Bingo,' I say, as Stu lets out a low whistle.

'Wow, you're good,' he says.

Ade stands up, slams the laptop shut. 'Right, now that's done, please can we go to the pub?'

'Be great to have you,' Stu's saying, but his words float past me. I'm thinking of Harry and the day I told him Gwynn's date with his patient had gone well. How he'd let out a 'whoop' like a kid opening a present. I shake my head.

'You guys go on, I've got stuff to do here.'

'You're sure?' Stu asks, shrugging. I nod as they begin to gather their things, Stu flinging an orange backpack across his shoulders, on top of his black padded jacket. I wave them off as they descend the stairs. At the door he turns, looks up, his eyes meeting mine one more time.

Chapter Nine

The only indication that Verity has entered my house is the slam of the door behind her. There's no 'hiyaaaa' and her footsteps sound through the hall slowly. I can hear her place her key down on the bench. Usually she thunders through, the keys landing with a clang on the tiled floor, her coat – always a big fake-fur number – shrugged off her shoulders and on the floor behind her. But today she comes up behind me as I'm stirring the sauce for our tea and wraps her arms around my waist, her head resting on my shoulder. She smells like vanilla and cigarettes. The fur from her coat – purple, to match her hair – tickles the top of my nose. I turn round, pull her into a proper hug. Verity's cuddles are amazing: she's got a shelf of a bosom, and she pulls you right in, squeezing you as if the world's shifted on its axis and she's stopping you from tumbling. Right now, her arms are limp by her sides.

'Hey, hey, what's wrong?' She breaks away, hugs her coat to her chest and then carries it to the hall, hanging it on a peg.

'Nothing, just a shit day, that's all.' Verity never likes to talk about her problems. 'There's bigger stuff going on in the world, Cait,' she'll say to me whenever I press her on things. 'How are you? How's the Morwena Star situation?'

This was why I'd invited her round, pretending that I wanted to celebrate finding Morwena's match. But really

I wanted to talk to Verity about Stu. I wanted her to help me assess the situation – could it be possible that only I had felt that intense electricity? That he was just being friendly? Was it just in my head, or had he felt the same heat as I had? But I also wasn't sure what answer I wanted from her.

'Good! I told her all about this Rowen guy and she likes the sound of him. She's not seen him yet but he's fit so I can't see that being a problem,' I say, going to the fridge and pulling out a bottle of pink Moët. 'So I think it's safe to celebrate.' I hold the bottle up to my ear, waving it around. Verity smiles back, but it's weak. Like watered-down squash. I hand the champagne to her to pop. She doesn't fire the cork into the sky, instead she twists it off, mopping up the excess with kitchen roll rather than slurping it straight from the bottle. She pulls down two glasses, pours us each a glass, handing me one and raising hers, just slightly. 'To my darling sweetie Caitlin, I'm so happy for you.'

On that very last line, she melts down into a puddle of tears. Verity's crying is almost as contagious as her laugh, that incredible honk of hers. Her tears are like endless hiccups, interspersed by apologies. 'Hic, hic, I'm sorry, hic,' she goes, her body juddering back and forth and this woman – this big, strong woman – turns into bones in front of my eyes. All I can do is hold her as she shakes, stroking her hair, the tight Afro curls bouncing gently underneath my touch.

With one hand still wrapped firmly around her shoulders I stretch my other hand to the gas knob, turn the hob ring off and guide her through to the living room, pushing her down onto my sofa: a soft squashy thing that was bought for comfort, rather than looks.

'There, let Hector take you in his arms,' I say.

She looks up from the cushion she's been blowing her nose into. 'You're so weird, naming your sofa.'

'Now, tell me, what's wrong?'

She pulls her knees up to her chest. Her voice, a low mutter. 'Oh I feel so stupid, I shouldn't be like this, not after . . . not after everything.'

I give her a light shove. 'Shut up, your problems matter. You have to tell me, it'll make it better.'

She pulls her head up from her knees, her face now puffy and swollen, a string of snot follows. I grab a box of tissues and hand it to her. She breathes in.

'OK, here goes. Jeremiah, Jeremiah . . . broke it off.'

She then pushes her face back into the cushion, muffling the explosion of tears that's awoken inside of her.

I remember the first time I saw Jeremiah. All three of us were in the pub, a glass-fronted Scream bar on West Street, and we'd managed to nab the best table – the two green leather sofas right in the window. The tables were sticky and the place smelled of stale hops mixed with BO. Verity sprayed her perfume around us, enveloping us in its sickly scent. It was back when I was working in PR, so I was in this nylon pencil skirt with a white blouse, which I'd managed to get a splodge of raspberry jam on, and Verity had brought me this silk dress to wear that was the colour of parma violets. She'd just chucked it to me when I spotted him looking over. Verity had arrived in torn-up denim hot pants, a tartan shirt and Converse. Her glorious thighs spilled out over the seat as she sat down and her hair had neon yellow streaks in it.

When I walked past him – this guy with tufts of blond hair spread all around his head like he'd just been electrocuted, and a body so skinny he could almost be a stick drawing – he grinned at me, then went right back to looking at Verity. Her feet were up on the table and she had pulled out a notebook and was sketching something. It had made my stomach tingle, the way he was looking at her. I felt sure that, if they met, he would look at her that way for the rest of her life.

When Harry arrived I had managed to convince him to go over and speak to Jeremiah, who was still sitting alone. 'He's on the table closest to the telly,' I'd hissed at him. 'Go and ask him about the rugby or something.' I'd had to promise Harry that this stranger wouldn't think he was weird, and then I'd scampered back to our table. It had been so hard not to keep craning my neck backwards to see what was happening, and I couldn't concentrate on anything Verity was saying. Eventually the pair came over and Harry introduced Jeremiah as an old friend of his from dental school. Jeremiah had grinned again – a gold incisor winking at us. 'Dental drop-out,' he remarked – and that sent Verity honking. We'd been such a good fit, straight away, the four of us: going from the pub to a comedy club and then back to our flat, where Verity and Jeremiah disappeared into her room. Cuddled up in bed I'd found myself completely unable to stop talking about how amazing it had felt setting the pair of them up. I remember feeling as if my smile had reached all the way down to my toes. 'I wish I could do this for work, not stupid PR,' I'd said – and Harry had kissed my cheek and called me his 'little Cilla'.

Now, as I sit here, rubbing her back, whispering to her that it will all be OK, I realise it hasn't been the four of us for a long time. In the years that followed that night Harry opened his own practice, I set up my business and we bought a house together. Verity began travelling to London for styling jobs and Jeremiah began doing animation work and they rented their place together. We went from the four of us meeting up in the pub almost every night to gathering just once a month for a Sunday roast. Harry would tell me how Jeremiah was after Thursday night football and Verity and I carried on as normal, snatching glasses of wine and gossip whenever we could. But even that had petered out recently, I was just always so busy with work, and, apart from the fight I witnessed recently, she hadn't mentioned that they were having any problems.

'He's right of course, things haven't been going well for a while,' Verity's saying, her tears abating, her voice calmer. 'We just don't laugh like we used to.'

My heart floods with guilt. I hadn't noticed.

'How long has it been like this for?'

'Oh, I dunno,' she shrugs. 'Six months, maybe? At first I thought it was a blip, but soon I just found that I wasn't excited about seeing him. And sometimes I'd catch him, while I was talking, just staring into space. Bored almost.'

I suddenly remember one night at the restaurant, Harry and I tucked away in my favourite booth, a bottle of white wine and pasta bowls in front of us . . . and nothing to say to each other. It felt as though the silence rested around us, in a cluster. I'd tried a couple of times to make conversation, asking Harry how his day had been, but he was answering in one-word sentences. I was so aware of Bobby looking over at us, what he must be thinking – the matchmaker with the failing relationship – but Harry hadn't wanted to come out that night, and he was making it very clear. Eventually I pulled my phone out, thinking that Bobby might presume I had important work to do. 'Oh, here we go,' Harry had muttered, as soon as he'd seen me reach for my bag. 'Time for Instagram . . . again.'

I carry on rubbing her back, grateful she's leaning forward so she can't see my eyes, glazed – just slightly – with tears. 'That's such a horrible feeling, Verity, but you know you're not boring,' I say. 'Relationships change, people change and sometimes there's not much you can do about it. But this, it sounds like, is for the best. You can't cling on to something that's no longer there.'

She opens her mouth. Shuts it again. Her eyes darting, sideways, and resting on my face. 'Cait . . .'

'Yep?'

She shakes her head and begins to sip at her champagne, the cheerful bubbles at an odd juxtaposition to her tear-stained face. 'I guess what's really bugging me is the thought of losing him as a friend. I love talking to him, even this morning I read something in the paper and I thought, "God, I want to tell Jeremiah that". But he wasn't there. He's gone to his brother's . . . I felt so lonely then.'

She starts to cry again. I think back to how much I always want to tell Harry about my day. Because that's what relationships become: past the crackling air, the 'will he kiss me' dance, past the thrilling sex, it's just having a confidant. What happens when that goes? Or they find someone new to confide in? I want to heal my best friend, smooth over her cracks with words as soothing as fresh concrete, but I don't know the answer.

'Maybe in time you won't have lost him as a friend?' I try. 'You can be one of those fabulous couples who still get on so well, but aren't together?'

'Like Chris and Gwyneth?' she says, and I think she looks almost hopeful. I nod. And then she begins to laugh.

'Come on, Cait, you know that's bullshit!'

I catch her honk, of course I do, and begin to laugh myself. Both of us laughing, and crying a little.

'It's for the best, I know it is. It'll just take a while for me to get used to not having him here.' She rubs her hands together, tugging at the skin. 'But, Cait?'

'Hmm-hmm?'

'Will you be there, at my house, when he moves his stuff out? I don't want to be all Carrie Bradshaw, slumped by the toilet, begging him at the very last moment to stay.'

'Of course I will. When is he going?'

'He's packing up right now. So tomorrow? But you'll have work?'

I pull her in. 'I'll cancel all my appointments, I'll be there.'

Chapter Ten

When I first moved into the flat with Verity she loaded all her things into a shopping trolley and wheeled it three miles from her old place to our new one. I remember waiting, boxes all around my feet, alone – Mum had had to drive off to avoid a parking fee – when I saw Verity, in mirrored aviators and red-checked dungarees, pushing her life's belongings up the street. When our lease was up, Harry – the ever-sensible presence in our life – said that, this time, we had to do it properly. So we got Joe. Joe, with his ginger beard and tiny frame who – like an ant – can carry twice what you expect him to manage, and who loads his van so precisely it's like watching a game of Tetris. He's been in and out of our lives ever since – he was there when Harry and I got the mortgage on our house, when I moved into my office and when Verity and Jeremiah moved here, to their rented flat with a salmon-pink door.

His van sits outside that door now, Jeremiah up front. His crazy curly hair is almost drooping, like he's been hit by lightning one too many times.

'A'right, Cait.' He says it too soon, when I'm still about a foot away, and I give him a small wave back, taking in his orange hoody, banana print t-shirt and baggy jeans.

'You not freezing?' I ask him. He's a contrast to the sky, which is a blanket of grey, dropping sleet onto my cheeks.

'Packed all my warm stuff, didn't I? Just didn't think.' He glances at the van, its back doors open and revealing old crisp boxes stacked all around his brown chair: the one he always sits in, rollie in one hand and the espresso cup he uses as an ashtray resting on the arm. Thinking about that, and the empty space in the living room where the chair should be, makes me want to hug him. I want to say thank you for all the times he's made me laugh, pulled me out of a slump just by the sight of his ridiculously bright clothing.

But I just shrug as he wraps his arms around himself and says: 'Course, it's a tough time.'

He shuffles on his feet and looks in towards the house. 'You'll be wanting the duchess, I s'pose? She's up in the bedroom.'

I nod. Joe's inside, toppling his way down the stairs, his face hidden by a pile of three boxes. 'A'right, Cait?' he says, his voice muffled through the cardboard.

'Yeah, need any help?' I reply, knowing the answer.

'Don't be silly, you'd just mess up me system. Go on up, she'll be needing you.'

Upstairs, Verity's hugging her knees to her chest on her bed, which is covered in a rumple of different-patterned blankets. She's sitting on a pink leopard-print one, her favourite, so I pick up the one with peacock feathers and wrap it around her. She's not as shrunken as she was the other night, the air around her seems firmer.

'He's just grabbing the last of his boxes,' I say. 'How are you?'

She lifts her shoulders a bit, drops them. 'Sad, I guess.'

The only words I have in my toolbox are pointless. The soundbites she'll have heard already, the things she'll know but won't be ready to believe. 'It'll all get better in time.'

'You'll find someone new, someone better.' 'Everything happens for a reason.' They always make me want to scream, 'But they mean fuck all!' whenever I hear them. Yet, as I sit beside her, putting one arm around her shoulders, I sigh and say, 'It's for the best. I know it doesn't feel like it now, but it is.'

She nods. 'I just want to forget about it all. Go back to how we used to be, before our world got a whole lot harder.' Outside I can hear the van doors slamming, Joe's whistling. I quickly stand up and put some music on to drown out the noise of him driving away.

'How about we go to Varsity?' I suggest. It's one of our old haunts – a sticky, cheap student bar where you can get pitchers of fluorescent-coloured cocktails in thick plastic jugs. We used to spend hours there, playing cards, occasionally pointing out the window at the men we'd sleep with.

That smile of hers cracks over her face, a lightbulb turned on. 'That sounds perfect, Cait.'

I love that she's the one who's cheered herself up. My best friend, the superwoman who can have a D-lister scream in her face for five minutes and then gently wipe the spit off, smile and say, 'Don't you think it's time for your nap?'

'I'm so proud of you, Verity,' I say as she stands up and begins raiding her wardrobe for something to wear. 'This stuff is so tough but you're coping with it all so well. I wish I could bottle up your strength, drink it like a potion.'

It was meant to make her smile, but she pauses, clutching a dress covered in poppies. Still facing the wardrobe, she says, 'Cait, I need to tell you something.'

Madonna's 'Material Girl' is playing and it's begun to rain harder, drops slamming against the windowpane.

'What?' She doesn't turn around to face me, she just stays there, speaking into the wardrobe.

'I cheated on Jeremiah.' She says it so quietly I have to ask her to repeat it. Which she does, but still, the words don't fully enter. And when they do it's like, inside of me, something rips. As if my heart is made of tissue paper and her words have tugged at it, pulled it apart.

'You did what?' I don't mean to sound angry. But the words come out that way, harsh and cutting.

She turns around, looks at me and drops her head. 'I didn't want to tell you but I just, I couldn't not tell you.'

'I'm glad you did.' It comes out hoarse, like a whisper, and I'm not sure I mean it. I want to rewind back a few beats, where she was just heartbroken and I was going to cheer her up with sequins and Strongbow.

'Caitlin, will you please look at me?'

I'm wringing out the blanket underneath me, squeezing it tight with my hands. I'm thinking of the way Stu had looked up at me from the bottom of the stairs, how I'd felt as if I needed to tie myself to the door handle, anything to stop me chasing after him and saying I'd changed my mind about going to the pub.

'I'm sorry, OK?' she's saying. 'But it wasn't right, we hadn't been right. My cheating isn't what ended it, it was just the sign we both needed that it was time for things to be over.'

There are so many things I could have done over the past year, in anger, in pain, that I haven't. That I've held myself back from doing. They flood me, and it's almost as if it's those memories that are taking over my mouth and making me speak. Like ghosts are controlling me.

'But you came round to my house crying. Heartbroken.' I look up at her, shake my head.

'So, I can still be upset about it. Even if I did mess up.'

'Mess up? That's an understatement.'

At that, she's throws her hands up. 'God, Caitlin, I know this stuff upsets you but don't you think you're being a bit unfair? You work in relationships, you know that this goes on. I've heard you say "cheating is the symptom, not the disease".'

I do say that, to clients who have been burned in the past, to reassure them that in the right relationships it won't happen. I even say it to those who have cheated, trying very hard to swallow my judgement and accept that it doesn't have to mean a lifetime of regret and loneliness. But this is different. She knows, first-hand, what hurt this can cause. I don't say that, though; I don't know if I can trust myself to.

'Yeah, I say it to clients, I've also had clients buy into my whole business because of you and Jeremiah,' I say, ignoring the real source of my anger, circling in red scrawls around my head. 'Fuck, that's how I got Morwena on board.'

'That's what you're thinking about just now? Morwena Fucking Star?' Verity's playing with a piece of her hair, tugging it back and forth, and her eyes are wide as she looks at me, like I'm a stranger that's been implanted in her bedroom.

'Well, it's going to be all based on a lie now, isn't it?' Even as the words come out I know they sound pathetic, that I need someone to come in, stand in between me and Verity and remind us both how much we love each other. Remind me how much none of this anger is really meant for her.

'Are you seriously having a go at me for lying?' She throws her hands up in the air. She'd been keeping them down by her sides, right at her hips, all clenched up. 'Come on, Caitlin, you of all people can't be mad about that stuff.'

'Don't.' I shake my head, look out the window. 'I thought.' I swallow my tears down, which are coming thick and fast up my throat. 'I thought you guys were perfect. I thought you would never do something like this, knowing the hurt it causes.'

She looks out the window. The light reflects a tear on her cheek. She darts her hand up, wipes it away, thinking I haven't spotted it. That swift movement presses into my stomach, settles there. I almost go over, wrap my arms around her. I wonder if she can feel the sadness, thick in my throat, the way I can feel her pain. I feel both our pasts collect in my bones, as I keep pushing them away.

'You're being naive, Caitlin. Nothing is perfect. You should stop pushing so hard for it, pretending that it is. It doesn't work, you know that.'

As she speaks it's not her voice I hear. It's Harry's. Harry saying, 'What does it matter if we're a bit late, it'll be fine', as we rush along the street, as I imagine what people are saying about us behind our backs. His face swims before mine as I yell at him for not tidying the kitchen, coming home to find it a mess – a total contrast to Polly Lee's, whose marble-topped, brass-handled kitchen I'd been looking at seconds before. I hear him, loud and clear, as if he's yelling in my ear right now: 'Caitlin, why are you always comparing your life to someone else's?' I snap my head up. The room is the same as it always was – she's still there but it's as if her face, her body have warped into something else – like I'm watching a TV show with bad reception.

'Is that what you're saying? That Harry was right in those arguments?'

'That's not what I'm saying at all, Cait. I'm just trying . . . I'm trying to defend myself. This has nothing to do with Harry.'

But I can't hear her. All I can feel are the words inside of me, like tiny balls of lava that I have no control over but that I have to release. 'You're the one that fucked up,' I say. 'Don't go trying to bring it back round to me.'

'I'm not.' She shakes her head, and there's that look again, like I'm an alien that's been transplanted into her best friend's body. 'Are you listening to me?'

I feel as if a fog has descended around me, like her words are all muddled up within that fog, and I can't separate what she's saying from what I really feel. Her voice floats around me, becoming all tangled up with my memories and I can't unpick what's real and what isn't.

'Look.' I can hear her using her softest voice, the one she uses when defusing a particularly tricky situation. It's patronising and it grates on me. 'I've been wanting to say this for a while now, but I think you need professional help. You know? A therapist. I can't . . .' She pauses. This time I know she's crying, but I won't look at her. 'I can't do this any more.'

And boom. That's all it takes for me to lose complete control, for the words to come spitting out of me. 'Maybe I can't do this any more. Our friendship. You clearly don't even fucking care about me, so why do I even bother?'

I don't mean this. I don't mean any of this. But the words won't stop. I'm shouting, shouting, shouting. Like I'm a can of fizzy pop and someone has shaken me up and released me, the rage I've bottled up exploding out.

Verity just stands there, stock-still. Her mouth slightly open. She doesn't say anything. And before she can speak, without waiting to see if she tells me that she does care about me, I fire down the stairs and out of her house, slamming the door so hard the ground appears to shake. Then I flip on my heel and begin to walk, in the opposite direction to home, down a hill so steep it takes my legs with it, as if they're walking with a purpose of their own. It's only when I reach the bottom, holding my thighs to calm down the energy within them, that I get the tiniest grasp on what just happened.

Everything about it felt like the dreams I'd been having lately, where I wake up with a tingling all over my body, having shouted at someone who didn't deserve it. A few nights ago I screamed at the lovely lady who comes in and cleans our offices each morning. The words I yelled at her were so vile that when I woke up, I couldn't even believe I knew them, that they lived in my head.

I take a seat on a low brick wall. The rain hasn't stopped and I'm drenched by it, it's soaked right through my jacket to my jumper and the t-shirt underneath. But the cold doesn't register – I just sit there, and let the water pour all around me, wondering if this is what will always happen to me now. My anger is going to break out from within me and into my reality. I'll just let it tumble out and turn the good things in my life poisonous. I don't want that. I didn't mean any of those things I just screamed at Verity – yet, one trigger, and I said them anyway. I know she loves me, that she cares. But perhaps I'd be best to leave her, let her get on with her life. My problems have already impacted her so much. I can't keep letting them. I remember her words, 'I can't do this any more', and know, like all my other friends who slowly retreated, disappearing into thin air, that I have become a burden to her.

I look through my phone. It's blinking angrily at me, annoyed at the water damage I've inflicted on it. My contacts is still full of names I recognise, names I used to call when I was upset about things, names I saw on week-nights, had cocktails with, went to the cinema with. But I can't call any of them now, it's been too long. There's just one person whose phone I know won't ring out on me, who will pick up. I find the number, press green. She answers on the third bleep.

'Mum,' I say. 'Can I come and stay with you for a while?'

Chapter Eleven

I press both hands against the living room wall. Rest my forehead on it, close my eyes. Even with my eyes shut I know the colour of this wallpaper: cream-ish, with bumpy raised flowers that have been gathering dust since my childhood. I stay there, leaning, head forward, until Mum comes through, pulls me away and places me on the sofa. I finger a rip in the cushion, tuck my knees to my chin and place my head on my thighs. The radio is blasting out from the kitchen, the hosts are rabbiting on about how it's almost the weekend. 'It's only Wednesday,' I say, into my knees. 'Time is moving so slowly, why won't it just stop?'

'What's that, duck?' Mum's holding a cup of tea to my face, I can feel the heat of the mug on my cheek. I peel myself up, remove the hair that's stuck to my nose. The tea is in a brown Smarties mug, which I wrap my hands around. Noddy Holder begins to yell 'It's Christmaaaas' from the radio.

'You always made all holidays so special,' I say, but Mum jumps up, jogs through and turns the radio off. The silence reminds me of something and makes me realise why I've felt odd since arriving here half an hour ago. I look up. The ceiling is bare. It should be covered in paper garlands, a riot of pinks, purples, greens and reds. I stand up and follow her into the kitchen.

Mum is staring at the oven. The paper sleeve of Aunt Bessie's Apple Crumble sits on the side. 'Where are all the decorations, Mum?'

There should be a Santa in here that sings a song when you walk past him. In the toilet there should be a seat cover and loo roll holder in the shape of Rudolph. But none of it's out. She bustles back through to the living room, with me in close pursuit, and flops onto the sofa, tearing open a packet of chocolate digestives and handing me one.

'Mum? The decorations?' The heating is up so high it makes my skin tight.

'Oh, I just thought I'd put them up later this year, maybe, if I bother at all.'

'Why would you not put them up? It's December now.'

She looks away, tugs at a lock of her bleached-blonde hair. She's been dyeing it for as long as I've been alive. I have no idea what her natural hair colour is.

'If you want me to put them up, I'll put them up. Just didn't think we would this year, that's all. Anyway, shall we pop the telly on? It's almost time for *Eggheads*.' She gets up, pushes the button for the TV. The control was lost ages ago – probably down some hole in this wretched couch. 'Then we'll have your favourite – posh pasta with crumble for pudding.'

The TV is tiny and fuzzy. All I can see is the blue of the background, and I have no idea who the contestants are. Mum pumps the volume up. 'We can't read the questions on the screen as the screen is so fuzzy,' she explains. 'So be quiet. I need to hear what they're saying.'

I sit on the sofa, trying to pretend I know the answers to questions about Tintin and the Great Fire of London. Mum pretends too, shouting them out and always getting it wrong. Each time the right answer is announced she mutters under her breath, 'But I was so sure.'

This was my childhood, sitting on this sofa after school, watching game shows with Mum. The kids in the street would be outside screaming, girls in pastel cycling shorts practising their cartwheels and boys trading football cards or Pogs. The incessant thud of a football hitting a wall. Sometimes I have dreams that are impossible to shake off, of being back in school, walking down the corridors while girls with shiny blonde ponytails that swished back and forth snigger at me.

This sofa was always a refuge from all of that: the white, toothy grins of game show hosts and the sound of buzzers and yelled-out answers always comfort me. But today it's not working. I keep shuffling about on the sofa, trying to get into a position that soothes me. I want to talk to Mum. To ask her again why the walls are bare.

'Where are your cards, Mum?'

'Ssshh, I can't hear the question,' she whispers back before shouting, 'Carol Vorderman.' On the TV the contestant says calmly, 'The Beatles.'

'Damn, I was so sure,' she says as I scan the walls again, looking for the red string, the green pegs that she hangs every card on.

'Cards, Mum? Where are they?'

'Sshh, will you? I just shoved them in a drawer.'

I get up and wander through to the kitchen, open up the 'messy' drawer. There's a pile of Christmas cards near the top. I begin to flick through them: I recognise all the names – people from the chemist, neighbours. I look for a man's name, but it's all 'Sheila' and 'Betty', and they are all signed: 'Do send my deepest love to Caitlin'. I shove them back in, pushing the drawer shut.

'Pop the pasta on while you're in there, will you, love? The little macaroni shapes?' she shouts through.

I fill up a pan with water, shove it on the hob and pull the cheddar out of the fridge, ignoring the trays of microwave meals 'for one' that are neatly stacked on the top shelf. I take the cheese through and begin grating it on my lap.

'Seeing anyone at all?' I ask, staring intently at the grater.

'Pffft,' she says, giving me a gentle shove. 'You know the answer to that one and'– she taps my jaw – 'no, you can't find me anyone.'

The TV fizzes in the background. I try another tactic. 'I could get you a new telly, if you wanted?'

'And why would I need one?' she retorts, as if she hadn't just told me we couldn't speak during *Eggheads* as she couldn't see the screen.

'Because it's clearly on its last legs!'

Mum has held tight to her 'make do and mend' policy throughout her life. She'd even darn tights when I was younger. Toys were second-hand: my Barbie's hair coloured in by someone else, my doll's face grubby with overuse. Back then it made sense as we couldn't afford it, but now I've got money, and she never lets me spend it on her.

'And when it kicks it I'll get another one. Jan from the chemist has offered me her old one.'

'What's the point in getting an old one when I can get you a brand-new one?'

'Because it makes no difference if it's brand new or not,' she says. 'Honestly, you're just like all the neighbours with their flash sixty-inch TVs and Michael Kors handbags. I don't get why everyone on this street is pretending they're not poor. We're all bloody skint.'

It's a rant I've heard a hundred times before and had it been any other day I would have just rolled my eyes, said 'Yes, Mum', and gone through and drained the pasta. But today I'm irked. It's like my body is covered in something itchy and irritating and I have no control over it, or what I feel inside. I just want to scream. But instead, I pick at her words.

'Maybe because they want to make the best of their lives? Have nice things?'

'Having loads of stuff doesn't mean you're happy.' It's a refrain I heard throughout my childhood – when I got given fake two-stripe Adidas trousers instead of three; when I brought my one doll over to a friend's house and she said it was crap as it wasn't an official Barbie. While our neighbours bought everything on credit, Mum refused. 'It's just showing off,' she'd tut, watching from the window as Lucy next door got her three-piece leather suite delivered. It's what she's tutting about now. 'Showing off, that's what it is. Honestly, just because something looks good on the outside, it could still be all shabby on the inside,' she says.

She means me, I think, picturing my office, how carefully curated it is, how everything in there matches something I've seen on someone else's Instagram page. How most mornings it looks so perfect I want to scream.

I feel for my little secret, at the back of my head. That small ball of tangled hair has settled at the nape of my neck. It's growing and becoming more unmanageable each day.

'Mum?' I say, in a soft and small voice. 'Can you untangle my hair?'

'Course, duck.' She reaches underneath the sofa, pulls out a basket containing a hard plastic brush and some leave-in conditioner. I settle myself in between her legs and she smooths my hair down with the palm of her hand, coating my hair with a coconut-scented mist.

'Oh,' she says, holding the ball between her hands. 'It's not been this bad for a long, long time, huh?'

When I was six I was invited to spend the weekend with my dad. I was so excited I packed all my best clothes into a pink, sparkly My Little Pony rucksack – my pride and joy – and brushed my hair one hundred times, every night for a week before going. I remember asking Mum, just before he came to collect me, 'Will he like me?' It was the question I asked every time I left the house, before school or birthday parties, and Mum always said the same thing: 'Who wouldn't like you, duck?' But when she said it that time she didn't smile or ruffle my hair, she just turned round and went and sat in the living room, leaving me to answer the door by myself.

That weekend I met my half-sister Louise for the first time, just a year younger than me. I also met my half-brother Joseph, who was a newborn with chubby hands and feet, who grinned up at me. I wanted to 'bop' his nose, or have his little fingers wrap tightly around mine, but I remember feeling, so strongly, that I couldn't. That he wasn't mine to touch or play with. With Louise I swallowed down my urge to throw myself on the ground, banging my fists, and instead played quietly with her. When I got home I refused to brush my hair for two months. Until eventually Mum had to chop the golf-ball-size tangle out with scissors.

We don't really talk about Dad very often.

'Mum?'

'Yep.'

'Do you think what happened with Dad still affects you?'

She chuckles, it's low and gruff. 'What are you? A therapist?' she says, pulling sharply on my knot at the same time – the familiar pain bringing tears to my eyes. Instinctively I throw my hand up, press it against the knot, yelp out an 'ouch'.

'Sorry.' Her brushing continues as she hums quietly to herself.

'Verity cheated on Jeremiah,' I say. I hadn't planned on telling her about the argument with Verity. I'd wanted to come here for refuge, for time to figure things out. She pauses. I can feel the bristles of the brush hovering just off the back of my head.

'Is she OK?' she asks.

My head jerks forward an inch. 'Why are you asking if she's OK? What about Jeremiah?'

She pulls my shoulders back, begins tugging the brush through my hair again. 'I don't know Jeremiah, and I know Verity. She's not the type to intentionally hurt someone, she'll have had her reasons.'

There's a pile of newspapers at my feet, their corners turning yellow. Our house has always been mayhem: plates fill the sink, dusty trinkets and half-drunk mugs of tea litter the surfaces. When I was younger, Mum was always treading on stray Lego blocks, yelping about how the house just wasn't big enough. The house Dad lived in, across town, had six bedrooms and carpets that were fluffy underneath my feet. I'd sometimes get letters from Louise, covered in glittery stickers and written in a scented gel pen that smelled of raspberry. I'd bring them through to Mum, bitterness coating my tongue as I told her what new toy Louise had that week. 'They have what they have, and we have what we have,' she'd say. 'And we're all very lucky.'

She's using that same measured tone now, and my head fills up with darkness. I try to mimic her. 'Aren't you angry at Verity?' I ask, feeling my heart begin to flutter.

'Are you angry at her?' she replies.

'Course I am.' The words come out like a dog's bark. I'm trying so hard not to explode at Mum the way I did with Verity. But it feels like someone has taken a biro and doodled thick black spiralling lines all across my brain.

'And why's that?' She thinks her voice, tinted with lavender, will soothe me, but I'm gripping my nails into my fists.

'I'm worried what she's done will have a lasting effect on Jeremiah.'

'He's a big boy, he doesn't need you fretting about him. I think this is more to do with—'

Before she can finish I cut her off, snapping: 'That's not fair, Mum. I've seen this happen, in my . . . clients. They can't move on, they're scared all the time that they'll be hurt again.'

She's completely stopped brushing now. I feel the back of my head – the tangle is still there, it almost throbs in my hand.

'I think we all know why you're being like this,' she says, holding my shoulders. 'But you're being unfair to Verity, and I hope to God you've not said any of this to her.'

My breath catches itself, sharp in my throat. My head is so full of darkness now, like my brain has been coloured in. I'm tired, so tired, but I know what I need to do. I thought coming here would help, that Mum would understand, but it's not helping at all. I push myself up. She thinks I'm going to drain the pasta, and asks me to stir some marge into it.

'I can't do this right now,' I say, shaking my head. I'm thinking of a text I received earlier. How it flashed up on my phone, and how I'd ignored it.

'Why don't you go upstairs, have a lie-down? I can heat the food up for you when you're ready.'

I nod, but as I get out into the corridor I pick my bag up, put on my coat. 'Duck? Duck?' I hear her yell just as I'm slamming the door behind me. As soon as the frosty air hits me, fills up my lungs with sharpness, I burst into tears.

Chapter Twelve

I begin to jog along Mum's street, the icy gusts of winds cooling down my hot, tired and teary face. I speed up as I pass our neighbours', their windows lit up with shimmering trees. Through one window I can see a family, all clustered on the sofa, bathed in blue light from their television. The bus stop is at the end of the road and when I reach it I find that I am gasping for breath. I check the time on my phone, find that there are two new messages. I shove it back into my pocket for now, checking the timetable. There's not a bus into town for another fifteen minutes, so I sit on the cold metal bench, banging my boots against the shelter, which shakes with every thud.

My phone rings: it's Mum. I don't want to answer but know that if I don't she'll just keep ringing and ringing. 'Hello?' I say, pretending everything is normal. That I'm not sitting at the bus stop at the end of her street, shivering in the cold.

'Caitlin.' Her voice is sharp. 'I'm worried about you. Please come back, we need to talk about all of this.'

My phone buzzes against my cheek, with another incoming message. 'I'm fine, Mum, just . . .' I trail off. I can't think of anything to say that will convince her this is what I must do.

'Oh,' she sighs. I can hear her voice cracking. 'You're not.'

Cars whizz past, their headlights dazzling me in bright white. I stay silent. I can hear her sniffing down the line. 'I spoke to Verity,' she says. I feel a tear land on my cheek. I am just so bored of crying. I wipe it away. 'She told me about your argument. She said she mentioned you going to a therapist?' I'm tempted to hang up. She keeps talking. 'I've thought for a while it would be a good idea, you know, it really helped Suzie in the chemist.'

Someone has carved J + C into the shelter. I trace it with my fingers, wishing I was wearing gloves. A coating of dark grey dust settles on my skin. 'I don't care about Suzie from the chemist,' I say, pressing the dirt onto my other hand, smearing it across my palm. 'I know what I need, and it's some fun.'

'Fun?' She says the word as if she's never heard it before.

'Yeah, fun, look, I know it seems as though I'm struggling, but I'm not. Verity and Jeremiah just threw me, that's all.' I rearrange my face into a smile, hoping she'll hear it through the line somehow. I don't know what I was thinking going to Mum's house after the argument; it's brought back some memories, unsettled me off my perch, but I *am* fine. 'Really,' I repeat. 'I'm fine.'

'And you'll speak to Verity?' She sounds unsure.

'Yes,' I reply. 'I promise. I just need to get back to the city, to the business, OK? I'll come see you again soon.'

I can hear the *Countdown* clock in the background, and can see her standing in her living room so clearly – still in her chemist's tabard, grubby from the day. I feel a pang in my stomach, a little voice telling me I should go back, look after her, stop her from being lonely. But then I think of the bare ceiling, the cards stashed away in the drawer and the concerned look that she wears every time she sees me lately. I'm tired of convincing her that everything is going well, that I've got everything I've ever wanted in my life. 'Mum, look, that's the bus coming, bye. Love you.'

I hang up, sit back down on the bench, looking at the road. The bus isn't actually due for five more minutes, so I open my phone up, read all of Ade's messages: *Dude, reads one, something SO exciting has happened. You have got to come out tonight, I'll show you it.*

I open up Instagram, check in on Morwena's page – her latest post is of her sitting in the lotus position, and resting in her palm are two candy-floss-coloured crystals. *Opening up my heart to love, opening up my very being to love. I have a feeling he's just around the corner*, the caption reads. I double-tap it to like, post a comment underneath: *Oh, he definitely is*, I type, adding in a winking face and then regretting it straight away.

I begin to hum something, I think a Taylor Swift song I heard on the radio earlier. The dark lines that circled my head have almost gone, as if they have snaked out of my ears. I did the right thing leaving Mum's. Being at work, in the life I've built for myself, is the right thing to do. I shouldn't feel guilty for having a little bit of fun, I think, opening the two unread messages. They're from Stu. *Hey, Ade's trying to get me to go out tonight, but it's your business we're celebrating, feels wrong without you . . . Come?* The second one, sent about an hour later, *God, now she's making me go to Babylon. I'll understand if you don't come now. But if you want to save a mid-thirties man from the terrors of a retro bar, please do.* My stomach begins to hum, a heady mix of excitement and nerves, something I haven't felt for a long time. I try to push past the feelings of guilt that also begin to swarm inside me as I reply: *Sure, what harm can one drink do?*

*

Harry's face was red-tinged, hiding under a den made of blankets, and I was laughing because it felt like no one knew where we were, even though we were in the centre of the living room. Licking the salt from the rim of a margarita glass, feeling the bump, bump, bump of the rough granules on my tongue. The memories come to me as I shut my eyes and fling a tequila down my throat, feeling that familiar burn, that rush. I drain the juice of the lime and grin, stickily, at Stu and Ade. Stu is gagging but Ade is serene. She looks as though she's just had a nice sip of water.

'Right,' she says, grabbing both our hands. 'Now you've done that, Caitlin, let me show you the reason I chose Babylon.' She begins dragging us to the door, weaving our way through the bar. It's nineties night and we dodge past men with their shirts undone by three buttons, bumping into women in scratchy sequin dresses, their once-perfect make-up smeared in black rings around their eyes.

'Ade! My coat,' I yell over the opening bars of Whigfield's 'Saturday Night', as a stampede of people rush squealing towards the dance floor. 'We'll only be a minute,' she says, so we dutifully trot behind her, the freezing air hitting me, sending goose pimples up my arms.

'Stu,' she instructs. 'Blindfold her.'

'What with?' he says as I begin to protest. He holds his hands up in the air, points to his body, the fact that he's wearing just jeans and a red t-shirt; I can see the faint outline where the cotton clings to his abs. I look down at my feet.

'Use your hands then,' Ade says, and because she's so impossible to argue with, he does as he's told, saying, 'Come here then,' which I do, dutifully but clumsily, accidentally treading on one of his toes as he wraps his huge hands around my face. I can feel his breath on my neck.

I hear Ade say, 'This way,' as he guides me a little further down the street. The tequila hits me and I begin to giggle. See? I want to say to Mum. Look how fine I am!

'Here,' Ade says. I can hear Stu whistle, low under his breath.

'Wow.' Then he pulls his hands away.

I open my eyes, adjusting them to what I'm looking at: a bright white light penetrating my skull. There, in a rectangle advert on the bus stop, right by Tesco, is my face – well, the side of my face – looking up into Harry's eyes. We're both smiling in a way that's almost unrecognisable, my hair is in loose waves tumbling down around my face and we're surrounded by so many butterflies, they're like brushes of colour across the portrait. *Find a love that gives you butterflies*, the poster reads, alongside a new website address.

'Oh my God,' I say, again and then again. I feel wobbly on my feet, sway to one side, then the other.

'Aw, she's so overwhelmed,' Ade says and, somehow, I manage a smile. 'A compromise!' she says. 'A brilliant marketing campaign but no photo shoot.' She claps her hands together. 'We've had over a hundred applications just this morning!'

Stu begins to talk me through the website, telling me he will show me tomorrow. His words float in one ear and out the other. I just stare at Harry, the way he's looking at me as if he's stumbled upon a precious jewel.

'Couldn't get through to him in the end,' she tells me, with a wave of her hand. 'But mate, I just decided to go ahead anyway. A good deal came up, and this is taking you to the next level! He can't be mad at you if you're both millionaires.'

'Unlikely,' I say, a smile trapped on my face.

'Now,' yelps Ade. 'We need to celebrate!'

I follow them both back down the street, a little dazed, until I'm hit by the flashing multi-coloured lights, the sound of 'Spice Up Your Life' blasting through me.

'You OK?' asks Stu, touching my back. And because there's nothing else that can be done, or said, and because I came here for fun, I nod.

'I'll get us champagne!' I say, imagining the bubbles whizzing around my tongue.

'You're not getting champagne in Babylon, Cait, don't be ridiculous,' Ade screeches before turning to the bartender. 'Three snakebites, please. She's paying.'

Then she's off, power-walking her way over to a woman in a black pencil skirt and red wine all down the front of her white shirt.

Stu winces. 'Remind me why we're here again?'

'I believe it's because there's a huge poster of my face outside,' I say, gesturing across the place. On the dance floor someone has been sick and a barmaid, who must only be around nineteen, is struggling with a hazard-yellow mop that's taller than her. 'Stay classy, Caitlin.'

'Hey,' he says, grabbing our pints and steering us into a vaguely quiet corner. 'First a bus stop in Sheffield, next a billboard in Times Square.' There's a pause, we both take a slurp from our drinks. 'Are you really OK with it? I tried to tell Ade to warn you first.'

'Yeah,' I say, trying to adopt the same laid-back attitude Ade had been displaying earlier. 'It's good for the business.'

I'd also – in a strange way – loved seeing Harry and me up there. It felt as though I'd frozen time, or maybe stepped into a completely new time zone, where, on that poster, everything was just perfect and it would stay that way. But I'm not going to tell Stu that, so I just shrug.

'So much for wanting to spend time with us, eh?' Stu points into the dance floor, where Ade is grinding against the red-wine-stain girl.

'Predictable.'

The air settles around us, reminding us both that it's just us now, out together, alone. It feels awkward, like I want to shake my shoulders out, break the tension with physical movement. I take a deep breath. I can do this. I can be out, alone, with another man. It's allowed.

'Tell me,' he says, 'who's the man the matchmaker picks for herself?'

'Apart from unwittingly famous?' I reply. I don't want to talk to Stu about Harry, not in this place, where it's so loud we have to pull our chairs in close, yell in each other's ears to be heard. But I have to give him something.

'He's a dentist, he's sweet, kind . . . The kindest, really.' I shake my head, let thoughts of Harry float out of one ear – I've just remembered that his surgery offers free dental treatment to homeless people every Thursday, and that memory constricts my throat, makes me want to run out of here and get back home. Instead I decide to quiz Stu like a client. Keep it professional. I'm good at that, turning the charm on, asking attentive questions about other people. Absorbing their lives until I have forgotten my own.

'What do you do for fun? Apart from climbing, of course.'

'Well, I have a dog, a wee sausage dog, called Jimi. Like Hendrix.' He grins, raises an eyebrow. 'I know, I know. Bit of a try-hard name.'

'Jimi. I think it's sweet. You a big fan then?'

'Not as much as my ex was. She's the one who named him.'

An image of his ex pops into my head: cool, straight blonde hair, kohl-rimmed eyes, the sort of woman who can wear flares and not look like she's heading straight to a fancy dress party. My stomach stabs with an odd jealousy, a tiny prick of it that I know I shouldn't feel but do anyway. Like how I feel when I see an old friend announce a pregnancy. It's guilt, wrapped up with envy, and it's acidic.

'Oh, when did you split then?'

He looks as if I've just pricked him with a safety pin. I remember where I am, that I can't just ask blunt questions outright. I throw my hands up to my face.

'I'm so sorry, that was rude of me to ask! I'm so used to asking clients every detail of their lives, I forget I can't do it in social situations.'

He shakes his head, gives me a ghost of a grin. 'It's all right. We split about six months ago. She didn't want to move to Sheffield. I got custody of Jimi though.'

He pulls out his phone, shows me a few pictures of his chocolate-brown sausage dog. In each he's wearing a dotted tie.

'Another drink?' he asks. We've both managed to drain our snakebites; I'd forgotten how good they taste. He rubs at his mouth. 'You've got . . .'

'A snakebite smile?' I say, knowing from years of drinking these things with Verity that, along with teeth coated in sugar, I'll also have a blackcurrant stain, pointing upwards at the corners of my mouth.

'I'd call it a Ribena smile . . . I like yours though.'

I don't know if he means my smile, or what I call it, so I just keep rubbing at my mouth, then I direct my chin up at him. 'All gone?'

He shakes his head. 'Here, let me.' He reaches across to me and I find, barely breathing, I lean forward. He takes his thumb and wipes my mouth, firmly but gently. His green eyes are more intense than usual – the colour of Christmas trees.

'White wine,' I say, simply to fill the air. 'Can I have a white wine, please? No preference.'

Three hours later, and Stu has just told me a joke that's made the wine come out of my nose. I can't remember what it was that made me laugh so much, or even if it actually was particularly funny, I just know that all tensions are gone. My shoulders are loose, partly down to the two extra tequilas we've had each – Ade sashayed over, her new conquest in tow, to slam them with us, before heading back to the dance floor.

Each time I knock the shots back I'm transferred to that first night with Harry, under those blankets. It had turned out exactly how Verity and I had scripted it: we'd found out that Harry's sister lived in the building, so we decided to throw a housewarming party and invite all the neighbours. I remember on the night wailing in my room, dressed in an embroidered white slip, that there was no guarantee *she'd* come, never mind him. Verity had told me sternly, in her best teacher voice, to quit my whining: that the best way to meet someone was to have fun. I'd strictly followed her orders, chatting to everyone and dancing, trying so hard not to watch the door. When he did enter I was in the process of building a den, throwing blankets over a clothes horse for our other neighbour's five-year-old daughter to play in. I'd heard a throat being cleared behind me and spun round – he was holding a bottle of tequila in one hand. 'Shot?' he'd said, pouring the amber liquid into a skull shot glass. But it's not just the taste of the tequila transporting me back to that night. It's the way I feel, the same as I did back then.

I remember speaking to Harry – we'd both crawled into the den, the children long gone home – and knowing he was really listening to me. I had this bubble of energy inside me, we were both telling each other our stories so fast, like we couldn't get them out quick enough. But also we wanted to take our time, cherish each word the other said – gobble them up until they became part of us.

I felt like I was watching my words go into him, fill him. He told me about his mum, how close they were but also how irritating he found her, how his mum always felt a little let down by life – simply because she was always comparing herself to other people.

With Stu I feel that same energy, that every story he tells feels important – more than small talk; something to remember, to cherish. But there's one thing that's not the same as it was with Harry – and that was how much I wanted Harry to kiss me that night, the fact it was definitely going to happen hovering in the air between us. With Stu I won't let that electricity in. Instead I learn about him, deflecting questions about myself, jumping up to get wine or request the DJ plays a song whenever the atmosphere comes too crackly to bear.

When the lights flash three times, telling us it's closing time, we both notice Ade has gone. The corner where she'd been kissing that woman, getting red wine all over her own mouth, lies empty. A discarded secret Santa present – a Rudolph teddy – sitting forlornly in their place.

'Did she say goodbye?' Stu asks as I realise I am struggling to stand up. I try twice, each time the wobble in my legs getting the better of me and I end up sitting down, laughing. He spots me, smiles. 'Here, let me,' he says, holding his hands out for me to grab on to. He pulls me up onto my feet, which tap across the floor, this way and that, as we walk. I'm swaying and bumping into people, letting out hiccup laughs each time I do, so he grabs my shoulder, pulls me into him. I forgot how wonderful that feeling is, being secured in place by a man's arm, feeling safe in the crook of his armpit. I inhale: he smells of aftershave, beer and something else, something biscuity and essentially him. It makes me dizzy.

Then we're outside on the street, the orange street lights bringing me back to who I am, why I am here. I unwind myself from him, spot a cab, which he waves down.

'You going to be OK getting home?' he asks, and words bubble up in my stomach, *no I'm not, please come back with me, not for anything, just for the feel of you beside me.* But I swallow them, nod and insist I'll be fine.

It's only later, as I'm lying in bed, one foot on the floor to stop the world spinning, that I realise the wine has wiped out chunks of our conversation from my memory. I have no clue what I've told him.

Chapter Thirteen

I've ignored my phone eight times already. But it won't stop ringing, the incessant buzzing as it bumps its way along my bedside table filling my ears and making my head constrict in pain. I know it can't be Verity, she has her special ringtone. When I looked at my phone last night she'd rung me twelve times. Mum had sent a text asking if I was OK, which I dutifully replied to, concentrating very hard on ensuring I spelled each word right.

My mouth is so furry, but the thought of brushing my teeth, that fake, clean, minty taste clogging up my tongue, is worse. The thought of doing anything at all is absolutely awful. I look at the clock ticking beside me patronisingly – it's 11.20 a.m. Can't I just go back to sleep? Harry and I used to do that, when we were younger, just stay in bed all day – have sex, order a pizza, watch reruns of *The IT Crowd* or *Black Books*, howling with laughter even though we knew exactly what jokes were coming and when. Sometimes Verity would crawl in, wrapped in a duvet, her hair jutting out at all angles. She'd always insist we watched *Don't Tell the Bride*, which Harry pretended he hated, but by the end of an episode he would always have an opinion on the bridesmaids' dresses.

Then I remember: I have a meeting with Morwena later to coach her before her date with Rowen tomorrow night. It's at her house, so I'll have to be feeling like this – like my body is permeated with filth and wine – in her haven of calm, gratitude and blessings. I can just picture it now, framed motivational slogans, Buddha ornaments and the stink of incense. My phone keeps ringing, insisting that I wake up and deal with it.

'Hello?' My voice sounds husky, I cough. 'Hello?'

'All right, sleepyhead.' It's Ade, and she does not sound like she was up until 3 a.m. snogging the face off 'Mandy, an HR representative from Doncaster', as her companion had introduced herself to us last night. In fact, she sounds – how dare she – chirpy.

'Just calling to check in on the Morwena meeting later,' she says as I scan my room for water. But there isn't any. I curse myself quietly. 'Are you listening to me?' she asks. I wasn't but I croak out a 'yes', which is satisfactory, it seems, as she begins to chatter on about the posters and Morwena's influence, and how both should see a threefold increase in sales. I'm simply fantasising about what pop I'm going to buy myself from our local shop – Sprite, Fanta or Lucozade – when it hits me she's been saying the word 'posters' quite a lot now.

'Wait, Ade, did you say posters? As in plural?'

'Yeah, did I not tell you? They're going to be all over Sheffield, smaller ones on the trams, sides of the buses, everywhere.'

My headache – which threatens to be lingering and persistent all day – flashes hot white. My stomach, swirling as if I'm on the Waltzers, sends bile up my throat. I'm going to be sick, I think, until I spot it: my saviour, at the bottom of my bedroom table. It's a champagne flute full of water that I must have filled up last night. I gulp it down. It's nowhere near enough, but it soothes me so I am able to keep talking. I pull the duvet over my head.

'You are happy with the posters, right, Cait?' Ade asks. If I tell her how I really feel she'll raise her voice in annoyance. I know she will.

'Yeah, yeah, they're good, as long as they're not costing me too much, you know. Um, look, I've gotta go. Get ready for Morwena.'

'Wait!' she yells, my head tingling. 'Did Stu show you the website redesign yet?'

My gut flips over again. Then there's the guilt, the paranoia – once just applicable to hangovers where I actually had done something wrong, now the affliction of every single time I dare to have more than one white wine.

'No, we didn't get a chance to look at it,' I say as Harry's face pops to the forefront of my mind. 'How about I come by the office tomorrow, before the date? We can look at it then.'

She agrees and I hang up, padding through to the shower. Last night's make-up is smeared all across my face – some pink lipstick has reached as far as my forehead. As I lather up, questions come firing through me. What did I say to him? Did I get too close? Was I being flirty? Over and over and over again they tumble about my brain, and I wish I could just shake them out of my ear, empty out my head and create space for the task at hand.

I wish I could phone Verity. She'd know exactly what to say to soothe me. I try to hear her, picture her hair changing colour as she shakes her head at me and laughs. 'Someone had too much wine last night,' she'd say. Then she'd rub my arm, get me an orange squash and explain to me that even if I did flirt, that's fine, I'm allowed. Harry's not the jealous type, I'm the one who is much more likely to kick off, let the swirling, irrational jealous thoughts in and allow them to ruin an evening. Like last time he let slip that it would just be him and one other dentist, a female dentist, going to the yearly California conference. We were out for the evening, after hardly seeing each other all week, and we ended up outside on the street screaming at each other.

Even now, after everything that's happened, I'm unsure who was right in that argument. It's hard for me to identify whether my feelings are born out of a paranoia to do with my past, or because I sensed something that's entirely valid.

I'm still debating with myself as I walk up the road to the bus stop, the light drizzle settling on my face in a film. My hair will be frizzy when I get to Morwena's and my outfit – a pair of black skinny jeans, thick black polo neck and camel coat – will smell of wet and the outside.

I get the front top deck seat, and stare down as the bus trundles off. There's a boy walking along the pavement outside Wetherspoons, walking like a gangster: he's waving his legs and arms like he's being controlled by a puppeteer. Following him is a woman, dressed in a purple tartan coat, her stride so wide and confident. I wonder how she does it? Feel so sure of her place on this world that she can walk like that, head held high. Then I see a man clad in neon yellow and orange, weaving his way on his bike through the traffic, nodding his head to music. He seems so vulnerable as he pulls up alongside a car in front, so small.

I dive down for my bag, pull my phone from its recesses. I plug my headphones in, keeping my eyes glued to the screen – and away from the cyclist – on Morwena's Insta stories. She's made the earliest yoga class, filming herself jogging there, showing her followers the golden light as the sun rises around her. She stands by the fountains in town, which jut up and around her, and it looks to be on a completely different continent – planet, even – from where I am sitting now, where everything is grey.

My stomach grumbles in envy as I watch Morwena tuck into her breakfast in a cafe in town; a wholemeal croissant smeared with chia jam, which she plops on before licking her fingers and telling her followers how 'bursting' with antioxidants it is. I didn't have time to eat before I left the house, so I promise myself I can get off a stop early to stock up on snacks: salt and vinegar crisps and chocolate for my journey home. I won't be able to eat that stuff in front of Morwena, so inside her local newsagents I grab a couple of fancy San Pellegrino cans of pop and a Special K bar. Surely she'll approve of them?

She answers the door dressed in navy-blue leggings and a soft cream jumper, her hair tousled and her face make-up free. I'm still not used to seeing this Morwena: acne sprinkled around her jawline, a chip on her oblong nails – flawed, but still entirely beautiful. She's much more ordinary than she makes herself out to be online, yet I can't help but look at her in fascination: there's something incredibly magnetic about the way she holds herself.

'Caitlin! Hello! How are you?' Her voice is babyish, questioning. Like she's carefully studied how a Californian celebrity speaks and has decided to impersonate that. She leads me through to her living room, where I settle myself on her sofa. It's hard beneath me – a deep, navy-blue corner number, definitely bought more for its looks rather than comfort. Morwena sits next to me, pushing a pile of *Real People*, *Chat* and *Take A Break* magazines underneath it with her feet. She glances over at me to see if I've noticed, so I quickly look around the room. It's a ground floor flat, with bay windows looking out on to the street. A postie sits out on a brick wall, directly outside. He's smoking a cigarette, his red trousers have ridden down so you can just see his bum crack, peppered with black hairs. She tuts at him, stands up and draws the cream curtains before lighting a Jo Malone candle on the mantelpiece. A dead cheese plant sits in the corner, its leaves bowed and brown-edged. She shakes her head at it, as if it's a naughty child she's disappointed with.

'So.' She sits back down, rubs her hands together. 'You going to show me him or 'owt?' The slip of her Yorkshire accent causes her hands to dart up to her face, before she swiftly regains composure and says, 'I'd so love to see who my dream man is!'

I swallow, my throat dry. 'I don't actually show pictures before a date.'

She looks at me, mouth open and then purses her lips together, juts the bottom one out. 'Why?'

'It's much better to see what you think of him in person,' I say. It's a well-worn line, which rolls off my tongue easily. I'll have to stick to the script, my headache has dulled but this hangover has replaced my brain with cotton wool. I feel less sharp than usual. 'So much of what makes someone fanciable is what they act like, how kind they are, how funny . . .'

'And is he?'

'Is he what?'

'Kind? Funny?'

I cast my mind back to calling Rowen. It was only a few days ago, but feels like it could be months. I can't remember anything about him.

'He is, yes, of course,' I reply.

'OK,' she crosses her arms. 'What else can you tell me about him?'

I'd love a cup of tea. I think of the cans of pop in my bag, wonder if it would be rude to take one out. I think I'll have to, fizzy liquid is all I can think about.

'He has . . .' I imagine cracking the can open, hearing the satisfying *psssht* and the light feeling of bubbles popping on my nose. 'Cheekbones! Sharp cheekbones!' I'm triumphant but she wants more, looking at me expectantly.

'Um, his eyes are . . .' I scan the room, looking for clues. Stu's eyes pop into my head, their warm, pine forest colour. There's a mug sitting on her coffee table, a wrinkled teabag on a coaster just beside it. I must stare at it that tad bit too long, as Morwena jumps up.

'Oh my God, I'm sorry. I'm being rude. Can I get you a drink?' Prayer answered.

'A cup of tea would be lovely.'

'Perfect.' She begins to scoop up the mug, the teabag, and wanders through to the kitchen, which appears to be under a small alcove off the living room. 'I have some gorgeous green tea, is that all right?'

It's not. Of course it's not. But I nod and smile.

'Lovely, of course.'

Green tea has to be the only liquid in the world that makes you thirstier the more you drink. I take a few sips, feel my cheeks almost wrinkle up with each one. The jasmine in it gives it a perfume-like flavour. I try not to wince as I reach into my bag, feeling the cool cans within. I pull one out. But she clocks it straight away.

'Oh, Caitlin, no!' she says, as if I've just started to chop up lines of cocaine on her coffee table. 'The sugar in those things! If you'd wanted a cold drink you should have just said.'

She gets up, prises the can out of my hand. 'Giving up sugar is one of the hardest things I have ever had to do.' I can mouth along to her as she wanders back into the kitchen. I've heard her speak about this so many times online. 'And wheat, and dairy and gluten. But I've found so many substitutes that taste, honestly, just as nice.'

I think of the 'carbonara' she touts, the sauce made of whizzed-up cashew nuts that congeals around courgette 'pasta'. I have to cough to cover up my gag.

'Here!' she says, placing a glass down in front of me with a flourish. It's a pint glass filled to the brim with a concoction of pond water, mixed with the slime TV presenters chucked on celebrities' heads in the nineties. 'My speciality!' I note she's not poured herself a glass. 'The Morwena hard green.'

'What's, um, what's in it?' I'm wondering if it's possible to be allergic to spinach. I'm sure I read somewhere that there are some foods it's impossible to be allergic to. If I lie will she see right through me?

'You'll have to taste it to find out!' she replies.

'I play that game with my husband,' I say, hoping to stall her. 'Guess the ingredient. Each time we cook for one another we have to guess what's in the dish.'

She puts her hands to her heart. 'Oh that's so cute! And I saw him, in town, on the posters? He's gorgeous!' She then mutters, so low I can hardly hear it. 'Bet you knew what he looked like before you went on a date with him.'

All the books on her shelves are horoscope or tarot-card related. I stare at their spines, all shades of purple with gold edging, anything to avoid looking at the juice, sludge-like, in front of me. 'Rowen has a few celebrity clients,' I say, his details slowly coming back to me. I'm remembering how he told me about his business, how he travels around in a van painted like a galaxy, visiting those who want their palms read or for him to contact a dead loved one on their behalf. My bones had turned cold at that point, despite having the office heating turned all the way up.

'Oh,' she says, edging closer to me. 'Who?'

'He couldn't disclose that to me . . . but he did tell me A-list.' The people he'd named had been a few bit parts in *Hollyoaks*. My stomach feels empty yet completely full up, all at once. It swirls angrily at me. Morwena cocks her head to one side.

'You OK? You look a bit . . . peaky.'

All I can think is, if I don't have a cup of tea, I'll die. Keel over and die.

'You should have some of my juice – your skin, it looks clammy. Like you're low on vitamin K. There's lots of kale in this.'

I'm going to have to do this. I pick up the glass. The thick liquid has made it heavy, and when I tip it to my mouth the sludge flows slowly and steadily towards me. It smells mossy, like the earth. Verity's brother, when we were younger, used to pluck worms out of their back garden and chase us around the living room, their squirming bodies all gathered in a clump of soil. That's what this drink smells of. When the liquid reaches my mouth it tastes grainy, like there's actual chunks of soil all over my tongue.

'Delicious, right?' she smiles at me. The liquid is still so thick and chunky in my mouth. I'm not sure I'm going to be able to swallow this, but she's started asking me more questions about Rowen, about the date. I tentatively swallow it, trying my hardest to think of nicer things: freshly squeezed orange juice, that first crisp glass of white wine . . . I start to cough, the nausea has come right up through my throat. If I don't get rid of this I am almost certain I'll vomit all over Morwena. She glances over at the window and in that time I manage to spit the rest of it out, back into the glass, a faint dribble of green running down my chin.

'Lovely,' I feign a smile, rubbing my chin. 'Intense . . . But let's get back to Rowen. I want to know how you're going into this date. Is it with a completely open mind? What are you looking for?'

'Well, that's simple. Perfection. I want someone perfect,' she replies, pushing the glass towards me once more. I try to retain eye contact with her, staring at her eyebrows – they look almost drawn on.

'You know that doesn't exist, right? You'll never find the perfect man.'

She reaches across to her phone, pulls up my Instagram page. One of the first photos is of me and Harry from the day of the Royal Wedding, the reality of that day completely wiped clean from both our smiles. 'You did! And I know I can, too. People told me I wouldn't find the perfect house, build the perfect career. And look around you.' She waves her arm as if she's an actress praising her audience. 'I did it.'

I stare at the dead cheese plant in the corner, its leaves droopy. Look back at the picture of Harry and me. Back and forth my eyes go, thinking of how much we all fake things.

'I just don't want you going in there and thinking things will be perfect right away. A good relationship takes time, and people aren't themselves on first dates. I always say give people two chances before you make your final judgement on them.'

She pouts. 'What, so you can't guarantee me the perfect date? I thought that's what your business was?'

'I'm in the business of love, Morwena. And I guarantee that if you go into this with an open mind and you trust me, it will all go to plan. Do you trust me?'

She looks from her left to her right. 'I trust you,' she replies, then she winks. 'But I trust myself more.'

Chapter Fourteen

'Looking swish, miss!' Elijah has appeared in front of me, all coiffed, in a love-heart-patterned shirt and jeans, yet shivering slightly in the cold. 'I've been wolf-whistling at you for ages!'

Lately, whenever I catch myself in the mirror, I'm amazed to see someone normal staring back. I'm not someone covered in scabs or skin that's been scrubbed red raw – there's nothing, apart from a soft greyness around my eyes, that indicates how I'm feeling inside. How full my head is with the argument I had with Verity, the things I yelled at her playing in a loop over and over around my head. I just see myself, in a blonde wig and fitted dress. That's all that stares back.

I gesture down at the outfit. 'Setting up another couple tonight.'

'Can't wait to hear about them,' he says, reaching for a strand of synthetic blonde. 'You'll come into the salon soon, won't you? My treat. I can't thank you enough for bringing Tom into my life.'

'It's my job.' I blush. 'How are things going with you guys?'

'Fantastic! Oh my God, I just love him so much.' He begins to rifle through his pockets, before fishing his phone out and swiping through. 'Wait until you see this!'

He pulls up a photo of him and Tom on top of two camels, silver sand spreading right into the distance. 'Wow,' I gasp. 'You didn't?!'

'We did! In that coffee shop, on our very first date, we booked to go to Morocco! Tom said I had to get over my fears in style. We just came back. Bit of winter sun.'

He is looking very brown. But there's something else within his skin, it's as if the sunshine and feelings of first love are glowing out of him. 'First holiday already,' I remark. 'Bit soon, isn't it?'

'If you think that,' Elijah says, 'you're not going to approve of this next pic.'

He swipes along to a selfie of the pair of them amid the bustling Moroccan markets, each holding up their ring fingers – a gold band on each. 'No!' My hands dart up to my face. 'You didn't!'

'We did!' squeals Elijah. 'We're engaged! We were talking about New Year, and Tom looked me dead in the eye and said, "I don't want to think about entering into another year if I don't know you're going to be in my life for ever". I know it's soon . . .'

I begin mentally counting backwards. I can't keep a grip on time these days.

'Around six weeks,' Elijah says, filling in the gaps. 'It had been a month when we got engaged. Everyone thinks we're mad.' He giggles. 'But you always say, "when you know, you know".'

My stomach kicks then. Reminding me of that rock-hard certainty I'd felt seeing Harry for the first time, a feeling that was cemented even further at our housewarming, the sight of him holding up that tequila bottle.

'You are mad.' I smile. 'But that's romance, isn't it?'

He claps his hands together. 'I was hoping you'd say that! And you must come to the wedding, New Year's Eve, bring that man of yours! Look, I've got to dash off, got a client . . . we'll send you the invite. Say you'll come, please!' With that he runs off, back into the salon.

Morwena's date is all set for 7 p.m. Bobby's reserved me my regular booth and is unreasonably excited about having someone 'Insta-famous' in his restaurant. He's texted me three times already this morning, showing off how he's polished his glasses and cutlery over and over until they're just right. I've got just enough time to pop into the office to tell Ade about Elijah and Tom: it may be a whirlwind wedding but it's my first ever, and I feel a flurry of excitement which masks my nerves for tonight.

I called Morwena this morning to offer some last-minute advice, a phone call that ended with her saying, 'He'd better be fucking perfect, OK?' and I could pretty much picture the snarl on her face as she said it. I couldn't get hold of Rowen though. I wanted to make sure he held his chair out for her and let her pick the wine. All things she seems to care about more than whether he's a nice person or not.

I climb up the stairs to the first floor, and I'm about to put my key in the lock when I hear a voice floating through it. There's something about Ade's tone that stops me walking straight in: her voice is lowered and she's talking more quickly than normal. I pause to listen.

'I'm telling you, Stu, there's something up with her. I dunno what it is, but it's weird . . .'

I hold my breath.

'I've never met Harry, don't you think that's strange? And Verity, her best mate, told me not to dig too much, to just accept that Caitlin keeps some things private.'

I'm trying to think back to that night with Stu, what it was I told him. But it's lost in my brain, washed away by white wine and tequila shots.

'That's not that strange, Ade. Lots of people want to keep their relationships private,' he says, his voice measured. 'You always get yourself in a tizz about things when there's no need. Chill out a bit.'

Her voice rises. 'Don't tell me to chill out! This is my job we're talking about. Your job, your reputation.'

He chuckles. 'In what way? That's a huge overreaction, mate.'

'This,' she says, triumphant. There's a pause. Shit, what are they looking at? I always knew there would be something out there that would expose me – the fear of it has been rumbling inside me for months – but I thought I'd be able to deal with it when it came. That I'd be able to come up with a reasonable explanation and deliver it with ease. Standing on the other side of this door has left me frozen and powerless.

'Let me see that more closely,' he says.

'That's Harry,' Ade says. I shut my eyes. 'And that's, I dunno, some pretty girl. But recognise him from Cait's pictures? The ones we've just done a huge ad campaign with?

What girl? I'm wondering. Who is it, Harry? Is it Kimberly, his receptionist? Or someone else?

'Yeah, it's probably a friend of his.' Stu sounds slightly patronising, exasperated. Like he's had conversations like this with Ade so many times before. 'Guys and girls can be friends, Ade.' I can picture her face: she'll be frowning at him, furious at his tone.

'Read the caption, duh,' she says, mimicking him. 'One year, followed by a heart emoji!'

'Oh . . . maybe. Oh, I dunno, she's in cycling gear – isn't Harry into that, could be something to do with biking?' Stu sounds less sure of himself now, more confused.

It must be Julia. Julia with her glossy brunette hair, that always looks blow-dried, even when she's returned from an eighty-mile cycle – all rosy-cheeked and enthusing that I should 'totally join them next time'. She must have got social media now; that was another of the many things that bugged me about her, how Harry would use her as an excuse when we argued, as I insisted that everyone our age was like this with Instagram, and he'd always reply: 'Julia from my cycling group isn't.'

I did try to cycle with Harry. I remember once packing a picnic, with our old checked blanket and lots of little tubs of treats, imagining that we'd cycle to a really pictur- esque spot, crack open a mini bottle of cava and lie on the blanket, looking at the clouds. Harry had other ideas. He'd selected a route out in the Peak District, 'An easy ten miles,' he'd said, neglecting to mention that most of those miles were uphill, and that, because I was on a hire bike and not used to it, my ass would hurt constantly. 'You have to cycle through it,' he'd shouted into the wind, always a foot or two ahead of me. 'How?' I'd yelled back. When we finally settled down for our picnic my face was the colour of tomatoes, my hair frizzy from the helmet and my blood sugar so low I ended up snapping as soon as he brought up Julia's name, telling me that she struggled at first but a few cycles in and she 'totally got the hang of it'. I'd said, 'Well, I'm sorry I'm not Miss Perfect Julia.' Harry had just shaken his head at me, told me to eat something to calm me down. We'd caught the train back to Sheffield in complete silence.

Through the door I hear Ade striding up and down, her heels clicking on the floor. 'She's a fake, Stu, it's the only explanation, a fake.'

But there is another explanation. I'm sure I'll be able to think of one, it's just right now my mind is completely blank.

'Will you keep your voice down?' Stu is saying. 'She'll be here any minute, we can ask her then. I don't think she's the lying type.'

My heart thuds down to the floor, hearing him say that. I don't want to listen in any more, but I don't want to face them either – Ade's eyes will bore into mine, while Stu will look on sympathetically. I have nothing I can say to them until I speak to Julia. I can get her to take down the picture. We may not get on but surely she's seen the posters? She'll have to understand. She owes me that much.

I walk down the stairs, rushing out into the fresh air, barrelling straight into the chest of someone. I pull away quickly, plastering on a grin to apologise to a stranger. He's tall, this man, so tall I have to strain my neck to look up at him, and the first thing I see are teeth. Glossy white teeth that half smile at me knowingly. Then I clock the jawline, the impeccable suit. It's Rowen. His presence casts a darkness over me, my stomach kicking about, like it is full of tiny little men banging their fists against its walls, screaming 'get away, get away'.

'Sorry, I didn't see you there.' He has a deep, plummy accent – the voice of an MP or a judge.

I keep my eyes low, focusing on a black lump of chewing gum on the pavement, hoping the wig and fake black wire-frame glasses I shoved on just before I left will do their job. Keep my identity hidden, not just because he's a client but also, I realise, because I do not want this man knowing anything about me.

'It's all right.' I begin to weave my way around him, but he blocks my path. I want to scream 'get out of my way' but instead I swallow, look up at him expectantly.

'Excuse me, dear, I hope you don't mind, but can I ask you something?'

His words roll like globs of slime off his tongue.

There's something about him that makes me nod even though I don't want to. As if he's cast a spell over me. 'Go on, I'm in a rush though . . .' It's my one stab at confidence, one he tries to halt in its tracks by holding up his hand, interrupting me.

'You're hiding something.'

My hand rushes up to my wig, checking it's still in place.

'Not that, dear. Whatever your need for a wig is no concern to me. I mean your loss. What you've lost. There's a great sadness in you, I can see it, floating all around your aura.'

The scabs on my skin. The reflection I am constantly expecting to see, he can. He can see it. How?

'No. No.' My tongue feels thick. I've lost control over it. Over my bones, which are now juddering under my skin. He just looks at me, nods.

'Yes, I can feel it. All around you. That special someone, and, hold on . . .'

He floats his hand just above my head, as if I'm in a glass bubble and he's resting his hand on it. 'Yes, a special day. A vital day. Something you're dreading. Soon. Soon.'

Is there a time I would have laughed him off? Dismissed him as a lunatic and gone home and told Harry all about it? I'm sure there was. But I can't find the person inside of me that would have done that. She's lost, hidden underneath this layer of raw skin and greyness that envelops my body. This layer no one can see. Apart from him.

His teeth smile at me once more, they speak to me. 'We know you. We know everything about you,' they hiss in low tones.

He's placing a card in my shaking hand. 'I can help with this.'

And with that, he's gone. Leaving me swaying back and forth on the street, feeling as if he's just spun me round and round.

I don't know how long I stand there for – completely unaware of the beeps of horns around me, the feel of a sharp wind whistling in my ears but something, perhaps the jostle of the street, snaps me back to my body. I look down at the card in my hand. In neat, cursive script it simply says: *Rowen Dagg, clairvoyant.*

I place it gently in my back pocket and pinch myself, until I leave a red mark on the back of my hand. Each step I take feels like I'm walking on uneven ground, like the solid, grey pavement beneath me has been transformed into a soft foam I could sink through at any second.

The sight of the restaurant should bring me comfort, remind me that everything is the same, but its familiarity makes me feel worse. I'm no longer the person I was last time I stepped through its doors. Bobby greets me as usual, a huge smile on his face. But I can't muster one back as he says, 'It's the big day!' I must sway slightly, as he grips me by the elbow. 'Caitlin? Are you OK?'

I nod, manage a, 'Fine, just a bit nervous, that's all.' It's just the wobbliness in my legs he can feel, my rational head tells me that. But then again, Rowen, in the space of a few short minutes, has torn my protective layer off. Can everyone see me now?

I take my seat, try and think of the steady wooden plank beneath me. All the conversation, the voices floating around, sound foreign, like they're in French or Italian. A woman at the table next to me grabs Bobby, asks him what the specials are. I know the words as he replies, 'Tomato', 'Truffle'. I mouth them out, but they don't compute, and become jumbled in my brain. I look over at the table that will soon house Morwena and Rowen. Before, I'd have been keeping my fingers crossed he'd arrive on time, stood up for her as she walked in, but now I know he lurks in the vicinity my only thought is: please don't let him see me. I can't have him stripping me down, crumbling me to dust with his eyes once more.

Then he enters. I see him at the door, baring those teeth at Bobby, weaving his way through the tables, tapping someone on the shoulder, requesting they move their chair in when there was plenty of space for him to squeeze through. He looks just as immaculate as he did in his photos. I try to concentrate on how shiny his shoes are, how sharp his jawline is. His hair has been styled, swept over to the left, and his chin is peppered with enough stubble to look manly but not unkempt.

He sits, his head so high it's like some string is attached to him, pulling him upwards. He has none of the usual nervous mannerisms I see before a first date: he's not scanning the menu, or checking his phone. He doesn't even glance at the door, he remains there, confident she will show up. Which she does, dressed in a grey slip of a dress, a faux fur coat on top that she shrugs off into the hands of one of the younger waiters. Her hair has been dyed neon, highlighter-pen orange for the occasion, and hangs around her shoulders in huge curls, and her eyes are rimmed with black. As she walks through to the table, on black platform heels, pretty much everyone turns to stare.

Rowen remains still, looking in the opposite direction, at the wall. The waiter indicates that this is her table and she hovers behind Rowen, before tentatively tapping him on his shoulder. Then he's up, spinning round, kissing her on both cheeks – I can see him exclaiming how wonderful she looks, and she giggles as he pulls her chair out.

'Morwena Star,' he says, his voice so smooth, the words coming out as if rehearsed. 'You're one impressive lady.'

She laughs, a little tinkle. 'You've done your research!'

'But of course, and if it's not too cheesy, may I say you look even more spectacular in real life.' Every word he says makes my heart beat faster. I feel as if I've lost control of it, it's beating in such a way that I can hear it reverberating in my ears.

Bobby glances over at me, gives a thumbs up. Their instant attraction to each other fizzes in the air – I should be happy. My phone buzzes with messages from Ade, asking how it's going, why she didn't see me in the office earlier. I mute her. Three words, you're a liar, circle my head and I don't know who they're aimed at. I try to look at just Morwena. Rowen's handing her the wine menu. 'Ladies first,' he says. Everything sounds scripted, and she's falling for it – she rests her chin on her hand, gazes at him. 'No, no, I'm sure you know all about wine.'

He runs his finger down the menu. 'Let's see, how about the chateau?' he says, picking the most expensive one there.

'We have a lot in common,' she says, her voice dropping to a whisper. 'You also believe.'

I don't 'believe'. I never have. I think psychics are cons. One managed to corner my mum once, about three years after Dad cheated on her – so I know how powerful their persuasion can be. That's what I felt when Rowen looked at me, my own distaste for his business. Yet I feel naked each time he glances around the restaurant, his eyes passing but never resting on me. I look at my watch. Morwena has asked me to stay for just one hour. I can do this, just fifty more minutes to go. I stare at the thin gold hand of my watch, willing the minutes to go faster.

Rowen is telling Morwena how he got into the industry, how he noticed a gap in the market that he had the skills to fill. She's asked him twice when he first realised he had 'the gift'. But each time he knocks the question back to her, quizzing her about her Instagram and how she grew her following. 'Really organically,' she's saying – as he stares intently at her, drinking her in. 'I was offering a genuine product, and people could see that.'

He clicks his fingers, smiles. 'But you make money, don't you?' He reaches over to the bottle to top her glass up, but she pulls it away.

'I don't think that's an appropriate question to ask,' she says.

He laughs, holds his hands up. 'I come in peace, but I'm just interested, that's all . . . we've all read the articles on "influencers" making a mint from doing very little.'

She pushes her chin back. 'That's a common misconception, actually. I work very hard.'

At that Bobby swoops in, taking their order. I look down at my arm. The tingling I feel under my skin isn't showing on the surface, neither is this juddering feeling – like my bones are knocking back and forth into each other. I can't do this. I swivel out of my chair, begin to walk to the toilet. Bobby appears beside me.

'What's the plan, boss?' he says. 'Want me to jump in? Spill a drink?'

I try to say words, tell him what I want to do next, but find I can't. They're stuck in my throat. I just keep thinking of Rowen, how he made me feel, like there's a waterfall that's been inside me this whole time and he's the one who has released it. I just have to get in the toilet, so I swing the door open and run to the furthest stall from the door, locking it tight behind me.

The toilet smells of cheap handwash, the type that lingers on your hands long after you've washed them. That and a synthetic pine scent emanating from a block of green jelly-like stuff encased in plastic sitting on the back of the loo. This place used to be a lot fancier; when I came to the opening the toilet was full of Jo Malone candles and creams. I remember because I smothered the hand cream all up my arms, so that when I came back Harry commented on how nice I smelled. That memory chokes in my throat, like someone has shoved cotton wool in my mouth. The business was in its infancy then, and I'd been so delighted to receive the invite to a fancy restaurant opening. 'It must mean they think I'm someone, Harry! Look, it says "we're inviting esteemed business owners from the local area",' I'd said, waving the invite – thick, cream, gold-embossed – in his face. 'Will you come with me? Please?'

He'd looked at the date and shaken his head: it was the annual meet-up for his cycling buddies, men and women who he mostly only nods to, or rolls his eyes at during a particularly tough hill in the Peak District. But each year they meet up properly, in clothes made of any material other than Lycra, and talk about best routes and carbon fibre bikes and stuff I could only feign interest in. He looked forward to it for months.

But when Verity couldn't come and I'd flopped on the sofa, too shy to go on my own, he'd tucked in beside me and said he'd miss his meet-up, that we'd have a fun night together. But we didn't. As soon as we arrived I was whisked off to meet other business owners, all of whom had come on their own. I felt silly for bringing Harry, like I'd brought along a chaperone and spent the night flitting from group to group, barely speaking to him.

The memory fills out my head, blocking all other thoughts: of Morwena, of Rowen, of how I promised I'd only come into this toilet for a minute or two, until I got my breath back. But now my breath is coming out of me in choked sobs and the red plastic walls of the stall are closing in on me.

I don't know how long I stay in there for, gripping my arms around my knees, my head buried in my legs to stop anyone else hearing my distress, my cries vibrating off my thighs. But it's Morwena's voice that breaks me out of it.

'Where the FUCK are you?' She's banging on all the toilet doors and I hear cries of, 'Hey, it's not me!' and, 'Bugger off!' coming from each stall. When she's outside my stall door I hold my breath.

'I can see your hideous shoes, Caitlin. I know you're in there.'

I open the door slowly. She launches into a tirade, her spit landing on my face as I stand up to face her. 'I hate him! Who is this rude, inconsiderate asshole you've set me up with?'

I know what I should say, that I should talk her into staying, that him asking about her salary can't be that bad, but I can't muster the energy. I just stare at her and shrug, pulling the rest of my hair out of the band I'd had it tied back in.

'Aren't you going to say something?' she demands. 'Justify why I'm paying you all this money?'

She's not paying me anything. Ade waived her fee, hoping she'd then post about us. But I remain silent. I want out of this toilet, out of these memories that are flooding through me thick and fast. I need to escape from the thoughts of Julia, of Harry, of my argument with Verity. All my regrets coming at me, circling around my head and taunting me. All I can manage is a short, swift: 'Leave, then.'

'Leave?' She has one hand on her hip and is speaking slowly, as if she's talking to a child. 'What sort of stupid idea is that? I can't let that man go on more dates, talk to women like they're his playthings. I'm Morwena Star.'

'I don't . . .' My voice comes out so softly. 'I don't know what you want from me.'

'I want you to do your job, go out there, tell him why he doesn't deserve a woman like me . . . no matter how good-looking he may be!'

'But, but . . .' There are no words in my head, nothing I can pluck out. I have no way to save this like I've saved so many before.

She spins on her heel, letting the door shut, saying, 'If you want a job done, do it yourself.'

I want to crumble to the floor, slide down the wall, bury my face in my hands. But I can hear shouting through the door, the clatter of a metal tray falling to the ground. Bobby saying, 'Now, can everyone just calm down,' and I know I can't leave him to deal with this. I take a deep breath, open the door and walk back out into the restaurant, just as Morwena swivels round to face me from where she's standing by her table, her wine glass in one hand. Rowen is covered, red droplets dripping down his hair, his cheeks. He remains sitting.

'You!' yells Morwena, pointing at me as everyone turns around to stare. My eyes are still ringed with black from where I've rubbed at my mascara, picking it out of my lashes. 'You must have known about this!'

She marches over to me. Rowen has stood up now, and the customers are no longer looking at him. He swiftly removes his coat, shakes his head, just slightly, and slips out the door.

'Know what?'

Bobby is standing beside me, his shoulder just touching mine. He feels solid, strong.

'That man is a fake. He priiiiiides himself on conning innocent, grieving people out of money.'

I'm confused. I can't shake any of my regrets away.

'What do you mean?'

'His. Clairvoyancy. Business. He uses it to make lots of money when he doesn't even hold the gift. He just told me! He hoped I was the same. That my, in his words, "crystal shit" was just to make me stand out on Instagram! As if!'

'But, but . . .' I think of how he knew what tomorrow was. How he knew everything about me, by just looking at me.

'No buts, Caitlin, you should have known. If you took any pride in your sham of a business, you'd have known—'

'Now, come on,' says Bobby. 'I know you're upset but Caitlin didn't know, did you, Cait?'

I didn't, of course I didn't. But I can't find the words I usually would. She begins to yell: 'I trusted you. I trusted you.'

I just shake my head, look to the floor.

'You're not going to say anything? You're pathetic. This business is pathetic. And believe me, Caitlin, I'm going to let everyone know about it. I'm going to destroy you.' And with that, she's marching towards the door.

Chapter Fifteen

A waiter sees Morwena out, so there's no door for her to slam. But still, as I watch her glide away, I feel as though her anger has made the walls shake and the floor wobbles beneath me. Bobby settles me into a chair and then signals for someone to get me a drink, and first hands me a glass of water and then a cup of tea, which he's added a generous slug of brandy to. I find it hard to even grip the mug, my hands are shaking so hard.

'Bobby, I . . .' I look up at him. He's standing above me, his hand holding tight onto the back of the chair. The other diners are back staring at their plates of pasta, but you can hear the whispers of 'What on earth just happened?' carrying over the air.

'Sssh, Çaitlin, you didn't know.'

'I didn't, I swear,' I say, but my stomach disagrees. 'He was creepy though, I could see that from the moment he walked in,' I admit. I don't want to tell Bobby about my encounter with Rowen in the street. It's sinking deeper into my memory and I'm beginning to feel as if I made the whole thing up, that it didn't happen at all.

'He was,' nods Bobby. 'Something very disconcerting about a man that good-looking. But still.' He squeezes my shoulder. 'There was no need for her to react like that, drama queen, honestly.'

A strangled chuckle escapes me. Bobby is one of the biggest drama queens I know. I've seen him greet new customers with a song and then a minute later storm out the back door as he couldn't find the cheese grater. I sip my tea, inhaling the strong scent of brandy and letting it soothe my frazzled nerves.

'I should go home, sort this,' I say to Bobby. 'I promise I won't let it harm any restaurant reviews.'

He waves his hand across the restaurant. 'No worries, they all enjoyed the show, gives them something to talk about.' A woman close by hears, smiles to herself as a bit of spaghetti slips into her mouth. 'But you're still a little shaken. Can I call your husband? Get him to collect you?'

I shake my head. 'He doesn't drive.' But the thought of Harry, coming by to get me on his bicycle, saying, 'Hop on, I'll give you a backie,' makes me happy.

'OK, I'll call a taxi for you then. Be one second.'

The black cab arrives quickly, and Bobby bundles me into it, with a slice of banofee pie in a styrofoam container. I let the music and the street lights wash over me until we're at my door. The whole house is in darkness.

I trudge through, turning each light on one by one. The Cat snakes around my feet mewing for food, which I give him mechanically. I slump down onto the sofa, open up my phone: I've been tagged in a video by Morwena. She's at home, sitting by the window, dead plants out of shot, and she's obviously redone her make-up – her skin is flawless, apart from one carefully placed smudge of mascara by her left eye. 'My dear Rubies and Sapphires,' she says, her voice slow, like she's the Queen delivering a speech. 'Something truly awful happened to me tonight, and I don't want to tell you it, to seem as if I'm trying to "call out" and send negativity, but also I can't have anyone else fall for her lies. You know me, I only ever want to surround myself with the genuine.'

I switch it off at that, there's no point listening to the rest. I know what happened, everyone at the restaurant knows what happened and now her eight million followers will too. And even then it's not the worst thing online right now. I go to Julia's page and, sure enough, there's Harry smiling out at me – green California hills stretched out behind him. He's wearing black shorts and a blue t-shirt. Julia's in a plum Lycra bodysuit which clings in all the right places, like she's Jennifer Lawrence in *X-Men*. The caption, which Ade read out earlier, is there, along with about eight comments, pretty much all a love heart or cycling emoji. I stare at it, the sky behind him is so clear and blue. He looks perfect, together they look perfect. I look around the home we built – only a few of his things remain, three cacti in grey pots on the bookshelves, which now house just my books and the hip flask he was given for his twenty-first birthday are the only remnants of him in the living room. Out in the hallway a barely worn rain jacket hangs limply, lifelessly on the hooks. His trainer collection has been packed and shipped away. My phone still sits in my hand, buzzing constantly, probably with comments and messages from Morwena's fans. I chuck it, hard, against the white wall. It clatters to the ground in the spot in the hallway where his bike should be. I find I'm screaming, directing the words into that empty space. 'Why the fuck aren't you here?' I shout, not caring if anyone hears me. I keep going, yelling the words over and over again until my throat is red raw, the angry energy within me released and I can collapse, sliding down the wall onto the hardwood floor.

*

I wake up feeling as though there's a thick, dark smog enveloping me. I made it to bed, and I lie here on my crisp white sheets and feel the smog as it holds me there, croaking at me, telling me the significance of the day. I try to push this darkness off me, tell myself that today doesn't matter, it's just another day, another one of the 365. That there are things in the present moment, things that have to be dealt with now, that simply can't be put off. I focus on them, as they come to me in flashes: Morwena's face, all screwed up, as she yelled that she'd destroy my career. That she'd destroy me. The other people in the restaurant, all glancing over and whispering. Rowen looking back as he dashed out the door.

I have to get to the office and sort it out. Or at least get there and let Ade sort it out. She may not be quite sure of me at the moment, she may even be readying herself to hand in her notice, but Ade can't leave behind a crisis. She thrives on fixing PR disasters.

I roll myself out of bed as if I'm pulling bricks off myself, not the pile of cushions I have built around my body. I don't bother to shower, or pull a brush through my hair, I just tug a pair of jeans on and a stained jumper, shove my curls back into a ponytail and under a bobble hat. It's so cold outside that my breath comes out of me in clouds. The air feels tight and stings my skin like daggers. I want to strip off my layers, let the cold air punish me. The other shopkeepers nod, say, 'Hello, freezing, isn't it?' to me as if it's just any other day. I keep my head down, raising one hand to wave, refusing to meet their eyes.

When I reach my office I find it's open, and there's a little Post-it note on the door that reads: *I let your guest in, she seemed pretty sad* followed by a smiley face. The room smells strongly of bleach, the surfaces gleaming; it must be the day our cleaner comes in. The lights are off, so all I can see is a shadow of a woman waiting for me on the sofa. I click them on, and there, curled up in a tiny ball, her face red raw from crying, is Morwena Star. She raises her chin just above her knees, and looks at me. Then she melts down into tears.

The Morwena of yesterday, jabbing her oblong finger-nails at me, is gone. Her long wavy hair is tied on her head in a messy bun. Yesterday it had raged around her face like Medusa's snakes. I am shocked how young she looks, how vulnerable. Her skin is milky-white, smooth, her cheeks round and childlike. Her bottom lip is actually shaking.

'I trusted you,' she says. It was what she had been yelling last night, over and over again, but today it comes out hoarse, almost a whisper.

I haven't had time to gather myself. I've only just messaged Ade, who hasn't seen it yet. I need her here. I send another message. Then I shove my phone in my pocket, and try my very best sympathetic smile.

'Just putting that on silent,' I say, and pull up a pouffe beside her, which I perch on, one butt cheek not quite fitting. 'Morwena, I can explain.'

'That was the worst night of my entire life. What could you possibly do to explain?' The whisper is gone, and has been replaced by a spoiled screech. I swallow. It's hard for me not to just say, 'For God's sake, it was one bad date. It really doesn't deserve these theatrics.' After all, everyone's had one. I certainly did, before Harry came along. I'd go home, feeling like crap, and then I'd see Verity on the sofa, bottle of wine ready, and we'd laugh about it. The date would then turn from a horrible night into a funny story: something priceless that would have the power later on to make someone else feel better, simply with the line: 'It can't have been as bad as the time I . . .'

Now I know there are things that happen to you that can't be turned into anecdotes. Things that leave a raw, angry scab all over your body that no one can see, or feel, but you. Those things deserve a hurricane of a reaction, like the one Morwena – now curled up, shaking and bawling – is putting on for me right now. Not last night. Not a bad date.

But still, thinking of how the business has been the thing keeping me going, how I don't want that block to fall, I attempt to tell her the truth.

'I'm truly sorry, I had absolutely no idea he was a fake,' I say, reaching to settle my hand on her forearm, but she pulls away. 'I'd spoken to him a lot before your date and, quite frankly, he spooked me out.'

I know I have to be as honest as I can be with her, about how Rowen made me feel. There's no other valid explanation as to why, when she was shrieking at him across the table, I wasn't there to get her out.

'He, um, well, he recognised something in me that not many people know. It felt so real, like he really was a psychic, and it upset me . . . That's why I wasn't there for you when you needed me.'

Her head snaps up and her eyes bore into me. 'Did he give you details? Did he know little, unusual things about what happened to you?'

I shake my head, trying to remember what exactly he had said. But all I can recall is how he made me feel. Like he could see right through me.

Morwena is still staring at me, but her expression is no longer soft and sad. It's one of scorn.

'That's what they do, God, how stupid are you not to recognise a cold reading?'

She says 'cold reading' in the same way someone else might say 'mattress' or 'computer', like it was something everyone knows. I have no idea what it means.

'It's when they use common techniques to pretend they know shit about you, but it's basic-bitch stuff . . . stuff everyone could relate to,' she explains, slowly. 'A true psychic will know details, places, events.'

Had he? He'd certainly known about today, about its significance. Or had he just mentioned a special event? That there was something coming up for me, something looming over me that had turned my aura black?

'He said there was a sadness in me that no one else knew about, that only he could see,' I say, as she shakes her head at me. 'It's, it's . . . kind of true, and it upset me.'

'God, Caitlin, you of all people should have seen it coming a mile off.'

His words float around my head: 'great loss', 'important day', 'special someone', and I realise that they're like letters on a Scrabble board. I'd put them together and created something significant. He hadn't seen a thing.

She continues droning on, scolding me for how stupid I've been. It all becomes part of the smog, joining Rowen's words as they float around me, mocking me. Apart from one sentence, which rings out crystal clear: 'You're supposed to be the master of instinct. How could you not tell who he really was?'

It snaps me back to what I've been fighting for. I may have let it slip recently, but I've always had a good instinct for people, I always have. Even when I was younger I could tell if someone was going to play a big part in my life – good or bad.

'I made a mistake with this guy,' I say, hoping she can't hear the falter in my voice. 'But I swear to you I do know who's right and who is wrong.'

'So why the mistake with me? What made you think Rowen was the one for me?'

I think of his teeth. How last night, seeing them all grin at me, he'd seemed knowing. But now I know what they were: predatory. How had I missed it?

'It was the pressure,' I admit. 'I wanted you to be happy and recommend me but there didn't seem to be anyone right,' I say, thinking of sitting in the office at midnight, sifting through applications while the special app Ade installed that let me know when someone unfollowed me buzzed in the dark. 'You and Rowen seemed to have so much in common. I hoped I'd feel the kick when I saw you both together, but it never came.'

'So,' she gulped. 'This happened to me because of my following?'

'It's intimidating,' I say. 'I wanted to get it right and I ended up getting it so wrong.'

'But it's all fake,' she suddenly shouts. 'I'm so fucking lonely. I'm MISERABLE.'

I think back to her feed: I don't think I've ever seen a friend on there. Maybe a couple of snaps with her yoga teacher? It all makes sense suddenly: that's what these tears

were all about. They weren't crocodile tears. She doesn't
have a Verity to turn all of this to comedy gold with.

'I mean, I love my crystals,' she's saying, now crouched
on the floor beside me, laying out a tiger's eye and a piece
of moonstone. 'But they just give me hope, they haven't
actually given me anything. No friends, no boyfriend, just
. . .' She reaches into the air, grabbing at it. 'Followers.'

'What about your friends, you know, from before?'

'They all disappeared, pretty much sick of me on my
phone all the time, or recording their every move.'

I think back to the Royal Wedding, and the countless
times before that, Verity and Harry rolling their eyes at me
as I filmed them. Verity holding her hands up to block the
camera and yelling, 'Not now, Cait, I look minging.' And
the way Verity had looked at me last time she saw me, as
if she didn't know who it was that was standing right in
front of her.

'I thought I'd make new friends, after all, my following
was growing constantly, but anyone I ever met, on blogger
trips or at events, was just like me. Always on their damn
phone! Either that or asking me to tag them in stuff, to
boost their own numbers.'

That's what I'd done. I had failed to see Morwena as a
person in her own right. I hadn't even got to know her
in the same way I do with my other clients, I had just
presumed I knew everything. But that was all from her feed.

'I'm so sorry,' I say. 'I should never have seen you just
as someone behind a screen. I will find you someone, I
promise. Can we please start again?'

She nods hesitantly, and I know I'm yet to convince
her. 'Let's have a cup of tea and get to know each other,
OK?' I say, getting up to click the kettle on, pulling out

a Teapig chamomile tea for her. I place the cup, bag still in, in front of her.

'What's this?' she says, looking into her cup and then descending – once again – into tears.

'It's chamomile, Teapigs, your favourite?'

'That's. All. Crap, I hate it!' she cries. 'They pay me to like it. Can I please have a normal tea, like yours?' She lowers her voice. 'With four sugars?'

A small bark of laughter escapes me. Morwena's entire feed is a shrine to sugar-free living. It's the first time I've let a real emotion out all day. And it feels good. But it also reminds me of what I'm pushing down, what happens later. I look at the clock. It's half one. I need to sort this girl out, get her away from the office in an hour and a half. I'm going to have to get to know the real her quickly. 'OK, we really need to get to know each other. How do you feel about yoga? Really?'

She grins up at me. 'That I really do love. It's the one place my head doesn't buzz with constant thought.'

I begin to fire questions at her.

'OK, great. And what do you love that you'd never dream of posting on Instagram?'

Without a beat she replies: 'Pot Noodles. Chicken and mushroom flavour.'

We both laugh then, but I stop abruptly when, through the glass wall that separates my office from the reception area, I see Ade walking in, talking to a woman with a harsh black bob.

'Shit, that's Sarah.'

She was supposed to meet me in the coffee shop. That's what her message had said, no question marks, no checking I was free. Simply a: *Wednesday. 3 p.m. Coffee shop. You know what it's about.* My desire to help Morwena has quickly been overridden. I have to get her away now. She can't meet Sarah, she can't hear anything Sarah has to say. I can feel my heart beating in points all over my body: my neck, my ears, my chest. The blood is rushing through me fast.

I can see Ade offering Sarah something, pointing at the door to the office. Sarah's dressed smartly, she always is. A hot-pink blazer over a pair of cropped grey trousers. Her skin looks tanned.

'It's, it's my husband's mum, she's early. I'm so sorry, Morwena, but you have to go.'

Her face flicks back to how it was last night. 'But we are getting to know each other? You're fixing your fuck-up, remember? Surely this woman can wait.'

But she absolutely cannot wait. She and Ade seem to be engaged in deep conversation. 'What the fuck is she saying?' I mutter under my breath, while scooping up the crystals Morwena has laid out on the floor, grabbing her handbag and shoving them in.

'Keep your hands off my crystals, you're muddying their auras!'

'For fuck's sake, they're not people, Morwena,' I snap. Sarah has spotted me and she's walking into the office. She's waving at me. Ade's behind her with a look on her face I can't quite pinpoint. Is it pity? God, I hope it's not pity.

'We'll sort this, I promise,' I say to Morwena, but it comes out a squeak and she just looks at me, her face screwed up in disdain.

'Whatever, you're fucking weird,' she says with a flounce, and pushes past Sarah and Ade without saying hello to either of them. 'I'm telling everyone about this.'

But, unlike last night, I fail to muster any ability to care. I just hustle her out, and hustle Sarah in, attempting to smile. This woman has never liked me.

I want to get down on the floor and stay there. I want to sink into a bath full of Epsom Salts. I want to be anywhere but here. Ade's beginning to follow us in, she's requesting an Earl Grey.

'Ade, I'm sorry, I'll have to talk to Sarah alone,' I say, and she shakes her head at me.

'We do need to talk,' she says.

I nod. 'Yep, later, but for now best to keep an eye on Morwena Star's Instagram account.'

'You young people and your social media,' says Sarah. 'I couldn't be doing with it.' She's settled herself on the corner sofa while I meticulously make her tea just how she likes it: the milk in a tiny jug, and the bag brewed for exactly two minutes. I glance at myself in the mirror. I look quite crazed after my Morwena encounter – my hair is sticking out at all angles, and there's dust on my cheek that must have transferred from her crystals.

I bring over the tea, apologising for my appearance. But instead of her usual, 'Well, yes, you really should use that serum I got you for Christmas', or, 'Go and tidy yourself up then we can talk', she shakes her head and says, 'You look fine, dear, don't worry.'

Settling myself in beside her, my hands wrapped around the warm mug for comfort, dread fills me from the top of my head to the tips of my toes. I notice that my left hand won't stop shaking. I place my cup down and hold my hands in my lap. Sarah reaches over and cups them in hers.

'I think you know why I am here,' she says, looking directly at me. I focus on her eyebrows, anything to avoid her eyes, which have begun to fill up with tears.

She wants to talk about him. I don't. I don't want to think about him. I tighten my body and make it rigid. I look away but she lightly pulls my chin around, holding her phone – a new iPhone, still with the protective film over the screen – and shows me my own account, and all the photos of Harry on there. 'I've seen the posters, too,' she whispers, followed by the words I've refused to take in. That I've never listened to. Today, in her clipped English accent, they're quite clear. The words float out of her mouth and land, thunk, into my heart.

'He's dead, Caitlin. Harry's dead. You have to face up to it.'

Chapter Sixteen

Had it been any other day I would have shouted, 'Forgotten your keys again?' and jogged through to let Harry in. But, for some reason, when I heard the doorbell that Wednesday in late December, I didn't. I walked from the kitchen, the house silent around me, and I opened the door, and saw them there, with their silly uniforms and solemn faces. They ushered me through to the living room and I felt as though I was walking through treacle.

'Might be best for you to sit down for this,' they'd said. I remember wanting to scream, 'No, just tell me!' but instead I offered them both a cup of tea, which they declined. I'd stayed standing, feeling my knees buckle, just slightly, at the sight of them on my sofa. They looked like aliens, sat there, like they didn't belong in my house, or even on this earth at all. Eventually one stood up and guided me to the armchair. I can't have known then that it was Harry; they could have been here to talk to me about anyone. But I must have known, somewhere, as I really hadn't wanted to sit there, in his chair. A timer began to go off, an incessant beep that let me know our dinner was ready, that he was supposed to be home by now.

When they did tell me I didn't listen. It was like I'd been shrunk into a tiny person, a little Polly Pocket. There were gulls shrieking all around my head, and it wasn't until that man's kind face had turned into a frown and he had said, 'Mrs Henry, can I call anyone for you?' that I realised they weren't gulls at all: I had been shrieking with laughter. At the realisation that that had been my reaction, I began to gulp for breath, rocking myself forward and then backwards. I don't know if I was crying. If it was crying it was like nothing I'd ever experienced before. It was too extreme to be classified as that.

It was Verity they called. She arrived, out of breath, at my doorway, which lay open – a gust of freezing wind snaking through to the living room where I sat, still in his chair, curled up. It was when she arrived that I grasped what had happened: 'A van driver, he looked the wrong way,' the policeman said to Verity, who stood there, a dressing gown flung over her clothes instead of a coat. At the sight of her everything had turned to grey, including Jeremiah's face, who stood behind her, car keys in his hand, staring at Harry's helmet, which was still hanging on its hook. Together they'd carried me to the car, it was evening – the sky was dark, and all along our road were commuters making their way home from work, putting their keys into doors and entering into brightly lit homes. They lay me down in the back seat, and Verity tucked that checked blanket over the top of me, and I inhaled it, how it smelled of him. I couldn't bear it so I chucked it off and shivered all the way to Mum's.

Her house looked exactly the same as it had two weeks before, when Harry and I had come over to help her decorate. I had held the bottom of the ladder as he'd climbed up the outside of her house, whistling as he strung up lights across the gutter. I'd been worried he'd fall and hurt himself, and he'd laughed at me, told me to stop being such a worry wart. I pushed through Mum, who stood in the doorway, saying I had to be alone. Then I'd rushed up to my childhood bedroom and stared at the ceiling, which was covered in paper garlands and tinsel. I tore them all down, petals of sparkly, colourful paper falling down around me the same way I'd been show-ered with confetti on my wedding day. Later Mum told me, from downstairs, they could just hear me screaming, and they'd rushed up, and she'd given me her strongest sleeping pill and put me to bed. Both Mum and Verity slept with me that night – and for weeks afterwards, curled around me.

I didn't see Sarah until the funeral. Weeks had gone by: weeks of forms, of choosing what catering I wanted, what sort of music he would have liked. I had no idea about any of it. I remember hanging up on a caterer as she asked whether I wanted 'mini bagels' or 'sausage rolls', yelling into a pillow about how none of it really mattered. At 3 a.m. one night I'd uncurled myself from Verity and gone to open his laptop, looking in his Spotify and finding it offered no answers, so I'd gone on Google, typed in 'songs for a funeral'. Verity was woken up by my laughter, after it was suggested to me that Mariah Carey's 'Bye Bye' would be an appropriate choice. She'd guided me back to bed, hushing me as I hysterically told her I couldn't remember what songs he'd told me he'd play at his funeral: it was back in a time when that was just an interesting question to ask on second dates.

Jeremiah ended up making the playlist. It was nice, I think. I can't remember much of that day – because by the time the funeral came around I'd realised that if I was going to survive this I'd have to do more than stiffen my knees. I'd have to stiffen my whole body, turn my bones into concrete.

It was raining, this sea of faces coming at me, as Jeremiah held a black umbrella over mine and Verity's heads as she shook people's hands for me, explaining that I was finding it hard to speak. I didn't know what to say to Sarah, her face was so different from the others. It wasn't pitiful like the rest, but warped and twisted – like mine, full of agony. Looking at her meant admitting who I had become, and that was something I refused to do.

A year on and her face doesn't seem as twisted as it once was. Her eyes are less haunted. They're still cloudy with grief and they're looking down at my hands, which are now juddering back and forth. She's in focus now, I can see her lips moving and I can hear the words coming from them. I don't know how long she's been speaking for.

'You just aren't the girl I know,' she's saying. 'You're so distant, living in this world where everything is the same. But it's not the same.'

I haven't actually spoken a word since she sat down. I've been thinking about every time I've uttered Harry's name to a new client. It first slipped out a fortnight after the funeral, and I came into the office and everything in here belonged to me, it was all things I'd picked out. It wasn't like being at home where every piece of furniture, every cushion, every tea towel signalled the life we'd built together.

I hadn't hired Ade yet and there was a bunch of CVs in my email account: all from people who didn't know me, or what had happened to me. It was the same with the application for my services – they just knew me as Cupid's Caitlin. A character there to help them find love: they didn't know I was now a widow who'd received 'in sympathy' cards and had to clear out my husband's wardrobe.

'It just seemed easier, somehow, to keep pretending here,' I begin to explain. 'At first it was almost a business decision. After everything, I couldn't bear to lose this as well . . . after all, who wants to be set up by a grieving widow?'

I knew that if my clients got a whiff of my agony they'd begin to see it in their future too. That there was no point in investing in love if there was no guarantee it would last. But also I liked being in this office, where I could sit in my desk chair and call Harry's mobile and pretend the reason he wasn't answering was because he was with a patient. Where I could look at my profile and see the pair of us so happy and smiling, and convince myself I hadn't lost that. Where I could tell people he was away, and use that as an excuse later, as I lay shivering in bed.

Everywhere else I went it felt like I was slowly being split in two down the middle. I'd turn down a street and come across a bar we stumbled out of together, or I'd go home and The Cat wouldn't understand why he wasn't seeing Harry and would wail at me in disappointment. Friends would try and make me talk about it, ask pointedly, 'How are you?' while cupping my elbow. I found I couldn't bear their pity so I phased them out, stopped returning their calls. I would spend hours in the office, putting together future plans and enthusing to every stranger I met about how wonderful Harry was. Then I hired Ade and she'd come in and say breezily, 'How's Harry? You guys going away this summer?' And I would say, 'Yeah, Spain, probably,' and feel the relief of not having to face up to my reality. But then she went from being a stranger, to a colleague, to then a friend, and I still couldn't tell her. I'd pulled the walls around myself so tightly.

And now Sarah is here, reminding me that this grief isn't just mine to own, that my actions have had an impact.

'I can't move on, not until you have,' she's saying. 'I know we'll never fully move on, but I need some closure.'

I open my mouth but can't find a thing to say. 'Um,' I say, faltering but she holds one hand up.

'Please, let me speak. I did try to just let you grieve in your own way, people kept coming up to me and saying, "Have you seen Caitlin's Instagram?" and I said, "Let her deal with this her own way". But then . . .' She pauses, touches her throat. 'But then . . .'

I fill the rest in for her, my shoulders drooping. 'But then you saw the posters.'

She nods, her eyes wide. She's sixty-three years old, but in that moment she looks like a child. A vision of her at the funeral comes back to me so clearly, her standing beside me, her daughter gripping her arm – Harry's younger sister, the bubblegum-popping, surly girl I'd grown to love over the years. She moved to London soon after, saying she couldn't bear to walk the streets that killed her brother. I closed myself off to her as well, I hated looking into her face and seeing his nose, his eyes staring back at me. But I should have been taking care of her, of his whole family. Instead I've made everything so much more painful. My tears come out in hiccups as I try to explain myself to Sarah, why I let it get as far as it did, but all that comes out is a strangled, 'Sorry.'

'Sssh,' she's saying into my hair. 'I understand, I understand.'

She smells of lavender and I inhale it, remembering her garden and the first time I went to their house and saw all the photos of Harry as a child. His sticky-out ears and goofy grin. In one he was wearing a Garfield the Cat t-shirt and I looked at him and thought, 'I love you, I'm never going to let anyone harm you.' I did let harm come to him. Why hadn't I spotted his helmet hanging on the hook?

I pull myself from her, roughly tug on my cheeks with both my hands. I have to fix this. 'Sarah,' I say, and I try to look at her properly. 'I will sort this, I won't use Harry any more.'

She stands up, brushes her skirt off. 'I'm going to leave now, Caitlin. But this is us, in this together now, you understand? I'll be back to check on you.' She says it strictly, in the same tone she used to use when she'd leave me chopping vegetables after giving me precise instructions on how she'd like them julienned. She kisses me twice on both cheeks and walks to the door. Leaving me there feeling like a sodden sponge, so heavy with tears I can barely move. My phone sits beside me, full of smiling Harry. Laughing Harry. Grumpy Harry. I pick it up, grip it tightly to my chest and begin, once again, to sob.

Chapter Seventeen

Everything around me is pitch-black. Wood is grazing the top of my head, my arms are curled around my knees. Natural light had flooded in earlier, and now the night sky outside seeps into the room. No one knows I'm here, tucked under my desk where I crawled earlier. But then I hear footsteps clattering their way up the stairs, Ade's and Stu's laughs coming up with them. 'You're a bloody workaholic, you,' she says. 'It's pub time.'

His voice is deep, gruff. 'I know, but just let me show you this one idea,' he says. 'I think it could help Caitlin, if you are right about her. Then we can go get a beer.'

I hear her key in the lock. 'That's odd, it's unlocked,' she says, creaking the door open and flicking on the switch. I remain hidden as I hear the clatter of cups, as she scoops them up off the desk above me. 'Caitlin never leaves cups to be washed,' she says to Stu. 'Is she here?'

Then it comes out of me, a tiny yelp, a mew almost. A cry, perhaps, for help.

'Caitlin?' His feet are inches in front of me. I reach out, touch his ankle. He crouches down and sees me, like crumpled paper underneath the desk.

'Oh my God, what's wrong?' I just stare out at them both. Ade has come over and crouches down. They both look at me, their heads to one side, like I'm a dying bird they've come across on the street and they don't know what to do with me.

'What are you doing down here?' It's a voice she'd use for a child: gentle but firm.

I can't say the words. I know I'll have to. But I can't. All I say is: 'Verity, please can you call Verity?'

She nods. 'We will, Stu, go and do that, will you? Her number is in my phone,' she says, then she reaches out to me and I grip her hand. 'Come on, out from under there.'

She guides me over to the sofa, wraps her coat around my shoulders, my whole body shaking like a wild animal. Stu comes over, sits on the floor at my feet, and hands me a cup of tea.

'She's on her way,' he says, and there's a silence – as if they're both afraid to speak.

'I heard you before,' I say, taking a sip of my tea. It's thick with sugar. It's hard to believe it was just yesterday that I was standing on the other side of the door, listening to them hypothesise over where Harry was. 'You're right, I am a fraud, Harry, he's, he's . . .'

Ade has settled in beside me and she rubs my back. 'Sssh, it's OK, we understand. We know.'

I don't know how they could have found out, unless Verity told them. There's no trace of his death online; Harry is one of his many middle names. They can't know. Yet they seem to, as they look at me with such pity. Ade's beside me on the sofa, Stu is sitting, cross-legged, on the floor.

'It happens,' Ade says, glibly. 'But we can fix it. Stu has a really good plan, that's why we're here.'

'You said you were going to quit,' I say, as Ade looks into her hands, begins to fiddle with them.

'I know, but then I remembered my heartbreak over Hannah, how it changes you, makes you do silly things.'

'Yeah,' nods Stu. 'With my ex, God, I didn't actually tell you this but she cheated on me, too, it was so awful. I get it, I really do.'

It dawns on me that they don't know. They've jumped to a conclusion. A better one. I look at him sitting there on the floor, his eyes all earnest, like he understands. My whole body crumples further into itself, as I whisper, 'That's not it.'

'What?' says Ade. 'Sorry, Cait, we can't hear you.'

I try to push myself up and forward. I'm going to have to say the words. But I'm not ready. 'I wish . . .' I say, louder, shaky still but clearer. 'I wish he'd left me. It would . . .' I begin to cry again. 'It would mean he was still here.'

I see them glance, confused, at each other. Then Ade's face changes, her realisation suddenly clear.

'He . . . died.' I choke the word out as Ade's face turns white. 'Oh God,' she says. 'Oh God.'

'Shit,' says Stu, his head bowed, staring at the ground.

'When?' she asks, and I can't look her in the eye. I look out, towards the window. There are no stars in the sky. I can hear people in the street below drunkenly singing The Pogues. I try to concentrate on them: how out of tune, but happy they sound.

'A year ago today.'

'I was, I was . . .' Ade's struggling to get the words out. Stu climbs up from the floor, squeezes himself in beside her. She throws her head on his chest.

'It's OK,' he whispers to her. I find myself saying it to her as well, rubbing her knee. Because it is. She could never have known. 'I was so angry at you,' she splutters out. 'Fuck, I'm so sorry.'

'It's not your fault, it was a reasonable explanation,' I say. My breathing has evened out, I feel back within my body, the panic I felt earlier quelled. 'That was Julia. A friend of his. I was . . . I was always so jealous of her.'

Memories of our arguments over Julia fill my head, so pointless now. How many times Harry insisted he didn't fancy her, that she was just a friend, and how much time I'd wasted refusing to believe it. I don't want to tell them about that. I don't want to talk any more. I lean my head back, shut my eyes and feel warm, callused hands take the cup of tea from my grip. Ade rests her head on my shoulder, after a while her breath becomes more steady. I can hear Stu moving around, washing cups up, wiping surfaces. Then I hear the door open, the quiet mutterings of 'hellos' and the coat is gently removed from my shoulders, replaced by a blanket, smelling of Marmite and washing powder. I open my eyes to see Verity, who pulls me up. Stu is on the other side of me as I discover my legs are shaky, it's hard to walk.

They pull me down the stairs, bundle me in the back seat of Jeremiah's car. I lie down on the seat – it smells of cigarette smoke. Jeremiah turns round from the driving seat and says, 'A'right, Cait? Let's get you home.'

We drive through the dark night and I stare out the window, unable to take in the streets we are driving past. It's the city I love and it looks just as it always has, and yet everything is completely different.

I wake up to a familiar noise. Like a drainpipe hissing. That's what I thought it was at first: I'm in my old bedroom, my floral duvet tucked in all around me. The curtains haven't been shut and the glow from the street light coats me in red. But then I realise the sound is so comforting I want to sink into my mattress, let the sound wash over me, soothe me. Like it is pouring concrete all over my cracks. It's Verity. It's the noise she makes when she's deeply asleep – I know it from hangover days on the sofa, from tents at festivals, from hostels in Europe. I know it from being twenty-one, with my whole life spread out in front of me. And I know it now: my face heavy, the skin around my eyes pulled at. At first, as I lie here, I just listen to her breath – in, out, in, out – it's like I've rewound the clock and any minute now Mum will come bundling in, a fresh basket of washing in her hands, and tell us it's almost time to get up for school. But then it comes flooding through me.

I look around my room. Mum's kept it exactly how it was when I was a teenager. Spice Girls, Peter Andre and 911 posters lined across the walls and the dresser covered in twenty photo frames – glitter ones, round ones, Forever Friends ones – and in most of those pictures there's just two people: Verity and me. At the very front there's one of us, in school uniform, sticking our tongues out to the camera. We were seven when we first met. Verity was the new girl in school and I remember spotting her sitting on a low brick wall, on her own, during playtime. I'd sat down beside her, offered her a jawbreaker. I knew straight away I wanted to be her best friend. Back then it was as simple as having the same hair: my curls blonde and tight, hers black and Afro – but it grew into more than that, she soon became the person I wanted to spend all my time with. When I married Harry she'd been beside me, in a gold sequinned dress, squeezing my hand just before I walked up to him. I'd promised her nothing would change as we entered into this new stage of life, one I assumed would involve her becoming godmother to my kids, long

Friday-night pub sessions replaced by walks in the park with matching buggies.

I pull myself out of the bed, trying really hard not to disturb her. My ancient radio alarm clock says it's 8 p.m., I must have slept all day and I feel groggy for it – my lips are flaking and the inside of my mouth is wrinkled and dry. I can hear Mum downstairs, bustling about, the clatter of dishes and the smell of Fairy Liquid wafting up the stairs.

'Hey.' I look round, Verity is awake. My pillows are pulled up behind her. It's been so long since our argument and I rush over to her, wrapping my arms around her, my head resting on her chest. I didn't think I could cry again but here I am, tears rolling down my face.

'I'm so sorry, I'm so sorry.' I'm repeating it over and over again, and she's just hushing me.

'It's OK,' she says as she rubs my back, our bodies pulled in so tightly to each other. We stay there for some time, until my fast, frantic breathing slows down and matches hers. I feel I can unwind myself, grab a tissue from the bedside table. I prop myself back beside her where I see fat tears wobbling on her cheeks.

'I'm the one who should be saying sorry,' she says, shaking her head ferociously. 'I handled our argument terribly. I wasn't here for you.'

'No, you don't need to say sorry, I do.' I hate to think of her ever blaming herself, my words vibrating through me as I yelled at her that she didn't care for me.

'No, I do—' she retorts.

'No, me!'

We look at each other and I break into a grin. 'Both as stubborn as each other,' she says, gripping my knee.

'How are you? Really?' she asks, looking me in the eye. This time I meet her gaze. 'I think after a while I forgot to properly ask,' she says, pausing, clearly grappling for words. 'I think I was afraid of the answer.'

Three little words that I'd begun to dread. They were bad enough from acquaintances, old friends of Harry's who'd ask me, their heads cocked to the side. I knew what they wanted from me so I'd grit my teeth, pinch my palms and reply: 'Fine.' But when Mum or Verity asked me, I'd find it even harder to respond: they knew I wasn't fine. But I wasn't ready to admit it.

Today I try. 'Angry. Terrified. Exhausted,' I say, with a sorry shrug. I don't know how to explain the feeling I get every morning, where my chest is so tight I feel like all the air inside of me has been pulled out. I've never known how to explain that to my best friend, to my mum. That there's this imaginary structure all around me and it's holding me up, because inside, bit by bit, I am crumbling. I've always been so afraid that if I make one false move, admit one tiny weakness, the whole thing will come crashing down.

She nibbles on the fabric of her collar. 'I should have done more to help you. I just didn't know what to do, no one teaches you this stuff.'

'I didn't know either,' I admit. 'I always thought that when something like this happened you felt like shit for a month, maybe two and then things went back to normal. Stupid, huh?'

'Not at all,' she says. 'I guess I thought the same.'

I breathe in, deeply. My ribcage feels like it can expand more, like it can give me more space.

'But it feels like. It feels . . . like . . .' I have to find the words somehow. Explain to her. Escape the 'fine'. 'Like someone has gnawed a chunk out of my side and left a gap there and that bit of me is lost. Gone. And there's nothing that can fill me in.'

She nods. The quiet weighs down on us. I wonder what she's thinking, as she realises there's nothing she can really compare it to. That's what our friendship has been based on. Verity telling me something and me replying, 'That's like when I . . .' or me confiding in her a fear of mine and her looking at me, wide-eyed, and screaming, 'I feel that way TOO.'

Now there's this chasm between us as she can't crawl into me, experience how I feel. But then I've never given her the chance to try.

'It's utter shite,' she says, the words breaking through the fog of silence. She says them in a Scottish accent, impersonating this guy who chatted her up once, years ago. A man we met only once, but whose mannerisms and sayings we've used constantly whenever 'something awful' happens. But that something awful is usually the shop running out of our favourite cans of pop when we're hungover, or a series we've been addicted to having a disappointing ending. Verity hasn't said it once, this entire year. It's so inappropriate, but it works. I melt into laughter.

'Total pash,' I reply.

We laugh until our sides hurt, until we're piled on top of each other in a tangle and Mum comes up and finds us like that, gasping for breath. She stands at the doorway, shaking her head.

'What is so funny?'

'Nothing,' I say, shaking my head. Because it's not funny really. It is utter shite. But God, it felt good to let that laughter rip through me. 'Can you get us some tea, Mum?'

She flip-flops her way down the stairs in her slippers as I pull myself out of the bed, out of Verity's grip. I look down – I'm in a pair of fluffy red Christmas pyjamas, the bottoms covered in a snowflake pattern. I've not seen them before – but Mum buys me a pair each year. I vaguely tap the duvet down, looking for my phone. I have no idea where I left it last night.

'Shall we go downstairs?'

Verity nods, pulling the duvet behind her, dragging it down the steps and onto the sofa where we encase ourselves in it. Mum brings through our tea – pasta coated in ketchup and mayonnaise, which makes Verity laugh and tell Mum never to change.

Once we're all squashed in beside each other, our bellies full of pasta, Mum and Verity sit silently, expectantly.

'So?' Mum says eventually. 'Are we going to be open now?' She says it in the same tone she used when she wanted me to confess to stealing the chocolate digestives, or to getting a bad grade in school.

I think of how good it had felt earlier, opening up, just a tiny bit. I take a breath. 'This isn't going to be easy. I'm sorry—' I begin to say but Verity cuts me off.

'Nope! You can't apologise for your feelings, your actions. You did what you had to do,' she says.

Mum pats her on the knee, playfully. 'So bossy!' Then she turns to me. 'But she's right. We've never blamed you or judged you, we just want to understand. And I think now, you have to tell us.'

'You're right,' I say, thinking of how much I've felt like a walking robot the past year, like someone else was controlling my actions. 'I didn't really know what I was doing, I was just doing it. It helped me, at first, not telling anyone else. I just so wanted to be normal again. The pretending helped.' I smile ruefully. 'Fake it till you make it . . .'

'But why wouldn't you ever explain this to us?' Verity says. 'I just came in the office one day and you whispered, "Don't tell Ade about Harry", and then when I tried to ask you why—'

'I always shut you down,' I reply. 'I felt ashamed of the whole thing.'

'You always looked so upset when we tried to push you to talk about it,' Mum says. 'Eventually, I guess, it became easier to stop trying.'

There were so many times both of them would gently sit me down and try and get me to open up. Each time it was like I developed a magic power to mentally block my ears with cotton wool and completely ignore them. 'I get it,' I'd say, snappily. 'I'm trying.' Or I'd just burst into tears and say, 'I don't feel like talking about this today.'

'I wasn't ready,' I say. 'I had to get ready on my own.'

'And you're ready now?' Verity asks.

'I don't know. Maybe I'll never be fully ready. I know I won't ever be fully better.'

Mum gasps at that, throws her hand over her mouth. 'It's OK, Mum,' I say. 'This is it, this is why I got afraid of talking. Because it's so shit. It's always going to be here with me but I think, I hope, it might not feel as big. Or it'll always be as big but it'll feel further away, like it's in another room. Does that make sense?' I smile. 'I'm shit at metaphors.'

'You're not,' Verity says. 'That makes sense. But we want to share this. It is shit. And I don't mean to . . .' She pauses, looks over at Mum, who nods at her. 'I don't mean to try and steal away your pain but it is big, it is huge, but it happened to all of us. You have to let us in, so we can all help ourselves heal together.'

'I get that.' I nod. 'I've been hoarding this, keeping it so tight to my chest. But . . . but . . .'

'What?' Verity says. 'This is the cloud of trust.' She tugs at the duvet we're all encased in. 'You can say anything, we will understand.'

'It's like I'm all caught up in the fake stuff,' I sigh. 'I cook for him, you know? Staring at the door, trying to imagine him coming home.' I feel so pathetic saying it aloud, and they're just looking silently at me, waiting for me to continue. 'I can't even describe what it's like to come through to my living room and see the blanket I folded the night before exactly the same as it was, or to see just my mug in the sink.'

'That's why you're always in the office,' Verity fills in.

'Yeah, it's safer there.'

'I've been doing that, too,' Verity says. 'Throwing wine down my throat, hoping it would help. Getting you over, pretending our friendship was just like it always was.'

'You stopped letting me talk about him,' I say. 'You'd both ask me how I was but you didn't let me share my memories. Verity, you'd change the subject every time he was mentioned.'

They glance at each other. 'We thought that would be encouraging you to keep living in the past,' Mum explains, slowly.

'I get it, I was acting crazy. But it felt good to talk about him at work, to be somewhere where people didn't look at me like I was about to have a breakdown,' I say. 'I was . . . angry at you both.'

'I practically had to force you to come over and spend any time with me. I was always showing up at your office or going to the pub at the end of your road,' Verity says. 'I felt like I was clinging on to our friendship so tightly, but it was only pushing you further away.'

'And you were never here, or if you did turn up you'd leave again quickly,' Mum adds. They're not saying it reproachfully, more as if they've finally discovered the answer to a cryptic crossword puzzle that's been hard to crack.

'I hated seeing how hard you were all trying to make me happy,' I reply. 'The tidy house and home cooking,' I say, looking at Verity. 'And the bare walls here, the cards all shoved in a drawer, Mum. Neither of you were ever normal around me. You weren't yourselves.'

'Shall we make a pact?' Verity says. 'That, from now on, we'll always be honest with each other? Be ourselves?' She grips my hand and then Mum's. I'm about to reply, 'Good idea,' but instead this noise escapes me. A strangled cry.

'I really, really miss Harry,' I say.

Chapter Eighteen

I smell cinnamon as soon as I wake up and can hear Mariah Carey blasting out from downstairs. I look at the clock: it's around half nine. We hadn't stayed up very long the night before, all three of us were wiped out. I pad down the stairs and the first thing I see is a red plastic Santa at the door, crouched and holding a finger to his lips as he sniggers. In the living room, the tree is up, absolutely covered in tinsel, coloured lights that flash in a riot of directions and baubles that each represent a different memory from our life. There's a big silver glitter-encrusted number one, from my first birthday party, and a pair of ballet shoes from the year I tried – and failed – to learn how to be a dancer. The sofa is covered in an icy-blue fluffy blanket covered in snowflakes, and dotted all around the TV are various gnomes dressed up as Santa.

In the kitchen Mum is standing precariously on a stool, a piece of red string coming out of her mouth. 'Come help me,' she mumbles through pursed lips. I stand at the bottom of the stool, rip some Sellotape with my mouth and hand it to her. She slaps the string to the wall and gestures to me to hand her a card from the pile on the counter. I do, then I hand her a tiny red peg. I know exactly what to do – it's like muscle memory, I've done it so many times.

It takes us about an hour to hang up everything, emptying all five of the boxes that Mum has unearthed that are coated in dust. Every inch of the ceiling is covered in tinsel or silver-paper garlands, and all our old friends are out: the Santa who sings with a lisp, the Rudolph toilet seat cover – she even pours me a bowl of cereal in a chunky bowl covered in gold stars. Verity comes down, rubbing her eyes in disbelief.

'What's all this, Susan?' she asks.

Mum sits at the table, still in the same outfit she was in last night, her eyes ringed in grey. 'It was time.'

'OK,' Verity says, smiling and sitting down at the table. 'But later can I turn off the plug-ins? The smell of cinnamon is bloody choking me.'

We laugh and begin to crunch through our Coco Pops in silence, Verity slurping the chocolatey milk from the bowl, when with slow horror I realise that Mum is crying, softly, into her bowl. I jump up, Verity following me, and stand behind her, wrapping my arms around her shaking body.

'Mum? Mum? What's wrong?' I say.

'Sorry, I didn't mean it about the cinnamon!' Verity says, in a bid to raise a smile. But Mum just keeps sobbing in her seat, the tears dripping into her bowl.

'Ssshh, ssssshh,' I say into her hair, soothing her like she did when I was a child. It takes her a few false starts before she gets her words out.

'I couldn't face it. It was so wrong to hang them without Harry here. I'm sorry, I shouldn't be crying. Not in front of you, Cait, I'm sorry.' The words come out gargled, like she's suppressing a hiccup. 'It's just . . . it's just . . . he was like my son. I miss him so much.'

My stomach fills up with this darkness, like I've swallowed tar. It's the same as when I saw Sarah, her face wrinkled and tired and reminding me, with those tiny little lines around her eyes, that this has never just been about me. About my loss. That I should have tried to share it.

'Oh, Mum, you're allowed to grieve for him. Of course you are,' I say, my voice breaking at the seams just slightly. I don't want to cry, I don't want her to think she's made me. 'And he loved your decorations, how you always made such a fuss. "It's always so Christmassy round your mum's", he'd say to me.'

She manages a weak, sloppy smile at that. 'I always got him things for his stocking. I even found myself putting aside a Lynx set for him at the chemist this year.' She nods to herself. 'That was always his favourite. The Africa one.'

It was the first Christmas present she ever got him, after we'd been dating about six months and I came round to help her hang the decorations. She said, 'Ooh, now I've got something for your Harry, do you think that's OK? He won't think it's too soon?' She took to Harry instantly that year as he unwrapped the Lynx Africa gift set and with a huge smile on his face said it was his favourite scent. She's been buying it for him ever since – and Harry never had the heart to tell her he doesn't ever spray the stuff.

She untangles herself from our grasp and stands up, wiping her face, which is now red and blotchy. 'What are we going to do with ourselves, girls?' she says, opening both her arms for Verity and I to come snuggle ourselves into.

'Thank you for hanging the decorations, Mum,' I say into her collar. 'I think it's important to keep these traditions up.'

'It's silly, all this, I suppose.' She gestures around her. 'But when your dad left it was important for me not to sink into myself, to keep things going for you, Cait. To give you a semblance of family life, I . . .' She blows her lips out, sighing. 'I wanted you to see that you can build a life, a happy one, without it being 2.4 perfection. Without a man . . .'

'You absolutely managed that, Susan,' Verity says. 'You've always been such an inspiration to us both.'

But I feel unsettled. I take a seat, to not show the wobbliness in my legs. So much of my pretending was to do with wanting to keep up the pretence of normality, to keep the memory of Harry in my brain as long as possible. But it was also borne out of fear, out of a deep worry that this wasn't something I could do by myself: go on, live, run a business, look after myself . . . I feel stripped of a limb without him.

I manage to smile up at Mum. 'You really did, what amazing Christmases we had throughout my childhood.'

'Remember that year it snowed?' says Verity.

'You sledged all the way here!' Mum says, squeezing Verity's hand. She lived just up the road, and had showed up at our door, in a neon pink tracksuit, absolutely sopping wet with melted snow. Mum had drawn her a bath, then wrapped her up in a towel, handing her a mug of Options hot chocolate.

'My favourite was when we both got rollerblades,' I say. 'And insisted, even though it was freezing outside, that we go and play on them.'

'Oh you fell so badly that year,' Mum recalls, and I remember the huge hole in my knee from where I fell flat on my face. How I was convinced it would never heal, but eventually it did, after I scratched and picked at the scab, causing the wound to scar. I roll my pyjama leg up. 'Still got the scar,' I say, fingering the oval-shaped mark on my leg.

'Look at that,' Mum says. 'Healed, but not forgotten.'

Verity begins to stack up the dishes as Mum and I remember our best Christmas moments: how I'd come crawling into her bed in the morning, and show her earnestly what Santa had put in my stocking – even keeping up the charade when I was definitely old enough to know better. We'd then head over to Verity's for breakfast, bringing her back with us at around 11 a.m. to swap presents. She always stayed far too long, and we'd munch our way through a Selection Box until eventually the phone would ring, we'd look at each other and hear Mum say, 'Yes, she's just left,' as Verity scrambled to put her shoes on. Then we'd eat our Christmas lunch, on our laps, in front of whatever movie was on that year.

We're debating which Christmas movie is our favourite, Mum arguing with Verity that *Die Hard* is not a Christmas film, when I hear a familiar beep. Then again. And again.

'Is that my phone?' I ask.

Mum and Verity stare at each other, like they're having a conversation with their eyes. I can almost picture the eyeballs chatting to each other: 'Should we?' Mum's green irises are saying to Verity's chocolate browns. Eventually they reach their conclusion.

'It's in the drawer,' Mum says, resolutely. 'You can have it. But just for ten minutes, OK?'

Mum hands me it, as if she's handing a sharp knife to a child. My Instagram is calling to me but I'm not sure I want to see right away if Morwena has posted about me again. Instead I'll check my email: much safer. I don't want to see the impact her post has had just yet. I breathe in: 118 unread messages. Most of those are applications – we're about to enter the busiest time of year for dating. People either looking for love for the New Year or because they spent so much time with their partner over the Christmas period they decide they can't bear them any more. I ignore

the applications, and instead open up a couple of account-
ancy things, enjoying the simplicity of numbers.

Verity and Mum are pretending not to look at me. Verity's
flicking through an old copy of *Take A Break* while Mum
fusses around behind me, wiping up the tea circle underneath
my mug, her eyes glancing to the screen every now and then.

'Stop it,' I say. 'I know you're looking.'

She smiles, holds her hands up. 'Guilty as charged. Just want
to check everything is OK. I don't like you being on Instagram
all the time. It's why I took the phone, popped it down here.'

I hold the screen up to her. 'Look! Just email. Let me be.'

But she grabs the phone off me, jabs her nail at the
screen. 'What's that?'

She hands it back to me. The email she's pointing to
has the subject: 'Influencer Trip Invitation: Maldives'. I'd
somehow missed it while I was trying to avoid opening any
applications. I tap it. Let out a tiny yelp. Verity looks up.

'What is it? Read it out!'

'Dear Caitlin, we've long been admirers of your business. We're a luxury—'

'LUXURY!' Mum yells.

'Luxury honeymoon company, and we'd love to send you
to try out one of our resorts, in exchange for a review on
your website. We appreciate this is incredibly last-minute,
but we do have a slot for over the Christmas period, flying
out overnight on the 23rd, arriving back on the 29th. It
would all be covered by us. Please let us know either way.'

They both stare at me, mouths open. Until eventually Verity
throws her arms up in the air. 'Well? What are you thinking?'

I shake my head, stay silent. There's one part of the
email I've not read out to them. I'm not sure I can bring
myself to. Instead I simply say: 'I can't believe they'd offer

me this, I'm not an "influencer".'

'I don't know what it means, but they certainly think you are,' Mum says, massaging my shoulder in a vaguely proud way.

'It's just a shame, the timing of it. I'd love to go to the Maldives but it's over Christmas and that has to be spent at home.'

'Who says it does?' Verity says. 'Seriously, who makes the rule that Christmas has to be all cold? It doesn't even bloody snow ever anyway.'

'We do,' I say. 'Tradition, remember? And I'd never leave Mum alone on Christmas Day.'

'Oh phooey, Lucy next door has invited me round theirs anyway,' Mum says with a wave of a hand. 'She knew I wouldn't be able to manage all the cooking this year anyway.'

Verity and I exchange a smile over her head. Mum buys everything in for Christmas. The Yorkshires are Aunt Bessies, the roast potatoes are frozen, the gravy is in a packet . . . She just shoves it all in the oven and sits watching the TV with a tin of Quality Street.

'I think it would be good for you, Cait, to get some sunshine, some time by yourself,' Verity is saying. 'Oooh and I bet they'll do yoga on the beach. What's the name of the resort?'

'Maruha,' I say, as she pulls her phone out, begins typing.

'Oh my God, it's incredible, a minimum stay is £6,000 a week!' she says. 'Caitlin, you have to go. I'll look after your mum. Seriously, when does stuff like this happen to people like us?'

I have to agree with her. It doesn't. When we were growing up, Verity's mum would always take me along on their family holidays – usually a caravan somewhere, Butlin's at a push. Certainly never anywhere sunny or hot. Still, I shake my head.

'No, I don't want to,' I say. 'Be weird to spend it on the beach.'

Mum nods. 'I like the sleet and the grey.' She holds out a pale arm. 'I'm not built for the sunshine. But still, Cait, I think you're making a big mistake. Some vitamin D is just what you need.'

'Vitamin Sea more like,' Verity says, sneaking up behind me, grabbing my phone out of my hand while I'm distracted. I jump up.

'Give it back! Verity, this is my decision!' I yelp as she begins reading out her response as she types. 'Thank you so much, I'd love to come—'

Then she stops. Looks at me. Looks at the screen. 'Oh, Caitlin . . . I see.' She stares at the email for a little bit, then she says quietly, 'They've offered the trip for you and Harry.'

I sink further into my chair. 'I can't tell them the truth,' I say. 'They'll think I'm crazy.'

Mum is still standing beside me, still massaging my shoulders. 'No, they won't, try them, they'll understand.'

'They want *that* Caitlin.' I gesture to my phone. 'The one with the perfect marriage, the unshakeable smile. Not this one. Not me.'

'You don't know what they want,' Verity says. 'The email says they're a fan of your business, not Harry, not your Instagram. See.' She holds the email close to my face. 'You.'

I read the email again and again. She's right. It does say they like my business. The only mention of Harry really is at the end, when it says, 'You are of course welcome to bring your husband.'

'Maybe I could say he's away on business?' I say, knowing full well what their replies will be.

'No, duckie,' Mum says. 'Remember last night? Total honesty. From all of us. Always going forward.'

'Even with strangers?' I say, and my voice sounds small and pleading – like a child asking for an extra bag of sweets.

'Even with strangers,' she says, firmly.

I swallow hard, tense my body, try to remember how I felt before emailing people asking for funding in the early days of the business. I found, back then, that if I just feigned confidence, asked firmly and nicely, I tended to do well. I could slay even the most sombre of meetings and come out feeling so proud. I clench my fists, bring them up to my ears and shake them – a 'power pose' I used to do in the toilets before each big event. Verity spots me, and smiles. She remembers that time well.

'You did all of that on your own,' she reminds me. 'You can do this.'

I type out my response, hold my breath and press send.

The reply comes back about five minutes later. We have all been distracting ourselves, crowded round my phone, looking on the *Daily Mail* website, Mum pretending she was disapproving but still completely absorbed. My phone pings, and I put my hand over the screen.

'Let me just read this myself, OK?' I ask. They oblige, stepping back, and try not to look at me as I read the email in silence.

We are terribly sorry to hear about your husband, sending so much love. You may not be interested but, as you are one of the biggest romance influencers in the UK, we'd still like to extend the invite – and you can bring along a plus one of your choosing. Please let us know.

I look over at Verity, who is clearly just pretending to read that copy of *Take A Break*. 'Verity, fancy coming to the Maldives with me?'

Chapter Nineteen

The water is choppy beneath me, and the air I'm inhaling feels different. Cleaner, lighter, fresher. Splashes of salty seawater are stinging my eyes but I don't care. Everything around me is blue. The sort of blue you don't think actually exists in real life – you think it only exists on digitally enhanced postcards or computer screensavers. But it does, and I'm currently in it, my best friend beside me, shrieking every time the boat goes over a wave.

I'm trying to avoid the voice in my head that keeps whispering, 'Harry would love it here', and instead look over at the couple opposite us. She's got the sort of deep brown tan that either indicates she goes on holiday a lot and wears oil on her skin the whole time, or that she's a big fan of the sunbed. Her hair is brassy blonde, cropped short, and she's wearing a huge pair of Gucci sunglasses, a turquoise kaftan and heeled flip-flops. She grips tight onto her husband's arm. He's got dark skin, a scruffy beard and is wearing a Hawaiian shirt. They're both in their mid-fifties, I'd say, and they're smiling, but not grinning manically like Verity and I: we are both staring at the ocean as if it's not really there, like this whole thing is an incredibly realistic dream.

Straight after receiving the reply, I emailed Ade and checked the company offering this was legit, that we hadn't just fallen for an elaborate phishing scheme. Even when they sent the flight confirmation through I tried to keep calm, deciding I'd only believe it when we were on the plane. Then we were on the plane, Verity dressed in a maroon Juicy Couture tracksuit she'd gone searching for on eBay as soon as I'd sent across her passport details. 'Paris Hilton in the noughties. That's my airport inspiration,' she'd said. She's now changed out of it, into a black dress covered in palm trees, and with huge mirrored reflective shades that I keep catching myself in, amazed at how relaxed I look.

'Can you believe it's Christmas Eve?' Verity shouts over the engine, which revs underneath us. 'And we're on our way to a five-star resort in the bloody Maldives! It's unreal. Just unreal.'

'First time here, huh?' the woman with the bleached crop says. She has a soft American accent that wouldn't feel out of place in a cowboy movie. We both nod quickly, like children on a school trip being offered sweeties.

'I warn you, it will spoil you. We came here five years ago and after that, no other holiday compared! So now we fly out every Christmas. Sure beats Texas and my questionable cooking.'

Her husband smiles at her, looking at her the same way Harry used to look at me. Something in my heart tugs. 'She makes a salad out of instant noodles, can you believe it?' His accent is pure Bronx, New York.

His wife slaps him on the chest. 'Hey, you like that salad!'
'I like the cups of mayo you shove in it, that's what I like.'
She leans over to us, hand extended. 'I'm Jan.'
Her husband gives a little wave. 'Usman.'
We introduce ourselves, and Usman pulls a cooler from underneath his seat. 'Beer, anyone? Get this holiday off to a good start.'

'So what brings you girls to paradise over Christmas?' Jan asks, as we clink bottles.

We'd prepared for this. Verity, who worked in an all-inclusive resort in Alicante one summer when we were seventeen, had warned me that there are lots of people who live for making 'holiday friends' that they'll never see again. We couldn't count on being alone the whole six days. 'If you don't want to bring Harry up, that's fine,' she'd said. 'But people will ask everything about your life. I'm serious, every day that summer I was asked about my worst memory, best memory . . . it's like these people bring conversation-starter cards and they're not afraid to use them.'

Verity steps in with our prepared answer. 'Girls' trip. I'm a bit heartbroken, see? So we thought we'd get away from all of that back home . . .'

'And where better to come than here?!' I chime in. It's not a lie, more an omission of information – so Mum and Verity had been OK with me not telling the whole truth. I wonder if Jan's desperate to ask how we afforded it. I would be.

'Poor poppet,' Jan says, reaching over and tapping Verity on the knee. 'But that certainly sounds a plan. Honestly, the resort is incredible. You won't even be thinking of your ex-fella by the time we get there.'

'I just can't believe we have to get there by boat!' I say. 'I was fully expecting to have to get a coach or something.'

She laughs – this big hearty chuckle. 'That's what they're all like around here, barely any roads and nothin' but the ocean for miles around. So, tell me, you staying in an Air Villa or a Water Villa?'

There's nothing about the resort that Verity and I don't know. In the week it took for the trip to come around we checked the website together daily, doing video tours of our room and reading the sample menus of every single one of the eight restaurants until we knew them by heart.

'Earth,' Verity says. We'd been quite disappointed not to have one of the little floating rooms on stilts, and then reminded ourselves we were getting a free holiday. It made me wonder if that's why celebrities are the way they are, how easy it is to get super-spoiled.

'Oh they're lovely. We were in one of those last year, weren't we, Usman?' She elbows him. He nods.

'Oh yeah, they're amazing. The beach is your front yard.'

'We're in a Water one this year, for a change. Hey, you'll have to come up for a drink one night, check it out.'

Verity squeezes my knee as if to say 'I told you so' and I smile at her. I wouldn't mind if Jan just talked at me the whole holiday.

'Look, there it is in the distance!' We've spotted lots of little islands on the boat trip so far, dots of brown huts stretching out into the ocean, like mini streets. And each time the boat just whizzed past. But now Jan is standing up, Usman holding tight onto her waist as she waves manically at a series of dots ahead of us.

The speedboat pulls up on a wooden stilted walkway, and we shakily step out onto it. Awaiting us are about thirty smiling faces, all dressed in pristine white uniforms. I can hear a strange whistling sound, to a jaunty tune. I realise it's coming from a man to my right, who is playing an actual conch.

'Welcome to new and old friends,' says one of the faces, stepping forward. All I can see are big, shiny teeth grinning at me and I feel dizzy with how wonderful everyone looks. The man is short, stocky and has four brown string necklaces around his neck. He removes them and places one over each of our heads. I look down, the charm is a star shape created from a palm leaf. 'My name is Charles and I am the general manager here. You must be tired after your long flight, so let's get you settled in your rooms, then later, will you join me for welcome drinks?'

He gently presses my back and we begin to walk down the wooden pier. Little huts pepper the beach, tucked back, each with a square blue swimming pool out in front of them. 'Wow, just wow,' Verity is muttering over and over under her breath. I don't need to look at her to know her smile has reached her ears.

We're led into a check-in area and directed to a bench where four ladies sit waiting for us. They put a glass of champagne in our hands and gesture to us to sit down. 'Let's get you checked in,' says Charles. 'While you enjoy a relaxing foot massage.'

It's almost too much. My brain is screaming at me, 'Enjoy the moment, enjoy the moment', while other parts of it are butting in and saying, 'This is awkward, I don't like the subservient nature of this woman massaging my feet', and another is saying, 'God, if only you could Instagram this, it would make great content'.

Verity has made me give her my phone, saying she will take pictures that I can post afterwards, but this week I have to not be showing off, checking in, worrying about Morwena or anything that involves being on my iPhone. It makes sense, but still I feel it is missing, like when you take off a ring that you've had on too long and you can still feel the ghost of it on your finger.

Eventually the woman stops massaging my feet and Charles comes over to take us to our room. 'We operate a no shoes policy here at Ozen,' he says. 'Much better to appreciate the feeling of your toes in the sand, don't you think?'

Verity drains the last of her champagne and we hop onto the back of a golf buggy, which drives us down winding streets under lush green trees.

We pull up outside a blue wooden gate, which Charles creaks open to reveal the most picture-perfect scene, framed beautifully by the entranceway. There's a sapphire-blue infinity pool directly in front of us that stretches out towards the beach and sea. A couple of palm trees shelter the pool, casting shadows in their recognisable shape on the sand. We both gasp, loudly, and at the exact same time. Charles chuckles.

'Your room is accessed by the key here, through this door.' He gestures to a door on the side. 'But you can also enter through the front, through these glass doors.' The whole front of our villa is a glass wall, with a bamboo and white linen corner sofa sitting on the porch. On the table is a bottle of champagne in a silver cooler.

He takes us inside: we have a living room, kitchen area and two bedrooms: one with wooden shuttered doors so you can look out to the beach from the bed.

'It's huge!' Verity says as she swings her arms around. 'Honestly, Charles, you should see my flat at home, my living room would fit in the bathroom.'

He chuckles again, a low, almost fatherly noise, as if we're two of his kids. 'Now you'll like this: the minibar is replenished twice daily, by your personal butler, Joseph. If you ever need Joseph for anything, anything at all, he can be reached by dialling zero on your phones. I'm going to leave you two to settle in, your bags are already here.' He gestures to the wardrobe. 'But I'll see you at the welcome drinks, at six, yes?'

We both nod obediently, and as soon as he's out the door, we begin to yelp and scream and say 'oh my God, oh my God' over and over again, holding onto each other's hands and jumping up and down. Verity throws herself onto the bed like a starfish and I pop open the champagne, pouring her a glass. 'Your Bolly, Patsy . . .'

She grabs it off me, takes a slurp of the bubbles. 'We've actually made it, Cait! We've made it.'

I take my own sip, look out at the bleached sand and think, 'Yes, I might actually make it through.' Then, with my flute in hand, I slide open the doors and rush down to the sea, Verity close behind, still whooping. The turquoise water laps at my feet, and I shut my eyes, feeling the sun beating down on my face. Verity sits down, letting the water rush over her dress, soaking it.

'Fuck it,' I say, and go and join her, yelping at the cool temperature of the water, the rush of it. She wraps one arm around me, pulls me in close.

'You can talk about him whenever you like,' she says. I rest my head on her shoulder, her skin is warm.

'Thank you. I will . . . But not now.'

We watch a speedboat on the horizon and the hazy sun in the sky. I have no idea what the time is and I simply don't care. 'You can, too, you know?' I say. 'Talk to me whenever you like.'

'About Harry?' she asks. 'I'd like that. I miss him.'

'Yes,' I say. 'But Jeremiah as well. I've not forgotten how tough this must be for you.'

She squeezes my shoulder. 'Thank you. I will . . . but not now. Right,' she says. 'You're going pink. Come on, let's unpack.'

She walks up the beach. Sand sticks to my wet legs as I follow her. My arms have gone a little rosy but I can't quite bear the thought of unpacking yet. It's like she reads my mind. 'You sit in the shade, read your book for a bit. I'll unload.'

'Are you sure? I can help,' I say, already settling myself down onto the wicker chair.

'You won't fold your clothes right, anyway,' she says. 'You know how particular I am about these things.' Before I can respond she's through the door, only coming back a second later to hand me my book.

'You've packed about three books too many,' she says.

'And you've packed fifteen pairs of shoes . . . for a no shoe resort!' I respond, my head lolling forward. I'm very tired. She pokes me.

'No sleeping!' she says strictly. 'The only way to get over jet lag is to keep to the hours of the place you're in! And it's 5 p.m. here.'

I try to concentrate on the words in my book – they swim in front of me as I listen to her singing away to herself. But I must have nodded off as the sky has gone cornflower blue when she shakes me awake.

'It's time for drinks, Caitlin,' she whispers, gently. I startle awake, look down – I'm still in my orange dress from earlier.

'You let me sleep!' I say, slurring slightly.

'I did,' she replies, smiling. 'You looked too cute. Here, I've found you an outfit.'

She smells of coconut shampoo and looks fresh – she's in a turquoise-blue dress that swoops along the floor and ties in a halterneck. On the bed is a strappy pink dress that I pull over my head; it's covered in tassels that sway in the light breeze. I yawn.

'We don't have to stay out for long,' Verity says. 'Drinks and dinner then bed, I reckon. How about you?'

'Sounds nice,' I say, but the evening shimmers with anticipation. There's so much of the resort we have yet to explore.

'Got the key?' I ask, and she nods, waving to all her shoes that she's lined up along one wall.

'Bye, my pretties, you are still loved, just not worn,' she says, blowing a kiss to them.

'I quite like the freedom of not having to wear shoes,' I say to her as we begin to walk down the path to the main bar. 'It frees up outfit possibilities, as you're not worrying you'll wreck your look with the wrong pair.'

'That's true. But then you're also not mega enhancing your look with them, plus'– she makes a childish face, sticking her bottom lip out –'I feel so teeny tiny.'

'But your feet aren't hurting. God, remember when we used to go out all the time? You'd always end up losing a shoe, as you'd take them off to dance and only take one home!'

'I lost many a hero that way. Many a hero.'

We link arms, bumping into each other as we walk. People cycle past us, tinging their bells to let us know of their presence. It's strange not to hear the hum of an engine, the smashing of bottles in bins, the beeping of horns: city sounds. It feels as though we've landed on a different planet – in a place where no one can get hurt, nothing bad can happen. And although my brain still whirrs with 'wish Harry could see this', it also helps that he's never been here. I can walk freely without being afraid of turning a corner and catching sight of a bar we once had a great night in, or a restaurant we had a silly argument in. Harry's memories pollute the streets of Sheffield, enveloping me in extreme emotions during the most routine of days.

The main bar is covered in Christmas decorations: foil tubes are strung across the ceiling, tinsel is wrapped around the beds that float in the huge infinity swimming pool at the front of it. A six-foot Christmas tree is beside the bar, topped with a silver star. The colours are all clashing and sparkling in the evening sunlight. It's like Mum's house has been picked up, shipped across here and tacked up with Sellotape. 'White Christmas' blasts out from the speakers and Jan and Usman are already at the bar, talking to a waiter with dark hair so shiny it reflects the lights. His cheekbones are sharp; he looks as though he's come straight off the set of a Bollywood film.

'Girls, come over here.' Jan is waving enthusiastically. She's dressed in a white off-the-shoulder dress, her bronzed shoulders shining in the light. Usman is in a tropical-print shirt, and smiles slowly, not waving.

'This is Willem,' Jan says, gesturing to the barman who has, worryingly, begun to lay out four shot glasses on the bar. 'He's our favourite, aren't you, Willy?'

'Well, you're my favourite lady on the whole island, Jan. Although it looks like you have competition.' He waves at both of us.

'Verity.' She puts her hand out and he kisses it.

'Caitlin,' I say, keeping my hand to my side, waving with the other.

'Want to see a trick?'

'Oh, girls, his tricks are the best! The absolute best.' Jan's hands are glued together at her heart in anticipation.

Willem's voice is this delicious mix of Indian and American, his words almost drip off his tongue. He pulls a deck of cards from his apron pocket and shuffles them as though he's playing an accordion. Then he fans them out across the bar, face down, and asks Verity to pick one. She does so, sneakily glancing at it, before placing it back down.

'Any card?' she asks, a hint of flirtation in her voice. But then it's rare to find a man, or woman, that Verity won't flirt with. 'It's not flirting, it's flattering,' she'll say whenever I accuse her of it. 'Nothing wrong with making people feel good about themselves.'

'Any card,' he says, with one eyebrow raised. Jan slurps her purple cocktail loudly.

She points at one. He nods, then, almost in a flash, all the cards from the bar are back up, neat in his hands. He shuffles them once more.

'I bet you I can find your card in this pack, with my eyes shut,' he says. 'And if I can't, the drinks are on me.'

'Nice try, buddy, the drinks are free anyway,' Verity retorts, laughing.

'Fair.' He nods. 'OK then, I'll pour you a glass of the most expensive brandy we have, £250 a glass, and usually only reserved for our most special customers.'

'Deal,' Verity says, shaking his hand heartily. I've always envied how easily she slots into any situation, with witty retorts and relaxed laughter. I've found I can come across a bit shy, perhaps uptight, until I can sit down one-on-one and chat with someone.

He squeezes his eyes shut. 'No peeking,' shrieks Jan, who keeps whispering to her husband, 'Oh, I just love a trick, I just love them.'

Willem holds a card out to Verity: three of hearts. 'This is your card.'

She shakes her head. 'Sorry, mate, it's not.'

His face drops, his chocolate-brown eyes now as sad as a Labrador's.

'You sure?'

'Sure,' she says and I'm thinking, 'I'd lie, anything to stop him looking that sad.'

'But, but . . . Willem, you never get it wrong,' says Jan. 'I'm serious, girls, we've been coming here for years and not once has he got it wrong.'

He shakes his head. 'This is a new trick, Jan. I am, how do you say it? Rusty. I must practise more. These girls and their beauty distracted me.'

'Don't try and charm us out of the prize,' Verity says.

He nods, turns around, pulls a square crystal bottle off the top shelf. With it comes a card, fluttering down.

'No, you didn't!' Jan's hands are over her mouth.

Willem bends down, picks the card up, a grin spreading across his face. 'Wait, what's this?'

He hands it to Verity: four of clubs. She looks at it, her mouth open. 'That's it, that's my card.'

We all begin to whoop and cheer, and Usman pats Willem on the back. 'You really had me there, you really had me there,' he says.

Jan whispers in my ear. 'The most handsome man on the entire island, I'm telling you.'

I whisper back. 'Usman?'

She slaps my knee, hoots with laughter. 'No, silly. Willem!'

He then winks at me, my stomach waking up and coming alive with butterflies. There's another whistle, the noise I now know is a conch, and in comes Charles. The room hushes and everyone turns to face him, as if he's royalty.

'Hello all, and welcome to my island!' he says, projecting his voice expertly. 'This is our home – and we can't wait to make you feel at home here, too.' He then begins to explain all the activities on offer as Jan whispers in my ear with her own review of each. 'Snorkelling, you have to, you see turtles!' she says, and then, 'Kayaking, not for me. Give me a margarita by the pool any day.'

Charles heads behind the bar and slaps Willem on the back. 'And if you ever need a cocktail, this is the man to make you one.' Willem grins, and takes a small bow. 'I hear some of us are fans of margaritas,' he says, and Jan whoops, raising her glass. Charles then begins going round, shaking hands with each guest. 'Such a lovely man,' Usman says. 'Do you know he's one of the best hoteliers in the Maldives?'

I shake my head.

'It's because he really cares for his guests,' he continues. 'Treats us all like family, doesn't he, love?'

'Well, a family that have made him very rich,' cackles Jan, before straightening her face and nodding. 'He'd do anything for his guests.'

'Hey,' she continues. 'Where are you all heading for dinner?' Verity looks warningly at me. 'We've got a table booked at the Japanese place, if you fancy joining us?'

Ignoring Verity's stare, I reply, 'That would be lovely.' Not out of politeness, but because there's something about this couple that makes me feel happy and welcome. Like I can be myself around them.

Usman looks at his watch: a big gold chunky thing that hangs loosely on his wrist. 'Better be heading then.' We weave our way out, shaking Charles' hand on the way. 'Have the teriyaki,' he advises Verity. 'You won't regret it.' The whole time I can feel Willem's eyes on my back, and I feel hot under his stare.

Settled at our table, overlooking the sea, now black as the night, Jan orders a round of lychee martinis for the table. 'So, y'all, tell me what you both do?'

I let Verity take the lead. 'I'm a stylist,' she says, which causes Jan to gasp and tug at her dress.

'No! Had I known I'd have dressed up better. You hear that, Usman? A stylist. Do you work with famous people?'

'Yeah, but you probably won't have heard of them. They're, like, UK reality TV stars . . .'

'Oooh,' she replies. 'Like the Kardashians?'

'The Kardashians if they got drunk and wet themselves,' I say, which causes Usman to hoot with laughter.

'And how about you, honey?' Jan asks. I swallow, settle my face into a smile.

'Um, it's a bit of a weird one,' I say. 'I'm a matchmaker.'

'Like, for love?' Usman asks.

'That's the one,' Verity says proudly. 'She's made so many people happy.'

I can feel myself blushing. 'I try,' I say. 'Anyway, how about you guys? How long have you been married?'

They both burst out laughing. 'Divorced,' says Usman, pointing at himself.

'It might not be the right thing to say to a matchmaker,' laughs Jan, 'but I'd say the secret to a happy marriage would be to . . . not do it!'

Verity raises her glass, the lychee on the rim dropping to the table, and says, 'Cheers to that.' I raise mine and clink it with theirs.

'OK, but just don't tell my clients!' Really I'm thinking about Harry's face on our wedding day as I walked down the aisle. Would we have made it if he was still alive? I wonder. I always wanted a marriage that would prove everyone wrong – the sort that stretched into our retirement, that would make people envious when they saw us both, grey-haired, rotating slowly on waxed dance floors.

Now I'll never know. I swallow down that sadness though, and tune back into the conversation. Verity's explaining her break-up with Jeremiah.

'In the end we were more like friends,' she says. 'But it still makes it hard, like I miss telling jokes to him, telling him about my day.' She glances over at me, as if looking for approval to continue. I smile, wishing I could empty our argument and all the things I said to her out of my brain. Or, better yet, rewind the clock so it didn't happen. 'Do you guys think it's possible to be friends with an ex?'

Usman looks to Jan and she looks back at him. 'I'm not sure,' he says. 'I still see my ex-wife a couple of times a year for a coffee. But it took us a long time to get there. I don't think it can happen straight away.'

'When did you last see this Jerry guy?' asks Jan.

'About a fortnight ago,' says Verity. 'He, he came to help me out with something.'

Verity said it had been instinctive, the moment Stu called asking her to come over she had just grabbed her phone and got Jeremiah to come with the car.

'That's too soon!' Jan says, gasping. 'You gotta learn who you are without him, before you become friends.'

'Well, being here certainly helps with that,' Verity says, nodding. 'It feels a million miles away from him, from everything.'

'And the place is full of hot waiters!' Jan says, giggling. 'Hey, what do you reckon to that Willem?'

Please don't fancy him, suddenly pops into my head. It's not entirely unexpected as I remember the heat from his eyes earlier, but I also want to squash it away – like I wanted to run away from Stu any time things got too personal, went too deep.

'Oh, he's not my type,' Verity says. 'Handsome gener-
ally isn't. I like 'em . . . how do I say this? A bit weird.'

Jan laughs, takes a slurp from her cocktail. 'He's definitely
my type,' she says, while Usman playfully taps her hand.

'We all know that, love!'

A few hours later, and Verity and I are feet to feet in a
hammock overlooking the sea, staring up at the sky – the
stars are like shards of glass. We're each slurping from a mini
bottle of champagne and Jan is blasting out Abba, dancing
around their villa. We headed here after the restaurant and
I now feel almost stoned with relaxation. I don't know
if it's the sway of the hammock, the sound of the waves
lapping or the champagne, but it's a wonderful feeling.

Jan and Usman are dancing now, shaking their hips to
'Dancing Queen'. 'Remember when this used to come on
when we actually were seventeen?' Verity says to me. I nod.

'That was the best age, it was so thrilling being underage
in nightclubs and our hangovers could be solved with a
packet of crisps and a can of pop,' I reply.

Jan comes over and begins pushing the hammock
like we're on a swing. 'Come on, girls,' she's shouting.
'You are still young now, get out that thing and dance
with me.'

Usman spins me under his arm while Verity and Jan grip
each other, swaying back and forth. Now I'm on my feet
the world feels squint underneath me, the swaying of the
hammock in my ears, rocking me back and forth.

'Right, last song. Then bed, I think,' Jan says, fiddling
with her phone, looking for something that's just right.
'Tomorrow is Christmas Day!'

'Weird,' Verity says. 'Do they acknowledge it here?'

'Oh, did you not read?' Usman says. 'They do the

whole shebang, but down on the beach, laying out these long wooden tables.'

'You can have as many roast potatoes as you like. It's magical. Aha, found it!' she shouts. The plink-plonk of a piano comes blasting out. It's so recognisable, the way I begin to dance, moving from side to side, is like muscle memory.

'Now I've had the time of my life.' Usman's voice is as deep as Bill Medley's and Verity and I look at him, amazed. Jan smiles, proudly, before kicking into her bit, 'and I owe it all to you . . .'

By the time the chorus has kicked in we're all singing, any vocal coordination out the window, shouting all together, 'THIS COULD BE LOVE!'

I'm taken back – once again – to my wedding day. The dance floor lit up in purple and blue, draping everyone in colour. Silver foil hearts rested in my hair – we'd had them fire out over the crowd at the end of our first dance, and by the end of the night kids were running around our ankles, scooping them up and pelting them at each other. During this song, while our friends drunkenly formed a huge circle, knocking hips, I'd grabbed Harry round the waist, gripping onto him so tightly. 'We're so lucky,' he'd whispered in my ear. 'We're so lucky.'

I wonder if Verity can remember. As she's come over and is holding my hand, swinging it in time with the music, squeezing her palm in mine. I can't get precious over songs like this, songs that are played countless times a day, bringing back memories for everyone. But I also can't stop my brain transporting me somewhere else whenever one is played, or when I smell his aftershave or see someone in a jumper he once owned. Even mouthwash reminds me of him – memories of him swirling it in bulbous cheeks, trying not to laugh while I teased him.

I've managed, somehow, to let these memories play out in my brain, a mini movie whirring away while my body takes over the motions and smiles and dances, so that by the time the song has ended, snapping me back to myself and this room, Usman and Jan haven't noticed. They just ruffle our hair.

'Night, girls, see you in the morning.'

We begin to amble back in silence, breathing in the view. We have to cross a huge bridge leading to the main bar to get 'home'. Circling around the rocks at the edge of the bridge are these tiny sharks, the size of small cats, and we watch them for a while.

I can hear, very faintly, Britney's 'One More Time' blasting out somewhere, a few people singing along. My moment of melancholy has lifted and been replaced by the urge to have fun.

'Can I tempt you with one more drink, girls?'

It's Willem, standing behind us. His apron is now splashed with some green liquid, his hair a tiny bit ruffled.

Verity looks over at me. 'It's up to this one.'

I notice that one of his eyes has a fleck of blue in it, contrasting against the deep brown. He has a mole under his left eyebrow and a dimple on his right cheek. I nod.

'Go on then.'

Chapter Twenty

The shots are pale pink, fizzing slightly at the top. The bar is empty apart from Verity and I, wobbling on high stools, while Willem adds a raspberry to each drink.

'Vodka, with freshly crushed raspberries, topped with champagne.' He grins. 'The Willem special. Ready?' He raises his and we clink glasses, the liquid going down my throat easily.

'That's actually really nice, Willem, where did you come up with that?' Verity asks.

'Better than the cheap tequila we're used to,' I add – and even though it's not particularly funny, Willem laughs, loudly, catching my eye.

'Mumbai,' he answers, the laugh still noticeable on his voice. 'I worked in the bars there, winning mixologist awards, and then I got headhunted to come here. I couldn't say no to paradise.'

When we arrived an hour ago he insisted on practising more magic tricks on us – and the four other guests in the bar. They've now left and Verity's head is dropping, the jet lag properly kicking in. We should go to bed really, but there's something bubbling and fizzing within me, my stomach whirring every time Willem looks over at me. It's like we're connected somehow, with an invisible piece of string. There's this thing in the air that we both feel but can't mention.

'And you live here all year round?' Verity's words are slurring a bit – whether it's the tiredness or the shots, I don't know.

'Yep, there's a staff island, over the bridge a bit that way.' He gestures across to where our villas are.

I attempt a flirty giggle but it comes out more like a hiccup. 'Oh my God, a staff island! That's amazing. You guys must have so much fun.'

He runs a hand through his hair, a piece flops forward over one eye. 'We do, yeah. Got a foosball table, kick back with some beers, you know, normal stuff.'

'Foosball! I love foosball, I used to play it all the time with my husband, Harry.' I didn't mean for it to come out. I didn't want to bring Harry here, have his name float in the warm wind. I wanted everything about being here to be kept simple. But it's out now, and Willem looks down at the bar, begins to wipe it with a blue cloth.

'You have a husband?'

Verity's eyes are on me, like I'm a precious vase resting precariously at the end of a table.

'No, um, not any more,' I say, trying very hard to keep my voice straight and hard. Not let it quiver. 'I used to.'

It breaks the spell. I feel the tiredness wash over me – and it feels like we boarded our plane three weeks ago, when really it was just this morning that we bundled into a taxi at 3 a.m. I listen to the wind blowing through the palm trees. Sensing the shift, Willem continues to wipe the bar. Verity looks at me.

'One more drink?' she asks. I can hear how shattered she is. I shake my head.

'You're knackered,' I reply. 'It's just the first night, and it's Christmas tomorrow.'

Willem turns round, his cloth now on his shoulder. He looks at his watch. 'No, ladies, it's Christmas now, it's past midnight.'

I remember being younger, trying so hard to wait up until midnight, hoping that might mean I'd see Santa. I'd lie there, straining to keep my eyes open, thinking I was going to make it – but then I'd wake up on Christmas morning, realising that, at some point, I'd fallen asleep.

'Happy Christmas,' Verity says to us both.

'One more,' says Willem. 'To toast.' He pulls a bottle of champagne from the fridge, pours us each a glass. It feels dainty in my hands, like I could just squeeze it and it would shatter. Willem pours himself a glass, too – holding a finger to his lips. 'Don't tell anyone.'

'Christmas is all about secrets,' I say, and he winks at me when we make the toast. I look away, at Verity, at the sea, at the floodlit pool, glancing back at him one more time as I down my champagne in a quick gulp.

'Right, bed,' I say to Verity.

'Are you sure?' she asks, looking from me to Willem to me once more. 'I don't mind walking back myself. You don't seem too tired.'

'Can I tempt you?' asks Willem. But I keep my resolve.

'Really, it's time to go – we were up so early this morning!' I mime yawning with my arms. Verity's champagne is only half drunk. She looks at me, quizzically, and shrugs at Willem.

'I guess that's us then. Goodnight, Willem,' she says to him.

'Goodnight, Verity,' he replies. 'And Caitlin?'

I turn, just as I've jumped down from the bar onto the sand. 'Yes?'

'Have a very Merry Christmas,' he says as a wave crashes in, reaching my ankles.

I didn't get out of bed last Christmas. I pulled the curtains tight, not allowing a crack of daylight in, and listened to the quiet of outside, staring at the wall. Mum came up every now and then, putting plates at the end of the bed, which I ignored.

Christmas always comes with this strange silence, as the world shuts down and locks itself in. Our street, usually busy with cars and kids, was empty – there was no thud of a basketball against the wall, or Mr G's car spluttering as he struggled to get it started. I felt as if I was drowning in the silence, like someone had filled the room with sand and it was choking me.

A year later and I wake to the sound of wind chimes clattering against each other outside. There's a warm body beside me, the sound of rustling, turning pages. I want to roll over and curl my own body around them, nestle my nose in the soft downy hair on the back of his neck, breathe in his minty smell. But it's Verity beside me, Verity handing me a glass of fizzy water and wishing me a Happy Christmas.

'Harry,' I choke out. 'Oh my God I miss him, I miss him so much.'

She pulls me into her, strokes my hair. 'I know, sweetheart, I know.' I don't let myself stay there for too long though, and roll myself off her, grabbing a towel. 'I can't spend the day crying, Verity, it's Christmas.'

'You can do whatever you like, Cait,' she replies. But I'm resolute.

'We're in paradise,' I remind her, heading for the shower. The day – even being so far away from everything I'm used to – still seems to have that Christmassy silence to it, a weight in the air telling me the day is special. I don't think I want it to be. I just want to make it into a normal day, lazing on the beach. But when I emerge from the shower Verity's sitting reading in a red swimsuit, a Santa hat plonked on the top of her head.

'You've got one too,' she says, gesturing towards the bed where another hat sits.

'Looks like I'm going to be forced to get into the spirit,' I say, feeling the soft red velvet in my hands.

'Probably,' she replies, 'if we go out there. But look, if you don't want to we can just order room service. Hide out in here.'

'No.' I shake my head, knowing if we do that I'll wallow. 'I think distraction, even if it's mega Christmassy distraction, is best.'

'I think you're probably right,' she replies. 'But hey, how about a compromise? We order in breakfast, chill and nap for a bit, then head out for the lunch about one? My book is mega addictive.'

'You and those crime thrillers.' I smile as I coat myself in suncream.

I settle myself on a sun lounger as she wanders inside to order breakfast. I shut my eyes and think about the Christmas before last, with Harry. It was our first in our house together, so we decided to spend it just the two of us. Usually we alternated, one at his family's house then one at my mum's. Each came with its challenges – I didn't like how his mum never offered second helpings, and made me feel guilty for adding an extra spoonful to my plate, her grey eyes trained right on me. He missed his mum's home cooking at mine, and I'd get cross with him. Silly fights really, but ones that mattered, all the same. They almost became as much a part of Christmas as the food and tree.

That year we didn't fight at all. We'd sat down a couple of weeks earlier to plan out the day. 'Do exactly what we want!' was the motto. I wanted to wear pyjamas all day – something I wasn't allowed to do at his mum's house – and he wanted to eat three square meals; he hated how usually he'd just have a breakfast and then one big lunch. 'It feels shameful, Cait,' he'd said to me. 'But I'm always hungry at six!' So we got up and had croissants, strawberry jam and lemon curd for breakfast – we'd each made each other a little stocking, which we were only allowed to fill with useful gifts. I'd teased Harry as mine had contained three different types of toothpaste. 'You get this stuff free!' I'd yelped, chucking a tube at him. 'No, I don't,' he protested. 'That's why it's a loving, thoughtful gift.'

We'd then watched two back-to-back *Wallace and Gromit* films, I drank champagne from an old mug and he had stout, with some blue cheese spread onto crackers with his fingers. 'Best flavour combination,' he'd said, smiling at me, some Stilton stuck in his stubble. We then had macaroni cheese with chips for our lunch, squirting tomato ketchup all over it, chanting 'Do what we want!' as we did so. By teatime, I'd had to change into new pyjamas twice as I'd first spilled wine down a pair and then sat on a pool of melted chocolate with the other. We were both pretty drunk, and had meant to put the roast potatoes on ages ago. I remember just looking at each other and mouthing, 'Chinese?' We'd fallen asleep on the sofa, slumped on top of each other at 8 p.m. It had been the most perfect day.

I try to remind myself that that was a different type of Christmas Day, a break from tradition, and it had been wonderful. So today can be as well.

On our way to the restaurant, every guest and staff member who walks past us wishes us a Merry Christmas. When we pass Willem's bar I look around for him, but he's not there. There's another barman in his place, busy shaking cocktails for two women in gold bikinis. Verity elbows me in the stomach. 'I know who you're looking for,' she trills. I try to pretend I don't know what she's talking about.

'Just wondering if Charles is about,' I say, keeping my eyes well away from hers.

'Yeah, right. You like him. I can tell. There's no fooling me.'

'He's cute,' I say, indeed trying to fool her. 'But a bit sleazy, do you not think?'

'I definitely think he's sleazy,' Verity replies. 'But you don't. C'mon, it's so obvious. And he's into you, too.'

It takes all my strength not to perk up at that, and I fight to keep my body moving in a straight line. But a smirk plays just slightly on my lips.

'Aha,' she shouts, triumphant. 'I see that smile!'

We approach the restaurant, where we see Charles waving at us. 'You could sleep with him, you know?' she says, as I ssshh her.

'Charles is there!' I whisper. 'Besides, I absolutely could not.'

'Yes, you could,' she hisses back, just as Charles opens his arms wide, shouting, 'Merry Christmas!' Behind him the restaurant is completely empty.

'Oh,' I say. 'Are we in the wrong place?'

'No, right place! But we have our Christmas meal some-where even more special,' Charles replies – pointing to a golf buggy with tinsel wrapped around the steering wheel. 'Your chariot awaits, ladies.'

The golf buggy trundles all the way to the end of the island, where we hop off and Charles directs us round a corner where there are five long tables spread across the beach, all filled with guests wearing Santa hats. We spot Jan and Usman, who wave at us, gesturing to the seats opposite them.

'We saved you these seats!' Jan says, hugging us both. Usman has a sprig of mistletoe tucked into his hat, and gives us each a peck on the cheek.

'Not that you'll get to stay in them very long,' he explains. 'First help yourself to the food up there, then the aim is to move about, get to know everyone's different Christmas traditions. Charles rings a bell when it's time to switch seats.'

'You're kidding, right?' asks Verity. 'It's like speed Christmassing?' She begins to look around her. 'That's my worst nightmare,' she adds, only half joking.

'That's what I thought too, honey,' says Jan. 'But honestly, it's a total riot. I knew if I told y'all what actu-ally happens you'd never come.'

'She's a sly dog,' chuckles Usman.

We make our way up to the table loaded with food and begin piling roast potatoes, mash, slices of turkey and cauliflower cheese onto our plates. 'Do you think we can sneak out?' Verity whispers to me.

'It could be fun,' I reply. 'Let's give it a chance.'

It feels so odd sitting back down, the warm temperature coating my skin and the sand beneath my toes as I pierce a roast potato with my fork, biting into it whole.

'So,' I try. 'What would you guys be eating if you were back home?' I ask them.

'Tamales, we always have them,' Jan says, explaining how Texas is so close to Mexico and is such a multicultural place that the towns enjoy a mishmash of different cultures. 'And Usman goes and chops down our tree,' she says proudly.

'There's a barbed-wire wreath that goes on our door,' he replies. 'It's in tribute to our cowboy roots – though it's pretty obvious there's not much cowboy in me.' He chuckles, while Jan loads some meat into a banana leaf and onto our plates.

'Here, try it,' she says. 'It's brilliant, Charles has all the Christmas food shipped in. So you can feel like you're at home.'

We both look down at the tamales, confused. 'You unfold it, and then use the leaf as a plate,' Usman explains, which I do dutifully. It's delicious. I smile at them both, my mouth still full.

'Next you have to have some fruit cake,' Jan says, bundling a heavy chunk full of red cherries into my hand.

'Ah, our fruitcake looks different to this,' Verity says. 'It's darker and we call it Christmas pudding, but I reckon the ingredients are the same.'

'We put a penny in the mixture before we cook it,' I add, remembering how this was always something Harry's mum insisted on, inviting us over two months before Christmas once she'd made her batter. 'If you're the one who finds it, you'll have luck for the whole year.'

'But what if you choke on it?' Jan finds this, for some reason, absolutely hysterical. I've noticed she's like this with everyone. 'No way!' she'll say to the most innocuous thing. 'That's so cool,' she'll enthuse, melting down into giggles. Her enthusiasm for quizzing people is infectious.

A *ting* breaks out and I see Charles, standing at the end of the table, a copper bell in hand. 'Time to switch,' he shouts. Verity and I decide to move but stick together, and plonk ourselves down beside a pretty Japanese girl in a candy-pink dress. She gives a small wave. 'Hello, I'm Aiko, from Osaka, Japan.'

We wave back and introduce ourselves, asking what she eats on Christmas Day. In a matter-of-fact manner, she simply says, 'Oh, KFC.'

Verity leans over, her mouth full of an orange cookie from Sweden. 'Like the chicken?'

'That's right,' nods Aiko. 'We're not a religious country, so our traditions are a little different. It's so popular, you have to order the special menu in advance! They even put Christmas pudding in the bucket!'

We both laugh, our eyes wide open. 'Have the resort got KFC in for you?'

'Well, not actual KFC, that would be pretty hard, but they've done some fried chicken – and look.' She points up to the table. 'They've hand-decorated some special buckets with the logo.'

'It's our favourite time of year to welcome guests,' Charles says, appearing behind us. 'The chefs love to learn new cooking techniques. So don't think you're getting away without sharing something. I hear your region is famous for puddings?'

'Oh,' says Verity, while I look puzzled. 'You mean Yorkshire puddings. Yep, but they're not sweet, they're savoury. And you have to get the batter just right, they're quite easy to mess up.'

'You must come show the chefs!' Charles says. 'And Caitlin, later you have to come and share a recipe with us. Maybe for, um, sounds so strange, but bread sauce?'

I nod, quickly pulling out my phone to text Mum and ask her to ask our next-door neighbours for a proper recipe. I sit for a little while as Aiko talks to the Swedish family across from us. Everyone's chatting away, sharing not just their country's traditions but the ones that are unique to their family as well.

A woman dressed in a black kaftan wanders over to me, her hair pulled back in a loose bun. Just from looking at her I can tell she's going to be French. 'Manon,' she says. As we speak she tells me about her Christmas Eve. 'We always watch the little ones perform their own version of a ballet,' she says. 'The adults paint their faces like nutcrackers and we all gather and watch, drinking champagne and eating cheese.' She moves her hands, telling me the story, every movement precise and elegant. But then Jan comes over, thrusting some Spanish shortbread at us, crumbs spluttering from her mouth as she says, 'You have to try this, it's so good.' Manon laughs and pushes a bit between her lips, as if she's smoking a cigarette.

'What are your traditions?' Manon asks Verity, who has returned from the table, her plate piled so high I'm amazed it doesn't fall.

'We open our presents one by one,' she says. 'The youngest of the family always has to hand them out and everyone watches as they do so.'

Manon does a fake shudder. 'That would be awful! What if you don't like your present?'

'It's all right, we're all pretty good at faking it,' Verity replies.

'I guess it's a British thing,' I say. 'Manners over the truth.'

Harry was never any good at getting me presents: I'd watch Instagram stories on Christmas morning and see other women unwrapping Mulberry bags, enthusing over how soft the leather was. Or jewellery: gold stacking rings or charm bracelets. Meanwhile, I'd have opened something strangely practical, like a handheld hoover ('You mentioned you wanted one in the summer,' Harry had said proudly, 'as The Cat sheds so much.') Or something just a bit odd, like a DVD boxset for a TV show I had absolutely no desire to watch, or a pen that came in its own collector's edition box. I'd sometimes moan about it to Verity and she'd remind me how thoughtful Harry is throughout the year – how he remembers that when I'm sick I only ever want to eat rice with cottage cheese mixed through, and that he always brings me cups of tea first thing in the morning.

'Yeah, it's fake smiles all the way in our household,' I say.

Manon disagrees, wrinkling her nose. 'You Brits!' she laughs. 'I simply say, "Thank you for the thought but this is being returned".'

'Never,' says Verity. 'My mum would tell me off so badly for being ungrateful!'

I'm so grateful, looking back, that I did shove on that fake smile. Because I did actually really enjoy *The Walking Dead*. Even that silly pen – which is way too heavy to actually write with – still sits on my desk in the office, making me smile.

'More champagne, both?' Manon swivels off her chair. 'Then I want to hear about your traditions, Cait.'

Verity uses the tiny amount of time we have alone to check in. 'How you holdin' up?' she says, squeezing my elbow.

I nod. 'I'm fine, I'm enjoying myself.' It's the truth. Last year, hidden under my duvet, the air stale with my own breath, surrounded by crumpled-up balls of tissue, it had felt like I'd never enjoy a Christmas ever again. The whole day, week even, had passed with me staying in that same position – curled up and staring into the dark. I don't think I even cried; it was like my insides had been stripped out of me and I was just a shell. Every now and then, throughout the day, I was aware of a presence beside me – either Mum or Verity, stroking my back, whispering to me. I don't know what they said. I wanted them to leave, to tell them not to bother, that I'd never feel better again. But I couldn't find the words, so they stayed, and every now and then the soft sound of their words or their hands gently pressing on me sent me back to sleep.

'So . . . what do you like most about Christmas?' Manon has returned, three glasses clutched precariously in her grip. We grab them, and as I begin to talk I notice that Aiko, Jan and Usman are all listening too.

'When we're . . . I'm at Mum's—' I say, faltering.

'Which is where?' Aiko asks.

'You know a place called Sheffield?' She shakes her head. 'It's in England.'

'Ah, London,' she says, nodding. I don't bother correcting her.

'Our families are from a little village just outside there,' I nod my head at Verity. 'And we've known each other since we were tiny, so my family will always go round to Verity's in the morning for breakfast. I love the food her mum cooks, plantain and callaloo . . .'

'Which you used to always call callalaaaaloooo,' Verity points out.

'Hey, it's hard to say! So we do that, and then head back to my mum's for lunch.'

'I don't come . . .' Verity says. 'As her mum is a terrible cook.'

I playfully punch her and carry on. 'Where me and Mum enjoy her *delicious* cooking in front of the telly, watching stuff like *Wallace and Gromit* and *Creature Comforts*.'

'Gromit?' asks Manon, managing to make it sound sophisticated somehow.

'He's a dog and Wallace is his owner and together they invent stuff and eat cheese,' I explain. Manon looks confused.

'It's funny, they always get things wrong,' Verity chips in.

'It's just you and your mum?' Aiko asks. Verity is about to interject – I see her mouth open like a fish and then shut again.

'No, sometimes Harry was there,' I say, trying on the past tense for size. 'My husband, that is.'

It's the closest I've come to telling the truth in a long time. I don't know what I'll do if they ask where he is, or what he does, or any more details, but they've moved on – as suddenly Aiko has remembered that she has seen *Wallace and Gromit* and she's laughing about his trousers. 'Shaun!' she is saying. 'He's Shaun the sheep!'

She pulls out her phone and shows us that Shaun the Sheep is actually incredibly famous in Japan. 'Look!' And there's Gromit made out of a pile of rice and Shaun stamped into mini pancakes.

'Where's Wallace?' asks Verity.

Aiko shrugs. 'Not as cute.'

'Poor Wallace,' Verity and I say at the same time, and then start to laugh.

The sun is beginning to set, casting us all in a golden light. 'Better than any decoration we could put on,' says Charles, resting his hand on Verity's shoulder. The others are now gathered round Jan's phone as she's showing them pictures of a cat cafe she went to in New York. 'Look at that one's little face,' she yelps.

'What do you do for Christmas, Charles?' I ask.

'Well, this!' he says, looking up and down the table proudly. 'This is my pride and joy.'

'What about with your family?'

'Oh.' He looks down. 'I lost my wife a few years ago. She was bar manager here at Ozen.'

'I'm so sorry.' Funny how, even when you despise hearing the empty words yourself, you still say them to other people. But, I realise, I am sorry. Sorry that this gentle, caring man who looks so cheerful on the outside – with his red bow tie, tinsel flung around his neck – has lost someone.

'She was a wonderful woman, yes. This was her idea – she used to say to me, "Charlie, there is so much anger in this world, people hating on other cultures, other ideas. Why can't we learn about each other? Treat each other with respect. Even if it happened for only one day, I'd be happy".'

'That's lovely.'

'I know it's just a luxury resort, and still sadness rages across the earth, but I feel like it makes a little difference, somehow, to the atmosphere,' he replies.

I can almost feel the world tipping as he says it. Like I'm aware of it moving, of us all being a tiny dot on this big round planet. I've never really believed in heaven, or spirits, and I hated it, wanted to scream, any time anyone said to me Harry was watching over me somewhere. But just now: black birds swooping across the sky as it turns to pink, its reflection in the blue sea turning almost purple, I believe it.

I think he can see this long table, Verity on it, tipping her head back to drain her glass of champagne. He can see Jan making her way round to everyone, and Usman sitting back, watching quietly. He can see Manon and Aiko showing each other photos of their families. Charles, elegant, tall and strong, topping up glasses. And me: he can see me, sitting here and thinking about us, our traditions. Tears pooling in my eyes as I smile, realising that there's so much more to come. That life is new and exciting and beautiful, and that even if you get ripped open, slowly you'll get sewn back up again.

Chapter Twenty-One

I'm awoken to the sound of Verity singing 'Under the Sea' in my ear. I groan, peeling my eyes open slowly. The curtains have been pulled back and a warm golden light permeates the room. I turn over, muffling the sound of her with the pillow as she goes into the chorus. 'No,' I say. 'I don't wanna get up.'

She rolls me back over, smiles down at me. She's already dressed, in a kaftan covered in a toucan print. 'But, darling, it's better, down where it's wetter,' she deadpans.

'Not on Boxing Day it isn't,' I protest. 'Boxing Day is for dunking cold roast potatoes in bread sauce in front of the telly.'

'Not here!' she replies. 'Here we're throwing everything out the window and embracing new things. That's what we learned last night, isn't it?'

'You were dead against yesterday,' I remind her, impersonating her voice and repeating her request to 'run away'.

'And you made me stay, and were right,' she says. 'Today it's my turn to be right. Come on, I've ordered in breakfast rolls.'

We'd stayed down at the beach until it was completely pitch-black and only the paper lanterns offered us any visibility. People began to disperse, couple by couple, until it was just me, Charles, Verity, Jan and Usman. Jan began to enthuse about their diving trip last year, how they'd seen turtles, and Verity got way too excited, booking us in then and there. I look over at the breakfast that's been wheeled into our room. She's never this organised, she must really want to do this.

'Fine,' I say. 'Only for you.' I crawl to the end of the bed and shove a cheese roll in my mouth.

At the diving school we're greeted by a completely bald man, his tanned head reflecting the sun. He smiles at us, his cheeks going into domes and showcasing the three scars across his cheek that are so thick he looks like he could have been attacked by a tiger. 'Vlad,' he says, pointing at his barrel chest. 'Have either of you dived before?'

We shake our heads, and Verity points to me. 'She's nervous.'

I nod, making a squeamish face. Vlad places a heavy hand on one of my shoulders. 'You're safe with me,' he grunts. 'I'm ex-military, Russian. We don't go down far, about thirty feet.'

'What's the deepest you've ever been down, Vlad?' Verity asks.

'About a thousand feet,' he replies, with a shrug. Verity gasps, while I just look on, slightly confused.

As we scramble into clingy wetsuits I have to ask Verity how deep that is. 'In buses, please,' I say. 'You know how rubbish I am at maths.'

'OK,' she says, sliding a flipper onto her foot. 'Let me think. So our dive, we're going down, like, the length of a little shuttle bus. Vlad's deepest dive is just under the length of the Eiffel Tower.'

'Whoa,' I reply. 'That is deep.'

'Yeah, so you'll be perfectly fine,' she says. We begin to waddle down to the beach in our flippers, like penguins.

'I'm shitting myself about this, Verity,' I whisper. 'A friend of mine did this course when travelling, and she said you have to practise all the bad stuff that could happen. They rip the mask from your face!'

'The best things in life are the things that scare you. Remember?' she reminds me.

All I can think of is Harry and how he always knew when I was afraid. He'd come over, squeeze my hand and instantly I'd feel safe. There's a point in our wedding video where we enter and see all our guests, who stand up and whoop and cheer. I remember feeling so overwhelmed by it all. And you can see my eyes dart quickly to him, and his hand drops down from a wave to grip mine and then my face fills up with a grin.

'The best things in life are what scare us,' I say, back to her. Hoping the words will reach my thumping heart. We keep going, one flipper in front of the other, until we're waist-deep in water and Vlad begins to load us up with our tanks. They're so heavy.

'Vlad, I'm not strong enough to carry this,' I say, a pain spreading across my shoulders.

'In water. Is light,' he says, reaching for me with those big hands and pushing me back into the sea where it feels suddenly as if the tank has fallen off me and there is nothing there on my back at all.

Vlad slowly talks Verity and me through everything we need to know. First we have to learn the hand signals, which I keep getting wrong.

'What's OK?' he asks, and I straight away do a thumbs up.

'No, no, that means you want to go back to boat. OK is this.' He puts his forefinger onto his thumb, to create the classic 'OK' circle I always associate with American TV shows.

'Oh yes, sorry, Vlad. Next time I will get it right.'

Verity nailed everything first time and is off practising on her own. Eventually she comes swimming over and pulls her mask off. 'You're doing this on purpose. Vlad, she is doing this on purpose.'

'What? No, I'm not. It's hard.'

'The OK signal is not hard, Cait.' She turns to Vlad. 'She's scared about the bit where you teach her what happens if your mask comes off. So she's trying to put it off for as long as possible.'

'Ah,' says Vlad, nodding. 'Yes. This is a common diver fear. But it OK. You can breathe, you have regulator.' He points at the mouthpiece attached to my tank. 'You have to not panic. Not breathe through nose. You'll be fine.'

'Not panic when water is flooding my nose, ears and eyes? Vlad, that's a big ask,' I say.

When he chuckles it's this deep booming thing. 'We will get there. I do this forty years. You are safe.'

My brain believes him but my body doesn't. Each time we go down, and he signals to me to remove my mask, I just can't do it. We go up to the surface and Verity comes swimming over.

'Remember Go Ape?' she says. I nod.

'What's Go Ape?' Vlad asks.

'Oh,' I say. 'It's this really scary treetop assault course, Vlad. You'd really love it.'

'Did you just describe Go Ape as really scary, to a Russian soldier?' Verity asks.

I put my hands up. 'It is really scary!' I look over at Vlad. 'It is,' I insist. 'You're entrusted with your own safety and you're super high up in the trees. So if you fall and the harness doesn't catch you that's your fault, as you didn't clip in properly.'

'But remember who was more scared of it than you?' she says.

It all comes flooding back. His face, white as a sheet as we had to practise clipping in on a much lower training course. How he'd darted his hand to mine and gripped it as the man spoke us through what we needed to know. 'Harry!' I say.

'That's right,' she says. 'And you were the one who persuaded him to do it. You took to it so naturally, while he was always lagging way behind the group, terrified!'

I remember coaching him to swing from monkey ropes, something I'd done with total ease. He'd stood on the edge of the platform, shaking his head, his lips pursed in a straight line. The very last obstacle had been a Tarzan jump, where you grabbed a rope and swung into a big net. I'd done it, managing to do the proper Tarzan call and everything. But, after much persuasion, Harry settled for the cop-out obstacle, and returned to the ground shaking. I'd completely forgotten about any of that, only remembering the whizz of air in my ears as I sailed to the ground on the huge zip line, and the pints the four of us, Jeremiah, Verity, Harry and me, had afterwards to celebrate our 'victory' at conquering the course.

With the memory fresh in my mind I duck back under the water and manage to pull my mask off straight away. When we surface Vlad pats me on the back. 'Well done,' he says. 'Now we ready to do it for real?'

The whole journey to our first diving spot I hear nothing. Verity is talking away to me, to Vlad and it doesn't reach my brain. The wind is whipping around me, my flippers are rubbing at my toes and I'm trying to remember all the things Vlad taught us. Repeating his lessons over and over in my mind to make sure they stick. But I'm more excited than nervous now, and when the anchor is dropped down from the boat and Vlad looks over at me making the 'OK' signal, I easily make it back, waddle to the edge of the boat and then, with one foot hovering over first, jump in.

The water feels spectacular, I flip onto my back and look up at the blue sky. 'We will go down slowly,' he says. 'It will feel like we are far from the surface but we are not. You can come up any time. Ready?'

On his count of three I duck under. At first I'm not aware of everything surrounding us. I'm just concentrating on my breathing, on keeping my head clear from 'what if' scenarios, reminding myself how much I trust Vlad. The sound down here is so strange – there's my breathing, but there's also a hissing and clicking sound coming from somewhere – it's almost as if I can hear the chattering small talk of the fishes that have begun to circle us.

There are so many, all different colours and shapes. There's a group of blue and yellow ones with black spots on their backs that come sashaying by, and then I see a little orange and black fish, just like Nemo. I want to smile but have been told that will adjust my mask slightly, so instead I give a little gasp and point at it, hoping Verity can see, too.

It's funny knowing she's right beside me but I can't speak to her. It's as if we're encased in two separate bubbles, each on our own adventure. I concentrate on the fish as they dart in and out of the coral, imagining little back stories for each: that one is bringing food for his wife, those two are falling in love . . . Vlad puts his thumb down, signalling that we can go even deeper.

We end up by some looming dark rocks, which Vlad swims right up to before beckoning to us to follow. Vlad turns his hand into a mouth, opening and shutting. I look between the rocks, and there's an eel his eyes swivel – up to me, as if he's saying hello.

Every now and then I'm hit with the thought of what a great photo this would make. How I could caption my Instagram post with 'found Nemo' and then another, new fish, comes swimming by and I forget it. Down here life is simple: the fish seem so happy darting about, almost playing with each other as they swim in circles around the coral. At one point we're all inside a huge shoal of black fish, which completely surrounds us, and then *whoosh*, they dart off again, clearing the path once more. With them comes another thought, pushing right through to the front of my mind. This is where he is – maybe not precisely here, or even underwater, but somewhere like this: in the uncomplicated peace.

Slowly Vlad brings us back up to the surface and each time he puts his thumb up I shake my head. I don't want to leave this beautiful, straightforward world. Eventually we break through the surface, rolling onto our backs, looking at the blue sky above us. I feel so crazily light, and even when we are pulled up the boat's ladder onto the back of the boat I don't feel my oxygen tanks heavy on my back. We sit on the hard wooden bench of the boat, pull off the tanks carefully and discard our flippers into a bucket. Vlad comes over, handing us each a can of lemonade and some banana bread wrapped up in tissue paper. He drapes towels over our shoulders like he's our father.

'You are a natural,' he says to Verity. 'And you—' He turns to me, gives me the OK sign. 'I knew you could do it, in the end, you a good diver. Both of you, come join the marines with me.'

'Sign us up,' Verity says, while I stare down at the ocean. The rippling surface gives no indication as to what magic lies below it. Verity sensing, somehow, that Harry is on my mind, pulls my hand into hers and squeezes it.

Chapter Twenty-Two

Back at the jetty we find that our legs are like jelly. It feels like they're still underwater and we find it hard to walk up the sand. We sway and bump into each other as if we're drunk, giggling.

'Did you find Nemo?' I ask Verity, and she nods and says, 'And how about that eel?' Then we settle into a contented silence, the only noise the squeaking of our wetsuits coming off and flopping onto the floor as we think about all the incredible creatures we saw down there.

Outside, Vlad is waiting for us, presenting us with our beginners' diving certificates, which we clutch proudly, holding them to our chests for a photo I can post online later. Just as Vlad shouts: 'Say under the sea,' and clicks the shutter button, I feel eyes on me. I glance around. Standing just by the entrance to the diving school is Willem. He's dressed casually, in a blue shirt and chinos, and he comes wandering over as I try desperately hard not to acknowledge his presence.

'Hello, ladies, hello, Vlad.' He tips an imaginary cap at Vlad, who ignores him and stomps off inside.

'Bye, Vlad! Thank you!' Verity shouts to his retreating back. 'Hey, Willem,' she says, smiling in a much more natural manner than I'm managing right now. My smile feels like it's made of plaster cast.

'Drinks later? I'll be starting my shift in a couple of hours,' he says, his mismatched eyes resting on me.

'Yeah, sure,' Verity says, then she looks over at me. 'I mean, maybe, sure, perhaps. We'll see.'

I remain silent. I'm not quite sure what I want and I'm worried if I speak it will come out as gobbledygook.

'Well, it would be great to see you . . . both,' he replies. Then he jogs off, waving to a group of guys sitting down near the shore, beer bottles in hand.

'He fancies you!' Verity says, elbowing me. 'The chemistry between you, mmm!' She holds her hands up to the air. 'I can feel it.'

'Shut up,' I reply, feeling the blush spread across my chest. 'He doesn't.'

'Other people could get away with these feeble protests,' she says, taking my arm. 'But considering your job, you just can't, Cait, you can't!'

She has a point. I hold my own hands up in defeat. 'Fine! He's gorgeous, OK?' I say, as we begin to walk, still swaying, back to our villa.

'So go for it,' Verity replies, as if it is that simple. The sand is uneven beneath our feet. I love the feeling of it between my toes but it's an effort to walk in, I feel like I'm dragging a huge weight with every step. I jog down closer to the waves, where the sand is harder. She chases me, holds onto my arm again. 'You'd be allowed to, you know?' she says, softer this time.

'I know,' I reply. But I don't. Not really. There's no rule book when it comes to this, and there was no drawn-out goodbye, Harry giving me his last wishes, telling me I should be happy. One day he was here, the next he wasn't. So I've tried to push down any stirrings of emotion I've felt towards other men and ignore them completely. But lately it's like my body has come alive again, and when men like Willem or Stu look at me I can feel their stare light up every inch of my skin, like I've been electrocuted.

When we get to our villa I plonk myself down on the sand, just in front of it. 'Do you really think I'm allowed?' I ask her.

'Of course, Cait,' she says, plonking herself beside me. 'He'd want you to be happy.'

'That's why I was angry with you, you know?' I admit. 'About Jeremiah.'

'I thought it was to do with your dad,' she replies.

'I guess it was a bit,' I say. 'But I couldn't understand why you'd want to mess up something so perfect—'

'It wasn't perfect, Cait. And I didn't want to mess it up, it just happened . . . somehow.'

'Yeah, sorry. I'm not explaining myself right,' I say. 'Maybe I was jealous. That you could move on, so easily.'

'It wasn't easy,' she reminds me, her voice a little stern.

'I was so angry at you.' I shake my head. 'I'm sorry. I read everything wrong. I don't know where it came from. I was thinking about how I was stopping myself from moving on, but also how I wouldn't have ever wanted to cheat on Harry. It felt wrong to me that you even had that choice. I don't know, am I making sense? Am I being a dick again?'

She squeezes my shoulder. 'You're not being a dick, you're talking, that's what matters. But . . .' She pauses. 'But Jeremiah and me, we're not Harry and you. You can't live your future through us.'

'That's it,' I say, shaking my head slowly. 'That's what I was trying to do.' I feel like screaming, shouting, jumping up and shaking my body out. There's a strange relief in hearing my innermost thoughts voiced.

'I have all these regrets with Harry,' I say. 'They swirl around my brain. Arguments we had, times I had a go at him because he didn't live up to what I wanted him to be in my head. My constant comparison of our life to other people's . . .' I sigh. 'Then when he died I had this awful realisation: we were happy . . . and I didn't even notice.'

'He noticed though.'

I look over at her. She's pulled a chocolate bar out of her bag and is chewing on it slowly, a little bit of caramel dripping down her chin. 'What do you mean?' I ask.

'When I was with you and Harry, the way he looked at you, how he laughed at all your jokes . . . even the really shit ones,' she says as I see Harry's face float to the forefront of my mind, as if he's there right in front of my eyes. 'There was no doubt he was so, so happy with you. He enjoyed his life, Cait. Really enjoyed it.'

I pick up a handful of sand, begin packing it all around my feet, burying them in the golden dust. 'Why did it have to end so soon then?' I ask, knowing it's a question that can never be answered. She begins to pick up sand, too, adds to my pile, encasing my feet further in it as the sand piles rise up to my shins.

I remember, in the weeks after the accident, waking up in the night, covered in sweat, gripping onto the sheets on the side he slept. How it would take me a minute to remember why he wasn't there, why I was screaming. How when I told Verity this she'd packed two big suitcases and moved in. Then about a month after that, I woke up once again and gripped onto her like I usually did and I scolded myself for being so childish that I needed my best friend to abandon her life, her boyfriend, to look after me. That morning I told her I was fine, that she could move out.

That night I woke up screaming once more, the bed empty. I'd wanted to phone her but felt I couldn't, I didn't want to keep burdening her with everything. My bright, bold friend brought down into the grey with me.

'I know I have to stop faking it, Verity. But how can I carry on now? Selling love when I know it only ever ends in pain?'

She pulls me in close to her as a tear trickles down my cheek. Her face too is wet, her big eyes glossy. 'I'd say that, what he was to you, what your life together was like, made him worth it.'

'Worth it? Verity, my grief isn't like money spent on an expensive meal.'

'I mean, if you could go back, press a button that meant he didn't show up to that housewarming, that you never properly met. Someone else endured this pain for you. Would you do it?'

All of a sudden all I can see are his hands. They were strangely smooth, with three freckles in a straight line on the right, just below his pinky finger. His nails were square, with milk marks scattered across them. I remember after our wedding how I'd sometimes grab his left hand, marvel at the plain gold band now sitting on it. How proud it made me feel, how happy and secure. I wonder if what she's asking is even possible – if we'd never met would someone else be taking this pain for me? Or would he still be here on earth? Did being with me set off the chain of events that led to that van crashing into him that day? Even if it did, I think, he would still be somewhere, waiting for me. I can't imagine a universe in which we would never meet.

'Yes.' I nod my head. 'This has been so awful, but it would be so much worse to never have known him.'

She picks up a shell that's beside her, hands it to me. It feels smooth as I flip it over and over in my palm. 'Well, there you have it. There it is.'

'I won't be able to go back, though,' I say. Because she's right, love is worth it but it's impossible for me to be the girl I was before, with rose-tinted ideas of what love is. 'Back to the old me.'

'No one is expecting you to,' she says, gently pulling her feet from the sand and shaking them off. 'You can change and grow with this, and I'll love you just the same. You can build someone new out of this pain.'

I try that on for size. The idea that I'm someone new. That I'll continue to grow into myself, that I've not stopped. 'Hmm,' I say. 'I wonder what she'll be like.'

'Brilliant. She'll be fantastic,' replies Verity, standing up, brushing the sand off her in a flurry. 'It's getting a little chilly, I'm going to go back inside, you coming?'

I shake my head. I want to stare out at the sky for a little longer, feel the shell in my hands, the sand packed around my toes. But there's something else I want to do. And once I muster the courage to stand up and head across there, I hope I won't regret it.

Chapter Twenty-Three

He's sitting at the bar when I arrive, sketching, glancing up at the ocean every now and then before bringing his pencil down, firmly and deliberately. I watch him from afar for a little while, assessing if this is something I actually want to do. The bar is quiet; there's a couple tucked into a corner, two rosy-pink cosmopolitans sitting untouched on the table in front of them. His arm is draped over her while she reads her book. Every now and then he ducks his head to kiss her. It's worth it, I think, and I go striding over, keeping my head up. As soon as he spots me he puts the notebook down, mouths 'drink' at me. I love the way he moves his mouth, like he's licking me with just the word.

I nod. 'Champagne, please.' He turns around, bends over for the bottle — his trousers are tight, I notice, glancing, just quickly. He turns back around, pops the bottle while looking right at me.

'You like your champagne,' he says. 'I've noticed this about you.'

'It's fun having it on tap,' I say. 'I feel like Beyoncé. So, anyway . . .' I lean forward, resting my forearms on the bar. 'What's your favourite thing about working here, Willem?'

He moves closer, so close I can feel the heat coming from his skin. He leans against the bar. If it wasn't there, we'd be touching. 'Meeting people,' he says, then pauses for a second. 'People like you.' I try my best to maintain eye contact with him as he locks me into it. The couple in the corner are now kissing, their drinks still untouched. I feel the urge to start blabbering on about how I love meeting people too, but instead I let the moment linger. I feel like I'm bathing in it.

'You dived today?' he says, still looking at me. 'Tell me about that.'

I do, enthusing about how I feel I've discovered another world and how it really did feel like I was in another realm, where none of my problems existed. He tells me that's what he likes about diving, too, that he tries to get out there most mornings. We go back and forth sharing our favourite animals and the best things we've seen in our lives. I gasp when he tells me he once swam with a group of five turtles. My champagne glass never gets empty; he keeps topping it up as the bubbles rush from my head to my toes and I feel full of amber, like I'm golden and sparkling.

The couple in the corner leave at some point, weaving their way back along the beach, giggling. Willem clears away their glasses, then pulls a stool up so he's facing me. The bar still separates us and if I could tear it apart with my hands, I would. A piece of his hair, dark and shiny, flops in front of his face. Instinctively I reach across and brush it to the side. He grabs my hand with his, holds it in between his palms. I feel as though I've stopped breathing. Like all the world around me has faded into a fog that encases us. I know what I want and I don't want to wait for it any longer. I'm sick of filling the time in between getting it with small talk and laughter for jokes I don't find that funny.

'What time do you finish?' I let the words come out, let them guide me. I have to trust my pounding heart, the electricity in the air. He looks up at the clock, the skin on his neck so brown, so smooth. I imagine kissing the natural dip of his clavicle. He looks back at me. My hair is frizzy from the dive today, I'm just in a tatty orange cotton dress, which is slightly misshapen so that one shoulder keeps sliding down. I don't have any make-up on and my cheeks and nose are slightly rosy – I didn't apply enough sunscreen earlier. But his eyes transform me. In his gaze I feel different, more powerful, capable of anything.

'I can,' he coughs, 'finish up now.'

'Will you show me the staff island?' I ask, shaking my hair out, letting it fan around my shoulders. His face spreads into a grin, more mischievous than I've seen before. This isn't his customer-facing smile – it feels like it just belongs to me.

He begins to slide the shutters down across the bottles of spirits. 'Give me five minutes,' he says, and disappears from behind the bar. I spin my stool around, look across at the sea, concentrate on the sound of the waves breaking onto the sand. The clock is ticking so slowly. I look up at the sky, it's inky black and scattered with stars. The air is so warm but my skin is peppered with goose pimples – I rub at my arms, swing my legs on the stool, anything to distract me from this period of waiting.

Then I hear a *ting, ting* and look round. Willem's there, on a white bicycle.

'Your carriage, my lady,' he says indicating the back.

'A backie? I haven't done one of those in years!' I squeal as I jump on. Willem stands up to pedal as I perch on the seat. It's pitch-black as he winds us through the streets, past lots of villas that look identical, their doors open to reveal sparkling turquoise swimming pools. The tree canopy stretches above us, and all I can hear are the sounds of tyres against the sand and a hooting from somewhere far away. We cross a narrow wooden bridge and I keep my hands firmly around Willem's waist, refusing to look down at the sea below me. When we step off I'm dizzy and stumble over my own feet and Willem catches me, his big hands holding onto my shoulders.

The foosball table is right on the beach, as are a few white sofas and a cool box. 'The staff room,' he says, grandly gesturing to it. I rush over to the table, grab the tiny white ball and circle it in my hands.

'We have to place a bet.'

'OK, if I win, you kiss me,' he says, smooth as anything. I swallow, remember the role that I am playing.

'And if I win . . . you kiss me.'

With that he's on me, his hands running all through my hair, down my sides, resting. I hadn't expected his lips to feel so different. He kisses gently and I'm trying not to think about how Harry's kisses were rough. Willem tastes of the sea, and he's slowly pulling each strap of my dress down, kissing the skin underneath, slowly, as he lays me down in the sand.

When I wake up the next morning I feel as though I'm on the beach still. There's sand gritty beneath me, and the sunlight is permeating through my shut eyelids. But when I prise them open I find I am in my bed, it's just that the sand from my encounter with Willem is now flooding the sheets. I'm completely coated in it, and my hair is knotted at the back of my head and itchy. The curtains have been drawn open and as I struggle into a seated position, I can see the sea – now turquoise, in stark contrast to how deep and black it looked last night.

I squeeze my eyes tightly shut. My lips feel tender, and I smell, unmistakably, of sex. I try to remember that feeling of Willem on top of me last night, his weight pinning me down, how I gasped at how much I'd missed that feeling; a man's heaviness on top of me. How incredible it had felt. At the time.

I shiver now, scratch at my irritated legs. My stomach grumbles – I didn't eat any dinner last night and it's angry with me. On the side table there's a can of Coke and a note from Verity: *Thought you might need this, gone to breakfast, can't wait to hear about last night.* She's drawn a winking face and a big thumbs up. I roll over, crack the can open and pour the dark, strange liquid down my throat. I push the covers off me, grab my sunglasses and slide the doors open, letting the sunshine and the heat come into the chilly air-conditioned room. There's a fruit bowl on the side. I grab a banana from it and plonk myself down. I struggle to eat it, it feels claggy in my mouth. I chew a few times, then spit it out in the sand. Why do I feel so wretched? This isn't fair. My emotions are coming through me, thick and fast and totally unwanted. I put my sunglasses on to mask my tears, but they're encrusted in sand. Sand from Mexican beaches, from that resort where we'd been so happy. And now I can feel the sweat of another man on my skin.

I'm aware of the shadow of a person above me, someone sitting down beside me. I smell artificial coconuts, the smell of tanning oil. I'm curled into myself, my chin resting on my knees.

'Caitlin, are you OK?' Jan strokes my arm.

Usually I'd plaster on a watery smile, insist I was fine. It's why old friends of mine have since said I 'pushed them away' after Harry died; I refused to listen to them as they tried to comfort me. But there's something about Jan's voice and how I know, after this week, I'll never see her again.

'No, I'm not,' I sigh.

'You're sobbing in paradise, I can see that. What's wrong?'

I want her to call me 'duck' like my mum does. I want her to cup my elbow, make me posh pasta and whisper to me that everything is going to be OK. I'm sobbing properly now, snorting with rushes of snot. Jan reaches into the basket she's carrying, unearths a crumpled tissue, hands it to me. I want to tell her the truth, about Harry, about my business, everything. But the words can't come out.

'Willem,' I splutter. 'I slept with Willem.'

'And what's wrong with that, honey? He's hot.' She's manoeuvred herself up beside me now, and is stroking my back, smiling gently at me to carry on.

'I'm married,' I twist my wedding ring round and round on my right hand. I'd moved it there recently, so it wasn't always there, winking at me, reminding me I am no longer a wife. 'But, but he's, he's . . .'

I begin to gasp for air and she hands me some water. 'Sip that slowly, sweetheart, don't rush yourself, I'm not going anywhere.' She whispers that last part again. 'I'm not going anywhere.'

I try to listen to the ocean, let my heart slow down in time with each lapping wave.

'Breathe through your nose, in, one, two, three, out, one, two, three . . .'

Her brassy, cowgirl voice has lowered into a yoga teacher whisper as she breathes with me, moving her hands up and down with each second counted.

'My husband, my Harry . . . he died.' Most people gasp when they hear that. They gasp and then they search around for words. But she doesn't. She nods, curtly.

'I see, oh my sweetheart, I see. I knew something was up. I knew it.'

'You did?' My crying has subsided, but my voice sounds childish, squeaky.

'Oh yes, that friend of yours, sweet girl, she's the one you've said is heartbroken. But she seems fine, laughing away, answering questions for you, looking at you like you are wrapped in cotton wool . . .'

That's how everyone looks at me. But Jan is looking at me with steely eyes, like she's just discovered I am actually a weightlifter, or an actress tipped to get an Oscar.

'My first husband died,' she says, so simply. Like she's telling me it might rain tomorrow.

'When?'

'Ten years ago now. When did your Harry die?' Most people are afraid of that word. I've become afraid of it too. Saying I 'lost' him, or he's 'passed', or sometimes I say 'he's just not here any more'. It feels physically painful to hear her say it like that, so bluntly. But it's almost a good type of pain, like when you press down on a bruise to remind yourself that you're here, you're feeling something.

'Pretty much a year ago,' I reply.

'You must still feel very angry.' It feels like she's torn my skin off, replaced it with something see-through. Like she can see the blood rushing through me, how it pounds at the walls of my veins.

'Sometimes the force of it terrifies me, like I don't want anyone to be happy,' I admit.

'I was the same, sweetheart, the exact same. I drank a lot, back then. Picked fights with random women in bars for no reason. Anything to release the deep anger within me.'

'Does it pass?' I say, thinking how I haven't been releasing it. How I've been bathing in a vat of my own anger.

She pauses. 'Yes, it does. But you have to let it, ride all the emotions, not pretend you're fine when you're not. You can't run from grief, it will always catch up with you. But tell me, sweetheart, have you spoken about this to anyone? Verity, does she know how you feel?'

'In the beginning, yes. She was amazing. But as time went on I found it harder and harder to explain to her, to anyone, that I still wasn't OK. I think that's what they wanted from me—'

'Who's they?'

'Everyone. Everyone always asking if I was OK, not ready for the answer. There was only so much that Verity could say. I got bored of hearing her, got bored of my own voice. So I began to pretend I was fine to her, to everyone . . .'

'Lots of people do that, it feels simpler somehow. I know I did.'

I take a deep breath. 'Bet you didn't go as far as I did . . .'

'I dunno, I think drinking until your smile and laugh feel real is quite a fakery.'

'But you didn't tell strangers he was alive, did you?'

'What?'

'I have been, pretending. I, oh God, this is going to sound so crazy but, in my work, I've been acting like he's still alive. Talking to my clients about him. Posting photos of him online. You see, I matchmake for my job. I help people fall in love. And that was too hard to do, without him beside me.'

'You've been helping people fall in love this entire year?'

I nod, a strangled laugh escaping me. 'Yeah, it's a bit nuts, I know.'

'Did you ever watch *Black Mirror*?' she says, while I shake my head. 'There was once this episode where a woman lost her husband and she had him digitally recreated. My friend in England sent me the episode and I remember thinking, "God, if I could do that, I would, I'd pay anything to have him back again". It sounds like that's what you were trying to do, keep him alive in your own way.'

'I guess it was a bit like that. I've stopped now, had to. Now I want more than anything to just feel normal again. That's what Willem was about, trying to be normal.'

She squeezes my knee. 'Sweetheart, I hate to break it to you – you'll never feel normal again. But, and this is the important part, you won't always feel like this. This torn up.'

That's exactly how I feel right now. Like someone has wrung out my stomach, twisting it like a wet dishcloth.

'I feel like I've cheated on him, like I got drunk and cheated on my husband and I know you're going to say that I'm allowed, that I shouldn't feel guilty, that Harry would want me to move on, but it's almost worse for that reason.' The words are coming out fast now, like they've all been caught up in a net at the bottom of my stomach and Jan has set them free.

'That's not what I was going to say at all, it's all horse crap, that stuff. You feel how you feel,' she says. 'Of course it's going to feel wrong to get with another man. And Harry wanting you to move on? I doubt he'd want you to move on with a waiter on the beach.'

'You're supposed to be making me feel better!' I say, but I'm smiling now. 'Hey – how did you know it was on the beach?'

She pulls me in for a cuddle. 'Oh, sweetheart, that's Willem's move. Staff island?'

I nod into her shoulder. 'Thought so,' she says. 'But hey, he's a sweet guy. Just a player, that's all.'

The thought of Willem using me like a disposable tourist causes my emotions to swing again. I begin to cry, quietly.

'Oh no, hey now.' She pulls me off her shoulder, grips me with both hands. 'Look at me. Caitlin, look at me. You aren't to shed any tears for Willem the Womaniser, you hear me?'

'But shouldn't it have been special? With someone who might end up loving me? My first guy since Harry, and he's a stranger.'

'How did it feel last night?'

I think back to the feeling of sand against my back, the sky twinkling above me, Willem breathing in my ear. How I knew I was drunk, I knew the next day I might regret it, with guilt twisting my intentions and memories, but how in that moment it felt right.

'Like it was something I needed to do,' I reply.

'Exactly. Sex is complicated, love even more so – you can't judge your actions, sometimes you just have to go with them. And, this is the most important part, you weren't hurting anyone. Repeat that after me. I wasn't hurting anyone.'

'I wasn't hurting anyone.' I almost want to scream it into the blue skies, break up the postcard-perfect landscape with my voice. I imagine the blue skies shattering, the palm trees falling down, the calm sea erupting into violent waves.

'There's my girl.' She pats me on the back. 'I'm going to leave you here now, we'll see you at lunch later. I need you to remember that how you feel is normal. You must never punish yourself for how you feel.'

I lie back on the sand, try and let those words sink in. I want to absorb them into my skin, in the way I rub on sun lotion. I want so badly to feel them. To be able to act on them. But instead I fall deeply asleep.

Chapter Twenty-Four

I find Verity at our regular breakfast table, which she's overloaded with fruit, toast, muffins and even a plate of sweetcorn pasta, which turned cold long ago. 'They were going to shut the kitchen,' she explains, gesturing to the mini buffet she's selected. 'I didn't know what you would want.'

I pick up some hard, cold toast and begin spreading some raspberry jam on it. 'Can you believe we've got to go back to empty fridges today?' I say, looking at the clock. The speedboat to take us back to the airport arrives at 4 p.m., for us to catch an overnight flight back home.

Verity holds a single hand up. 'Don't!' she cries. 'I'm happily living in denial.' She puts her book down, the pages fanned out, and takes a long, happy slurp of her drink, which is the colour of clover. She points at it. 'There's rum in here.' She laughs, honk honk honk. 'Figured it's the last time I'll be able to drink at breakfast for a long time.'

'Good idea.' I signal to the waiter, pointing at her drink. 'Two more, please!' I say as he comes over and pours some fizzy water into each of our glasses, raising an eyebrow at us both.

'Certainly,' he replies, then saunters off.

'Was that eyebrow shady?' Verity whispers. 'Is he judging us?' She honks once more. 'I don't care, I feel delighted with myself. Anyway!' She rubs her hands together, a gleeful look spreading across her face. 'I need a drink, I want to hear about last night . . .' She drops her voice. 'With Willem.'

I smile. The naughty look that she's got on her face takes me right back to when we lived together. Whenever I brought a guy home and she didn't know who it was, she would drag her bean bag out into our hallway and settle there with her duvet and a pile of gossip magazines. When they tried to sneak out, shoes in hand, they'd find her there, waving at them, munching on a bag of salt and vinegar Squares. Then she'd dive into my room and ask for all the details.

'Well, we slept together,' I say now, glancing around to make sure none of his bosses are there.

'Duh!' she says. 'You couldn't be near that man and not sleep with him. God, he's gorgeous.'

'I thought you said he wasn't your type!' I reply.

'He's not,' she protests. 'No tattoos. But still . . .' She does a low wolf whistle. 'So tell me, how was he?'

'Good.' I blush.

'You know I want more than that! Tell me about his penis!' she hoots, just as our waiter places down our two drinks with a flourish. He tuts, loudly, as he does so.

'Now he's definitely judging us,' I whisper, waiting for him to leave earshot before carrying on. 'And I'm not telling you about his penis.'

She juts her bottom lip out. 'Fine, spoilsport. What can you tell me?'

I pause, thinking of Willem's lips on my neck, how he traced kisses all down my body as I looked up at the night sky. 'It was on the beach, at the staff island.'

'Rebellious, hot,' she says, nodding in approval.

'And he was . . .' I pause. Different, is what I want to say. Different to Harry. 'Gentle, kind, um . . . attentive.' I'm finding this so much harder than I used to. Verity used to ask questions about his body, his moves, and I'd giggle and tell her until she said, 'Gross, stop now,' and then we'd order a pizza and gossip about all the other things that happened on the night out. Then it hits me: back then all these men were the pathway to the love of my life, it didn't matter if the sex was bad or if they turned out to be total assholes. As I would always tell myself, I was learning from them, and they would lead me to the right person. Now, Willem is the first man on a new path – the path away from Harry.

'And did you . . .' She takes another, long slurp from her drink. It's almost finished. I copy her, downing a good few inches from mine, then pick up the slice of kiwi placed delicately on the side and munch it thoughtfully. 'Come on! This pause is killing me!' she cries, and then I nod, smile at her and she raises her hands up high and cheers, clapping loudly. The couple at the table next to us glance over and smile.

'Go Willem!' she says. 'I mean I expected it of him, you know my speciality—'

'You can always tell if a man will deliver on an orgasm,' I say. She puts her hands together in a prayer pose.

'And I thank God for that,' she laughs.

Then she looks at me, the smile not quite erased from her face – it's still there, dancing naughtily in her eyes. But her mouth transforms itself into a small pout and I know she's about to ask me a serious question.

'How do you feel today?' she asks, scanning my face for clues. I've kept my sunglasses firmly on my face, masking my itchy, red eyes. I didn't want them to be the first thing she saw.

'I felt shit this morning,' I shrug. 'Had a good long cry on the beach.'

'Oh, Caitlin,' she says. 'I'm sorry.'

'It's all right, I needed to be alone . . . But then Jan came along.'

'Oh no!' Verity shakes her head. 'Curse of the holiday friends.'

'No, she was great,' I say, thinking of how kind Jan had been, how reassuring, how real. 'She lost her husband too, a long time ago. It was nice talking to someone who understands.'

Verity nods. I hope I've not upset her, but she just carries on talking. 'What did she say?'

'That I can't beat myself up for how I feel, that it's OK to feel angry at the world, at my friends . . .' I pick up a bit of the pasta, nibble on it, then put it back down again. Look at her. She smiles back at me.

'Wise woman,' she says. 'Your friends, well, this friend, will be here for you no matter what. No matter how badly you behave.'

'Even when I don't tell you about the size of Willem's penis?' I say.

She nods, solemnly. 'Even then.'

We both break out into these big grins, the type that will eventually hurt all along your jaw. I can feel the air between those smiles – warm, golden and unbreakable. If I could dive into it I would. I wrinkle my nose up.

'She told me Willem's a player, that he's always getting with guests,' I say. Verity signals to the waiter, two more, she mouths at him.

'Of course,' she says, totally unfazed.

'You knew that?'

She looks at me, baffled. 'So did you!' she says.

I think back to the way Willem looked at me, to all the compliments he paid me. I shake my head. 'I don't think I did,' I say.

Our drinks are plonked down. The waiter steps back, surveys our table. 'Can I clear all this away, please?' There are crusts of toast swimming in the pasta sauce, half a muffin in the bowl of fruit, its crumbs clinging to some browning banana slices. Verity shakes her head.

'No, we're still eating,' she says. 'Oh, in fact. Some chips would be lovely. For dunking.'

He looks at her, then at the table, then back at her again. She grins up at him. 'What in?' he asks. She points at the pasta. 'The sauce. Waste not, want not and all that.'

'Whatever you need,' he replies, through gritted teeth. 'Chips are on their way.'

'Now, back to Willem,' she says, as I pluck out the crust from the sauce and pop it in my mouth. 'You're telling me, Caitlin the Matchmaker, that you didn't know he was a player? My special skill may be spotting men who give orgasms, but yours . . . yours, my dear friend, is hunting out the good ones. You've built a career on it!'

'Ha,' I say. 'I never thought of it like that before, I guess you're right. Maybe deep down I did know.'

'Your first man after Harry couldn't have been a nice guy,' she says. 'Someone that would get attached to you – because, let's face it, they all fall in love with you—'

'No they don't!' I protest.

'Agree to disagree.'

'You're very kind to me,' I reply, shaking my head. 'So you're saying I used my special skill to seek out the perfect shag?'

'It's like you're coming after my crown. I warn you, it's not easy at the top. But seriously, I do think this is what you needed, in the strangest of ways . . .'

'You're right, actually. God, how irresponsible. My grief needed a barman to sleep with!'

She honks. 'Yeah, it probably did, I mean obviously it's more complicated than that, but you could have come here, done yoga, meditated, all those things and still not come to any conclusion. Returned home with glowing tanned skin but still shitty insides. Looking at you now, I think you seem more OK than I've seen you in a long, long time.'

I look up at the clock. It's almost noon. 'We're going to have to go soon,' I say, just as our bowl of chips arrives. 'We need to pack and that wardrobe is a bomb site.'

'Don't try and distract me,' she says, scooping up a handful of chips.

'I'm not, I agree with you. So much waits for me back home, but I'm really glad I came, and I'm so glad you were here with me.'

She reaches across, squeezes my hand in hers. 'Me too,' she says, tears beginning to pool in the bottom of her eyes. She releases her hand, wipes them away. 'But I actually meant you were distracting me from my chips.'

We both begin to laugh, the waiter looking on disapprovingly and the couple next to us, obviously sick of our noise, push back their chairs to leave. But I don't care. The laughter bubbles within me, and I have a strong feeling that she's right. I'm going to be OK.

As we drag our cases up towards the jetty to where the speedboat waits for us, Verity mutters to me, 'We could

just not go,' I mean, claim squatters' rights or something.'
'What they going to do about it?'

Charles is waiting for us and comes rushing up to take
our cases off us. 'Girls! You should have called, we'd have
taken them for you,' he scolds.

'We need a taste of reality, Charles,' I say. 'You've
spoiled us.'

'I'm going to miss being Beyoncé so much,' says Verity.

'I thought you might say that,' says Charles, chuckling
as he reaches for the two beige bags he has hanging off
his arm. 'These are your gift bags, look inside.'

We pull them open and there, nestled amongst a hat
and a fridge magnet in the shape of a palm tree, is a mini
bottle of champagne. 'For your journey,' he says, nodding.
'Now, let me help you board the boat.'

He holds one hand out and I'm about to grab it when
I hear a squeal, and the clatter of footsteps making their
way up the wooden pier. 'Wait! Don't let them go yet!'
Jan and Usman are racing towards us, waving frantically.

'Oh phew, we caught you,' Jan says, gasping for breath as
she arrives. 'Bloody Usman ordered an extra round of cocktails.'

'You asked me to!' protests Usman. She lightly punches
him on the shoulder. 'Sshh, don't tell them that!' she says,
before pulling us both into a big hug. 'Can't you let them
stay?' she asks Charles, who simply shakes his head.

'Not unless you pay their bill,' he says.

'One day,' nods Jan. 'I bloody well will, that'll show
you, eh, Charles?' He smiles at her fondly.

'Stop distracting them,' he says. 'They'll miss their plane.'

She keeps a hold of us, and then whispers in my ear.
'You feel what you feel, you hear me? You have my
permission.' Then she lets us go, and she says to Verity:

'Don't go breaking any more hearts, eh?' And Verity laughs, shrugs and tells her she'll try.

We climb onto the boat. It's been four days and yet it feels only hours ago we were last on it and Usman was pulling beers out for us. But it also feels like years have passed, we've changed so much in this time. It's an odd feeling, but one I like. We're waving so hard at everyone now, Charles is hooting on a conch shell as the boat revs up and begins to whoosh away. My arm starts to hurt and eventually I place it down in my lap. Verity keeps on waving, tears forming in her eyes. She keeps going until the island is so far away, and Charles, Usman and Jan are just tiny dots on the horizon.

'Caitlin?' she asks, as I reach for the cool box.

'Hmm,' I say, not looking up as I scramble around for it. It should be under here somewhere.

'When we get home I'm moving into yours for a bit, OK.' It's a statement, rather than a question. I find the cool box, hand her up a bottle of beer, which she cracks open expertly with her hands.

'You don't have to,' I say. 'I'm f—'

But she holds up one hand. 'Don't tell me you're fine. Besides, this isn't about you.' She looks out at the sea, the boat is picking up speed now; we're rocking together, almost flying over each wave as water sprays us. 'I need it, OK? Otherwise I'll go running back to Jeremiah, out of sheer boredom. And we can't be having that, can we?'

'No,' I say, smiling, gripping her hand. 'That's true.'

I watch as our island disappears into a dot, as if it was never really there at all. I pull her in for a hug and realise that I'm not scared of going home at all. In fact, now, I'm rather looking forward to it.

★

We arrive back at mine around midnight, shivering, our warm, tanned skin just isn't used to the freezing UK temperatures, and my heating hasn't been on all week. 'Where's Joseph when you need him?' Verity says, pulling in her gigantic suitcase. 'I'd love a bath right now.'

'I'll run you one,' I say, shouting through the kitchen as I flick the heating on. 'Let you be Beyoncé just a little while longer. There's some clean pyjamas in the drawer for you.'

'I could pop open my little champagne!' she says. 'Bring a taste of Ozen to Sheffield.'

'Exactly,' I say, carrying through two cups of tea. 'You know it's about 5 a.m. there. Isn't that strange?'

'Ugh, I don't want to think about it,' she says.

I take a slurp of my tea. I've definitely missed that. There were only herbal teas beside the kettle in our villa – we didn't flick it on once. Seemed pointless when there was a minibar full of champagne. 'I'm seeing Ade tomorrow,' I sigh. 'Ade thought it would be best to get crisis mode in operation as soon as possible.'

'She's so bossy, remember you can take charge. You are, after all, the boss,' Verity reminds me.

'I know, but I trust her. She's got my best interests at heart.'

'Yeah, she does,' Verity agrees. 'And then it's the wedding. God, they planned that in record time.'

'I know,' I say. 'I'm sure everyone thinks it's too fast, but I think it's sweet in a way. How quickly they knew.'

'Each to their own,' muses Verity.

Dread swirls in my stomach, which I try to ignore but can't. 'I said Harry could come,' I say, remembering how

I'd just ticked the box that said we both could come and posted it with my eyes glued shut.

'They'll understand, Caitlin,' she says. 'As soon as you wake up tomorrow, write them a little email explaining. I can help you phrase it. Remember—'

'We're now being nothing but honest. You don't think they'll think I'm mad?'

'You said they're nice, didn't you?' she asks. I nod, cradling my tea. 'Well then, they'll get it. Only dickheads wouldn't. And you don't want to go to a wedding of two dickheads, do you?'

'They're not dickheads,' I say, thinking of Elijah's face as I'd rounded the corner in that bright orange fish hat. His warm smile breaking across his face. She's right, I can tell them.

'Thanks, Verity,' I say, yawning. 'I'm going to go run you that bath now.'

Chapter Twenty-Five

I haven't been back to the office since Stu and Ade found me under my desk. As I unlock the door and step in it feels like walking onto a movie set. Everything is so familiar – my motivational pictures, the grey couch . . . The mug I was sipping from has been washed up and placed on the side, like a haunted relic from another time. It's the thirtieth of December, that dead time between Christmas and New Year, and the streets are quiet. I like that even if I did send any emails no one would pay attention to them for days. Even Morwena's followers have calmed down. I haven't received a nasty comment since Christmas.

I walk around, fiddling with everything: the house plants have been watered, and mostly it's neat and tidy so there's not much for me to do to fill the time until they both arrive. I take a seat at my desk, open up my laptop and look at the web design Stu has already worked so hard on. The background is a dusky, millennial pink and he's taken the old pictures of Harry and me and made them look like they've been taken in an old-fashioned photo booth, the strips of pictures scattered around the edge of the site like it's a scrapbook. 'I've found love,' the banner reads, 'now I want to help you feel as happy as me'.

I remember when they first showed me it, how I'd looked at those photos and read the words and felt this crushing feeling in my chest. Like someone had taken my lungs and squeezed them, pushing the air right out of me. 'It's beautiful,' I'd managed. 'Really beautiful.' Stu had looked so proud of himself, dropping his head down, his hair flopping over his eyes, his cheeks turning red. Now I am going to have to tell him to change it all. Hopefully he'll understand why.

I open up Instagram on the browser. I deleted the app on the way home from the Maldives – having been reunited with my phone I found I had no desire to post any pictures from our trip just yet. I thought of the people following me, how it might diminish the good times they'd had over Christmas to see this gorgeous five-star resort. I didn't want them looking around their living room, at their drunken auntie napping, and feel bad.

I'll have to post eventually, it was one of the conditions of the trip, as well as a write-up on my website, but I'll consult Ade on the best time to do so. Although Ozen might not be too happy with what I can offer them now: the nasty comments may have stopped, but since Morwena's post about me I've dropped about 3,000 followers.

Ade and Stu come bundling in, brandishing plastic horns, which they toot at me. 'Happy Christmas!' shouts Ade, with Stu just out of step behind her. I smile and clap but the whole thing falls a bit flat – I could almost imagine Ade cornering Stu just before they came in and whispering, 'Let's go in big, to cheer her up.'

It feels a lot less tense when they put the horns down, settle on the sofa and Stu looks me right in the eye and says, 'How are you?'

I pause, trying to think how I really feel. 'Embarrassed, sad . . . but better, now everything is out in the open.'

'You don't need to be embarrassed.'

'Ade, I faked a husband to thousands of people and then had a meltdown that involved hiding under this very desk.'

'Hey, he was real once,' she says, and then her hands dart up to her mouth. 'Shit, sorry, was that the wrong thing to say?'

But I'm already laughing, as is Stu. 'Seriously, she did think you'd made him up for a while. Hired a model or something like that . . .'

'To be my imaginary friend? God, Ade, how sad do you think I am?'

'I dunno, we knew you were hiding something and I tend to go a bit far with my theories sometimes.'

I know if Harry was here he'd say, 'If she was going to hire a model do you not think she'd hire someone more attractive?' I'm tempted to make the joke, but it feels unfair somehow, like laughing at someone behind their back. Instead I shrug and say, 'I guess he is a bit like an imaginary friend . . . I still talk to him all the time, you know?'

Stu nods. 'I know it's not the same, but I do that with my granny sometimes. Tell her what I've been up to. I remember telling her I'd broken up with my ex . . .' He shakes his head. 'Granny always hated Kim.'

'High five to Granny,' says Ade, holding her hand up, which Stu dutifully slaps, rolling his eyes at me.

'I'm going to go get myself a coffee, anyone else?'

I point to my mug. 'Please.'

He gets up and goes through to the tiny kitchen area that's off to the side of the office. Ade watches his back as he goes.

'He's nice, Stu,' she says to me, once she's certain he's out of earshot. I know what she's getting at. I don't take the bait, murmuring a 'mmm-hmm' under my breath, so she presses further. 'Single, too . . .'

'Thinking of adding him to the books?'

She laughs at that. 'Touché, Cait,' she says.

Stu comes back over, hands me the mug. 'What we talking about?' he asks.

'Nothing.' I shake my head. 'The . . . the holiday. Anyway,' I say, clearing my throat in a manner I hope sounds businesslike. 'Obviously I've kind of fucked the business up a bit . . .'

'Oh, you haven't,' says Ade, protesting.

I cock my head at her. 'Ade, come on . . .'

'OK, yeah, it is in a bit of a state.' She shrugs. 'I've saved worse, though.'

'Exactly! What you guys have done before, we just need to do that . . . but you know, it needs to all be true,' I say.

'We can definitely help you with that,' Stu says.

A memory of Harry comes to mind. Him sitting in his holey jogging bottoms on a Saturday night, watching me as I applied eyeliner and moaned to him about not wanting to go out that evening. 'You don't have to always "be", Cait, all the time, doing all this stuff for them.' He'd gestured widely with his can of beer. I'd felt annoyed at him, he didn't get it: why I tried so hard, why I felt I had to go out with some local business owners, that it was all about being the very best. Those were the people that succeeded, the ones who tried all the time. If only I could go back now, get him to budge up, and snuggled into him. He'd tugged at his jogging bottoms as I left, said, 'This would look pretty sexy on Instagram right about now,' and I'd laughed as he'd made some lame hashtag joke and I thought, 'I can't wait until you're a father.'

'And with the new look I do want to honour him, have him be a part of it—'

Ade cuts in. 'Yes, definitely,' she says. 'I—'

I hold a hand up, smile at her to let her know I wasn't finished. 'But this business was never all about him. My biggest career achievement can't be "I found a husband now you can too". I did this.' I gesture around the office. 'I'm the one who has made all of this happen. I don't want people to think that they have to have what I had in order to be happy.' I shake my head. 'That's not what I want to sell, not any more.'

I trail off, look over at them both. Ade is furiously scribbling notes down, the paper in front of her now filled with impossible-to-decipher doodles. Stu, once again, is looking directly at me. 'That's what I've always said, isn't it, Ade?' She looks up from her notebook.

'It is actually,' she agrees.

'Before, y' know,' he says, quickly darting his eyes to his hands. 'I said to Ade, "Why is this all about him? She's the one that's built this business, who has this great instinct for what makes people right for each other, that's what the whole website should be about", but Ade—'

'I told him he was talking rubbish,' she says, pulling a guilty face. 'I just figured he was jealous—' Then, before she says anything further, she throws her hands up to her face, over her mouth.

Stu gives her a look. 'Anyway, moving on,' he says. 'What did you have in mind, Caitlin?'

I reach into my bag, pulling out a ring binder note-book. 'Obviously you can make this look so much better, and I trust you guys so much,' I say, opening the pages I quickly sketched this morning and laying them out on the coffee table. My design is still quite similar to what they'd originally created: there are still photos of Harry and me, but there's a big mixture. There's our wedding day snaps, the honeymoon, and the amazing holidays all mixed in with ones of us at the supermarket laughing at the size of vegetables, pictures of us on the sofa, ugly selfies with The Cat. On some of them I've drawn little arrows, and then written explanations like, 'Five minutes later had an argument over how to get home', or, 'I was really annoying him that day by taking too many pictures'.

'I want to show the realities of relationships,' I say, pointing to each picture. 'How sometimes even first dates will be crap and that maybe you won't be with this person for ever, but that doesn't mean you shouldn't try . . . I don't want all the pictures to be of me and Harry, I want my other couples in there, too. I'm sure they'd agree to it.'

I'm excited, I'm babbling, going too fast, and I'm not looking up, just staring at the notebook as I don't want to see their faces. When I do eventually look up, Stu is smiling but Ade is frowning, shaking her head.

'I'm sorry, Caitlin, it's so sweet and I get it – but it won't work. People want perfection, that's what they're buying. They don't want reality – that veg picture' – she points at my silly sketch – 'was the worst-performing of all the pictures we put up of you and Harry. All those picture-perfect honeymoon shots were the ones that did well, that got you more clients . . .'

'What if we forget about the numbers for a moment? Forget that's what we're chasing?' I say, keeping my voice as firm as possible.

'Forget numbers?' she splutters. 'Forget the way we make money?' She holds her hands up mockingly. 'Fine, whatever you say, boss.'

'The thing is, I don't want perfection. I thought I did – but as soon as I stopped following all the Morwena Star types on my account and followed those who are a bit more real, I felt better about myself,' I say. 'There must be other people out there like me who we're missing out on as they look at my Insta or website and think, "That looks too perfect, it's not for me".'

'She has a point,' says Stu. 'That's what I'm like, what a bunch of my female mates are like. We don't want rose-filtered romance, we just want to meet someone who we'll have fun with.'

Ade chews on her bottom lip. Her eyes dart to mine, to Stu's. 'But the charts . . . you will lose followers.'

'I've already lost so many,' I say. 'And if I don't get as many applications as I used to, that's fine. I'm overwhelmed anyway. I want to ensure I don't make any mistakes, that I can find the right person for everyone.'

'When you hired me you said you wanted me to double your followers, to make the business soar . . . I've . . . I've failed already! Even more so if I allow you to do this.'

'You've not failed.' I reach for her hand. 'I've just changed my mind about what I want. And this is what I want. I'm a matchmaker who didn't get her fairytale ending. I'm a widow. I can't sell long-lasting love to people any more, it wouldn't feel right.'

She nods. 'If this is what you want and you accept it might not be the best – money-wise – for the business, then of course I'll help you. Stu?'

'I think it's brilliant,' he says. 'It's like, love's not perfect, but it's worth it.'

'That's amazing, Stu!' I say. 'I wanted something to go across here.' I gesture to the banner that used to read, 'No bad dates . . . just perfect ones'. 'But I couldn't think of anything that worked. But that would!'

'And below here we'd have your manifesto, a little blurb about you and your reasons for the relaunch . . .' He picks up a pencil, begins expertly drawing a much better version of what I've drawn.

'We can get some good local press for you,' Ade adds, and I can detect excitement in her voice. 'And restart the Instagram from scratch, delete all the photos and relaunch the account with a nice picture of you and Harry – any one you want – with the caption detailing your love for him, but telling the truth . . .'

'I love it,' I say, nodding, swallowing hard. I look at Stu, at Ade, at Stu again. Down at my notebook and around the office I decorated, that I pay for. This is all real, I tell myself. And it's good.

Chapter Twenty-Six

Harry didn't approve of weddings on New Year's Eve. I know exactly what he'd have said if he'd received Tom and Elijah's invite. 'It's selfish,' he'd say. 'Stealing guests away from the party like that. Making them fit into their plans on the best night of the year.' Because, unlike most people in England, Harry absolutely loved New Year's Eve. 'Verity, it's only an anti-climax if you make it that way,' he scolded her once, early on in our relationship when she dared to say she thought it was often a let-down. 'You've just never spent it with me before, this year will be your best yet.'

And it was. We'd always spent it down the pub with the Druncles and Julia, where we delighted in getting a free party popper with every drink, but that year Harry hired us a flat in the centre of Edinburgh and the four of us spent a week up there. New Year itself, or Hogmanay as they call it, was like nothing I'd ever experienced before. Fireworks erupted at midnight all around us, while millions of people in the street below danced, sang, sprayed cans of beer – it was electric, and we spent hours just weaving our way through the streets, amazed at how many people would stop and talk to us and wish us Happy New Year. After that Harry always took charge of the occasion, making us do something different every time. Whether it was throwing a big party at home, or when we went to this

little village in Cornwall where the main street was lined
with pubs and everyone was in fancy dress, hopping from
pub to pub. It worked, between us, him being so excited
about New Year and me being a Christmas nut. It made
our holidays so special as we'd always kick off the first of
December by piling in the car and driving around, looking
at all the festive lights that had been freshly strung up, and
end it on the first of January with Harry's famous hangover
breakfast, and everyone would come round to ours and
relive the night before together.

I was going to skip New Year this year, but that decision was taken out of my hands the moment I received the
invite. Verity's found me a dress for the occasion – white
pleated and with these big, almost watercolour flowers
splodged all over it. She's painted my lips a bright hot
pink and even hopped in a cab to collect a pair of rose-
gold chunky heels from her place, which tie the whole
look together. She waves me off in the taxi, like a proud
mother, and the taxi driver glances at me nervously – as
if I'm a child hidden in a woman's body.

I look out at the streets of people – it's 2 p.m. and there
are already crowds of people gathered outside pubs, smoking
and clutching pints. It's one of those bright, freezing-cold
days where the sun and the white sky hurt your eyes when
you look up and the air bites at your skin as you walk. I
pull my coat – which is an old one of mine, made of pink
fake fur – round myself tightly as I get out, and make my
way to the entrance of the theatre, shyly glancing around
to see if there is anyone I know. Tom and Elijah have
chosen the Crucible for the venue: Sheffield's most famous
theatre, more well known by most for hosting the snooker
each year than anything else, but Elijah had texted me a

few days before: *Gonna be on the same stage Maggie Smith has graced eeeek*. For their present I've tracked down the vintage poster of the show she'd starred in, and had it framed and sent across to their house.

I've never been to a wedding on my own before – I got invited to one wedding before Harry came into my life: the couple were twenty-one and doing it as a rebellion against their parents more than anything. Verity had known them too so we'd gone along, and like the rest of our friends, treated the whole thing as an excuse for a massive piss-up. Verity had got off with the best man and I'd ended up leading most of the wedding party in 'The Macarena'. After that I always had Harry by my side, and although we all got older, we did always end up too drunk and dancing. I loved watching his face, confused as he concentrated on his moves, being lit up in blue, purple and green. I'd decided not to tell Elijah and Tom what had happened to Harry – it felt too dark a secret to share just before a wedding. Instead, I just apologised, explaining I'd tell them another time why he couldn't make it.

As I take my seat in the auditorium I grip my card in its envelope for comfort, fiddle with the gold chain around my neck as I wait for the ceremony to start. It's going to be held on the stage itself, and we're all in the stalls, waiting for it to begin. It's just as the lights begin to darken that someone pulls down the seat beside me: I glance across to them. In the dim light I can just make out that it's a man – who must be fairly tall, with a sharply defined jaw and floppy hair. He smiles at me in the dark.

The vows echo out through the theatre. Tom is in a red tartan suit, his long hair – pulled back into a low pony-tail – looks shiny and clean, as do the black Converse on his feet. Elijah's in a smart, skinny-legged grey suit with a yellow flower pinned to his lapel. An elderly lady is helped up by two bald rugby-looking men and assisted onto the stage, where she kisses both of them on each cheek and takes the mic. 'I used to read this to Elijah when he was a little boy,' she says to the room, clearing her throat.

'*The Velveteen Rabbit*,' whispers the man next to me.

It's been the reading of choice at at least three weddings I've been to. But today is the first time I properly listen to the words, the meaning of them.

'"Does it hurt?" asked the Rabbit. "Sometimes," said the Skin Horse, for she was always truthful. "When you are real you don't mind being hurt",' she reads, slowly and a little shakily into the mic. I glance over at the man next to me. I thought he was taking the piss when he correctly guesses the reading, but now I can see him, mouthing along to the words, a soft smile settled on his face.

'"I suppose you are real?" said the Rabbit. And then he wished he had not said it, for he thought the Skin Horse only smiled. "Someone made me Real," he said. "That was a great many years ago; but once you are Real you can't become unreal again. It lasts for always".' She takes a little bow, while the room claps for her – and Tom and Elijah step forward. The tears fill my eyes quickly, urgently – I feel them wet on my face, and I'm glad for the dark. I root around my handbag for a packet of tissues but I must have forgotten to pack them. I wish I had worn a different dress, as I'm sniffling now and could have at least resorted to my sleeve. Then something soft lands in my lap: a mini pack of Kleenex has been dropped there. I look to the man next to me, who is facing forward, concentrating on the registrar's final words. 'You're OK,' he mouths, his eyes fixed on the stage.

When the lights come up and we all begin to shuffle out of the auditorium, I smile at him. 'Thank you for that.'

'No worries, I know the readings can be tough.' He's got a Geordie accent and rough stubble around his chin. In one hand he holds a square, flat package wrapped in black and silver paper, and with his other he grabs two flutes of champagne off a waiter, hands one to me.

'What did you get the happy couple then?' I ask, pointing to the package.

'A Metallica record.'

I laugh. 'No need to ask which member of the wedding party you know then?'

'Exactly. Elijah,' he says with a straight face. 'Tom's my buddy from university, we used to mosh together.'

'Looking like this . . .' I wave my hand to his appearance: despite the stubble, he's incredibly well put together, his suit sharply ironed and his shoes shining.

He puts down his record, hands me his glass to hold. 'Let me show you,' he says, pulling his phone out and flicking backwards through his photos. I look for evidence of a girlfriend or boyfriend, and don't see any. I file that away for later. 'Here it is.'

It's a fuzzy photo: a picture taken of an old paper photograph. There's Tom, his hair longer and greasier than I've ever seen it, a huge spike through the bottom of his nose, like a bull. Beside him is a man with a proper tall mohican – neon, highlighter-pen green, the spikes spread across his shaved head.

'Oh my God, is that you?' I say, looking at him and then back at the picture.

'Guilty as charged.'

'It's incredible! Is it true that it's all held together with egg whites?'

'It is indeed. I didn't smell that great back then. Though that was probably all that moshing more than anything.'

'Those are some big piercings,' I point to his ears, which have huge holes in them, each encased in a black ring.

'My flesh tunnels? Yeah, they're a regret.' He brushes a bit of hair behind his ear to reveal a hole in the flesh of his lobe.

'Oh my God, will it ever heal?'

'Never. Hence the floppy-hair look.'

'At least it's a look that works, you've got that whole Harry Styles thing going on.'

He holds his heart as if he's been shot. 'Did you just tell an ex-mosher that he looks like Harry Styles? You're killing me.' His eyes are this really beautiful brown, like a Labrador's, and his hands are bare from rings, I notice, as he holds one out for me to shake.

'Ian, by the way.'

'Caitlin,' I say, gripping his hand. His shake is firm.

We begin to weave our way out into the reception area, which is a huge glass room that opens out on to the main square. I look at the fountains – they've been shut off because of the cold, and a layer of frost rests on the windows. Waiters keep drifting past, silver trays balanced precariously on upturned palms, offering us canapés. Ian lets me pick the morsels off first.

'I'm always starving at these things,' I say, shoving a vol-au-vent in my mouth. His cheeks are full of two quail's eggs, giving him a hamster-like appearance. Looking at him, I feel something stir deep in my stomach. I'm about to ask him a question when a woman in a yellow dress comes over. 'Ian!' she cries as her little boy, who's wearing mini Converse, hugs his legs.

'Sally! Oh my God, look at you! When did you get rid of the dreads?' he gasps.

'After the second,' she smiles mischievously. 'I hung onto them way too long.'

She introduces herself and they begin to reminisce about their early twenties. It's nice to hear all their stories, how they once ended up on a band's tour bus because Tom had got off with the drummer, and they woke up in Glasgow. And the time they ran out of money at a festival in Prague and had to trade their belongings for food.

'Do you ever miss it?' I ask.

She moves her head from side to side. 'Sometimes, when I'm up at 3 a.m. 'cos one of the kids has wet the bed and the other is screaming, I think, "God, I'd love to be smoking joints round Tom's right now", but then everything settles again and I realise what made it so good was that it couldn't last. We had to savour that time, you know?'

'Absolutely,' says Ian. 'Hey, cheers to that, to savouring time.'

'To savouring time,' we all echo, clinking glasses.

Sally looks over at her son, who's pulling at a waiter's leg. 'Best go get him and find that husband of mine. But I hear they're playing all our old tunes later – see you in the pit, Ian?'

'You betcha,' he says, and just like that, we are alone again.

'She seems nice,' I say, to fill the silence.

'Sally? Yeah, she's the best. You should have seen her back then – multi-coloured dreads down to her ass, piercings all over.' His eyes follow her as she walks away. But it's a look of fondness more than anything. 'I'm not looking forward to seeing that husband of hers,' he adds.

'Why?'

'Oh, I used to have a little thing with Sally. And he's the jealous type.'

Straight, I think, banking that one away. I'm about to carry on our conversation when a booming voice comes through the speakers. 'Can everyone please take your seats for dinner.'

'I guess I'll see you on the dance floor later?' Ian says, and I nod, thinking I'll probably duck out before then.

'Yep, definitely.'

The table information is all pinned up on a noticeboard, handwritten instructions scrawled onto tacky, bright postcards. I search for my name: I'm on the Palma table – our postcard has a donkey carrying around a naked woman with long blonde hair.

'That'll be Elijah's touch, he collects these things,' I tell Ian. 'What table are you on?'

'Palma.'

'Snap . . . sorry, guess you're stuck with me.'

'Must be fate,' he replies.

Joining us on our table is Mike, who has a shaved head with a snake tattooed all around it, as if the snake is sleeping on there. Ian greets him warmly with a slap on the back and asks him what he's up to these days. 'Head teacher,' he says, rather sheepishly. Then there's a Scottish couple, both thin as meerkats, their necks longer than most: they're Tom's cousins and both work in law enforcement. I wonder if they'd eyed Mike suspiciously before sitting down.

I begin firing inane questions at everyone on the table. Mike used to teach English before climbing the ranks, his tattoo makes the kids a little scared of him, which can only be a good thing. The police couple both live in Inverness, and it was a long journey down, and Ian's just come back from a work trip to Kenya, where he did get to go on safari and he did see an elephant . . .

The easy conversation dominates the starter and the main as Ian keeps topping up my glass with white wine, which I glug down easily. The feeling in my stomach grows with every nugget of information that he offers about himself, until I just can't help myself any more.

'Do you believe in healing crystals?' I blurt out. He looks amused, as he'd just been talking about the 11-plus exam with Mike, who was now debating the harm private schools do with the rest of the table.

'Absolutely not, you don't, do you? Are you hiding a piece of quartz in your purse?' He looks down at my bag, which I've kept tight in my lap.

'Nope, a friend of mine does,' I say, suddenly embarrassed. It's been a while since I've done this, chased a man for information about himself. 'Weird question, I know . . .'

'You must have seen something in me, I suppose,' he says, tapping his creme brûlée with his spoon until it cracks. 'I'm a geologist, so I know a lot about crystals and their properties. But all that healing stuff? Not judging those that are into it but I prefer to deal with facts.'

There's the soft tapping of a mic, and we look over at the top table. Tom has got to his feet and is looking around the room, his other hand twisting at the bottom of his shirt. Everyone is still talking, ignoring him. Ian reaches for his knife, taps at his glass. 'Speech!' he booms – and Tom looks over, mouths a small 'thank you'.

'Now for those of you who think Elijah and I met in a bar . . . I'm about to hit you with the truth. We were put together by professional help, a matchmaker,' he says.

The room mock-gasps and someone shouts out from a table at the back, 'Worst-kept secret in history,' and Elijah hoots with laughter. He grabs the mic for a second. 'Sorry darling, I kinda spilled to, well, a lot of people . . .'

Tom playfully punches him in the arm. 'That's that joke ruined, then. Anyway . . .'

He begins to recount the story: 'Elijah had actually asked the matchmaker to come along and chaperone the date in case he didn't like the guy . . . which, by the way, he didn't. And the feeling was mutual . . .' I'm turning redder and redder.

'Same page bitch,' shouts Elijah. 'That hair.' Some whoops and cheers come from a table to my left, full of people with beautiful hairdos.

'If you thought my hair was bad then you should have seen the matchmaker's,' Tom says. 'No shade intended, she has gorgeous real hair – in these long blonde curls usually . . .'

Ian glances over at me. I look back at him, smile sheepishly. He points at me, and I turn back to the speech.

'But on that day, so I wouldn't recognise her, she'd worn a wig. A big, Annie-style, curly wig.'

The room erupts into laughter as I feel myself going even redder, the blush rising up through my body and blooming across my chest in clusters like a world map.

'She'd suggested we meet in the zoo, but she'd forgotten that Elijah here has a really weird fear of germs—'

'I won't even wash people's hair in the salon!' Elijah hoots, while the table of gorgeous-haired people shout, 'Lazy bugger!'

'To get us both out of there, she borrows a zookeeper's uniform and evacuates the whole place, citing a problem with the gorillas.'

By this point the Scottish couple on my table are laughing so hard they're clutching their sides.

'The point was for me to never know she was there . . . but I'm no fool, I clocked her straight away. But we both went along with it, leaving and going to a coffee shop the' – he holds his hands up in quote marks – '"zookeeper" suggested for us.'

I wore my hair long and loose today, it hangs down my back like a big sign that reads 'This is her, this is the matchmaker'. I'm embarrassed as more and more people begin looking around the room, and then spot me – the colour of cherry tomatoes – shrinking, just slightly, in my seat. I try to concentrate on the rest of what Tom is saying.

'The thing is, as crazy as the whole thing was, when we reached the coffee shop we were both incredibly touched by how hard she'd worked to ensure we still got to know each other,' he says, and I feel my embarrassment fading, replaced by something else: I'm proud as I watch them both up there. 'At first we bonded by laughing at how mad it was and then, we realised, how wonderful it was to meet someone who was still that optimistic about love that they'd evacuate an entire tourist attraction for us to be together.'

That was why I did it. A small giggle escapes me. By now Tom and Elijah are looking directly at the table, and I beam back at them. 'Both of us had been hurt in the past and were growing bitter,' Elijah says, taking the mic. 'She gave us that hope and spark we needed to actually try, and for that – and so much more – we really can't thank her enough. So as much as I'd like to raise a glass to my new husband . . .'

The crowd whoops. 'I'd first like to raise a glass to her, to Caitlin.'

'To Caitlin.'

My table all encourage me to stand up, which I do, dutifully – even curtsying when Elijah shouts 'QUEEEEEEEN'
at me.

'I knew that was you,' Ian whispers to me, as Tom and
Elijah make their way to the dance floor, the opening chords
of Aerosmith's 'I Don't Wanna Miss a Thing' blasting out.

'Guilty as charged,' I say.

The pride has settled in my body like a warm blush. I
watch Tom and Elijah move with each other, fairy lights
twinkling all around them, and I sway and sing along, in
this roomful of strangers. Ian's beside me, his shoulder
brushing mine. He smells of fresh lemons. 'Next up,' he
says. 'We mosh!'

'Yes, it's a requirement of the wedding,' says Sally,
joining us. Her kids have rushed onto the dance floor,
are sliding all over it on their knees. Tom gets down with
them, shows them how to do the air guitar.

'I've never moshed before,' I say. '"The Macarena" is
more my speciality.'

'You can teach us that afterwards,' she says, as this
clanging, screeching noise begins to blast out and Mike,
Ian and Sally rush to the dance floor, moving their heads
up and down at an alarmingly fast rate. The group with
the beautiful hair gesture at Elijah to come over to them,
which he does, jumping over and embracing them all in
huge hugs. Ian beckons at me to come and join him, and
I bop on over, reluctantly.

'Just go wild!' Sally says, moving her head as if she still
had dreads and stomping her feet. I give it a go, moving
my head up and down like a nodding dog, then raising
my feet up high and clanging them back down again.
None of what I am doing actually goes with the music,

but looking at the others, it doesn't seem to matter. By the end of the song I'm panting for breath but smiling. I throw my hands up. 'I need a drink!' I say, retreating as another song – which sounds pretty much exactly the same – begins to play. 'Can I get anyone one?'

They all nod enthusiastically, shouting 'beer' and 'wine' at me as I weave over to the bar, waving at Elijah, who is telling a story, gesturing around while his friends laugh. The waiter gives me a tray for all the drinks and I'm about to pick it up when Ian appears by my side. 'Thought you'd need a hand,' he says, picking up three pints between his fingers. 'Worked in bars for years.'

I carry over the pint for Sally and white wine for me, and watch, happily from the side, as they all jump up and down, transported right back to their youth. At one point Sally drags me over, makes me show her 'The Macarena' – which she copies, dutifully, while Metallica's 'Whiplash' plays. 'There's a first,' she says afterwards, wiping sweat from her brow.

Elijah comes strutting over. 'Caitlin,' he says. 'You read my mind, it's definitely time for the cheesy stuff. Darling,' he shouts at Tom. 'You promised no more metal after 11 p.m.'

'Of course,' says Tom, jogging over to the DJ, who swiftly swaps Metallica for Kylie's 'Can't Get You Out Of My Head', at which all the hairdressers come rushing to the dance floor. I find, as the lights flash green, purple and red, that I'm utterly exhausted. It's a happy tired though, like you get after a long countryside walk or a swim. I pull out my phone, sneakily pressing the button to order a taxi.

Just as I'm leaving, the taxi pulling up, coating me in its white light, I feel a shoulder brush mine, smell fresh lemons.

'Hey,' Ian says, his breath hot in my ear. 'Before you go. Got anyone for me?'

'As a matter of fact, I do . . .' I say, handing him my card and stepping into the cab. 'Drop me an email.'

I don't expect Verity to be in when I arrive home. She'll have been invited to so many parties, she always is. But the lights are all on, and through the window I can see her sitting there, clad in tartan pyjamas. I wave at her, and she jumps up to let me in, pulling me in for a big cuddle.

'You did it!' she whispers in my ear. 'How was it?'

I make my way through to the living room, flop down onto the sofa. 'So much fun!' I reply. 'I learned how to mosh.'

'You didn't!' she says, pouring some champagne into a mug for me.

'I did.' I nod, trying to show her my moves by bobbing up and down on the sofa.

'You little rocker,' she says, glancing at the muted TV. 'Hey, it's almost midnight.'

I pick up the control, turn the volume up and snuggle into her as we watch the fireworks erupt all over the world, the checked blanket tucked over our knees. 'Happy New Year, Caitlin,' she says, kissing me on the top of my head.

'Happy New Year, Verity,' I reply. 'This is going to be a good one.'

Chapter Twenty-Seven

When we arrive at the pub, on New Year's Day, the Druncles whoop and cheer us and give us their party poppers. 'We know you don't like to miss out,' they say to us, while Julia treats us to a cider each on the house. We take our favourite spot in the corner, looking out at the street, where a group of men stand smoking, laughing and patting each other on the back.

Verity slurps from her cider, leaning forward to do so rather than picking the pint glass up – her hair is tied back with a silk scarf covered in melon print.

'How are things, Verity?' I ask. 'You know? With Jeremiah?' I've not really had the chance to ask since our break, whether she's messaged him or not.

'We've not spoken that much,' she says. 'I'm trying to listen to Usman's advice, not push it with the whole "let's be friends" thing.'

She glances down, then reaches back and tightens the scarf, pulling and releasing the knot at the back of her head.

'It'll be weird, the first . . . well, second, I suppose, time . . . not with him, I mean,' she says, pausing, looking out at the men. She points to one with a shaved head and a tattooed neck. 'That guy's fit,' she says. I look at him, glancing quickly back at the bar when he turns around.

'Stop distracting yourself, Verity.' I click my fingers in her direction. 'But yes, he is fit. Hey,' I say, remembering something from the last time I was sitting in this chair. 'The other guy . . . it wasn't . . . was it?'

She looks at me, confused. 'What you on about?'

'You know . . .' I say, gesturing my head towards the bar. 'Was it?'

'I really have no idea what you're talking about.'

'Jack,' I say, a lot louder than I had meant to, as Jack swivels round on his stool from the bar and shouts over, 'What is it, Cait love?'

Verity's hands fly up to her face as she suppresses a laugh. 'Caitlin, no!' She shakes her head, looking at me through her fingers.

'What?' I ask, indicating to Jack that I didn't mean him. 'You were flirting that night.'

'Jack is a sixty-year-old alcoholic,' she says, still shaking, the laugh bubbling up within her. 'Of course it wasn't him.'

'You have weird taste!' I say in defence, looking at Jack. His hair is salt and pepper, and his belly is rotund, like a pregnant woman, but he has sparkle in his eyes. 'And he's not so bad . . .'

'Add him to your books then, I ain't going near him,' she laughs. 'It was just some guy from work. He was all right.'

'Think anything will come of it?'

'Definitely not, I'm not looking to date this year.' She looks out the window at the neck tattoo guy. He catches her eye. 'I just want to have fun. I need to remind myself of that. It's crazy — you tell people you're single and all they want to do is set you up with someone.'

'Guilty as charged,' I grin.

'When single is fun. I love it so far.'

'Cheers to that,' I say, lifting my glass to meet hers, just as Julia comes over, placing our burgers down in front of us.

'What we cheers-ing to, ladies?' she says, pulling a handful of sauce sachets down and placing them between our plates.

'Fun!' Verity says.

'And that guy,' I say, pointing subtly to the guy outside, who has just lit his second cigarette with his first. 'And being single.'

'I'll join you in that,' she says. 'Let's grab a drink later. It's great to see you smiling again, Cait.'

'Thanks, Julia,' I say. 'It'll take time, but I'm feeling brighter. There's this guy . . .' I begin to tell Verity, and she glances up.

'Oh yeah, who?' she replies, but I find I'm not ready to tell her yet. I need to gather my thoughts, just a little longer, before I can.

'He's helping Ade out with the website,' I say.

'Oh yeah, Stu, is it?' she asks. 'She's mentioned him a few times. What about him?'

'Oh nothing,' I reply, taking a chip off her plate.

'Hey,' she says, slapping my hand away. 'There's plenty still on yours.'

'I know, but yours taste better . . . Stu's just had some good plans for the relaunch. I reckon it's going to be all right, I can recover from this whole thing.'

I tell her about how we're planning on getting everything up and running in time for Valentine's Day. How busy Stu and Ade have been, even working up until 10 p.m. on New Year's Eve to get everything done. 'It feels good, like I'm working towards something I actually believe in.'

'There will be a party, right?' she says, her eyes swivelling across the room. The tattooed-neck guy has just swung open the door, and is making his way across to the bar.

'Yep, of course,' I say. 'Valentine's evening, Bobby's said we can have the restaurant.'

Ade's been keeping me up to date with everything, texting me constantly. I'll go back into the office tomorrow, share the photos of Elijah and Tom's wedding – which they've said we can upload onto the site.

'That's brilliant,' she says, her mouth full of burger. 'I've actually been working on something.'

'What?'

'I can't tell you that yet.' She winks at me. 'You'll think I'm totally mad. But, well, the party will be the perfect time for it to all slot into place, I reckon.'

I mock-gasp. 'You have to tell me!'

'I will . . . but in due time. You're going to have to be patient.'

We chew our burgers in silence as I try to rack my brains as to what she could have planned. I try a few guesses – 'Is it to do with Jan?' I ask, and she shakes her head. 'Mum? You've found someone for her?' It's not that either, clearly, as she honks, 'You wish!' in response.

'I know,' I say, holding up a chip triumphantly. 'You've arranged for us to go back to the Maldives – we fly out the day after.'

'That's what I wish!' she says. 'But seriously, I do think we should book another holiday, really soon. There's great deals in the sales. You know, in the spirit of being as fun as we possibly can be.'

'Deal,' I say, clinking my glass to hers. It's almost empty. She eyes it, checks the bar to see if the tattooed guy is still there. 'Another?'

'Sorry,' I reply. 'I'd love to, but you know I've got something to do this afternoon.'

'Ah yeah,' she says, draining her pint, wiping the liquid from her lips. 'How are you feeling about it?'

'Totally dreading it,' I admit. 'But it's the right thing to do.'

'It'll be like a plaster, Cait, the quicker you pull it off, the better,' she says, noticing that my eyes have gone to the bar. He's up there, ordering a round of tequilas for his mates. We hear him shout, 'First shot of the year,' and Verity smiles across at him from underneath her long lashes.

'You know what?' I say. 'Go up there, get yourself a pint, get me a half.'

'You've got time?' She looks at the clock behind the bar.

'I'll chat to Julia for a bit, then head, now please . . . go and talk to that guy. You're killing me, you know I love a good romance.'

She shakes her head. 'Oh, Caitlin, you know there will be nothing romantic about this encounter.'

Chapter Twenty-Eight

Harry's childhood home is the grandest I've ever seen. I remember when we first went there, about six months into our relationship, and we were walking up this road where every house had a big black gate and a winding path that went all the way back. You had to get on your tippy toes to look over the walls to see what the actual house looked like, or what cars were in the drive. I was pointing things out excitedly to him. 'Look, that house has a green Jaguar!' or, 'Wow, look at that one, it has an actual doorway made of roses!' He joined in, playing my game of 'if you could live in any house on this street, which would it be?' laughing as I kept changing my mind with each new one we passed.

I had absolutely no idea that he lived in one of these houses — further up the road was a Toby Carvery where Verity and I would sometimes go, catching the bus from town. I knew the area and figured Harry's family lived in the normal, new-build block about ten minutes away. So I was pissed off, probably out of embarrassment, when we'd stopped outside a big brass gate and he'd said, 'This is me.' I was hissing at him as we crunched up the gravel drive, 'I can't believe you let me play that game when you actually live here.' But he was just smiling, telling me it was still a fun game to play. The house at the end of the winding path was covered in ivy, the two front windows had floral stained glass in the top panels and Harry banged an actual brass door knocker instead of ringing a doorbell. When he did so, a dog's barking began to ring out from inside, getting closer and closer, along with a woman's cut-glass voice saying, 'Gerty, sssshh, it's just Harry, it's just Harry.'

Seeing Sarah for the first time was like seeing an oil painting, or a statue in a museum – she was so different from anything I had ever known, it was as if she'd popped out of a storybook and into my life. Her black hair was coiffed all around her ears, which had two big diamonds sparkling from the lobes, and she was wearing loose black velvet trousers, a deep ruby-red vest top and was wrapped up in a mustardy-gold shawl. I'd worn jeans, a fluffy blue mohair jumper and a pair of bright yellow ballet pumps ('Happy shoes,' I'd said to Harry as I'd popped them on. 'They win over everyone'). She'd smiled at me, the corners of her mouth only slightly tipped upwards, and kissed me on both cheeks. When I stepped back from her embrace I noticed that some of my jumper had come off onto her shawl. We'd been in her presence two minutes and already my face had turned bright red.

She never quite stopped having that effect on me. Neither did the house. I stand outside it now, getting ready to bang on the door, and feel myself reddening already. This feeling of unworthiness washing over me – a feeling I've kind of created all by myself, as Sarah has always been, on the surface, so welcoming of me. I was invited to every family occasion, and from the moment she met me she treated me the exact same way as the rest of the family.

But she had this way of looking at me that made me feel so nervous, I was clumsy in her presence. Spilling over the water jug when she asked me to pass it, screwing up recipes I had cooked a thousand times before just because she was over for lunch. If we ever stayed the night I'd emerge early for me, 9 a.m. say, and she'd remark, 'Nice lie-in?' her face tilted downwards, like she was literally looking down her nose at me.

She didn't look at me that way last time she saw me. Last time she was full of pity, her eyes filled with tears but also with a steely determination: like she knew what was best for me. It was, I guess, in a motherly way. I hear Gerty's nails skid across the tiled floor of the hallway, shortly followed by a clicking of heels, then the turn of the lock, and all the time I'm holding my breath, willing myself to calm down.

'Caitlin.'

She pulls me in, planting just one kiss on my cheek. She smells of cashmere and Chanel No. 5 – the soft wool of her bright yellow cardigan brushes my neck. Inside, she directs me towards the living room upstairs – they have two, the one at the front of the house usually reserved for drinks parties or unexpected guests. The second living room, I was told on the first visit, is for 'family and close friends only', and it is a little more homely than the other: with plump mustard velvet sofas that you sink into, and bookshelves lining three out of the four walls. I settle on one of the sofas and she pours me a red wine, without asking if I want one.

'I'm so glad you called.' She squints at me, looking me up and down. I'm wearing a striped multi-coloured jumper tucked into a brassy gold pleated skirt, with chunky lace-up boots. I'm suddenly conscious that I should have taken them off downstairs and left them in the hallway. 'You look . . . you look, well.'

'I've actually been away – um, the Maldives. I was offered the trip, for free, lucky old me, I suppose. Couldn't not take it, ended up bringing Verity along, it was good, good for me.'

I realise I could probably blabber forever about the trip, excusing myself for going, apologising for having even a tiny bit of fun.

'I've been thinking about what you said.' I pause, smooth my skirt down, trying to remember the words I rehearsed to myself all the way here. 'And, um, first of all, I want to apologise again. Losing Harry, I now see, made me incredibly selfish—'

She holds up a hand to make me stop. Which I do, dutifully.

'Not selfish, dear. You reacted how you reacted, we all grieve differently.'

It's something I've heard constantly in the past fortnight: from my mum, Verity, Ade, Stu . . . I know I didn't act out of a driven maliciousness, but in a robotic, survival mode kind of way – but still I caused Sarah hurt, and for that I do want to say sorry.

'OK, maybe not selfishly. But I did things, plastering his image everywhere, that hurt you. I'm sorry for that.'

She nods, quickly, curtly, and I carry on. 'I'm going to stop doing that now, the posters are coming down this week and I've spoken to the people I work with and they're redesigning the whole website so it's more truthful. It's what I want – I think it's what I want. But the reason I'm here today . . .'

This is the hard bit. Putting into words the worry that I've carried around with me, like a saddlebag permanently attached to my hip. The truth that is so hard to acknowledge, I've tucked it deep into a hidden part of my brain. It feels like I've placed all of this sand on top of it, just poured anything I can onto this thought to stop it from surfacing. Tears suddenly spring to my eyes and begin to trickle down my cheeks. Sarah, ever the hostess, pulls a hand-sewn, monogrammed hanky from inside her sleeve and hands it to me. I blow my nose on it, loudly.

'Did . . . did Harry think I neglected him for the business? Did he think he was second fiddle to it?'

Images of myself, late at night, in the office, surrounded by papers now follow me around. Or memories of being out with him but too busy thinking about whom I'd match with who rather than what he was telling me about his day. These memories hang, like unworn clothes in a closet, inside my mind, taunting me for the things I took for granted, because I thought they would last for ever.

I can't look up at her. I'm fiddling with a piece of loose skin on my thumb and everything else is blurred out. She's the person who would know how Harry really felt. They were close; he phoned her almost every night and was round most weekends, and whether I was there or not they'd always take time for a little wander round her garden outside. I'd watch them from the window, this cold woman's face suddenly so much warmer now she was with her son: as if the roses surrounding her had infiltrated her complexion and made it shine.

She pulls my hand into hers, moves my fingers in one firm movement away from the nagging piece of skin. 'Look at me, Caitlin,' she says, and I do. She's shaking her head.

'No, he never thought that. He was so proud of you, he'd always tell my friends about what you did, the people you helped. He'd text me whenever you had some success or other.' I smile through my tears, even though I can sense a 'but' hanging in the air. Sarah will never just tell you what you want to hear, which is the other reason why I asked. But still, sitting here, the seconds ticking by loudly on a grandfather clock in the hallway, is excruciating. I wish I'd never come.

'But . . .'

I breathe out, there it is.

'He did worry you got sidetracked, forgot your reasons for doing it in the first place. He'd tell me you were caught up on that Instagram thingy, or that you were chasing down someone for status, rather than your original goal.'

'Which was to help people.'

She nods. 'Which was to help people.'

I wipe at my face with the flats of my hands. 'That's what the new business message is all about, showing people that love can be hard work, that it isn't perfect. I want to spend more time with individual clients and less time trying to become the next Tinder.'

'The next what?'

I shake my head. 'Never mind, I just won't be trying to be something I'm not any more.'

'And Harry?'

'He'll still be part of it. He has to be. I can't just wipe him from my history, build a generic-looking website with cartoons of cupids. I have to tell people about him, about what happened to me – for them to understand.'

Tears have begun to pool in her eyes. She reaches across and pulls a box of tissues from the coffee table. She dabs at the droplets, smudging her mascara slightly. 'I'd still see him? On the site? As a way of selling?' She spits the last word out. I realise I'm unprepared for this, for her to object.

'He's not a marketing tool.' My voice sounds firmer than I expected. That was my initial fear, at first, as Ade and Stu got stuck into the new rebrand. 'I just can't go on telling people that love never causes hurt, that it will last for ever.'

'Love does last for ever. I'll love my husband for ever, and you'll love Harry for ever.' Harry's dad had died a few years before we met – a heart attack – and his photo is all over the house. He looks like Harry, with his wide grin and kind eyes. I stare at him sometimes, wondering what it would be like if we'd met.

'Of course I'll love him for ever. Of course I will. But people are going to ask about my own love life, it's inevitable – they want to know they can trust me. And I want to be able to tell them the truth.'

'So why not just wait until they ask? Why plaster him all over the website, like he's some kind of model?'

'Sarah, if you don't want me to do this, I'll think of another way.' It's not what I want but I know it's true – just as I can't carry on lying, and I want to tell my clients the full story, I also couldn't do something that would cause Sarah any more hurt.

'It was a stupid decision,' I add, 'to post photos of him like that, and there were so many reasons behind it. None of those, really, were to get more clients – though it looked like it on the outside. It was all to do with how I was feeling inside. It was this temporary plaster to my grief. But I can't now go back and completely delete every trace of him . . .'

She gasps at that, her hand flying up to her mouth. 'No! You can't erase him like he didn't exist.'

I pull out my phone to show her the link Stu sent an hour ago – a rough imagining of what the website will look like. 'That's why I really think this new way is a compromise. For me, it's a way of including the man who helped me so much – without pretending any more.'

She stares hard at the phone, scrolling through, and I hold my breath. She looks up. 'And what about everywhere else? On those socials?'

'They'll be photos of real-life love stories, captions underneath that are sweet and funny and true – what they like about each other . . . and what they don't. Kind of like *Humans of New York*.'

'Human of . . .?'

'Never mind. But it'll be other people. One of me and Harry, but that's it.'

She nods. I can't read what she's thinking. 'It's certainly a beautiful-looking website with a nice message.' I smile at her, as a way of thanks, but also waiting for the 'but' I sense coming. 'But I need to think about it.'

'OK, I understand. I'll come back, give you your space.' I begin to gather my bag, which is slumped at my feet. She presses her hand against my thigh, to stop me.

'No, don't go. Just wait here, OK? There's more wine in the bottle.' She gestures to a crystal decanter on the side that looks so heavy I know I won't be able to lift it.

I'm confused, but as always with Sarah, I do as I'm told. 'OK,' I bleat, and with that she's out the room, the scent of her perfume still lingering in the air. I sit, fiddling with my hands in my lap for a bit, concentrating on my breath – in through the nose, out through the mouth.

My phone's on the chair where she left it and I could just have a quick distracting scroll, but I don't want to. I want to be able to think about our conversation, and what the future holds. It's been such a rush since Tom and Elijah's wedding, I've not had much time on my own that hasn't been spent writing down plans and sketching out ideas.

I stand up, wander over to the decanter and pop the crystal off the top. When I place it down on the table it makes a thunk, and, as predicted, I can't lift the bottle to fill my glass up. So instead I wander over to the window, look out at the expansive gardens below. The next-door neighbour's patch has a huge trampoline on it that's gathered leaves over winter – a frosty sheen crisping their edges. The other side is a little outgrown, nothing terrible but it isn't nearly as neat as Sarah's pristine garden. I know she's complained about it before to them, to get it sorted. Which always seemed a little unfair to me – their messy garden doesn't affect how hers looks. But I always smiled and nodded and said 'mm-hmm' when she moaned to Harry and I about it. She has a winding gravel path that leads all the way through bright green mown grass, to a greenhouse at the end. Even now, in the depths of winter, she has flowers blooming – and the bushes look so healthy, their leaves a rich green. Three gardens down, a man sits out on a bench, a mustard tartan scarf wrapped tightly around his chin, clutching a cup of coffee. He's just staring out into space and I begin to wonder what he's doing out there – perhaps he used to be a smoker and now simply takes time outside, instead of puffing away. Or maybe he has kids inside running riot and he just needs a small break from the madness of the Christmas holidays and everyone being cooped up inside together for days.

I'm so busy distracting myself that I don't spot Sarah come out onto her lawn, not at first anyway. Then her movement catches my eye; she's walking in circles, round and round. Every now and then she'll wander up to her rose bush – empty of buds – and reach her hand out to stroke a leaf. I can see her breath coming out of her in puffs of grey smoke, and her arms are wrapped tightly around her waist – she's wearing the same outfit she was wearing up here, and hasn't put a coat on. It feels wrong, somehow, to watch her out there, like I've caught her doing something she shouldn't. And it's only when I notice that her mouth is moving that I realise why. I'm witnessing one of her most private moments; she's speaking – walking round in circles and speaking into the air.

'Are you there?' I whisper to myself. 'Are you listening to her?'

The only sound in the room is that of Gerty softly snoring, lost in her dream. I shut my eyes, remember standing in this very same spot a few years ago, and watching Sarah and Harry wander through the garden. It was summer and all her rose bushes were in full bloom, these marvellous creations of red, fuchsia and blush pink. Sarah was proudly pointing each flower out to Harry and he was listening intently, I could tell from the furrow in his brow. A wasp was lingering around his neck and he didn't move his hand up to bat it away, or shuffle into a different spot to lose it, he just stayed there, standing by the bush listening to his mother.

Now the garden is almost bare: some snowdrops have gathered in little groups in the soil beds and there are a few tiny white flowers dotted about, and I wonder what she's planted, what seeds are going to blossom and grow in the next few months. When she planted them, gently pressing them into the soil, she'll have known that Harry would never see what was going to grow. She told me once that during the spring, when Harry was a little boy, she'd take him out and plonk him in one of the beds. He'd sit there for hours, running the soil through his fingers, marching his toy digger up and down the wooden edges, while she weeded and planted and raked. How did she find the strength to go out there this spring and work through her list as normal? Was she thinking of him? Or was she pretending that nothing was amiss? That he'd be round on Sunday and she could show him excitedly the flowers she'd ordered from the gardening catalogues she collected?

I can't remember what I was doing in spring. Since losing him I lost track of the seasons, not once pausing to recognise the warmth on my skin, or noticing the first time it was OK to go out of the house without a cardigan. I didn't notice the first leaves of autumn, or look up in the sky on the fifth of November at the fireworks displays above. I'd just felt irritated at the bangs, worried for The Cat, who'd taken to hiding out underneath the coat pile in the hallway. Standing now, looking at her, chatting away, I know where I should have been: here. He'd want me to take care of her, he always worried about her getting lonely, especially as she stopped going to church after his dad died.

'There are so many things I've done wrong in the past year, Harry.' I still keep my voice low, but the ceiling is so high, and my words echo around the room. 'But I'd lost myself, I hope you understand that. I'm going to be better, make you proud, you'll see.'

'He's proud of you. He'll always be proud of you.'

Sarah's words make me jump. I don't know how I didn't notice she'd gone from the garden – but it's empty now, with no sign she was ever there. I spin around to see her standing in the doorway; she's smiling at me, even though there are tears running down her face. In her hands she clutches a bunch of snowdrops, their heads drooping in melancholy.

'I talk to him too. It helps. And I really think he hears me. I don't think he's here, but I do know that wherever he is he hears me. He'll hear you, too.'

She hands me the snowdrops and then proceeds to crush them by pulling me in for a long hug. I feel her breath in my ear as she whispers, 'You do what you need to do. I believe in you.' And then both of us begin to cry.

Chapter Twenty-Nine

February has rolled round quicker than expected and, as we approach the relaunch, I find myself stuck in a daydream, remembering when I first launched. Harry had insisted on a bit of normality. I'd wanted the party to be an elegant affair, with candlelight and white tablecloths. I'd already emailed three five-star hotels when he got hold of my plans. 'Think about how you felt on our first date,' he'd said, standing opposite me, pressing down on my shoulders. I'd humoured him, shutting my eyes, saying, 'I'm thinking back, way back. OK, I'm with you, looking at you properly and I feel . . .' I'd paused for dramatic effect. 'Sick, bored and like I wanted to get out of there.' He'd cracked up then, having fallen hook, line and sinker for the joke, but then quickly composed himself.

'I'm serious, Cait, I was so nervous. I just wanted you to like me. If I'd been somewhere mega fancy, where I didn't feel like myself, I know for sure I'd have ballsed it up.'

'Some people do feel themselves in fancy places. Your mother certainly does,' I'd replied.

'My mother is not your target market,' he'd retorted. 'You know you should have it in Bobby's restaurant, it's where you have your dates, and he loves you.'

The idea behind the launch was that I'd get all my singles together in one room, almost like a speed-dating party, but without the pressure. Show them that dating and meeting new people was fun. 'I'm telling you,' he'd said. 'It's the only place to have it.'

He was right, and the night went off brilliantly. I loved walking around the party and every now and then glancing over at Harry, always with a full pint in his hand, chatting away to someone.

This time I didn't email any other venues – I knew exactly where the party should be held. I'd spent an evening with Verity individually handwriting each invitation, both of us laughing as we massaged our hands, which ached and spasmed.

Ade had rolled her eyes when I told her the date we were working towards. But now she's here, pumping helium into metallic pink heart-shaped balloons, singing along to Elton John and loving the schmaltziness of it all. 'We'll make it really cheesy,' I had said. 'The Valentine's Day everyone imagines. Clusters of red roses on the tables, spotlights across the floor, Roses chocolates going around on trays with pink champagne. It'll be a bit tongue-in-cheek as essentially what we're saying is this type of romance isn't real – oh, I wish we could get puppies!'

We didn't manage to get puppies, but the rest we've almost managed. And Stu has brought along his dog, Jimi – a sausage dog whose belly hangs down so low it almost touches the floor. Stu has dutifully tied a pink ribbon round his neck, instead of his collar. We're all a bit nervous as we run around the room, trying to busy ourselves with tasks – even though pretty much everything is done now, with just an hour to go until the guests should hopefully arrive.

'Do you think people will be relaxed?' I say to Bobby, who has just finished moving the final table – with Stu's help – to the side, making a central space in the middle of the room. 'The champagne's not too much?'

'Well, for one, it's not champagne, it's cava,' he says, making me laugh. 'And for t'other, they can still get pints at the bar. People might be a little uptight at first, but get a few drinks down 'em and they'll unwind, trust me. As will you. It's going to be a great party.'

'It's so stressful not being able to look at Facebook to see what the numbers are,' Ade says, sidling over, her heels clicking against the wooden floor. She's dressed in a neon pink lace dress layered on top of a black slip, and her shoes have big gold plastic hearts on them – for someone who found the theme cheesy, she's certainly embracing it. She'd really wanted to create an event online and when I had said no to that, wanting it to be much more traditional, she'd insisted that people could RSVP via email. I reluctantly allowed that, and all day today she's been refreshing the inbox, recounting the emails accepting our invite.

'It's going to be fine, Ade, we've already seen an uptick in interest on Instagram and people are still applying to be members. Morwena's posts didn't have as much impact as we first thought.'

'Speaking of,' Ade narrows her eyes. 'I can't believe you invited that witch. And she said yes! Does she have no shame?'

'We know the answer to that: of course not!' I say, laughing. 'But she's just lonely. That can send you a bit crazy, I definitely know that. Besides, I have someone coming for her . . . we might get our "influencer" fan after all.'

Ade waves her hand. 'Ach, I'm no longer interested in that. It's all about micro-influencers now, anyway.'

Since I've stopped caring as much about our numbers, Ade has as well. She's still obsessed with making the business attract as many people as it possibly can, but has begun to look into new ways to do so, and has been spouting off facts about time-per-view on the website and how much engagement our social media posts get. I phase it out a little, and just let her get on with her job. As for Stu – who has chosen a pink and white spotty bow tie for the occasion – he's been in the office a lot, working on his freelance projects at my spare desk.

It's nice having him around. He gets involved with the matches and suggesting new places for them to go on dates – we've even gone to a few places together; he took me to check out his climbing wall back in January, and we went on a walk out to the Peak District together. But, despite Ade's obvious desperation for us to get together, they're not dates. I'm still not ready for that.

'Almost time, how are you feeling?' Stu checks his watch and I can see the gold hands indicating it's five minutes to seven. 'People probably won't arrive bang on time anyway.'

'No,' I agree. 'So I'm glad I've got all of you guys here around me, makes me a lot less nervous.'

'It'll be fine,' he says, putting his arm around my shoulder and giving me a squeeze. 'You've done a fantastic job.'

'It was a group effort.'

Stu, Verity and Ade had all arrived to meet me at the restaurant at 3 p.m. today, after staying up well past midnight the night before placing roses in copper vases and gluing together props for our homemade photo booth in the corner. Today we scattered my newly designed business cards across the tables, and Stu carted speakers in to create a DJ booth. He even strung up a disco ball, so shards of light scatter our faces.

Verity picked out my outfit: I'm in a pale pink fifties-style dress, with a layer of white lace underneath, which I love to twirl in. She's styled my hair so I'm wearing it up, with some roses woven through the incredibly complicated bun-style thing that she's crafted at the nape of my neck.

Verity comes over. She's been in the toilets getting changed, and we all whoop and cheer at the sight of her: she's opted for a bright red suit, with tiny matching roses woven through her Afro curls and a gold clutch bag in the shape of a giant heart. We all cluster together, staring at the door waiting for our first guest, until Bobby comes over and tells us we'll probably intimidate whoever comes in and that we should just get a drink down ourselves and relax. He's right – and I'm laughing at a joke of Verity's when I feel a tap on my shoulder. I spin around to see Jan and Usman, grinning at me.

'Oh my God,' I squeal. 'You guys made it! That's insane. I just wanted to tell you about it.'

'We were so touched to be invited,' Jan says. 'And I've always wanted to see England, we're going to go to London tomorrow. Meet the Queen.'

'Tan's faded though,' I say, reaching for her arm and comparing it to mine. She's still a deep honey colour.

'Mine's fake,' she cackles, just as I spot Tom and Elijah enter. Elijah's in a white suit, pink bow tie, while Tom's in skinny black jeans and red Converse. I wave them both over, taking part in Elijah's elaborate air kissing on three cheeks, and introduce everyone. They all begin engaging in small talk, as Tom tells everyone about the pair's honeymoon (they're both very tanned) and I place my hand on my stomach, try to calm the party of butterflies inside it. This is the first time I'm seeing a lot of the people who I lied to. My skin itches with embarrassment when I think about it, even though Stu and Verity have both spent a lot of time reassuring me that I don't need to feel that way.

Elijah gives my elbow a squeeze, Jan and Tom are chatting away, while Usman stands silently beside her. Verity and Ade are discussing which of my newest clients they have their eyes on and their game plans for talking to them, and Stu has gone off to help Bobby with the disco lights we've hired.

'I was sorry to hear about Harry,' Elijah whispers. I swallow, this is going to be the first of many similar conversations I'll have to face tonight.

'Thank you. I'm sorry I deceived you.' Every time I used to bump into Elijah in the street, smoking on one of his many breaks, I wished he'd sign up to my service just so we could be friends. When he eventually did I was delighted . . . but then I remembered, during small talk, I'd mentioned Harry. I regretted it, as it meant we could never have the friendship I'd hoped for.

'Don't worry about that,' he says. 'Me and Tom, we both get it. We're just glad we've got to know you, and we hope to carry on knowing you.'

'I'd really like that,' I say, as James and Elena walk through the door, hand in hand.

'Oh God,' Elijah says, spotting them. 'That guy comes into the salon sometimes. He's so boring, utterly obsessed by wine.'

'He's not so bad,' I say as I wave them over. Although I do spot James sniffing the glass of cava he's handed suspiciously. He whispers something to Elena and she laughs, slapping him lightly on the thigh.

'Slagging off the wine, are we, James?' I say, smiling at them both. James' face begins to go pink. 'Don't worry, one day I'll be able to afford the stuff that suits your tastes.'

'Yeah, if you win the lottery,' Elena says, clinking my glass. 'Tastes great to me. Gorgeous party, Caitlin.'

I look around. It's begun to fill up a bit now, with groups of people gathered in small clusters together, chatting. I'd been worried earlier that I'd gone overboard with the Valentine's-themed accessories, but with people in the room, offsetting the kitsch, it really works.

'Where you guys had your first date,' I say, and Elena laughs, rolling her eyes.

'And he almost bored me to death!'

'Hey!' says James. 'It wasn't that bad, was it?'

'I believe at one point you told me the minute differences between a Shiraz and a Merlot.'

'Vital information for you to know!'

Ade hovers beside me, gripping her camera. She gives me a sharp jab on the thigh. 'We have to get pictures of all the couples you've put together tonight,' she'd instructed earlier. 'I'm going to be strict about it.'

'Actually, on that note, would you guys mind posing for a picture for my Instagram?' I say, and Elena begins to ruffle her fingers through her hair. 'I dunno if you've seen but I'm doing something new with it, telling real people's love stories. The fact your first date didn't go off that well, I think, is such a nice lesson for others – not to judge their dates too much on their nerves.'

'I'd be single for ever if everyone did that,' says James, pulling Elena in and smiling for the picture.

'I love what you're doing with the new look,' says Elena. 'And we were sorry to hear about Harry.'

I'd decided that I didn't want to have to make an announcement or anything in person at the party, as it would seem too macabre, so, with the help of Ade and Stu, I'd crafted a blog post for the website explaining what had happened and my reasons for keeping it secret. It had been picked up by the local press and a lovely journalist called Jessica had come round to the house to interview me for a sensitive piece that hit the news stands last week.

But still I feel something stirring in me. I swallow it down and decide to remove myself, just for a second, in order to check what it is. I'd made a promise to Verity that I'd take as many breaks as I possibly could in order to keep my head in the right place. 'You're the host,' she'd said earlier. 'You can escape for so many valid reasons. And just send me the signal, and I'll come meet you in the back corridor.'

'Thank you,' I say. 'I'm just going to go check on the canapés.'

The signal for Verity is a WhatsApp message with a simple wave emoji, but I can see she's begun to talk to a guy with plenty of tattoos all up and down his biceps. I don't want to interrupt her. So instead I weave my way through the crowd, smiling and saying 'hello' to everyone as I pass, until I'm in the back corridor.

It's there I realise I haven't been breathing properly, that my heart is racing – fluttering away in my chest. I start to breathe in through my nose and out through my mouth as I try to figure out how I'm feeling. There's a strange sensation in my body that I can't quite name.

'You didn't send the signal!' Verity has appeared beside me, an extra glass of cava in her hand, which she gives to me. We both sink to the floor, our legs out.

'You were talking to that guy with tattoos, Rory, I think his name is. Graphic designer?'

'You got it. God, how do you remember all those details?'

'It's my job. He also has a cat named King Diddy and he skateboards in his spare time.'

'It's over then. I could never date a man who still skateboards in his twenties.'

I elbow her in the stomach. 'You should give him a chance. I'm fine, go back out there.'

'No, you're not. That's why you're practising yoga breathing in a corridor, instead of enjoying your fabulous party.'

'I'm worried everyone's gossiping about me. That they all think I'm a loser for what I did. I dunno, I was so confident in this new plan but, now I'm here, I just wish Harry was here to tell me I'm doing the right thing.'

'You're doing the right thing.' The voice comes from the other end of the corridor, and I recognise it instantly. Sarah is standing there beside my mum, clutching a bunch of flowers. She walks over, her heels clicking on the concrete, and my mum scampers behind her in a pair of squeaky ballet flats. I scramble up and Sarah hands me the flowers and gives me a hug, followed by Mum, who whispers, 'I'm so proud of you,' in my ear.

Now I'm standing within this cluster of women, my breathing slows down. I inhale the flowers: lilac. Verity breaks the silence.

'People are gossiping about you.'

'Verity!' my mum gasps, but she carries on talking.

'They're gossiping about how brave you are, how much they like you, how much they want the best for you. That's what they're talking about.'

'She's right,' says Sarah. 'Everyone in my church came up and said they'd read your article and thought what you were doing was bold. They liked how honest it was. And I know Harry would think the same.'

I catch a tear with my hand as it slides down my left cheek. I notice that Mum, too, is crying. Verity hands us both tissues. 'Stop it, you two, I'll start.'

'It's OK,' I say, sniffing. 'Of course tonight wouldn't go off without a few tears. I'm glad you're both here.'

'If you don't want to go back out there, sweetie, you don't have to.' Mum's back to treating me with kid gloves as well, calling me each day, randomly popping by the office for no reason. I shut her out for such a long time, so I reason it's entirely fair.

'Of course she does!' Verity and Sarah both speak at the same time, their words overlapping each other.

They're right. Harry absolutely hated public speaking – he always had. If he ever had news that the whole team at the dental practice should know, he'd choose to tell them each separately rather than calling a meeting. I remember one time, at a group training day, he came home with his face sheet-white. I thought something terrible had happened but he'd flopped down on the sofa and said, 'Caitlin, it was awful . . . I had to introduce myself! In front of thirty people!'

But then, a fortnight before the launch, Harry had swaggered through the front door, into the kitchen, plopped a kiss on my cheek and said, casually: 'I'm going to do a speech about you. I'm so proud of you.' He'd smelled yeasty, of the beers he'd been having with Jeremiah, so, the next morning, I fully expected him to change his mind. But he didn't. And on the night, despite his hands juddering back and forth, and the paper in them shaking, he'd delivered a beautiful speech. I had to muster some of his bravery and go back out there and tell people all about him, make it right.

I drain my glass. 'I'm fine, Mum, let's go.' Outside the party is buzzing – the room is full up now, and there's even a few people on the dance floor: Stu is on there, alongside Ian, Sally and her two kids – one of whom is leading Stu's sausage dog round in circles. I head over, greeting them all with a hug.

'Taking her for a walk, are we?' I say, and Sally looks down and laughs at the poor dog whose big brown eyes are looking at the child, perplexed.

'More like a drag.'

Seeing Ian reminds me of my other mission of the night. But has she even arrived? Will she even actually come? It's then I feel a shift in the crowd, they all move a little left, and a few heads turn in one direction. It has to be her – and sure enough, there she is, wearing a practically see-through white shift dress, the outlines of her nipples poking through the barely-there fabric. One of them is obviously pierced. She's wearing a long silver pendant round her neck and her now-lilac hair is piled in tumbling curls on top of her head. She looks like a mermaid who has stepped out of the sea, and she's walking straight towards me. But when she arrives there's none of her usual bravado, she doesn't squeal or tell me she is just 'delighted' to see me. She nods at Stu, Sally and Ian, reaches down to pat the dog's head and then whispers: 'Can I chat to you for a moment?'

As we leave I hear Ian say, 'Who is that?'

Morwena finds us a table tucked away in a corner. There are already two people sitting on it, but as soon as she approaches they both, on instinct, stand up and allow her to sit down – which she does, nodding a thank you to them. As they walk past, I fluster, 'There's no need . . .' but she's already beckoning to a waiter to bring her a drink.

She looks at me, her eyes huge and wobbling. 'Caitlin, I'm so sorry. I didn't know.'

'You didn't know because I didn't tell you.'

'But I should have known. I should have sensed it,' she says, her voice getting squeakier. 'And when Ade called to tell me, I couldn't believe it, I'm normally so good at these things.'

'Really, don't worry,' I say, wondering if all hippy-dippy types beat themselves up if they don't manage to predict exactly how their friends are feeling at any one time. 'I shouldn't have lied.'

She's not really listening, but carrying on, telling me how she – of course – has deleted all the posts about me, and that she shared my article on her Instagram stories and she'll do anything she can to help with the relaunch. It's sweet, but it's also not what I want to talk to her about. I hold my hand up to shush her and she looks at me, mouth agape, but does stop talking.

'I appreciate that. But I'm just going to carry on doing the best job I can and hopefully spread the word that way,' I say. 'And in order to do that I need to find you what you came to me for. But you have to do some work for it too, I can't magically find you a man who's going to fit everything you want. He doesn't exist.'

'You're not going to make me see Rowen again, are you?' she says, a hint of a grin playing on her face.

'No, but the man I'm introducing you to tonight, I want you to show him the real you. The one who takes sugar in her tea, who reads trashy gossip magazines, who's a little vulnerable. That Morwena. Not this curated version of yourself.' I wave my hand up and down, and she looks down at herself.

'But this is who people like.'

I shake my head. 'I'm sorry, Morwena, they don't.' I swallow. This is the harshest I've ever been with a client. Usually I win them over with compliments, flatter their egos until they glow with confidence. But Morwena's ego is already too inflated. And for all the wrong reasons. 'Your followers may like that, and I'm not asking you to change what you do online. But in real life something has to give – just like how you wouldn't want to be friends with a Disney Princess, people can't be around you.'

'You think I'm like a Disney Princess?' She's blushed a little pink and I realise she's taking that part as a compliment.

'Well, yes, but that's not a good thing. No one wants to hang out with Snow White, she's too much of a goody-two-shoes and then she slept all the time. And Cinderella is sickly-sweet! She never stands up for herself.'

'Ariel would be a good laugh.'

'OK, I'll give you Ariel. Wait! Morwena, we're off topic. The point is, unless you're yourself with this man it won't work out. He'll want to know all parts of you. And I so want this one to work out, I have a really good feeling about it.'

Her face reverts back to vulnerable, her lip jutting out. 'And you think he will actually like *that* me?'

'I know it for a fact.'

'OK, I'll give it a go then,' she says, standing up, wobbling a little on her heels. I grab her hand and lead her across the dance floor. 'What, we're meeting him now?' she whispers in my ear.

'It's now or never,' I reply, tapping Ian on the shoulder. 'Ian, there's someone I'd like you to meet. This is Morwena, Morwena, Ian, Ian, Morwena.' He grabs her hand and kisses it, before staring directly at her chest.

'I love that necklace, quartz, is it?'

She reaches up, cradles the pendant in her hand. 'How did you know?'

'I'm a geologist,' he explains. 'One of the strongest materials around, that is.'

'I hope it makes me strong,' she says, glancing over at me. 'It's clear quartz,' she blushes. 'Sorry, you probably already knew that. It's supposed to encourage me to see things more clearly. To view things not so much through a lens . . .'

Sally's little boy then comes rushing over, tugs on Ian's arm. 'Excuse me, Ian, will you play hide and seek with me?'

'Only if this lady plays too,' Ian says, gesturing to Morwena. To which the little boy gasps, 'But she's a princess!'

'Princesses play hide and seek too,' says Morwena. 'Ian should count to ten and then we can find somewhere to hide, OK?'

I stand and watch them play for a while, Morwena and Alex pulling themselves under one of the tables, the red and white tablecloths masking everything except their excited giggles as Ian stands near, shouting loudly, 'Now where could they be?'

'Looks like another successful match,' Stu says, standing beside me.

'Hopefully.'

'How do you do it? I would never have put those two together.'

'It really is just this feeling I get about people, I guess I must know what makes them tick. I did lose it for a while, but it's coming back, slowly.'

A bit of his hair flops down in front of his left eye. He has a round mole, the size of a pencil eraser, just above his lip, on the right-hand side. I can look at him now, a lot more clearly. My stomach does gymnastic flips as I do so, as I watch how he takes a drink in big gulps, the muscles in his forearm tensing. He also has light grey eye bags, signalling the late nights he's spent with me, checking every last detail of this relaunch.

I think of my mum a few weeks ago: 'Harry would want you to end up with someone kind,' she'd said, completely out of the blue, while serving up tea. I'd been able to nod and say, 'Yes, he would.' Thinking of that night, the stars twinkling above us, and Stu hollering for a taxi for me, his hand resting on the small of my back as I climbed inside. His cheery wave as I'd driven off.

'Stu?' I turn to him, and he looks back, his eyes catching mine. It's like there's a current of electricity between us, sparks of light on a piece of rope connecting us. But I don't know what to say, what the right thing is to say. The air feels thick between us.

I'm about to say something, *anything*, when Verity appears beside me, pinches my elbow. 'Don't be mad,' she whispers to me.

'Why would I be mad?'

I look over at the door. A woman I don't recognise has entered, and she scans the room desperately before spotting Verity and hop-running over. 'Verity,' she says, biting her bottom lip. 'Hello!' Then she puts her hands over her eyes. 'Oh God, is this going to work? Will she ever forgive me?'

It all clicks into place now. I hold a hand out. 'Hannah, is it?'

She nods, begins scanning the room once more. 'You just have to talk to her,' Verity says. 'She's outside, smoking.' Hannah turns on her heel and practically runs to the door.

Jeremiah appears behind us, squeezes Verity's shoulder. 'Mate,' he says. 'You managed it!'

'You knew about this?!' I ask him, my mouth agape. 'Yeah,' he replies, sheepishly. 'The duchess told me about it, wanted my advice, to check she was doing the right thing.'

They've been meeting up, going to comedy gigs together, having settled into an easy, relaxed friendship. 'We're better this way,' Verity had told me a few weeks ago. 'He's even seeing someone new. A seamstress, if you'll believe it – he's finally sorted out those damn t-shirts.'

He's in one now, I can tell it's one of his designs as the print is tiny cartoon spacemen, but the shoulders are perfect, like he's bought it from a shop. 'What did you say?' I ask him.

'I told her to stop meddling!' he says. 'Of course she didn't listen.'

'Hannah sat down with her parents a few weeks back,' Verity explains. 'I went down to London, had a drink with her afterwards. She says they're slowly coming round.'

'And Ade, do you think she'll forgive her?'

Verity looks towards the door. Ade and Hannah have just walked in, holding hands. 'There's your answer. Now, isn't it time to do your speech?'

'I thought you could do it standing in front of the DJ booth,' says Stu, pointing to a small raised stage. 'I set a mic up for you.'

I can feel my bones shaking underneath my skin. As I walk through the room I try to concentrate on everyone's smiles. 'They all want you to do well, Caitlin,' I say to myself in my head, over and over again.

Then, all of a sudden, I've stepped up onto the tiny stage – it's just a few inches off the ground but still feels a sizeable distance, with the spotlight glaring at me. I tap the microphone gently, but no one in the room notices, the chatter in the air is too loud. I try again, thumping it with two fingers this time. A few people look up, which is even worse, as now they're witness to my futile attempts at commanding a crowd. Ian, Stu and Morwena are trying at shush those around them, pointing across to me, but still my heart is beating fast and I find I'm frozen here, looking into a blur of faces. Then I feel warmth around my fingers, and can sense Verity prying the microphone out of my hand.

'Ladies and gentlemen,' she says loudly, commanding attention immediately and giving me time to catch my breath and slow my heart down. 'I know you're loving the drinks, but the lovely Caitlin has a few words to say. Then you can go back to drinking, promise.'

She hands me the mic and I'm so grateful – her presence on this stage has shrunk it, made the crowd into a sea of smiles, and I no longer feel afraid.

'My husband wasn't perfect,' I say, my voice shaking as I try to project my words further and louder. 'He left piles of pencil shavings around the house, he forgot to let me know when he was staying out for an extra drink and he played computer games way too often. He also – and you'll only really appreciate this if you've ever spent any time with a dentist – never let me have a sneaky one-minute brush when I was tired. He'd stand over me, like a parent, until I'd done my full two minutes.'

The crowd laughs at that one – and I'm glad. 'Don't do too many dentist jokes,' Verity had said, taking a biro to my earlier speech. It had contained about four more.

'You all might have thought otherwise. Anyone taking a look at my Instagram feed lately would have, too. But behind every image posted there's another story in the background. Of a humdrum life of arguing about who would wheel the bins out when it was raining and, "Are you seriously going to play another damn computer game?" Sometimes I wished my husband was someone else, someone who bought me Mulberry bags for my birthday and took pictures of me, captioning them and telling the world how much he loved me.' I pause. 'I regret that now, because he may not have been perfect, but he was mine.'

The room is completely silent, apart from the sniffling of someone in one corner. I wasn't sure whether I needed to explain what had happened with Harry. Or if they'd have all seen the article in the paper. But this silence, heavy in the air, tells me that they all know. That they're listening.

'I don't want you to make the same mistakes I did. To look at the snapshot of other people's lives and make the assumption that yours doesn't match up. That because your partner has a strange, boring obsession – with wine, say . . .'

I hear Elena laugh, and imagine her elbowing James in the ribs. 'Then that's OK. I want everyone to know that your partner, or future partner, isn't going to be everything to you. You can find other people to share your strange hobby or your love of mosh pits. Look at the full picture: your best friend, your mother, your dad, your colleagues. They all fill you up, make you whole.

'Every kind of relationship is valid, having people to love is the most important thing of all – but that should include yourself. I learned that the hardest way, that love is so much more than just the person you're dating, the person you're married to. It's in everything. And we should cherish it every single day. So, here's to love – in all its glorious forms,' I say, raising my glass, my voice breaking just slightly.

'To love,' the room echoes back at me.

I feel my knees buckle – but then I look up, out at all the smiling faces, hear the chorus of their voices in the air, and I feel something, almost like a whisper in my ear. A solidness drifts through me and I know, despite standing on this stage all alone, that he's right beside me.

ACKNOWLEDGEMENTS

Like Caitlin, I wouldn't be whole – the person I am today – if it wasn't for the love of the people I'm about to thank. And this book wouldn't be a whole, real book – with proper pages and an actual plot – without the love and care of others. The main being, of course, my wonderful editor Katie Brown, who always managed to know exactly what this story and these characters needed, voicing the niggling thought at the back of my brain before it had even fully formed yet. She's one of the hardest working people I've ever encountered, and I hope *The Matchmaker* has set me up with a strong, funny and talented new friend. The book really wouldn't be here if it wasn't for her, and the rest of the Trapeze team – Leanne Oliver, Jennifer Kerslake, Sam Eades (who was the first person I ever spoke to about a lying matchmaker), and Elaine Egan, who first introduced me to Sam after hearing me spout on about how I had written a book many, many times over breakfast. Then there's my loveable, totally nuts agent Diana Beaumont (I would have written this for free, so I really needed her) and fellow author Lucy Vine, who introduced me to Diana and has been utterly kind and supportive from the very start, despite only knowing me as someone who drank too much wine and banged on about wanting to write novels.

Then there's my Super Cool Writing Club (yep, that name has officially stuck): Stacey Halls, Claire Frost, Cyan

Turan and Sophie Hines, who were some of the first readers – our meetings were always the thing that kicked me into action to actually get some words down on paper. I also couldn't have dragged myself out of bed to write at 6 a.m. before work if I didn't know my colleagues for the rest of the day were going to be so kind and fun. Amy Grier, in particular, for always being a steady presence by my side, and Farrah Storr for teaching me the power of a strong edit. Never fear red pen. They, alongside Lottie Lumsden, Daniella Scott, Kate Pasola, Hannah Jones, Stephanie Jackson, Jennifer Savin, Claire Hodgson, LC, Amy Bannerman and the entire *Cosmopolitan* team make every long day a joy.

I absolutely wouldn't have coped without the support of my friends who listened when I explained that I wouldn't be able to come out for drinks as I had a book to write (and didn't remind me of these words when I went out for drinks anyway)! They are also the people who pulled me out of my own grief – and for that I won't ever be able to thank them enough. I pooled together all of their personalities and love to create the bond that Verity and Caitlin have in this book. The Power Seven, whose friendship has kept me going for decades, including the real Verity, who is actually little like Caitlin's Verity (for one, she's an incredible cook) but she does give the greatest hugs in the whole world. And Jennie (whose comforting breathing in a yoga class inspired a scene in the book, which sounds odd written down), Eleanor (my wee metadata whizz), Anne (whose amazing family and aunty I stole the concept of 'drunkles' off of), Louis (who I'm almost married to) and Amber (whose smile I always want to see). Then there's The Power Seven partners: Gary, Ewan, Eliot and James

– who all show me what real, happy couples look like, which helped me pick out Caitlin's matches. Edway and Annabelle – so many of our Sheffield memories (two-for-five pound wine) are weaved into this book and I love that we still laugh and love each other just as much as we did back then. Thank you Ed for being one of my first readers, and for feeling passionate about Harry's kindness – I knew I'd created a strong (well, despite being dead) character when you were so aghast that he'd ever cheat. Dale Lewis, I'm very grateful you're also a part of our little three. Heather, I'm sorry, you'll get a proper character named after you one day (though I'm fond of the seeing eye dog who has lost her sense of smell). Stu 2, no, this isn't a sign I'm in love with you (Stu in the book actually has game). Also Mattmate, Corinne, Isla and Neel for always cheering me on. Brad and Klaus for keeping Ian entertained while I worked. My lifelong friends Seth, Gill and Conan (thank you for reading the emails I wrote you when I should have been editing this) and my newest friends, the Greece girls who steadied my buzzing brain when I really needed it: Hannah, Meg, Roxie and Ciara.

I really wouldn't be a whole person if it wasn't for my dad who I must have inherited the writing gene off of, thank you – and my incredible little family: my sister Bex, who is probably more excited about this book than I am, Brendan, who endured the endless episodes of *First Dates* that I watched for inspiration, Alex, whose life brought new and much-needed joy to all of us and, of course, Caitlin – one day I hope you'll think it's cool to have a book character named after you (who's not a seeing eye dog, sorry again, Heather!). Richard and Lynda for always being there. My newer, but just as dear family, Rose,

Graeme, Paul and Becca thank you for welcoming me, and Rose especially for showing me the best way to do Christmas decorations (which definitely inspired certain parts of this book).

And, of course, my husband, Ian Hunter, who, not only dealt with my bird's nest hair for weekends at a time while I was writing this, but taught me what steady, long-enduring love looks like. There's no one I'd rather talk to about my day more than him.

But finally, thank you to my mum, for everything that she has given me. I wish that she could be here to read this, but, like Harry, I know she's somewhere – hopefully in the uncomplicated, quiet peace.

Lia Louis interviews
Catriona Innes about her debut novel
The Matchmaker

LL: What inspired you to write The Matchmaker? What came first for you – the characters, or the niggle of an idea for a plot?

CI: Weirdly, the idea of a matchmaker lying about her relationship is something I've had going around my head since I was about sixteen. I used to write short stories in which a matchmaker would look at odd couples and wonder why they were together. Then, during a meeting with Trapeze editor Sam Eades, she mentioned doing something around *First Dates,* the TV show, and whether there was a novel idea in that somewhere. That's when the idea popped into my head again! Then I spent loads of time really thinking about Caitlin and what drives her, what her past was – and realised the idea had more legs in today's ultra-competitive online environment, where we're all lying a little, than it did back when I was a teenager!

LL: The main character Caitlin's job is a professional matchmaker, which is just so fun. Did you do much research on matchmaking as a profession?

CI: When I first moved to London about ten years ago, I applied to work for loads of matchmaking companies! I thought it was the coolest job, and I'd personally set up my friends in relationships that worked out. Turned out I needed a CV a bit more meaty than that, as I didn't even

307

get one interview. When I was writing the book, I did look into the job and read lots of interviews from those who work in the romance game for how they choose who's right and who's wrong for each other. I also spent ages charting the history of Tinder and its explosion on our dating lives – which is also something I'm very aware of in my job at *Cosmopolitan* as it's had such a massive impact on our readers. It made me realise that someone like Caitlin, today, probably would get lots of people signing up for her services – everyone's getting a bit tired of meeting people through their screens, I think.

LL: When we find out what really happened with Harry, it comes as quite a shock, and perhaps a darker truth than the reader might have expected. Was it always the plan to have Harry be dead?
CI: Originally it was just going to be that Harry had cheated on Caitlin, and the big showdown in the restaurant with Morwena was going to be because he walked in with his new girlfriend. I imagined Caitlin storming over to Harry and tearing off her wig to reveal herself! But my brilliant editor Katie came up with the darker element of the story, and I thought it was genius straight away – and it's really helped to elevate the novel into something more complex, I think. I'd still like to see Caitlin tear off her wig in a showdown though, just shows how addicted to drama I am!

LL: You write about grief so beautifully, rawly and honestly. Writing can be so cathartic, but also the opposite when it comes to sadder subjects. Did you find these scenes particularly difficult to write?
CI: Thank you. I lost my mum when I was nineteen

and I've always found one of the things that's helped me through that time (and even now, as grief, I think, lasts for ever) has always been writing. So I'm pretty comfortable getting into the dark stuff. I enjoy taking myself into really dark places, I find it helps me in so many ways. It was the lighter scenes I found much tougher to write; at first, I was just cringing at myself and writing through my hands. It's funny as I'm actually a really positive person in real life but when it comes to writing I can go dark, quite quickly.

LL: The book explores social media and its pressures to present a perfect life to the world, which in this day and age is such an important issue to broach. Do you think we are getting better at being more transparent, more honest in our social media posts, like Caitlin is in the end?

CI: We definitely are – you see so many big-name influencers discussing their flaws and the reality of their lives now. I also really love seeing how social media has become a place for people to share the realities of their mental health and use it to make others feel less alone. However, I do think that because it's becoming popular to be honest in our social media posts, this is also being used in a different, more contrived way that could end up making people feel worse about themselves. For example, no make-up selfies where the person still looks utterly stunning and they point out that they have 'bad days like everyone else' or people using body positivity as a way to strip off and say they have tummy rolls . . . when they don't really. That sounds super cynical and, ultimately, I think honesty is a force for good, but often when something becomes popular online it's then co-opted as a marketing technique and the original point is lost, which I think is sad.

LL: There are some gorgeous chapters set in the Maldives and the scenes were so emotive and vivid! Was this trip-based experience, or on somewhere you have been in real life? (If so, please lie to us and tell us you met a Willem and had a hot night on the beach with him.)

CI: All those scenes are based on a real place! And now I'm praying that they'll read the book and find it to be so complimentary that they invite me back . . . for free. There really is a staff island too, and unlimited champagne in the mini bars. It's the most amazing place. There also was a waiter who did magic tricks, but I don't think he was a womaniser in real life . . . or if he was I never got to find out. Probably because I was there on my honeymoon (or because I was sunburnt wearing a baggy Jurassic Park T-shirt the whole trip).

LL: The book ended with Caitlin finally showing everyone the truth about her life, and who she is. She isn't saved by a man, but by friends, family, and mostly, herself. Did you always know it would end like this or did you have alternate endings?

CI: I knew I didn't want it to be a typical happy ending, with everything tied up in a big shiny bow, as grief isn't like that and isn't ever 'solved'. But I also didn't want to end the book on a sad note like 'and then Caitlin missed Harry for ever' type of thing, as that wouldn't be an enjoyable read! I just knew that when I lost my mum, it was my friends who pulled me through, so I wanted the ending to reflect the power these other relationships can have. I certainly didn't want anyone to leave the book feeling that because they haven't found their 'one', or they're not in a relationship, that they don't have love in their lives. So I knew all of that and that it would probably end in the restaurant the book began in (as I love *Save the Cat!*, a book that helps with plot and that's one of the piece of advice in it), and then I just let the ending come naturally to me while writing.

CREDITS

Trapeze would like to thank everyone at Orion who worked on the publication of *The Matchmaker*.

Agent
Diana Beaumont

Editor
Katie Brown

Copy-editor
Joanne Gledhill

Proofreader
Jenny Page

Editorial Management
Sarah Fortune
Charlie Panayiotou
Jane Hughes
Alice Davis
Claire Boyle
Jeannelle Brew

Audio
Paul Stark

Amber Bates

Contracts
Anne Goddard
Paul Bulos
Jake Alderson

Design
Lucie Stericker
Joanna Ridley
Nick May
Clare Sivell
Helen Ewing
Madeline Meckiffe

Finance
Jennifer Muchan
Jasdip Nandra
Afeera Ahmed
Elizabeth Beaumont
Sue Baker
Victor Falola

Marketing
Tom Noble
Lucy Cameron

Production
Claire Keep
Fiona McIntosh

Publicity
Leanne Oliver

Sales
Jen Wilson
Victoria Laws
Esther Waters
Frances Doyle
Ben Goddard
Georgina Cutler
Jack Hallam
Ellie Kyrke-Smith
Inês Figuiera
Barbara Ronan
Andrew Hally
Dominic Smith
Deborah Deyong
Lauren Buck
Maggy Park
Linda McGregor

Sinead White
Jemimah James
Rachel Jones
Jack Dennison
Nigel Andrews
Ian Williamson
Julia Benson
Declan Kyle
Robert Mackenzie
Sinead White
Imogen Clarke
Megan Smith
Charlotte Clay
Rebecca Cobbold

Operations
Jo Jacobs
Sharon Willis
Lisa Pryde
Lucy Brem

Rights
Susan Howe
Richard King
Krystyna Kujawinska
Jessica Purdue
Louise Henderson

Jo McMillan grew up in the UK and has lived and worked in China and Malaysia. She is currently based in Berlin. *Motherland* is her first novel.

Praise for *Motherland*

'For those of us who remember how well youthful politics can entangle teenage love, this funny, sweet, sad first novel is both a delight and a glorious journey back to a time and place many of us only recall with a wry shake of the head'
Stella Duffy

'A touching and poignant read, which uniquely explores this period in time in a way in which few other authors have attempted to'

Herald

'In its warm and witty portrait of offbeat mother-daughter relations, *Motherland* often recalls Nina Stibbe's *Man at the Helm*. Jess's gift for wry observations also gives rise to some wonderfully quotable lines'

Lady

'A funny and poignant first novel'

Daily Mail

'An ambitious coming-of-age story, filled with quirky details and descriptions'

Scotsman

'Funny, smart, and packed full of all the melancholy you would expect from a novel that slowly sheds a child's innocence'

Red

'I'm sure that these are characters (and the voice of a new novelist) .... gain ...A be⸻⸻⸻⸻⸻⸻⸻⸻t'
kbag